Taken by Storm

Perfect Storm
Book 1

Mari Carr

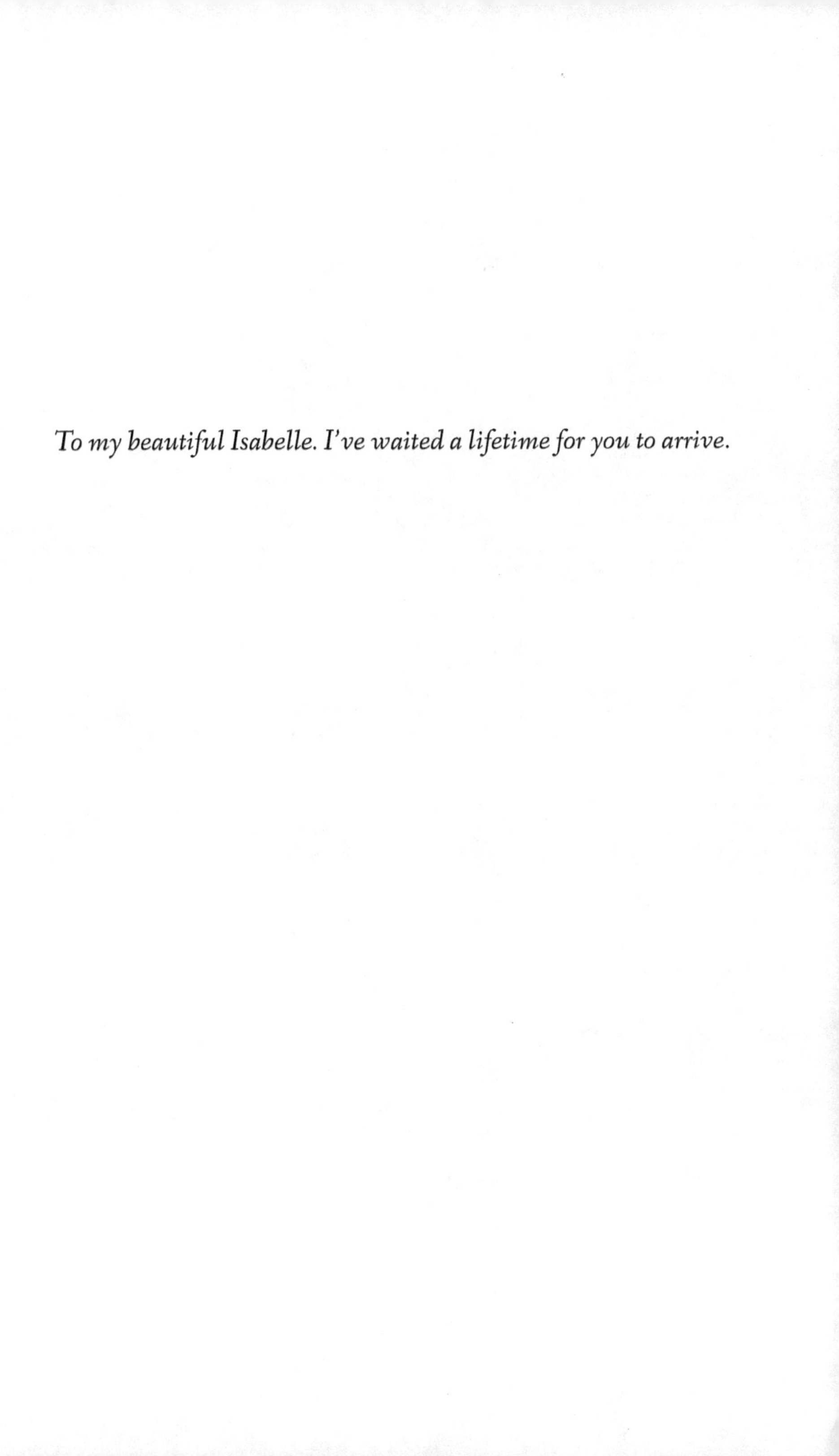

To my beautiful Isabelle. I've waited a lifetime for you to arrive.

Taken by Storm

There's a storm coming... and he's not taking no for an answer.

Life has dealt Kasi one blow after another. Following her mother's untimely death, her family implodes, leaving her alone to run the farm. Fatigue and stress have become her new best friends, every day passing in a blur of work, work, and more work. When Levi Storm, her lifelong crush, keeps her from face-planting due to exhaustion, she's mortified...and more than a little bit turned on.

A person could set a clock by Levi's daily routine, right down to his afternoon trip to the Mills' farm market to buy one of Kasi's delicious pies. He's known Kasi her entire life, so when the beautiful young woman faints in front of him, coming to in his arms, Levi is stunned by the sudden realization that she's meant to be his, and he's prepared to move heaven and earth to claim her.

Kasi should at least try to shake the sexy new six foot five shadow she's acquired, but Levi's much-needed help around the farm, his comfort as she struggles with grief, and his breath-stealing kisses are reigniting the hope and happiness she's lost.

Until reality crashes in again, forcing her to choose between the dominant, possessive, amazing man who makes her heart race and her family's beloved farm.

Chapter One

August was a bitch.

Because it was hot.

Too freaking hot.

Kasi Mills felt a bead of sweat roll down the back of her neck and along her spine. She sat still on her stool, marking the progress of the perspiration all the way to the waistband of her shorts, cursing the summer heat.

Every now and then, she got a brief blast of less-hot air from the two rotating fans she'd set up in the back corner of her family's small roadside fruit stand, the "storefront" for all the produce grown on Lucky Penny Farm.

This current stand was an improvement on the original as at least now, it was a permanent structure with electricity. Her father had replaced their old stand—which had been little more than a series of three long wooden shelves covered with a bit of awning—five years earlier.

While this new stand was larger, it would be a stretch to say they'd stepped up from fruit stand to farm market. Regardless, the stand had a concrete floor and an actual door so shoppers could walk into the shed, which boasted three full walls lined with shelves containing large baskets of green beans, apples, peaches, berries, tomatoes, corn, and more.

The front was a bisected wall, with a hinged top half that served as an awning when opened. There was a tiny checkout station in the center of the space, which was where she was perched. Daddy had built the stand so that she and Mama weren't constantly reloading their truck at the end of each day with all the buckets of unsold fruits and vegetables. Nowadays, she simply lowered the large piece of plywood at the front that revealed all their wares, padlocked it, and called it a day.

Kasi did a visual scan of the table along the front wall where she kept the home-baked goods, such as pies, bread, cakes, and cookies that made their stand so popular. Kasi's mother had been the world's greatest baker, and she'd passed those skills—and recipes—on to her. While they did a fair amount of business with the produce, the pies were the true star of the Lucky Penny Fruit Stand show.

Which was why, with only a half an hour until close, Kasi was completely out of the loaves of home-baked bread, Bundt cakes, and apple pies—today's featured flavor.

Well. Not completely out.

There was one tucked away, saved—as always—for Levi Storm, though he'd never made that request of her. In truth, Levi didn't know that she started every single one of her days trying to determine which pie was the best so that she could tuck it on a shelf behind her, hidden away until just a few minutes before his arrival.

It was a completely silly thing to do, but her schoolgirl crush on Levi had started...well, when she'd been a schoolgirl.

Ninth grade to be exact.

Levi's cousin, Remi, had been her best friend since birth, so Kasi was no stranger to Stormy Weather Farm, a large property nestled on the side of a mountain and home to the hottest men in Gracemont.

No, strike that. The hottest men in Virginia.

The Storm men had been setting hearts aflutter in their tiny neck of the woods for decades. Seven brothers, all single, all so pussy-meltingly hot, they sometimes didn't seem mortal.

Levi was the oldest brother, and even though he was thirty-seven, the fair women of Gracemont hadn't yet given up hope on the stubborn bachelor finding love with one of them and settling down. Not that it made a damn difference in Kasi's life if he *did* have a change of heart regarding his single status.

Because...again...Kasi was and always had been Levi's *baby* cousin Remi's best friend. So when Kasi's crush began in ninth grade, she'd been fourteen, Levi twenty-seven. He'd spent a great deal of that summer working in the family's vineyards without a shirt on, and while Kasi had never noticed or given a shit about such things prior to that year, puberty kicked in hard because, damn...

She *saw* him that year, with his long brown hair, full beard, mahogany-colored eyes, chiseled jaw, and even more chiseled abs. He was tall and broad in a sexy lumberjack way, and he struck her as the kind of guy who could pick a woman up, toss her over his shoulder, and carry her off to the bedroom without even breathing heavy.

Not that she knew that for sure. Or from personal experience.

Because ten years later and well into womanhood now, Levi noticed one—and only one—thing about her, apart from her status as Remi's bestie.

Her pies.

Every single day for the last few years, at the end of his workday and just a few minutes before she closed, Levi drove off the mountain to buy a pie. It was, and always had been, the highlight of Kasi's day. She'd watch his truck make the turn onto the country lane that ran in front of her family's farm, which was the cue for her to grab her best—hidden—pie and place it on the table. Levi would come inside, give her a quick nod of the head—the quiet man's hello—pick up the pie, bring it to the counter, and hand her a twenty. Every single day, she tried to give him his change, and every single day, he said, "Keep it," in that dark-chocolate voice of his that sent her pulse racing. Then he'd give her another nod—this one a goodbye—and that was it.

The sum equivalent of her daily bright spot.

How fucking sad was that?

Kasi lifted her hair away from the back of her neck, desperate for some relief from this unbearable humidity. She closed her eyes, trying to imagine colder things.

Ice skating on the pond at Gracemont Park.

Sledding down the hellacious hills on Stormy Weather Farm with Remi.

Building a snowman with her kid brother, Keith.

The visualization didn't work.

Probably because being hot and sitting in a pool of her own sweat wasn't her predominant complaint at the moment.

Exhaustion was.

So, instead, she kept her eyes closed, steadied her breathing, and started counting down the hours until she could climb between the crisp, cool cotton sheets on her bed.

Sadly, the hourly countdown would take some time because she was a long way away from bedtime, from laying her head on her soft pillow and falling asleep. Back in her carefree days, she was a champion sleeper, the queen of REM dreams, hers always vivid and epic and wonderful. Nowadays, the best she could muster were a few hours of restless, tossing-and-turning sleep that left her even more exhausted come morning.

Being tired had become a regular thing in her life the past eight months, but that didn't make it any easier to deal with.

She jerked when someone cleared their throat.

Kasi's eyes flew open, and she was shocked to discover Levi standing right in front of her counter. How the hell had he parked in front of the stand and walked in without her noticing? Had she actually fallen asleep sitting up?

She lowered the arms that were still holding her hair and realized she hadn't put his pie out on the table.

"Oh, Levi," she said. "I, um, I held a pie back for you because they were going so fast today." It was a lie, but she doubted he'd see through it. After all, he *was* her most reliable customer.

She rose from the stool, moving a little too quickly. Gray spots blinded her as she was overcome with a wave of dizziness. She tried to reach out for the counter but her hands found nothing but air, and for a split second, she became aware that she was going down, her gaze focused on the concrete floor.

Her last thought was *this is going to hurt*, before things went black.

When she opened her eyes, Kasi realized two things simultaneously. She was lying on the floor and her head was in Levi's lap.

"Did I pass out?"

Levi nodded, scowling, though not with anger. He looked worried as hell. About her. If she was more lucid, she'd probably have some sort of misplaced feelings about that.

As it was...

"I'm going to call nine-one-one."

Kasi shook her head as she reached out to grip his wrist, preventing him from grabbing his phone from his back pocket.

"No. That's not necessary. It was just the heat. I didn't drink enough water today."

For a second, she was afraid Levi was going to ignore her and place the call anyway.

"I'm fine," she insisted, attempting to rise. Levi helped her, a steady hand on her elbow, a firm arm around her back.

Those touches would have thrilled her if her sticky shirt wasn't clinging to her skin.

Real sexy, Kass.

Once she was off the floor, she sank back down on her stool. Levi hovered close, his hand still on her arm, until he was sure she wasn't going to fall off it. Then he walked over to the tin she filled with ice and bottles of water every afternoon, returning with one. He twisted off the cap and held it out to her. The ice in the tin had melted long ago, so the water was basically lukewarm rather than cold, but still...it was wet.

She drank a few small sips before starting to put the bottle on the counter. Levi crossed his arms and lifted one eyebrow, making it clear he expected her to drink it all.

She lifted the water and drained it. Putting the bottle container on the counter, Kasi felt her arms, looking for scrapes, feeling for bumps.

"What are you doing?" Levi asked.

She frowned. "I didn't hurt anything when I fell."

"That's because I caught you."

"Oh." She could feel herself flushing, but this time the heat didn't have a damn thing to do with it. "Uh. Wow. Quick reflexes."

Why? Why couldn't she speak to Levi without sounding like a complete moron?

Levi must have noticed her red cheeks because he grabbed another bottle of water and handed it to her.

She uncapped it and pretended to take a sip, just to appease him.

"How much sleep did you get last night?"

His question took her aback. So much so, she just answered it, albeit in a vague way.

"The usual amount." Which was about four hours. Not that she mentioned that part.

"When did you last eat?"

"Breakfast," she replied again, wondering if he would consider a few slices of the apples she was using in her pies as breakfast.

"What happened to lunch?" With each question, Levi's voice got deeper, his frown more pronounced. Again, she didn't get a sense he was angry at her. It was more like he was worried, but in a grumpy, sexy way.

Kasi worked hard not to let herself read anything into his concern, even as her romantic heart swooned. Levi was a nice guy, who'd known her most of her life, and she'd just fainted. He'd be concerned about anyone in the same position.

"I didn't have time for lunch. The farm truck got a flat, and I had to change it before I loaded it with the trays of baked goods and buckets of produce."

Levi glanced around, and she could practically read the question he left unspoken. She was surrounded by food right now, which meant, she could have literally eaten all damn day if she wanted to. The thing was, she didn't eat the fruit stand food because they needed every penny they could earn from it.

Levi raked his hair out of his face with his fingers. God, she loved his hair. All of his brothers were more clean-cut, their hair shorter and more stylish. Levi didn't go for that, allowing his thick, unruly hair to grow long enough that it brushed his shoulders, giving him this wild mountain man look that was ridiculously hotter than it should have been. Kasi knew his long hair and beard weren't style choices so much as Levi was just a hard worker, and shit like getting his hair cut and shaving probably fell very low on his to-do list.

"You changed the flat?" he asked.

She narrowed her eyes, silently warning him to tread lightly. She might be a woman, but that didn't mean she couldn't take care of herself. "I did," she answered shortly.

"Good. Sounds like my lesson stuck."

It took Kasi a minute to remember that Levi had been the one to teach her and Remi how to change a tire the summer they turned nine. She wasn't sure why he thought two young girls needed that particular lesson at that point in their lives. It could have simply been opportunity presenting itself because he'd had a flat, and they'd been driving Remi's aunt Claire crazy, running around the yard and howling like wild banshees, while she was hanging laundry on the line. For thirty minutes, Levi had kept them entertained and somewhat quiet while instructing them on how to change a tire.

"It did."

Levi crossed his arms again, drawing her attention to thick biceps she wouldn't mind grabbing hold of and swinging from like a monkey in a tree.

"You've lost weight, Kasi. You're too skinny. And those circles under your eyes are so dark it looks like you've got two black eyes."

Kasi didn't reply for a second because there was way too much to unpack in all of that. For one thing, she didn't think Levi ever noticed anything specific about her, since her presence in his life was that of a background character. She was someone he acknowledged but didn't pay much attention to... sort of like the mailman you give a quick wave to when he hands you your mail, or the grocery clerk you thank before picking up your bags and leaving the store.

And for another thing, she couldn't remember the last time he'd actually said her name, their conversation limited to that damn "keep the change" exchange.

No. That was wrong. She did remember the last time.

It had been just after her mother's funeral in January. He'd taken her hand, squeezing it gently, and said, "I'm sorry, Kasi."

Half the town had said those exact same words, but for some reason, Levi's were the only ones that had offered her a split second of comfort.

Shaking off that dark memory, she put one hand on her hip and tilted her head, trying to make light of his too-astute observations. "Levi, please. Stop with the compliments or my head will swell."

His lips tipped at the edges. Not really a grin, but she still felt a sense of pride in it because Levi's smiles were too few and far between. He wasn't a miserable man. Not at all. Just a serious one. Whenever she caught a glimpse of his smile or heard him laugh, it felt special, so the idea that she'd almost made him smile...well, that was a big win.

Kasi rose from her stool, aware Levi was hovering close in case she went down again. Reaching for the lower shelf, she pulled out his pie. "Apple today."

He took it from her, reaching for his wallet.

Kasi waved her hand. "On the house. For catching me," she said with a grin.

Levi grunted, another part of his unique communication skills—like the nods—that she'd come to understand. This grunt meant no. And he proved her right when he pulled a twenty from his pocket and put it in her hand.

"Do you want to do the dance where I ask if you want change, and you say keep it?"

Levi grunted again. This one amused. "We can skip that today."

"Suit yourself, but it seems a shame to break the streak, big guy. I thought we really had something going."

"Have you always had such a smart mouth?" he asked.

She laughed. "Hell yeah. You seem to be forgetting my best friend is Remi Storm."

Levi nodded, probably because that response made sense. "I didn't forget." Remi was the reigning queen of sarcasm and quick quips, with Kasi coming in a very distant second.

"Besides," she continued, wondering if she hadn't hit her head at least a little bit because normally she wasn't quite this chatty, especially with Levi. "You've never paid much attention to me. Let's face it, for most of my life, you saw me as the tomboy running around your family's farm, causing havoc with Remi."

"You were a kid," he pointed out.

"Yeah. I *was*." Kasi didn't have a clue why she stressed the word *was* so hard. That certainly hadn't been her intent, but when Levi narrowed his eyes, taking a harder look at her, she wasn't sorry she had.

Score one for passing out.

Or maybe it was utter exhaustion causing her loose lips.

"Well, I hope you enjoy your pie," she said dismissively, feeling a bit awkward under his too-intent gaze. "See you tomorrow."

She spun around, not bothering to wait for his goodbye nod, and took a minute to grab the trays she used to transport the baked goods from the farmhouse to the fruit stand. She was surprised when she turned and realized Levi hadn't left. Instead, he grabbed the empty baskets she'd stacked earlier to replenish with produce back at the farm.

"What are you doing?" she asked.

"You're closing up, right?"

She nodded. "Yeah."

"Well," Levi said, like she was six eggs short of a dozen. "I'm helping."

"Why?"

Levi rolled his eyes, then jerked his head toward the doorway. "Come on, Kasi. We're losing daylight," he said sarcastically.

He led her out of the stand and over to her truck, helping her load it with the trays and baskets. Today had been a good day, so they each had to make a couple of trips. Once the truck was loaded, Levi remained where he was.

Kasi hesitated when it was clear he wasn't leaving. "Shouldn't you be getting home for dinner?"

"What else do you need to do?" he asked, instead of answering her question.

"I just need to turn off the fans, grab the cash box and iPad, and lock things up."

"Okay." He nodded, returning to the stand—and stopping at the door when he realized she was still by the truck.

Kasi frowned, confused. "What are you doing?"

"This would go a lot faster if you actually helped."

She smirked, walking past him and into the stand. "*Now* who's got a smart mouth?"

Kasi wasn't sure, but she thought for a second she heard Levi chuckle. However, when she turned to look at him, his face was just as solemn and serious as always, so she decided it was her tired brain playing tricks on her.

While she turned off the fans, Levi lowered the front plywood, snapping the lock in place. Then he returned to the counter, grabbed his pie, and followed her out, holding the cash box and iPad she used for credit payments, while she locked the stand door.

"Okay, then," she said, taking her tech from him. "Thanks again for everything."

Levi lifted his chin toward her truck. "Get in. I'm going to follow you back to your place."

Kasi gestured to the dirt road. "It's only a mile down the driveway, Levi."

"And you just passed out. So I'm going to follow you."

Kasi, like everyone else in Gracemont, was no stranger to Storm stubbornness. Remi had it in spades, as did everyone else in her family. "Arguing about this will be pointless, won't it?"

This time, there was no mistaking anything because Levi gave her a genuine, bona fide grin. Well, it was probably more smirk than grin, but it was still sexy as fuck.

"What do you think?"

Issuing her girlie bits the "down girl" command, she shrugged. "Suit yourself."

She climbed into her family's ancient "farm use only" truck and started it. She always said a small prayer before turning the key because they needed this truck, desperately, and there wasn't enough money in the coffers to buy a new one. Or even a new-to-them, used piece-of-shit one.

Kasi considered the ever-growing pile of bills in the kitchen and, as always, her chest tightened with anxiety. Paying the bills and dealing with the farm finances used to be her mother's job, but since her death, it had fallen to her.

Hell, all of it had fallen to her.

Mama had been the driving force on the farm, the one basically pulling the strings, for as long as Kasi could remember. It wasn't that her father was incapable. It was just that her parents simply knew where their strengths lie and, in their case, it was with Mama making the decisions and Daddy doing the backbreaking manual labor.

Daddy was a simple man, with simple pleasures. He preferred digging in the dirt, singing along to country music on the radio, and watching TV. Not that he was lazy. That wasn't the case at all. His brain was just wired differently. He had trouble prioritizing and organizing and even making to-do lists, so every morning, he'd come downstairs, grab his honey-do list of daily chores from Mama—ranked in the order he needed to perform them—and went on his merry way. And the best part about their relationship was the fact Mama had been his polar opposite, a type-A personality from the word go, who'd loved ruling her roost.

It had worked for them, and Kasi had always viewed their marriage as one of the best ever. Because despite their differences, they were the most "in love" people Kasi had ever known. She lost count of how many nights she'd come downstairs to spy them slow dancing together in the kitchen. The first time she'd seen it, she had only been seven, but finding someone who would dance with her in the kitchen had rocketed to number one on Kasi's list of #lifegoals.

Parking in the driveway between the farmhouse and the barn, Kasi shut off the engine and climbed out of the truck. She expected Levi to wave and turn around, so she was surprised when he parked his truck right behind hers and got out.

"I'm home," she announced, waving jazz hands in his direction. "All safe and sound."

Levi nodded as he headed toward the bed of her truck, reaching in to grab the buckets.

"What are you doing now?" she asked.

"Helping you off-load. These go in the barn?"

"Uh. Yeah." She grabbed the second load of baskets, trailing him. Once they entered the barn, she pointed to a table by the front door. "I just leave them there. Pete and Paul will refill them first thing in the morning."

The Riley twins had worked on her family's farm for the past twenty years, both men starting part-time when they were still in high school, then coming on full-time after graduation. They lived with their mom just a few miles down the road.

Unlike the Storms, the Riley brothers hadn't been blessed

with good looks, both sort of doughy faced with pockmarks left behind from too many years of acne. They also hadn't scored much in terms of intelligence or personality, either, and Kasi was one-hundred percent certain neither of them had ever gone on a date before. God, they'd probably die of mortification before they could even work up the nerve to ask someone out.

Both men were seemingly satisfied to live out their days at home with their widowed mother. Their dad had been killed before Kasi was born, but she knew the story of how he'd died after his tractor rolled, crushing him beneath it when the twins had been just three years old.

Kasi could count on one hand—with fingers left over—the number of conversations she'd had with the Rileys in the past two decades that hadn't involved farm business. But they worked hard, and they'd been a godsend since Mama's death. Kasi wasn't sure where she'd be without them, but she feared she might have to find out sooner rather than later, if she couldn't find a way out of the farm's financial straits.

Levi placed his stack of baskets next to hers, then followed her out of the barn.

"Okay, well, thanks for all your help today, Levi. I really appreciate it. I, um..." She wasn't sure what else she could say. "I need to get dinner on the table. Bye."

Levi turned to go. She remained where she was because watching him walk away was the icing on the cake when it came to her favorite part of the day. Damn, his ass was fine.

He'd only taken a half dozen steps when she realized he wasn't walking to his truck but to her house. Then he stopped when he noticed she wasn't walking with him.

"What are you doing *now*?" she asked for what felt like the hundredth time in the last thirty minutes.

"Walking you to your door."

"Why?" It was a stupid question, but she couldn't quite

keep up with this version of Levi. She was used to the strong, silent type who barely spared her a sideways glance. This guy seemed to be in no hurry to leave. And while she liked it, she was struggling to understand his motivation.

The crush she'd harbored for too long wanted to interpret his actions as interest. The pragmatist figured it was just Levi being a good guy and a good neighbor.

Le sigh.

He crossed his arms. "You ask a lot of questions. Or actually just the same one. Over and over."

She grinned, amused by his observation. This Levi, the one who talked, made her want to push his buttons just to see how he'd respond. "Not that's it's doing me any good. You're only answering about half."

Levi walked back to her, not stopping until he was about a foot away. He was so close, she had to tilt her head back to look at him. She wasn't sure she'd ever been this close to Levi in her life—with the exception of when she'd just had her head in his lap—and the way he was gazing down at her meant their faces were close together.

Close enough that she could see the flecks of green swirling within those deep mahogany eyes of his.

"I'm walking you to your door because that's what a gentleman does."

She detected the slight scent of peppermint on his breath, and she wondered if it was from toothpaste or mints. Not that it mattered. Peppermint had just climbed to the top of her list of aphrodisiacs. She licked her lower lip, her heart fluttering when Levi's gaze slid down, watching her tongue swipe across it.

"Oh," she replied, cursing how fucking breathless she sounded. It took her a second or ten, but Kasi finally managed to break herself from the spell that was Levi, taking a step back.

"You don't have to walk me. I'm perfectly capable of getting to the house on my own."

Levi's scowl was back, and this time, it wasn't concern but annoyance driving it.

Yeah. That felt more normal.

She and Remi had been twin tomboy tornadoes when they were kids, so she was no stranger to the countless exasperated looks Levi had flashed her way over the years. Clearly, he still viewed her as his baby cousin's friend. The idea that he would forever see her as a kid rather than the woman she'd grown to be, hurt a little. But it was also a good reminder that her crush was destined to always remain just that.

A crush.

"Okay, well. Goodbye," she said, infusing her words with as much cheer as she could manage before turning and heading back in the direction of the barn, wishing it wasn't so hard to walk away from him.

Chapter Two

Levi watched Kasi walk away, trying to decide if he was more annoyed or turned on.

She wore denim cutoffs that framed her peach-shaped ass to perfection, which swayed as she walked. The fact that he was noticing anything sexual about Kasi, whom he'd known since she was a kid, should have had him averting his eyes.

But it didn't.

Not at all.

Because she was all grown up.

Of course, he knew that. He'd seen her pretty much daily for the past few years when he stopped by the Lucky Penny stand for one of her pies. The pies had become his and his brothers' guilty pleasure, and he'd caught enough shit from the guys early on whenever he failed to bring one home that he'd gone ahead and included the trip to the fruit stand as part of his daily routine.

Once it was sliced and divvied up after dinner, Levi only got one piece of it. And it wasn't even a big piece. Never anywhere near enough for him. He'd considered, on more than one occasion, buying two pies and hiding the second from his brothers because sharing sucked.

So yeah. He knew Kasi Mills was no longer a kid, but what he'd failed to let himself admit was that she was a very beautiful woman.

Her long chestnut-brown hair hung straight down her back, reaching down to where her T-shirt ended, and the tiniest bit of her bare skin showed.

She was nearly back to the barn when he realized she was walking away from the house.

"Where the hell are you going?" he called out to her.

Kasi glanced over her shoulder, and he saw yet another glimpse of surprise in her expression. Apparently, his actions were as shocking to her as they were to him. He didn't have a clue why he'd followed her from the stand to her farmhouse. Though considering she'd just passed out, he figured it was common courtesy to make sure she got home okay.

But that hadn't required him to get out of his truck and help her unload. Or stick around to see what she did next.

However, leaving felt as hard as sharing her delicious pies with his brothers.

"I need to feed the animals first," she yelled back. "It won't take long."

He studied her for a minute. Long enough that she must have thought the conversation was over because she turned away from him again and walked into the barn.

Levi sighed, then headed away from his truck, following her once more.

By the time he arrived, she was scattering feed to the chickens in the pen attached to the far side of the barn. There was a long row of henhouses inside a coop. The Lucky Penny Farm also sold eggs and had amassed quite a few regulars who swore their eggs were the greatest. Levi's mother was one of those devoted fans, so every egg consumed at Stormy Weather Farm—either by the family or in the B&B—came from this farm, and Kasi personally delivered God only knew how many dozen to Mom every Sunday morning.

Once the chickens were fed, Kasi hung up the bucket, reaching for a small bale of hay. He intercepted her, picking it up himself. Levi expected her to ask him what he was doing again, but it seemed as if she'd finally given up questioning him and was just rolling with it.

That, or she simply didn't have the energy to fight him anymore. He'd noticed the dark circles under her eyes the last few times he'd come for his pie, but he and Kasi didn't have the type of relationship where he felt as if he could ask questions.

Cutting the string holding the bale together, Kasi scattered it in the pen that held the goats, the baying creatures quickly surrounding them, chomping away happily. She did the same for her three horses. Then she emptied a bucket of slops for the pigs. After that, she grabbed a hose and dragged it from pen to pen, filling the troughs with water.

"Where's your dad and your brother?" Levi wondered why neither of them were feeding the animals.

"Daddy will be in the house," Kasi replied. "And I didn't see Keith's motorcycle when I pulled up, so he must be out with friends."

Levi wasn't sure, but he thought he heard her mutter "again" under her breath.

"Shouldn't he be helping you with some of these chores?"

Kasi shrugged wearily. "He's eighteen, and he just graduated from high school in June. You know how boys are at that age. Gotta sow their wild oats or something."

Levi didn't agree with that assessment at all. He'd been eighteen once too, but that didn't mean his father wouldn't have tanned his hide if he'd failed to do his chores. There was no age limit where the expectations lessened on a farm. Hell, once he graduated, he'd been expected to take on more work.

Rather than argue the point, he decided to see what else needed to be done because Kasi should be inside her house with her feet up. Levi wasn't completely sure he bought the excuse that she'd just gotten overheated. When he'd walked into the stand, she'd been sitting on the stool with her eyes closed, and he'd wondered if she'd managed to fall asleep like that.

Maybe she was getting sick.

"Is that all the chores?"

Kasi nodded.

"Good."

They left the barn together, walking side by side. She'd gone quiet, her gait almost sluggish. He was glad he'd stuck around to help, since her father and brother didn't seem to offer her any.

She glanced at him when he bypassed his truck, walking all the way to the porch with her.

Kasi gave him a smirk. "Still being a gentleman?"

He bowed slightly. "Always."

She stopped at the front door, waiting. "Is there something else you need?"

Levi crossed his arms. "I'm just making sure you actually go inside. Starting to suspect you're trying to get rid of me so you can go plow the back forty."

Kasi grimaced, the expression hitting Levi right straight in the chest because the second she replied, he regretted his joke.

"You don't have to worry about that. The back forty burned."

Levi sighed, cursing his wayward tongue. "I remember."

Her family had lost a whole season's corn crop due to that fire. "Did they ever figure out what started it?"

Kasi shook her head. "The ground was pretty dry thanks to the drought, but with us watering regularly, it was still going to be a good harvest. Fire marshal suggested a lightning strike, as there'd been some storms in the area that night, or maybe a lit cigarette. But none of the farm hands or my father smoke."

Levi suspected losing those crops had dealt them a bit of financial blow, but that was the nature of farming. "Burning can sometimes be good for the soil. I bet your yield this year will be better for it."

"We, um... We didn't plant anything there this year."

Levi frowned—because that was a hell of a lot of farmland to leave unplanted.

However, before he could ask why not, there was a loud crash inside and the sound of glass breaking. Kasi quickly opened the front door, dashing inside, and Levi followed.

She pulled up short in the doorway to the kitchen and quickly threw her hands up. "Daddy. Don't move," she said.

Levi took a second to study the scene, concerned by what he saw. Kasi's father was standing in the middle of the kitchen, surrounded by several broken dishes. A tray lay nearby on the floor as well. All of that was easily enough explained. Mr. Mills got clumsy and dropped a tray.

What Levi *couldn't* reconcile was this version of Mr. Mills to the man he'd known his entire life. He did a quick calculation, trying to decide when he'd last seen the man.

Then it occurred to him.

At his wife's funeral.

It wasn't that his path and Mr. Mills' crossed on a regular occasion, but they usually ran into each other at least a dozen times a year, either at town events, the grocery store, or even at Rain or Shine Brewery. Mr. and Mrs. Mills had spent more than a few restful Sundays doing tastings there, and enjoying the changing colors of the leaves or the return of spring.

But it had been eight months since he'd seen the man, and that time hadn't been kind to him.

Always a tall, lanky guy, Mr. Mills seemed to have lost weight he didn't have to lose. Same as Kasi. His thinning hair was almost completely gone, and his tanned complexion had faded to a chalky white, something unheard of in professional farmers, who spent their days out in the bright sunshine.

The worst part was the man's vacant expression.

He was looking at Kasi as if confused.

Kasi moved forward slowly, trying to avoid the larger pieces of glass. "Stay where you are, Daddy. You're not wearing shoes. Let me clean up this glass so you don't cut yourself." She knelt down, intent on picking up the sharp shards with her hands.

"Where's the broom and dustpan?" Levi asked.

Kasi pointed to a closed door. "In the pantry."

Levi crossed the room to grab them. "Don't try to pick it up with your ha—"

That was all he was able to say before Kasi gasped. She'd sliced the end of one of her fingers, blood instantly welling.

"Ouch." She quickly covered it with the other hand, applying pressure.

Levi grabbed the broom and dustpan, sweeping the glass into a pile and scooping it up. It took several trips between the pile and the trash can to get most of the glass.

In the meantime, Kasi walked to the sink, running her cut finger under the water.

"How bad is it?" Levi asked, looking at her from the floor as he scooped up the last of the mess.

"Not bad at all. Little more than a paper cut," she said, though Levi wasn't sure he believed her. Kasi was fairly accomplished at underplaying things.

Levi captured her gaze from where he knelt on the floor. "Mmm-hmm. Let me finish cleaning this mess and then I'll take a look at it."

"It's fine," she insisted, reaching into a cabinet by the sink and pulling out a Band-Aid. Wrapping it around her finger tightly, she grabbed a washcloth from the sink, wet it, then knelt next to him, running the cloth over the floor to pick up any tiny shards left behind.

Through all their efforts, Mr. Mills remained still, wringing his hands.

"Are you okay, Daddy?" Kasi said, both of them rising once they'd finished cleaning the mess.

"I carried my tray down," he said, his voice so quiet, Levi had to strain to hear him. "I smelled..." Mr. Mills swallowed heavily, his hands shaking, a tear sliding down his wrinkled cheek. "I smelled pot roast. I thought...your mother always made...it smelled just like hers. I thought she was here."

"It's okay," Kasi said softly. "It'll be okay. Are you hungry? I bought some rolls to go with the roast. I just need to pop them in the microwave. Why don't we eat together down here?" Kasi was using that same cheerful tone she'd used with Levi, even though he knew she wasn't feeling happy.

Mr. Mills shook his head. "No. Tray in my room is..." His words faded as he rambled out of the kitchen, heading upstairs.

Kasi watched him leave, then turned to Levi. She opened her mouth but closed it again without saying anything.

He watched her swallow heavily, watched her blink back tears, never shedding a single one.

Levi's heart broke and came to life simultaneously as he reached out, gripped her upper arms, and pulled her toward him.

Kasi stood stiffly, her hands balled in fists against his chest, as he ran his hands up and down her back, slowly rocking her.

It only took a moment for her hands to open, pressing flat against his chest, leaving him to wonder if she was going to push him away.

Levi didn't loosen his grip, but he didn't tighten it either.

A full minute passed before her shoulders sagged and her body gave way. She wrapped her arms around his middle, pressed her cheek to his chest, and just held on.

Levi knew in an instant that he would hold her like this for the rest of her life if that was what she needed. It was a heavy, misplaced, strange thought, but it was the truest, most real thing he'd ever felt.

She was shorter than him, most people were, the top of her head brushing his chin. He bent lower, placing a soft kiss to her hair, loving the way her hold on him tightened in response.

And between one beat of his heart and the next, Levi fell.

She was his.

Kasi Mills was *his*.

And just like that, his entire world clicked into place.

After a few minutes, Kasi lowered her arms and stepped away.

Levi resisted the urge to drag her back. The inches she put between them felt like miles, felt wrong.

He studied her face. Damn. She hadn't shed a single tear. Levi couldn't decide if he admired her strength or if he was worried about the way she kept her emotions bottled inside.

"Sorry," she whispered, her gaze locked on the middle of his chest.

Levi cupped her chin, tilting her face upward, waiting until she lifted her eyes to his. "There's nothing to be sorry for, little bear. You're quite the warrior, aren't you?"

Kasi cleared her throat, looking away first, as if uncomfortable under his gaze. She glanced toward the counter, where Levi saw the Crock-Pot.

"I need to make a tray for my father." Kasi bent down to pick up the one her father had dropped.

Levi took it from her, guiding her toward one of the chairs at the kitchen table. "Sit down."

She started to step back to the counter, but he halted her with a look.

"*Now*, Kasi."

She blinked twice, her brows furrowed in confusion, then did as he said, sinking down.

If the moment wasn't steeped in so much newness, Levi would have found her response to his command a turn-on. As it was, he was still reeling with the knowledge that she was his.

Levi opened a couple cabinets before finding the bowls. He dipped out three portions of the pot roast, steam rising, the smell making his mouth water.

"Where are the rolls?" he asked, recalling her telling her father about them.

She pointed to the refrigerator. "Freezer. I bought them at the store. I didn't have time to make any from scratch." She sounded as if she was apologizing.

Levi grabbed the bag. "These are the same ones my brothers and I eat. They're good. Quick and easy."

Sliding a half dozen of them into the microwave, he set the timer. They only needed a minute. While he waited, he loaded a tray for Mr. Mills with the bowl of pot roast, a small plate with a couple slabs of butter waiting for the bread, silverware, and a glass of water. When the timer buzzed, he added two rolls to the plate, then put the rest of the bread and the butter dish on the kitchen table. He carried over the other two bowls, glasses of water, and spoons.

"Eat," he said to Kasi, as he turned back to grab the tray.

She popped up. "I can carry that to him."

Levi lifted one eyebrow. "Sit back down and eat. Which room is your father's?"

"Really," she insisted, still reaching for the tray. "It's not a problem for me to—"

"Little bear, if you keep arguing with me about every single thing, the two of us are going to have a problem," he said sternly.

Kasi dropped back down in her chair.

"Good girl," he purred. "Which room?"

"Top of the stairs. First door on the left."

Levi nodded then walked upstairs. The door to her father's room was open. The man had climbed into a bed that looked like it wasn't just serving as a place to sleep but as an entire home. There were books scattered on the mattress, half a dozen used tissues, a couple newspapers folded in such a way that the only thing showing was the crosswords. There were countless glasses and other dishes on most of the flat surfaces. Next to the bed was a small table that was cleared off. No doubt, that was where the tray had been before Mr. Mills carried it down.

"Dinner," Levi announced, carrying the tray in and setting it down.

Mr. Mills didn't even acknowledge his presence, his attention completely focused on the television.

Uncertain what else to say, Levi returned downstairs.

Kasi looked like her father when he entered the kitchen, staring off into the distance, her food untouched.

She glanced up when he joined her at the table. "How is he?" she asked.

"Not sure he even realized I was in the room. He was watching *Jeopardy*, so I just left the tray."

Kasi smiled sadly. "He and Mama never missed *Jeopardy*."

Levi reached across the table, sliding her unused spoon closer to her.

She smirked, then picked it up, digging in. Levi did the same, tempted to moan when the first bite hit his tongue. Tender meat and potatoes in a savory sauce. He quickly took another bite, and this time he didn't hold back.

"Holy shit, that's good," he praised.

Kasi smiled, clearly pleased, even as she said, "Don't think I didn't notice how you invited yourself to dinner."

Levi grinned. "I figured it was the least you could do after all my help today."

She narrowed her eyes playfully. "Is that right?"

Levi winked, then the two of them kept eating, neither of them breaking the silence. It wasn't awkward, rather it was peaceful, easy.

He was pleased to see Kasi wasn't holding back, devouring every bite of the roast and two of the rolls. He'd been worried about her weight loss, but it didn't seem to be the result of not eating. Which sparked his curiosity about just what in the hell was going on in the Mills' home.

"How long has he been like that?" Levi asked.

Kasi put her spoon in her bowl then carried it to the sink, rinsing both before putting them in the dishwasher. Levi followed suit, thinking her actions were an attempt to avoid answering his question.

When she turned to face him, leaning on the counter, she sighed. "Since Mama died." Her voice wobbled slightly at the end, and it took everything he had not to sweep her back into his arms. While he knew that was exactly where she belonged, it would probably be a good idea to let Kasi catch up to him.

"That was back in January, right?"

Kasi nodded. "Eight months ago."

"He able to work on the farm at all?"

She shook her head.

Levi didn't like the picture forming in his mind. Suddenly,

he understood the unplanted fields. "Your brother helping out?"

Kasi shrugged. "He's taking Mama's death hard too. Only not in a take-to-bed way."

Levi crossed his arms. "What's his way?"

"Escaping the house, which is actually preferable to when he's home because when he *is* here, he's a gigantic pain in the ass."

"Pain in the ass how?"

Kasi rubbed her eyes tiredly. "He's been getting into a little bit of trouble."

"What kind of trouble?"

"Vandalism, speeding on that motorcycle of his. Last week, he got caught drinking underage with a couple of his friends. Luckily, Sheriff Anderson and my father have been friends since high school. So far, he's been bringing Keith home and letting him off with a warning, although he did have to pay for the damages from the vandalism. I'm just afraid Keith is going to abuse the sheriff's compassion one time too many."

Kasi covered her mouth, trying to hide her yawn. The comfort food was obviously working its way through her system, making her full and sleepily.

As much as Levi wanted to stay with her, he knew she needed sleep. A lot of it.

He stepped next to her, leaning against the counter beside her. "If I leave, are you going to go to bed?"

Kasi didn't respond right away, which told him her answer wasn't going to be honest.

"Don't lie to me, Kasi."

Her gaze flew to his, and he wasn't sure what he saw in those pretty eyes of hers. Confusion? Annoyance? Arousal? Any or all of those looked about right.

"No. I'm not going to bed. I need to start prepping the baked goods to sell at the stand tomorrow."

"Prepping what?" he asked.

"I put the pie crust and bread together. Refrigerate the crust overnight and leave the bread to rise. Then I bake the cakes."

He frowned. It was nearly eight o'clock. What she was talking about would take hours.

"Give me the cake recipe."

Kasi blinked, startled. "What? *No.*"

Levi stepped in front of her, cupping her cheeks in his hands. God, her skin was soft. She flushed slightly, and the innocence of it caught him off guard. He started playing over what he knew about Kasi, trying to recall if she'd ever had any boyfriends. Sadly, he'd been a blind fucking fool for too long.

"What did I tell you about arguing with me, little bear?"

He felt the way her pulse accelerated, saw her eyelids grow heavy. That adorable pink tongue appeared, swiping her full bottom lip and sending his thoughts to a whole bunch of places he couldn't go tonight. She was dead on her feet...and apparently, still several hours away from bedtime.

Levi released her and stepped back, Kasi visibly shaking her head as if to wake herself up.

"Fine. I'm nothing if not a quick learner, and the past hour has shown me nothing I say will matter anyway," she relented, turning her back on him to reach for a recipe box on the counter. She pulled a card out and handed it to him. "I triple it. The mixer is over there. The ingredients are in the pantry and fridge."

Levi nodded once. "I used to bake with my mom when I was a kid. She insisted me and my brothers learn our way around a kitchen so we could feed ourselves and any future wives who might come our way. I can figure it out. You get started on your crust and bread."

The two of them worked together in companionable silence. Well, relative silence. Kasi turned on the radio, country music playing softly in the background.

Once his cakes were in the oven, he helped her knead the bread dough.

"That it?" Levi was worried she might rattle off twelve more things she needed to do before bedtime.

Kasi nodded, her gaze landing on the clock on the stove. "Oh wow. It's only ten thirty."

"Only?" he asked, but Kasi didn't pick up on his tone.

"That went so much faster with your help."

Levi decided he'd bake cakes every night for the rest of his life if it meant getting to see the smile Kasi was giving him right now.

But then her comment clicked, and he frowned. "What time do you usually finish?"

"I don't know," she said, washing up the countertops. "Eleven thirty, midnight."

Levi had asked her at the fruit stand how much sleep she'd gotten last night, and she'd successfully dodged the question by saying "the usual amount."

He was wise to her tricks now. "Is that what time you normally go to bed?"

She nodded. "Yeah, after I take a shower."

"And what times does your alarm go off?"

Kasi bit her lower lip.

Levi took her chin between his forefinger and thumb. "The truth."

"Four thirty."

It was worse than Levi had even imagined. He was an early riser, up and out of bed most mornings by five. Such was the life of a farmer. But he sure as shit wasn't crawling between the sheets at midnight. Things in the house he shared with his brothers settled down around nine, all of them retreating to their own rooms since every single one of them was up with the birds.

He now understood the dark circles under Kasi's eyes—and he wasn't happy.

"So you're getting four hours of sleep a night," he growled. "When is your day off? You take the weekends?"

Kasi really needed to get better at reading his tone because her laugh was the wrong response. It took at least twenty seconds before she realized he was being serious.

She tilted her head. "It's a farm, Levi. You know there are no days off. Animals like to eat every day, and on the weekends, I open the stand even earlier because those are our best-selling days. People drive down here from the city for fresh produce."

He knew because of his daily pie purchase that the only day the stand wasn't open was Monday, but given Kasi's response, it was clear she still worked on that day too, doing other chores.

So if he was understanding what she was saying, she was working long-ass hours, seven days a week. "And you've got no one helping you?"

"The Riley twins work here. They keep the crops going."

"Thought Jeb Wilson and Cal Rogers worked here too?"

Kasi's eyes darted away, only for a moment, but he could tell she was uncomfortable with his question. "Not anymore," she said, offering no further explanation.

Levi had a million more questions he wanted to ask, but doing so would just cut into her sleep time. Considering the work he'd done to help her finish her chores early, it would be counterproductive to keep her talking.

"I should be going," he said, forcing himself to step away

from her. Leaving her alone in the middle of all this felt wrong, but he didn't belong here.

Yet.

That was going to change very, very soon.

Kasi walked him to the door, thanking him again for all his help. It was a friendly enough farewell, but it was clear Kasi was viewing tonight as an anomaly. No doubt in her mind, tomorrow they would be returning to their acquaintance status, and she'd be on her own again.

His girl was in for a rude awakening.

Chapter Three

Kasi had just poured some creamer into her coffee when she heard a knock at the door. A quick glance at the clock told her it was a little before five a.m. It was still dark outside, so who the hell would be knocking on her door? The Riley twins usually didn't arrive until six, and they never stopped by the house first, always just bypassing it and heading straight out to the fields. When they'd first started working here, Mama had offered them breakfast and lunch, but they'd refused, claiming their mother always made sure they had a big breakfast before leaving the house and packed them bagged lunches.

Walking out of the kitchen, Kasi glanced toward the front door. The top half was a window, the bottom solid wood. She always left the front porch light on these days, since Keith came in all hours of the night.

As such, it was easy to make out Levi Storm standing on the porch, looking back at her.

Kasi crossed the foyer and unlocked the door. "Levi?"

"Mornin', little bear."

Kasi wondered how this man could throw her for such a loop with just three words. For one thing, this was the fourth time he'd called her little bear, and she was starting to like the sound of it way too much. For another, even though it was an easygoing statement, hearing it issued in Levi's deep voice had parts of her body that typically lay dormant waking right the hell up.

"Did you leave something here last night?"

Levi frowned, and she realized she hadn't offered him a very neighborly greeting.

"Sorry," she backtracked. "Good morning, Levi."

His expression cleared. It looked like he'd come here straight from the shower. His hair was still damp and brushed back off his face, and he smelled good. Very good. Woodsy, musky, testosteroney.

Shit. It was way too early to be this turned on.

"You gonna invite me in?" he asked, the edges of his lips tipped up, leaving her to wonder if he could read her mind.

"Oh. Um, yeah." She stepped back, allowing him to enter.

Levi closed the door behind him, clearly intent on staying awhile.

"Did you need something?" She was still trying to puzzle out his presence here so early in the morning.

"Wouldn't mind a cup of that coffee I smell," he said, heading in the direction of the kitchen without waiting for an invitation.

Kasi followed in his wake, trying to keep up physically and mentally.

She opened the cabinet that held the coffee mugs and handed one to Levi, who'd already grabbed the pot.

"Do you want cream or sugar?" she asked.

He shook his head. "Drink it black."

Levi glanced around the kitchen, nodding toward the crusts

she'd pulled out of the fridge. "You getting ready to put the pies together?"

"Yeah." Kasi lifted a peach from the counter. "Peach pie today."

Levi gave her a quick grin. "Another one of my favorites. So what do you need help with?"

"Help with?" Kasi frowned. "Nothing."

Levi crossed his arms in that way she was coming to understand indicated annoyance. "Tell me what's on your list for today."

"Shouldn't you be home doing your own chores?"

Levi leaned forward until his face was just inches from hers. For a second, she let herself imagine what it might feel like to kiss him. Would his lips be as soft as they looked? Would his beard tickle?

"Shouldn't you be answering my question?" he retorted.

Last night had proven Kasi wasn't as adept at winning arguments with Levi as she might have liked. "I've got the oven preheating. Once it's ready, I bake the bread while assembling the pies, then they go in. While the pies are baking, I run out to feed the animals and gather the eggs, then I check in with the Rileys, letting them know what produce I need for the stand. Then I come back and make breakfast for Daddy and Keith. And after that..." She sighed. "This is kind of a long list. You good if I just stop there? I need to get back to work peeling those peaches."

Levi's scowl was back, but just like last night, it wasn't anger she was feeling from him.

"That your brother's bike parked out front?"

Kasi nodded. "Yep. Heard him roaring down the driveway around two a.m."

He reached out and ran his thumb gently under her eye. She knew exactly what he saw there. The same dark circles that had become a permanent part of her makeup these days. She'd started referring to it as her "extreme smoky eye" look.

"So he woke you up," he grumbled in a tone that shouldn't sound so fucking sexy.

Kasi shrugged. "I fell right back to sleep."

That was a lie. She'd tossed and turned, replaying her evening with Levi, then stressing out about the ever-growing pile of bills, before making a mental list of which chores needed to happen first today. There was no way she could do everything that needed to be done around here, so she'd started prioritizing the tasks, much like her mother used to do for Daddy.

"Which room is Keith's?" Levi asked.

"Why?"

Levi raised one eyebrow. She recalled him mentioning that they'd have problems if she kept questioning everything he said and did. She couldn't help but wonder what kind of problems he meant.

She pointed to the steps. "Top of the stairs, second room on the right, but—"

Before Kasi could point out that her brother wouldn't crawl his lazy ass out of bed before noon, Levi was climbing the stairs.

"What the hell?" she muttered, moving to the bottom of the stairs curiously.

She heard Levi pounding on Keith's door, though she couldn't make out her brother's murmured reply. She had no trouble understanding what *Levi* was saying because he wasn't exactly using his inside voice.

"Get out of bed," Levi bellowed.

Keith muttered something indistinguishable.

"You either get out of that bed on your own, or I'll drag your ass out," Levi threatened.

More mumbling, and then footsteps.

Kasi had shuffled away from the stairs and back to the

kitchen when she spotted a furious Keith, in just his boxers, coming downstairs with Levi hot on his heels.

"What the fuck, Kasi?" Keith said, the second he walked into the kitchen. Her brother had been the mildest, most gentle of souls before Mama passed, so it was still jarring for her to see this new, always-present angry side.

Levi, who'd followed him to the kitchen, whirled him around, putting his finger in Keith's face. "Don't you dare talk to your sister that way. The animals need to be tended to. Get dressed and do it."

"Go fuck yourself," Keith spat back.

Kasi thought perhaps she should caution Keith that his response was stupid as shit because, Jesus Christ, Levi had at least half a foot on her brother and probably fifty extra pounds —all of it sheer muscle.

Levi beat her to that warning. "You want to rethink that answer?"

Keith blinked a few times as Levi's deadly tone penetrated, clearing away whatever lingering drowsiness was impacting her brother's ability to think. He'd only been in bed a couple of hours, and it looked like Levi caught him right in the middle of a deep sleep.

Keith swallowed hard once, then looked away from Levi. Unfortunately, that shifting gaze landed on Kasi like he expected her to save him or something.

For one thing, she couldn't win her *own* battles with Levi, and for another—and more importantly—she didn't want to win this one. Because she wanted Keith to do exactly what Levi was telling him to.

Before Mama's death, the animals had always been Keith's to care for, and he'd done so with enthusiasm, naming each of his precious chickens and bottle-feeding any baby goats whose mothers died or rejected them. Daddy used to call him Dr.

Doolittle, claiming there wasn't an animal alive that Keith couldn't "horse whisper" into undying devotion toward him.

"Your sister has her own chores to do," Levi continued, when neither she nor Keith spoke up. "Too *many* chores. So you're going to take some of them on. As of today, gathering the eggs and taking care of the animals is your job. You got it?"

Keith clenched his jaw, but it was obvious he didn't want to go up against Levi—so he turned on Kasi.

Because of course he did.

Kasi had been Keith's whipping boy for eight months, the recipient of every single drop of rage in his system. The first time he'd lashed out had been three days after Mama's funeral, and the utter venom he'd spewed on her had left her so numb and taken aback, she'd gone to bed and stayed there for four-teen hours. When she crawled out, she'd discovered Keith gone and Daddy sitting in the living room, staring at a picture of Mama. Nothing had been done on the farm, and that was when she realized she didn't have the luxury of falling apart.

"Are you fucking this guy or something? Isn't he too old for you?" Keith spat at her.

Levi reached out and shoved her brother against the wall roughly. "Apologize to your sister," he demanded through gritted teeth.

Keith narrowed his eyes, glaring at Levi. "Sorry," he said, in the least-apologetic voice Kasi had ever heard.

Levi slammed Keith against the wall again, applying more pressure. "Apologize. To. Her."

Whatever belligerence Keith had been holding on to slipped away, and for the first time, he appeared to realize he had no hope of winning this fight. His eyes drifted over to her. "Sorry, Kasi," he said quietly.

Levi released him. "Now go get dressed and take care of the

animals. Once that's done, find me, and I'll let you know what other chores you're taking on."

Keith scowled as he left the kitchen without speaking another word, but the way he stomped up the stairs told Kasi this was far from over. Her brother was smart enough to hold his tongue until Levi was gone, which meant she had an upcoming confrontation to look forward to.

The idea of having to deal with a pissed-off Keith sparked her own temper. Because, dammit, she didn't have time for this shit.

"What the hell was that?" she asked Levi, her fists planted on her hips.

"You can't run this farm, Kasi."

Those words stung. Because she *had* been running this farm.

And because she knew he was right.

Too much stuff was getting left undone. She'd had to let two of their hands go since she couldn't afford to pay them, which meant nearly two-thirds of their farmland was sitting unplanted because there was no one to work it.

It was a vicious circle. No one to plant meant no crops, which meant no money. Short of doing exactly what Levi jokingly accused her of last night, and plowing the back forty on her own, she had no hope that they could dig themselves out of this. She was fucking kidding herself if she thought she could save them with just the money from the stand and the weekly produce and egg deliveries to local businesses.

Of course, she had too much pride to let Levi know how much his words hurt, so she swallowed it down. "Another compliment, Levi?"

He raked his fingers through his hair. "What I mean is, you can't run it alone," he said in a gentler voice, something that looked like regret in his expression. Like he knew he'd hurt her feelings.

But how? Before yesterday, she and Levi had been little more than acquaintances. She was Remi's friend, and he was her crush. Two roles that meant they'd hardly exchanged more than a hundred words in the past decade.

"I'm doing the best I can." She hated that her voice wavered.

Levi stepped in front of her, cupping her cheeks in his large, calloused palms. "I know that. But it's too much to do on your own. Until your father gets back on his feet, your brother needs to do his part."

Kasi's temper had been banked, but barely. Levi's obvious observation tweaked it again.

She threw her arms out. "No shit, Levi. You think I don't know that? But as I've been told too many fucking times in the past eight months, I'm not his mother, and I can't tell him what to do. He's eighteen and grieving. He won't listen to me."

"Then he'll have to listen to *me*," Levi said, as if that was the simplest solution in the world.

"And what makes you think he'll do that?"

"Because I'm the man of the house."

Kasi laughed.

He didn't.

She sobered up quickly. "Um...no, you're not?"

Levi stepped closer, and Kasi hated herself for stepping away until her back was pressed against the counter. He caged her there, his hands resting on the counter on either side of her.

"Your father can't do it, and your brother *won't* do it, so it falls to me."

Despite his attempts at intimidating her with his size, Kasi laughed, more than prepared to call him on his misogynistic bullshit because what the hell kind of game was he playing?

"Actually, it's fallen to me, Levi. Which means I'm the woman of the house. And I—"

"That's right," Levi cut her off. "You are, and you're mine, so now it's fallen to both of us."

Kasi frowned, bewildered.

Because she was what now?

"Yours?" she asked. "Since when?"

"Since you passed out in my arms yesterday at the fruit stand."

She couldn't smell liquor on his breath, so she didn't think he was drunk.

There was no noticeable lump on his skull, so she didn't think he'd hit his head.

She'd known him her whole life, and she'd never seen any signs of insanity.

"That was a one-off. I'm not the kind of girl who passes out regularly, so you don't have to worry about following me around, waiting to catch me."

"Good to know," Levi replied, amused.

His response annoyed her. "I'm not yours, Levi."

He didn't reply immediately. Instead, he just smirked as if *he* was the one acting perfectly sane here, while she was off her rocker. Which was definitely NOT the case.

"Levi," she insisted. "If my passing out has triggered something inside that's telling you I'm a damsel in distress and in need of saving, let me go ahead and reassure you that's not the case. I'm perfectly capable of taking care of myself."

"I know you are."

Kasi lifted her hands, placing her palms on his torso, intent on pushing him away. She couldn't think when he was standing so damn close to her, and given the crazy shit he was saying, she needed her wits about her.

Unfortunately, her hands had a different opinion about

their purpose when she felt his rock-hard abs through the thin cotton of his T-shirt.

Holy. Fuck.

What was this guy made of? Steel?

She reluctantly applied the tiniest bit of pressure, hoping it would be enough for Levi to take the hint and move away, but he only pushed back until his chest pressed against hers, brushing against her breasts.

She had to swallow down a whimper. "I...um..."

What the hell had they been talking about?

"I know you can take care of yourself, little bear," he repeated.

Kasi was grateful for the reminder because she'd totally lost the plot. She just wished he hadn't tacked on the "little bear" part because it made her melt a little more every time she heard it. "Good," she said lamely. "So you get it. I'm not yours."

Levi brushed her hair over her shoulder. She usually pinned it up in a ponytail, but she'd been too groggy when she first woke up to remember, and by the time she was downstairs, she was too tired to go back for a hairband.

"You want to bet on that?" he asked.

Kasi had started to look at her life as if it were broken down into two parts. There was the Kasi she was before her mother died, and the Kasi she became after.

The first Kasi had been playful, carefree, with more than a healthy dose of wildness mixed in for good measure. It was one of the reasons she and Remi had always been such good friends. Neither of them could resist an adventure or a dare.

This Kasi, the new one, was too serious and tied down with responsibilities so heavy that they threatened to break her back. Nowadays, the most adventure she enjoyed was finding a few minutes to watch a little more of *Bridgerton*.

For the first time in months, she felt a bit of her wild side emerging because she really—REALLY—wanted to take Levi's bet.

But she couldn't.

New Kasi existed for a reason, a good one, so she snuffed out the wildness and shook her head. "No. I don't want to bet."

"You sure about that?"

Once again, she got the sense Levi could tell what she was thinking, and it turned her on as much as it unnerved her.

"There's no way you could prove something like that, so why bet?" Yeah. So much for shutting old Kasi away. Why didn't she just wave a red flag in front of the man? Why didn't she just scream the words, "I dare you!"

Levi grinned. God. She loved it when he did that. His eyes crinkled at the edges, his white teeth sparkled, and it drew attention to that thick beard of his that she was dying to run her fingers through.

Levi closed the distance between them even more, something she wouldn't have thought possible.

"Little bear," he said, his lips less than an inch from hers.

"Hmm?" she hummed, her eyes closing in anticipation.

"Here's your proof."

His lips touched hers softly at first, almost as if he were coaxing her out to play.

Kasi hadn't kissed a lot of guys in her past. Hell, she hadn't even had a real boyfriend. Sure, she'd gone on dates, but none of those guys had ever stuck around long enough for their status to upgrade to relationship.

Probably because she'd always measured every man who had ever asked her out with the Levi yardstick, and they'd all come up short.

Now, she was royally fucked. Future dead-end dates wouldn't be measured by an unexplored crush. Because this kiss wasn't fiction, wasn't fantasy, wasn't wishful thinking.

It was real and passionate and mind-blowing and over-whelming and...

She was screwed.

Her fingers closed around the soft material of his T-shirt, gripping so tightly she feared she'd tear it. One of Levi's hands made its way to her cheek, cupping it in equal part affection and possession. His other hand was wrapped around the nape of her neck, the touch making her feel safe and claimed all at the same time.

She started when he nipped her lower lip, her gasp the opening he was looking for as his tongue slid inside. He tasted like coffee, his bitterness mingling with the sweetness of her cream and sugar.

Levi pushed her harder against the counter, every part of his body flat against hers, allowing her to feel the effect this kiss was having on him too.

There was a large—holy fuck, too large—bulge beneath his jeans, and just the thought of him getting hard over a kiss with her was making her dizzy. Dizzy enough, she worried she might have to eat her words about not being the kind of girl who passed out all the time.

Kasi had no idea how long they stood there, Levi devouring her mouth, her lips, her tongue. He laid claim to it all, and damn if she didn't hand it over without hesitation.

Levi broke the kiss, resting his forehead against hers. She expected him to do a bit of crowing, bragging about making his point. She sure as shit hadn't resisted the kiss, so if that was what he considered proof of ownership, then yeah, he no doubt thought he'd won the bet.

However, Kasi had kissed plenty of guys in the past without handing over the deed, and she intended to set him straight on that.

As soon as she remembered how to breathe.

"Make me a honey-do list," Levi said.

Where was the crowing?

Kasi blinked a few times, trying to make sense of his words in the wake of...*that kiss.*

"What?"

"Make me a list of chores that need to be done around here," he reiterated, his change of subject nearly giving her whiplash.

Did he truly think that kiss had been answer enough to his assertion that she was his?

God. Did *she?*

Suddenly, she wasn't so sure. Probably because it was on the tip of her tongue to demand that he kiss her again.

"Kasi," Levi said. "Did you hear me?"

"You want a list. For Keith?" she asked stupidly, failing miserably at keeping up with whatever the hell was going on here.

Levi shook his head. "For both of us, though one list will be fine. Write down everything that needs to be done around here. Put the most important things on top. I'll divvy up what I do and what I give to Keith."

"But isn't it harvest time?"

Levi was a farmer too, working in the vineyards his grandfather planted over fifty years earlier. Remi told Kasi that for the past few years, Levi had also started growing hops for the brewery, but he wasn't happy with the yield due to the lack of farmland available to him since the vineyards took precedence.

"Only a couple varieties of grapes are ready to harvest right now, and we've got plenty of help with the picking. My family and crew can carry on without me for the day."

Kasi snorted. "Yeah well, you might as well head back up the mountain because my list won't be done in just one day."

Levi didn't seem the slightest bit bothered by that. "Then I'll keep coming back."

"You can't."

Levi let go of the counter, his hands gripping her waist in a firm and oh-so-sexy way. "Make the goddamn list, Kasi."

She drew in a slow breath, then nodded. She'd lost sleep, mentally worried about the very list he was asking for, so she would just write down the things she'd planned to do today and give him that. There was no way she could list everything, but she figured she could come up with enough stuff to keep him busy for a day or two. That should satisfy him.

At this point, his request felt like a win-win. She'd get to spend a couple more days with Levi *and* get some much-needed repairs done around the farm. He'd already worked one miracle by getting Keith out of bed and helping, even though she knew that phenomenon would be a short-lived one that ended the second Levi headed home.

Levi narrowed his eyes, cupping her chin in his calloused palm and tilting her head back to make her look at him. "I want the *whole* list," he stressed. "If you leave anything off, I'll find out—and believe me when I say, there will be consequences if you hold out on me."

"Consequences?" It felt like a threatening word, so why was her pussy suddenly clenching in response?

Levi nodded. "Yep. I'll bend you over that kitchen table, push those tight shorts down to your knees, and spank that sexy ass of yours. Then I'll drive three fingers deep inside you hard and fast, fucking you with them until you come so hard you see stars."

"You... What?" she breathed, her eyes dilated, her cheeks flushed.

"And then once you've suffered those consequences, I'll

kiss it all better and make you come on my mouth. After that... well, let's just say *that's* when I'll get serious."

Kasi opened her mouth, but when nothing came out, she closed it again. Surely, she should respond to that. Right? She opened her mouth again before she realized she had no clue what to say.

Levi pushed her mouth closed with one finger, smirking. "I didn't ask a question, so you don't need to say anything. Just nod so I know you understand."

Kasi nodded.

Because...Jesus.

Was Levi saying he wanted to punish her? With sex?

She might not be super-experienced, but she was pretty sure sex and orgasms weren't punishment. Although, now that she thought about it, he didn't call it punishment. He called it consequences, so...

Yeah, she had no idea if that made a difference or not. No one had ever said anything even remotely close to that to her in her entire life. And she'd sure as shit never imagined Levi saying stuff like that to her.

Kasi had indulged in a couple—thousand—fantasies of Levi over the years, and none of them had even approached this level of "yes please."

She was shocked she wasn't panting like a dog in heat.

This whole conversation was so far out of the realm of reality, Kasi actually stood there an extra minute, trying to make sure it had really happened.

Maybe she finally had gone over the deep end while standing here, imagining Levi saying all these wonderful, horny things.

She studied his face. He was looking at her with an all-too-cocky smirk, and it jerked her back to the here and now.

There was no way he really meant he'd do all that. He was

probably going for some kind of shock factor to get her to do what he wanted.

If only she could remember what that was…

"List, Kasi," he said. "Now."

Oh yeah.

When Levi pushed away, she moved to the catch-all drawer, pulling out a pad of paper and a pen, then forced herself to the table on weak legs.

While she wrote her list, Levi slid the prepared loaves of bread into the oven, then started peeling and chopping the peaches.

Kasi started with the tasks she'd intended to do herself today, the most pressing ones, then she listed at least a couple dozen more items—drifting into fantasyland because no one could accomplish all of this.

Levi walked over to her, reading the list over her shoulder. "Is that everything?"

"It's everything I can think of right now," she answered honestly.

His hand landed on her shoulder, giving it a light squeeze. "Okay. If you remember anything else, add it to the list."

"This is too much, Levi," she said, not entirely certain if she was talking about the chores or him.

"No, Kasi. It's not. It's just right."

With those parting words, he took her list from her and left the kitchen, whistling like he didn't have a care in the world. Like she hadn't just saddled him with a shit-ton of back-breaking work.

Like he was happy.

Before Kasi could dwell on anything that had happened— like that kiss because damn, she'd love to spend a little time dwelling on that—the buzzer to the oven told her the bread was done.

She rose from the table, pushing aside all thoughts of Levi as much as she could and focusing on her own work. Her own overwhelming list.

Unlike Levi's, hers didn't have an end.

~

"You about ready to go to the fruit stand?" Levi strolled into the kitchen.

She put the last pan in the dishwasher, closed the door, and started it. "Yeah. I just finished loading all the trays and cleaning up." She gestured toward the table. "I made you and Keith sandwiches for lunch if you're hungry."

Levi gave her a quick kiss on the cheek and a smile before picking up the roast beef sandwich and taking a big bite. "This is great. Thanks."

Grabbing a seat at the table, he crooked his finger, pulling her list out of his back pocket for her to look at. He'd drawn lines through the first six things.

"You finished all this? Just this morning?" The first item on the list alone would have taken Kasi hours.

"Keith took care of two of those. Begrudgingly," Levi added.

"Not warming up to you, huh?" she asked with a grin. "Can't imagine why not."

"Smart-ass," he teased, chuckling before giving her a quick, hard slap on the ass that was probably meant to be playful. It missed the mark because her nipples tightened instantly and her panties were suddenly damp.

"Keith took the farm truck to work on repairing the fence, so I thought I'd drive you to the stand. I need to head home to take care of some stuff there. I'll come back at the regular time to pick you up, and then we can have dinner with your father."

"Don't remember inviting you to dinner." Kasi felt compelled not to make things too easy for the cocky man, but damn if she didn't also really want him to stay for dinner.

Levi didn't take offense, merely grinning in that way that told her, invitation or not, he would be here for dinner.

Kasi turned the Crock-Pot on low so that the macaroni and cheese she'd tossed together would be cooked by the time they returned home. Levi quickly finished his sandwich, then together, they loaded his truck with all the items for the stand.

Twenty minutes later, Kasi watched his truck disappear around the turn down the road, and it wasn't until nearly an hour had passed that she realized she was still smiling.

She'd noticed the first few customers giving her curious looks. Considering there hadn't been much to smile about lately, she now understood why they were suddenly wondering about her newfound cheerfulness.

Unfortunately, the smile faded when a new customer walked in.

"Hello, Kasi. You look pretty today," Scottie Grover said.

She looked the same as she always did. Tired.

Scottie was the mayor of Gracemont and a major douchebag. His family owned and operated a horse breeding farm next door to her family's land. Despite being neighbors for nearly twenty years, Kasi could count on one hand the number of times his parents had come to visit. And none of those had been social calls, but instead complaints about poor fencing or Keith riding his four-wheeler too close to their property line and spooking their horses.

"Uh, thanks. What can I get you?" she asked, aware he probably wasn't here to buy anything. He never bought anything. Up until last fall, Scottie had never stopped by the stand. Not until Lucy Storm rejected his suit, and he turned his attention in Kasi's direction. Since then, this "stopping by" bullshit had become a more regular occurrence.

She wasn't sure what made her runner-up, but she wished he'd find someone else. The guy gave off major creep vibes, and the fact he always managed to arrive at the stand when she was alone made her uncomfortable. If he'd stopped by twenty minutes ago, she would have had the buffer of Edith Millholland and Genevieve Rogers to keep her from having to make conversation with him.

Scottie glanced around, and she thought perhaps he was looking for something in particular this time rather than just dropping by to flirt with her and remind her that her family was in debt to the town. That hope was dashed when he stepped closer. Scottie had definite issues when it came to understanding and respecting personal boundaries. He also thought he was quite the ladies' man.

She took a step away from him when he ran the back of one finger down her arm. The touch was too familiar and inappropriate, considering they weren't dating. Hell, they weren't even friends.

Scottie scowled when she recoiled from her touch. He'd become increasingly irritated by her continual rejections during each visit.

However, when he spoke, she realized this wasn't a social call.

"I wanted to stop by and speak to you on behalf of the town government again."

Kasi frowned. "I understand you're trying to help, Scottie, but we're fine. I called Herb last week." And she had, but Herb hadn't answered, so she'd been forced to leave a voicemail.

Scottie placed his hand over hers where it rested on the counter. She pulled away again, and he sighed heavily, acting as if she was being needlessly difficult or something.

"Your family is still behind on paying their personal property tax."

Kasi was aware of that. That bill was just one of many sitting in a stack back at the farmhouse, waiting to be paid.

"As I said last time, I wasn't aware it was part of the mayor's duties to collect taxes," she said, striking out due to her over-abundance of pride.

"And as I said," Scottie began, not masking his annoyance, "I'm merely doing it as a favor for you. And for Herb. I told him I was heading home, and he asked if I could stop by to chat with you."

Kasi supposed that sounded reasonable enough considering she had just left the voicemail. Herb Cline was the Commissioner of the Revenue, and his office was in the same building as the mayor's. Herb also served as the clerk of court because Gracemont was about as big as a postage stamp. As such, all the town officials and government offices, as well as the police department, were housed in the same three-story building on Main Street. That also meant it wasn't uncommon for others in the county offices to "pass word along" for each other. It was one of the curses of living in a small community.

"Herb and your dad are close, and I think he's uncomfortable bringing up such a delicate subject," Scottie continued.

Kasi was suddenly less sorry to be dealing with Scottie. She'd managed to hide the worst of her father's mental break by offering a steady stream of excuses whenever friends stopped by to call on him. He'd visited with a few close buddies early on, but the conversations had all been one-sided and awkward as Daddy sat crying quietly. After a while, his closest friends stopped coming by and instead called her weekly to check on him.

Her relief over dealing with Scottie was short-lived, however, when he added, "Just like Sheriff Anderson didn't want to add to your family's grief by pressing charges against Keith for that vandalism."

There was something in Scottie's tone that let her know the end of that situation would have been different if Scottie had been the sheriff. The mayor had shown up the day after the event to "gently"—ha ha—let her know her brother clearly needed a man in his life to keep him in line. Sadly, that wasn't the first time Scottie had dropped the hint that he'd like to be that man...as her husband.

As if.

"I've reached out to Herb a couple times about getting an extension. He was more than happy to extend the first time."

"The first time," Scottie reiterated, making it clear the same courtesy wasn't likely to be offered again.

"We're going to pay our taxes, Scottie. We're just going through a rough time with the drought last summer, and the fire, and..." She paused, not wanting to use the last as an excuse but hoping perhaps it would buy her some time. "And Mama passing away."

Scottie nodded, even as he sniffed haughtily. God, he was an insufferable ass.

"We've never missed payments in the past," she added, trying to sound more contrite.

Scottie tried—and failed—to look compassionate, and when he reached out, putting his hand on her shoulder, Kasi fought not to shake it off this time. "I'm sure it hasn't been easy, Kasi." He started squeezing his grip, like he was giving her a massage. She'd hit her limit on his creepy touches, so she lowered her shoulder and twisted until his hand fell.

He scowled again...and she knew she'd pushed the wrong button when he said, "But that's not exactly true, is it? Because you've missed the last *two* years. Herb already gave your family an extension on the first year. It's not the town's policy to extend longer than that. Failing to pay your taxes—"

"We're good for the money. You know that. We just need more time."

Scottie sighed heavily, making Kasi feel as if she were asking him to part the Red Sea or single-handedly straighten the Leaning Tower of Pisa, as opposed to just asking for more time.

"I'll speak to Herb for you," he replied, like he was doing her the world's biggest favor, "but you have to understand that this town depends on those taxes to function effectively."

And to pay his salary.

Wisely, she held her tongue, her face flushing with anger and embarrassment. She hated being made to feel like a pauper. "I'm only asking for a little bit more time."

"You realize there is another solution, one I mentioned in the spring."

Spring, my ass, she thought.

Scottie had first dropped the marriage suggestion on her just four weeks after her mother died because apparently his ego was so large he genuinely thought he'd be the cure to her grief.

"I'm not interested in getting married. To anyone," she added, simply to appease him. Unfortunately, she didn't want to piss him off so much that he started making waves for her with Herb.

Scottie nodded, walking over to a basket filled with apples. Helping himself to one, he took a large bite, then nodded before stepping next to her again. "You know I'm on your side, Kasi. I'd do anything for you. I hate seeing your family in this position. I'll talk to Herb. See you soon, sweetheart." He gave her a smug smile, like he was some generous benefactor, pausing with one eyebrow raised. It was obvious he expected her gratitude, even though it was on the tip of her tongue to tell him she wasn't his sweetheart.

"Thank you," she choked out.

"Anything for you." He stroked her arm again in that overly familiar way, and she swallowed down the bile his touch produced. With those parting words, he left.

Without paying for the apple.

The petty part of her considered calling the sheriff to report the theft, but she decided it probably wasn't wise to piss the mayor off, since she was asking for more time to pay their debt.

Keith walked in just as Scottie was climbing into his BMW.

"Was that Grover?" he asked.

Kasi nodded.

"What the hell did he want?"

She shrugged, trying for nonchalant. She was unwilling to burden Keith with any of this. "Just trying to drum up votes."

Keith gave her a hard look, and she realized her mistake. Up until eight months ago, she and Keith had been close. Which meant he knew her tells when she was lying.

She'd been avoiding his gaze, so she forced herself to look him straight in the eye as she added, "He's up for reelection."

Keith scowled, clearly unconvinced.

"Whatever," he said finally, reverting back to this new version of himself as he walked out.

Suddenly, Kasi didn't feel much like smiling anymore, so she did what she always did whenever she ran into Scottie. She put him out of her mind completely.

Chapter Four

Levi parked his truck next to the fruit stand, closer than usual. He figured he'd save himself and Kasi some steps as they loaded her empty trays and baskets. As he walked into the stand, there was a strange spring in his step that even he didn't recognize.

He'd spent the better part of the afternoon grinning like a damn fool. Theo had caught him doing so in the brewery, when Levi had brought by a sample of the new variety of hops he was growing. His brother had taken one look at his big-ass grin and asked him if he'd gotten laid last night.

Levi hadn't responded. Instead, he'd just rolled his eyes, whistling as he walked away.

Another brother, Maverick, had asked the exact same question an hour later as the two of them walked through the vineyard checking on the grapes, and he'd given him the same nonresponse.

It wasn't that he didn't want to talk to his brothers about Kasi. Truth was, he and his six brothers were best friends, and there was very little he didn't share with them, including the big old farmhouse on their family farm.

Four generations of the Storm family had called Stormy Weather Farm home, starting with Levi's great-grandparents, who'd bought the two-hundred-plus acres at the beginning of the twentieth century. They'd built a farmhouse—the one Levi's parents now lived in and operated as a B&B—and planted an orchard of apple trees. Granddaddy Lloyd, their only son, had built the second farmhouse a little way down the lane from his parents' place shortly after he and his wife, Grandma Sheila, married.

Upon his parents' passing, it was Granddaddy who'd had the vision of starting a winery, so he'd chopped down most of the apple trees and planted the vineyard. Grandma and Granddaddy had two sons, Rex and Ronnie, and when Levi's dad, Rex, married his mom, Claire, they moved into the original farmhouse that had been vacant for several years. When the second son, Ronnie, married Diana, a third farmhouse was built, and that was the one Levi and his brothers shared, each of them moving in after they graduated from high school.

Sadly, Ronnie and Diana had been killed in a car accident eighteen years earlier, after which their four young daughters—Lucy, Mila, Nora, and Remi—had moved in with Grandma and Granddaddy. Lucy, the oldest, had only been ten at the time. After their grandparents had passed, the girls remained in that farmhouse.

Levi's mom claimed that sometimes it felt like all the Storms did was play musical chairs with the three houses, and Levi had to admit she made a good point. With the exception of his parents, everyone else had house-swapped at some point in their lives.

Remi had taken to calling the home he shared with his

brothers the Frat House, and considering there were seven single men living there, it not only fit but stuck.

Once Levi had finished his chores at Stormy Weather Farm, he'd headed inside, fired up his computer, and started fiddling with his personal work schedule, trying to carve in some time each day to help Kasi. He didn't have a problem working a few extra hours every day if it meant lightening her load. The problem was, harvest time had started. Currently there were only a couple varieties of grapes ready to be picked, but the others weren't far behind. Which meant he was going to have to put a big dent in Kasi's honey-do list in the two weeks before September arrived, when it would be all hands on deck in the vineyard.

Once he'd realized how short his time was, his smile was less prevalent as he considered what Kasi's life had been like since her mother's passing. He could kick his own ass for not asking sooner if she needed help. He'd seen the dark circles under her eyes, noticed the lost weight, but he'd chalked it up to grief, not exhaustion.

He should have asked.

Not that it would have changed a damn thing. He knew Kasi well enough to realize if he *had* asked, she would have put on a fake smile and reassured him everything was fine. He'd never noticed her stubborn streak before yesterday, but that was because he'd been a blind fucking idiot, failing to recognize what was standing right in front of him.

Those days were over.

When Levi stepped into the stand, Kasi had her back to him, combining two baskets of green beans into one. The empty one would be taken back to the farmhouse and filled with today's yield by the Riley brothers. As he always arrived just before quitting time, he was somewhat familiar with her process for closing.

"Did you save me a pie?" He walked over to take the now-empty basket from her to add to the pile she'd already made.

Kasi grinned, gesturing at the empty pastry table. "Sorry. Sold out."

Levi reached for her, wrapping his arms around her waist. "What about the one you always hold back for me?"

Kasi's eyes widened. "You knew about that?"

Levi chuckled. "Not until now. Though I'll admit, I wondered over the years. More than a few times, one relative or another would try to save me a trip down here, letting me know they'd been by the stand and you were sold out of pies."

"So why did you still come?"

"A couple times, I didn't. Then one day, I was running into town anyway and thought I'd take a chance. Sure enough, there was a pie. After that, I came even after the warnings and the funny thing was, every time I showed up, there was always just one pie left, sitting there like it was waiting for me."

Kasi blushed slightly, her pink cheeks so adorable, he couldn't resist stroking one with the back of his knuckles. "You're one of my best customers and I, um...well..." she stammered, clearly embarrassed.

Levi bent down and gave her a kiss on the cheek. "Thank you, little bear," he murmured, touched by her thinking of him, even though it drove home how little he'd been paying attention to her. "You 'bout ready to go?"

He walked to the counter and caught sight of a spreadsheet with numbers. It looked like a budget. Levi sighed. In addition to doing all the chores, it appeared Kasi had taken on the responsibility of paying the bills. Not that he should be surprised by that. Just bothered that there didn't seem to be an end to all the things that had fallen to her after her mother's death.

"Need help crunching numbers? I've got mad calculator skills," he said, joking.

His teasing felt less funny when Kasi quickly grabbed the ledger and closed it. "Nope. All good."

Two days in, and he was getting pretty good at recognizing when Kasi wasn't being honest. Her eyes darted to the left, the pitch of her voice rose an octave, and she plastered on a too-bright smile.

"You sure?"

She nodded, turning away to retrieve something from behind the counter. He started to call her on her lie, but then she stood up with a peach pie in her hands. And not just any peach pie. The best one. He knew that because he'd watched her assemble it, fully aware the one with the lattice top had just a little bit more fruit in it than the others.

So she hadn't just been saving him a pie each day. But the best ones.

Levi slid a twenty into her open cash box, winking at her as he said, "Keep the change."

Her responding giggle was the sweetest thing he'd ever heard.

Then Levi took the pie from her, carrying it in one hand and her pile of baskets in the other. "Let me put these in the truck, then I'll come back for the trays."

"I can get the trays," she replied, as she locked up the cash box and closed the tablet.

"I'll get the trays, Kasi," he repeated, waiting until she focused on him.

She crossed her arms, annoyed. "Fine."

Levi grinned. It was going to be fun spoiling her, mainly because she was so bad at letting him. It also looked like he was going to have the opportunity to give her that lesson in consequences he'd promised, sooner rather than later.

Jesus. His mother would rip him a new one if she heard him threatening to spank Kasi the way he had. Truth was, he'd never said anything like that to a woman before, never even considered it one of his kinks, but something about Kasi had awakened a primitive part of him he didn't even know existed. He'd always considered himself a nice, normal, easygoing guy, but with Kasi, that all went away, leaving behind this crazed, possessive lunatic who wanted nothing more than to lock her in his house and take care of her for the rest of his days.

Levi was overwhelmed by this sudden compulsion to take away her worries and sadness and wrap her in a soft cotton blanket and feed her pie. The problem was, he also wanted to strip her naked, tie her up, spank her sexy ass, and claim every inch, every curve of her body until she begged him for mercy. And then begged him for more.

Once they finished loading the truck and locking the stand, he drove them back to her farmhouse. Now that he was familiar with her routine, they worked quickly to place the baskets in the barn before carrying the trays to the kitchen.

The savory smell of cheese hit him as soon as they walked inside, and his mouth instantly started watering. Kasi was apparently a big fan of the Crock-Pot, which made sense. She didn't close the stand until six each day, so it made life easier for her if she could come home to an already-prepared meal.

Once he put the trays in the pantry, he turned to her. "Tell me what I can do to help you get supper on the table."

She nodded to the cabinet where he'd found the bowls last night. "Mind grabbing some plates? I'll heat some of the green beans I canned from last year's harvest to eat with the mac and cheese."

Levi found the plates and started dipping out three servings. Keith's motorcycle was gone again. "Keith not eating here?"

Kasi shrugged. "He came by the stand on his way out. Just said he'd be back later. If he doesn't eat in town, he'll reheat the leftovers."

Levi picked up the tray he'd used to serve Mr. Mills his meal last night. "Think your father will join us?"

Kasi shook her head. "No."

"Does he ever eat with you?"

Kasi was slower to respond to that question, and when she did, he couldn't help but notice it was one of her nonanswers. "He's just having a couple bad days."

Levi wanted to ask if something prompted those bad days or if they were all bad, but the tight way Kasi held herself and her closed-off expression told him it wasn't something she wanted to discuss.

He put the tray together, adding a big scoop of green beans to the plate once they were hot, then picked it up.

"I can—" Kasi started.

"Set the table for us. You have any beer?"

She smiled. "I might have a six pack of Rain or Shine IPA in the fridge."

He gave her a little hip bump. "Good girl. My favorite. I'll be right back."

Levi quickly delivered the food to Mr. Mills. If the man was surprised to discover Levi delivering his dinner for the second night in a row, he didn't let on. Unlike last night, he was more alert and even said hello before turning his attention back to the television.

When Levi returned to the kitchen, he was pleased to discover Kasi had set the table for the two of them, steam rising from the plates of delicious-looking food, a bottle of beer open for both of them, and she'd even lit a candle as their centerpiece.

Levi decided to take advantage of that, dimming the lights

so that the ambience of the kitchen changed from homey to romantic.

Once he sat down, she lifted her bottle, so he followed suit, tapping his against hers before they each took a sip.

"Your brother keep working after I left?"

Kasi nodded. "I think so. I know he fed the animals before he left. He made sure to let me know."

"Is he still being rude to you?"

Kasi took another sip of beer. "Honestly, I'm not sure I even view his actions as rude anymore. I'm starting to think this is just his new personality."

Levi didn't care for that response, but he didn't pursue it because Kasi looked just as tired tonight as she had yesterday. Even with him helping, she wasn't getting enough sleep, and he wasn't sure how to fix that. She wouldn't take a day off, no matter what he said, and until her father got back on his feet and Keith started doing his fair share of the chores, she would work herself to exhaustion every night.

"This is nice," he said, after they'd eaten in comfortable silence for a few minutes.

"The mac and cheese?"

Levi shook his head. "Eating dinner together. Just you and me."

She gave him a curious look, no doubt trying to figure out if he was sincere. He thought he'd made it clear yesterday. After all, he'd point-blank told her she was his, but he supposed a proclamation like that—made after only a few hours of being together—didn't hold much weight. Which was why he was going to put in the time, make sure she understood he was here to stay.

"Why haven't you ever had a long-term girlfriend, Levi?"

The fact Kasi knew he hadn't, let Levi know she'd been keeping tabs on him. He recalled the way she saved the pies, and he wondered about her feelings toward him. When she was younger, he was pretty sure she'd had a crush on him, but he hadn't gotten the sense that was still the case until today, when she'd admitted to saving the pies. And while she'd kicked up a fuss after he'd used that "you're mine" line, she hadn't tossed him out on his ass or blocked the door when he'd returned this morning.

"Never found a woman I wanted to spend that much time with," he confessed. "I've always known I wouldn't settle for just anyone, and I figured if I ever *did* find the one, I'd know. Like my dad did."

Kasi leaned forward, placing her elbows on the table. "Like your dad?"

"My mom wasn't originally from Gracemont," Levi started, wiping his mouth and leaning back. He stretched his legs out under the table until they touched hers. He drew the toe of one of his boots along her calf playfully. "She came here right after graduation to visit her great-aunt for the summer. After that, she had planned to go on back home to Pittsburgh, where she grew up. She had a job lined up there in a department store."

"She didn't go back?"

Levi shook his head. "Nope. Met my dad at the town's annual Fourth of July picnic. According to Dad, he took one look at my mom and fell head over ass in love. Asked her for a date fifteen minutes after meeting her. They went out every single night for two weeks, and at the end of those fourteen days, he proposed to her."

Kasi's eyes widened. "After just two weeks?"

Levi was used to that response whenever he told someone this story. "Dad swore he would have proposed to her at the Fourth of July picnic, but he didn't have a ring, and he wanted to do it right."

"And your mom said yes? I mean, obviously she said yes. But did she say yes that time or make him wait?"

"There was no waiting for either of them. Mom said she was just as smitten and positive as Dad that they were meant to be. They had a small wedding the next month and by the end of their first year of marriage, I was born. Dad calls her his soul mate. I can count on one hand the number of times I've seen them fight, but even then, they don't let their anger linger. They subscribe to that idea of never going to bed angry, so they always find a way to fix whatever's wrong."

Kasi rested her chin on one hand. "That sounds nice."

"When you spend your life around that kind of love, that kind of happiness," Levi continued, "it makes it impossible to think of settling for less."

"Do your brothers feel the same way? I mean, you're all still single."

Levi toyed with his fork. "You know, I've never asked them, but I have a feeling if I did, they'd agree they were waiting for the same. True love."

"Must be nice having a big family. Sometimes I wish my parents had had more kids. It gets..." She looked away.

"Gets what?" he prodded, tapping her leg with his foot.

She bit her lower lip. "Kind of lonely sometimes. I didn't realize how much life my mother brought to the house until she was no longer here."

Kasi looked away, and Levi could see her starting to close down. It occurred to him, that had become the standard operating procedure for the Mills family. Rather than talk about their loss, they shut it all up inside. Which was why all of them were falling apart.

"What was your parents' marriage like?" Levi asked, determined to get Kasi talking about her mother.

She hesitated for a moment, but he didn't let her off the hook. Just continued to look at her until she gave in.

"Their marriage was pretty similar to your folks'. They didn't have a whirlwind romance or anything. In fact, they dated for four years before they tied the knot. Mama said she was starting to worry Daddy would never pop the question, and she said she'd been prepared to do it herself if it came to that. Daddy always laughed whenever she told that story, saying they'd have been married a lot longer if she'd just gone ahead and done it. Daddy's kind of the nervous sort, and he was too afraid to lose," Kasi finger-quoted the next bit, "the prettiest girl he'd ever seen. I think it's safe to say theirs was sort of an opposites-attract thing."

Levi had always been curious about the Mills' relationship because he'd never seen a couple so different—in appearance and personality—as Katrina and Tim Mills.

"Nothing wrong with opposites," he mused.

"That's true, but damn if Mama and Daddy didn't stretch that saying to its limits. While Daddy's timid and quiet, Mama could have talked the paint off the wall. She had an opinion on everything, a saying to fit every situation, and a laugh that could split your eardrums wide open." Kasi's smile as she spoke was the first genuine one he'd seen on her face in ages.

"And none of that bothered your father?" he asked.

"Oh my God, no. He loved her laugh, loved listening to her talk. My daddy is..." Kasi paused, clearly looking for the words. "He's quiet and a gentle soul. The kind of person who traps a bug in the house to set it free outside. He never raised his voice to me or Keith when we were little, which meant Mama was the disciplinarian. He says the greatest feeling on earth is when those first rays of sunshine heat your skin every morning. Daddy is one of those guys who would give someone the last dollar in his pocket if they were hungry."

Levi could see how much Kasi loved her father. The man, up until his wife's death, had been one of the hardest workers Levi had ever known, and generous almost to a fault.

"How did they meet?"

Kasi smiled. "Mama was ten years younger than Daddy, so they were never in school together, though she said she'd always noticed him around town and such. After she graduated from high school, she went to college and had a serious boyfriend for a time. She moved to New York with him, working in the finance sector. She hated everything about big city life, so she moved home, back to Gracemont after a few years—without the boyfriend. She said she never forgot Daddy, so after many—MANY—attempts at catching his attention, the queen of confidence just gave in and asked him out on a date."

"I take it he said yes."

"He did. She was thirty when they married, Daddy forty. After the wedding, they moved in here with my grandfather, who was still alive at the time. This farm has been in my family for a long time. I came along when Mama was thirty-three, and she had Keith when she was thirty-nine."

The Mills family, like the Storms, had deep roots in Gracemont.

"After Granddaddy passed, Mama stepped in and ran the farm because of her background in business. She was the brains. Daddy was the strong back," Kasi added.

Levi wasn't surprised by that, given Mrs. Mills' take-charge attitude. She'd served as president of the Ladies Auxiliary for the fire department, his mom the vice president. Between the two of them, they'd raised enough money over the years to buy a much-needed new tanker truck for the department.

"Mama made Daddy a list every morning of chores. She decided what we would plant, when and where. She was the one who came up with the idea to open the stand and to deliver eggs. She struck the deals with the local grocery stores, getting them to stock our produce. It was all her. Daddy used to say the greatest day of his life was the day she walked up to him outside the barbershop and asked him out to dinner."

"Sounds like your parents had a relationship very much like my mom and dad, despite being one of those opposites-attract couples," Levi mused, glad she'd grown up surrounded by love. It was the exact kind of life he wanted to give her...and their kids.

He could imagine the two of them telling their own story on his cousin Lucy's *Kiss and Tell* YouTube show, sharing how they'd met and fallen in love. They'd sit on the couch together and he'd look at Kasi and swear the best day of his life was the day she passed out in his arms.

"God, they were even opposites in appearance," Kasi added. "As you know, Daddy is tall and skinny, while Mama was short and fluffy."

Levi chuckled. "Fluffy?"

Kasi's eyes traveled around the kitchen as she spoke. "That was how Mama liked to describe herself. Food was her love language, and she strongly believed in sampling what she cooked before she served it. I've wondered...worried...well, I think now maybe her weight contributed to the heart attack. Her doctor had warned her about her high blood pressure and cholesterol, but Mama refused to cook without salt and butter, and she swore everything was better with bacon. I should have tried—"

"Don't," Levi said, leaning forward to place his hand over hers. "No good ever comes from what if."

Kasi considered that, then nodded. "She died in this room."

Levi didn't know that. How hard must it be for Kasi to spend hours in here, day in and day out, with that memory tucked inside her head. He squeezed her hand.

"I found her."

Fuck.

Kasi was staring at the kitchen floor. Levi used his grip on her hand to tug her out of her seat, pulling her onto his lap. She sat there stiffly, but when he wrapped his arm around her waist and tucked her closer, she loosened up, sinking into his embrace.

"I'm sorry, Kasi."

Something in her eyes softened. "I've never talked about this."

Levi cupped her cheek, forcing her gaze to his. "You need to."

"Yeah. I think I do." She swallowed hard, then took a steadying breath before continuing. "Keith and Daddy were out in the barn, repairing the roof because it was leaking and the forecasters were calling for some bad weather that night. Mama and I were baking in the kitchen, just like we always did, getting things ready to sell at the stand. We were a few eggs shy for a cake Mama wanted to make, so I offered to grab some from the chicken coop. When I got back, she was on the floor."

Every word she said felt like a dagger in his heart, but he didn't stop her.

"I yelled for Daddy, then called 9-1-1. I tried to do CPR, but... The doctor called it a massive heart attack. There was a total blockage. She didn't even mention feeling bad that morning and she didn't act sick. One second, she was there and the next...gone."

Levi pressed his cheek against the top of her head, slowly rocking her, though Kasi wasn't shedding a single tear. He couldn't tell if that was because she'd cried them all out or because she was holding them in so tightly.

She kept talking, her eyes distant as if she was replaying it all in her mind. "I don't remember much about the days that followed. You know how it is after someone passes. There were lots of people stopping by, bringing food. Edith Millholland was here a lot, walking us step by step through writing the obituary and planning the funeral."

Levi smiled when she mentioned Edith's name. Edith Millholland was a Gracemont icon. If the town ever decided to elect a First Lady, she'd be it. She'd lived in Gracemont her entire life —all eighty-two years of it. She knew everyone and everything, had a sharp wit, and was probably one of the nicest people Levi knew. He was glad she'd been there for Kasi and her family.

"I'm not sure what I would have done without Edith because Daddy and Keith were... Well, they weren't able to help much."

"You did a fine job, Kasi. It was a nice funeral," Levi assured her.

Kasi nodded slowly. "I just tried to hold it together. I had to pick out an outfit for Mama to be buried in, had to find freezer space for all the damn casseroles, had to get Daddy and Keith to eat."

"You're a strong woman. Like your mother," Levi murmured, his lips pressing against the side of her head.

"Not that strong. A few days after the funeral, Keith sort of...unleashed."

Levi frowned. "What did he do?"

"He blamed me. Said I shouldn't have left Mama alone in the kitchen, said I should have realized she was sick. He said she was dead because of me."

"Jesus," Levi muttered. "Kasi, you know that's not true."

She nodded slightly. "I do. Now. At the time, I wasn't exactly in a good headspace, so I locked myself in my bedroom, cried forever, then slept twelve hours. When I came out, I realized nothing had been done. Keith was gone, Daddy hadn't eaten or done a single chore. That's when I knew I couldn't do that again."

Levi frowned. "Grieve?"

Kasi looked at him and shook her head. "Stop." Then she looked away when she added, "The grieving will always be there."

"My little bear," he whispered, hating her response. "So fierce."

He didn't know what she saw on his face, but it broke the spell as Kasi pushed herself off his lap. It took everything he had not to pull her back down and hold her there until she cried out all her pain, then slept in his arms for the next week or two. She needed at least that much rest.

"I need to get going on the stand food," she said, grabbing their plates and carrying them to the sink.

Levi rose and helped her clean the dinner dishes. Then he demanded the cake recipe, even though she insisted—as always —that she didn't need any help. Luckily, he only had to give her a look before she relented. He was sorry she didn't push him on the issue because he thought a spanking and an orgasm might do her just as much good as a nap. She was coiled tighter than a rattlesnake ready to strike.

It was nearly eleven before they finished, and he hated that, once again, she was getting to bed so late.

They walked to the front door together, his arm hanging loosely around her shoulders. He found it impossible to be near her and not touching her.

"I can't come in the morning," he said when they stepped out onto the porch. "My family holds a monthly meeting where we discuss all the farm's businesses."

"You realize you don't work here. You don't have to show up at all."

Levi narrowed his eyes. "Thought we'd already sorted that out. You belong to me, and I take care of what's mine."

"I don't remember agreeing to that." Her grin was pure mischief. Yep. This woman was going to enjoy pushing his buttons. And he was going to enjoy letting her.

"Maybe I should jog your memory."

Levi didn't give her a second to consider what was coming next as he drew her into his arms and kissed her. He'd spent too much time today thinking about their first kiss that morning. The memory of it kept sneaking up on him, distracting him.

Kasi hummed softly when his tongue found its way into her mouth. God, she tasted sweet, like berries and sugar. His cock thickened when she lifted her arms and ran her fingers through his hair. He pushed her against the screen door, pressing his thigh between her legs, loving the way she started riding it, pushing her pussy against him, seeking stimulation.

She was going to be a firecracker in the bedroom, and he couldn't wait to watch her explode.

Sadly, that wasn't going to happen tonight. For one thing, her father was asleep in the bedroom right down the hall from hers, and more importantly, the dark circles under her eyes needed to go away. His girl needed sleep way more than sex.

Dammit.

He slowly gentled the kiss, thrilled by her resistance, by the way her fingers tightened in his hair in an attempt to keep his lips on hers.

Levi pushed away, only a few inches, watching as Kasi blinked a few times, trying to shake off the remnants of the kiss. When her eyes cleared, her forehead furrowed. Her damn brain had kicked in.

"I don't think I understand what's going on here," she admitted.

Levi grinned. "I know you don't, but I don't want you to

worry about it. You're dealing with a lot of hard shit right now, but this..." He pointed his finger at her and then himself. "This thing between you and me? It's going to be the easiest thing in the world. Trust me."

Her expression cleared and she nodded. "I do trust you. And I like the sound of easy."

He chuckled, then stole one more quick kiss before saying good night.

As he drove down the dark driveway, he couldn't help but smile.

Levi liked the sound of easy too.

Chapter Five

Levi put the hammer down when his cellphone started ringing, frowning as he glanced at the screen.

"Paul?" he said, answering quickly. He'd exchanged phone numbers with the Riley twins yesterday, telling them to let him know if they had any issues on the farm.

Kasi would kick his ass all the way to next Tuesday if she knew he'd done that, but he didn't care. He was determined to take as much off her plate as possible.

"Hey, Levi. Wanted to let you know Pete's going to open the stand, so we're not going to finish picking the green beans today like we planned."

"Why is Pete opening the stand? Where's Kasi?"

"Her brother drove her to the hospital."

"What?" Levi left his tools where they lay, dug his keys out of his pocket, and headed to his truck.

"Took a tumble in the barn. Hit her head on a shelf. I cleaned up the blood."

"Blood?" Levi threw his truck into drive and kicked up gravel as he pulled away from the cabin. In addition to the B&B

his parents operated, there were ten rental cabins located around the farm. Mina had pulled him aside after the family meeting this morning to ask if he could fix a few loose boards on the porch of this one, since it was vacant the next month.

Mila intended to give it a bit of a facelift. Every two or three years, she chose a cabin to renovate, so they didn't all get run-down at the same time. Once he was done, he'd intended to head to Kasi's to try to mark a few more things off her honey-do list.

"Head wounds bleed," Paul said matter-of-factly, like every word he spoke wasn't shaking Levi to the core.

Pete and Paul Riley were good workers, but damn if they didn't have the personality of rocks. He wasn't sure he'd ever seen either man laugh, just as he'd never seen them get upset or angry or...anything. Their lives consisted of work, home, and church. And that was it. They didn't go out to bars, didn't date, and didn't attend any of the local town events.

"Was she conscious when Keith took her to the hospital?" Levi took a turn a little too quickly, struggling to keep his phone pressed to his ear with his shoulder. He should have put the damn thing on speaker.

"Yeah. Kicked up a fuss about going, but her brother was pretty shaken up and insisted."

That made two of them. Levi's opinion of Keith just rose a few levels.

"Good for him. I'm heading to the hospital now. I'll see about getting one of my cousins to man the stand so you and Pete can finish harvesting those beans."

While Kasi hadn't said as much, he got the sense when he'd mentioned her ledger that she was worried about money. Pete had confided yesterday that the green beans they were harvesting were supposed to be delivered to the local grocery store, as well as a couple of restaurants tomorrow. If money really was an issue, Kasi wouldn't want to miss those deliveries.

Paul grunted, which Levi assumed was his way of saying goodbye because the call disconnected right after that.

Tossing his phone in the center console, he tried to calm down as he drove off the mountain. It wouldn't do any good for him to wreck his truck trying to get to her. Of course, that didn't mean he slowed down because he couldn't get the image of Kasi hitting her head on a shelf out of his mind. Once he got onto the main highway, he called Remi, who promised to head over to Lucky Penny Farm to work the stand for Kasi.

If Remi was wondering why the hell he was racing to get to her best friend and the hospital, she didn't ask. Obviously, her brain hadn't kicked in on that fact yet—too worried about Kasi's accident—but she'd start asking questions soon enough. Not that he had a problem with her asking because he was going to tell her the same thing he'd told Kasi.

She was his.

Period.

He made it to the hospital in less than twenty minutes, which meant it was a miracle he hadn't been pulled over for speeding because ordinarily, that trip took closer to half an hour.

Walking into the ER, he spotted Jessica James behind the desk. He and Jessica had graduated from high school together and she now worked as a nurse.

"Hey, Jess."

"Hi, Levi. What brings you here today? You alright?"

"Yeah. I'm fine. I understand Kasi Mills was brought in by her brother."

Jessica nodded. "Oh yeah. She's here. Doc already fixed her up, and I'm just working on her discharge papers."

Levi released the breath he'd been holding since Paul's call.

If they were letting her go, her injuries couldn't be too serious. "Can I go back and see her?"

"Um. Sure, I guess. She's in exam room three." Jessica grinned, clearly intrigued by his request. She was a big gossip, so he suspected she was currently working on how she was going to spin this conversation later when she called her girlfriends.

"Thanks," he said, hastily walking toward the exam rooms. He heard Kasi before he saw her, her raised voice carrying down the hall.

"I don't give a shit if it *is* policy, Monty. I'm not getting in that thing."

"Kasi."

Levi recognized Monty Bly's voice, noting the resigned tone. Gracemont wasn't a large town, and Levi had spent every single second of his life in it, which meant he knew pretty much every person who lived here.

"Don't you 'Kasi' me. I'm not getting in that wheelchair. I'll look like an idiot."

Levi peered through the doorway of the room and spotted Kasi sitting on the edge of the exam table. She was wearing yet another pair of cutoff denim shorts and a pink T-shirt that was splattered with drying blood. She had a small bandage near her hairline, and she looked madder than a wet hen.

Keith stood off to the side, leaning against the wall, looking at his phone. If he'd been concerned back at the farm, it appeared to have worn off because now he just looked bored.

Levi stepped inside before Monty could continue the battle.

"What are you doing here?" Kasi asked, still scowling.

Levi crossed his arms, not bothering to hide his annoyance at her tone. "Paul called me."

"Why?"

"Nope. That's not the question. The question is why didn't *you* call me?" Levi was looking at Keith as he asked.

Keith replied with a scowl. Levi figured Kasi's brother probably had some choice words he wanted to add, but he held back.

Levi crossed the room to her. Now that he was closer, he could see a lump beneath the bandage and a large, painful-looking bruise on the side of her forehead. "You okay?"

Kasi nodded.

"She passed out," Keith replied. "Hit her head when she fell."

Levi looked over at Monty, who'd been an ER nurse here for close to twenty years. "What did Doc say?"

Monty spared a glance toward Kasi, who shrugged. Monty interpreted that as permission to respond. "Doc put in a half dozen stitches and said she might have a slight concussion. Bruised up her arms pretty good too. He gave her some pain medication and she's supposed to take it easy the rest of the day."

Kasi scoffed. "All caught up now?" Damn, she was not a happy camper. "Can I please go? The stand should have been opened by now." She hopped down from the table, clearly intent on walking out.

"Kasi," Monty started again, rolling the wheelchair toward her.

Kasi held up her hand. "Keep that thing away from me."

"Here we go again," Keith muttered.

"Little bear," Levi said, loosely wrapping an arm around her middle to halt her escape. "You can either sit your cute ass down in that wheelchair, or I'm carrying you out of here."

Keith snickered.

Kasi whirled on her brother. "You think that's funny?"

"I don't think it's *not* funny," Keith replied, pure smart-ass. Apparently that trait ran in the family.

She scowled, then turned back to Levi. She clearly intended to give him the what-for as well, but he wasn't in the mood. Every bit of her face was lined with exhaustion and pain. He was finished playing nice.

"Sit down, Kasi. *Now*," he stressed.

She blinked a few times at his heated demand, then gave in, dropping down into the wheelchair. She started muttering something, but the only words Levi heard were "look stupid" and "cocky asshole."

As he rolled her out of the exam room, Levi glanced over his shoulder at Keith. "I'll drive her home."

Not to *her* home, but Kasi didn't need to know that.

"You don't have to come back to the farm. I'll ride with Keith," Kasi said.

Levi ignored her. "Why don't you head on out, Keith. We'll see you later."

He pushed Kasi to the front desk, where Jessica waited with the discharge papers. The nurse's eyes lit up when she saw Levi pushing the chair. Gossip was as treasured as gold in Gracemont, and he and Kasi were about to star in whatever romantic tale Jessica cooked up to spread around.

"Okay. I'll see you guys there." Keith left the hospital, while Kasi signed the discharge papers. Jessica made some comment about how nice it was of Levi to pick her up, but Kasi didn't take the bait, merely shrugging without saying a word.

The second they hit the exit to the hospital, Kasi hopped out of the wheelchair, storming toward his truck so quickly, he had to jog a couple steps to catch her. When he did, he wrapped his arm around her waist. She'd just passed out. The last thing he needed was for her to take another tumble.

"Slow down," he said.

Kasi shot him a dirty look but matched his more leisurely pace.

Levi opened her door, helping her inside before leaning over to buckle her seat belt.

"Seriously?" she muttered. "I'm not an invalid, Levi."

He gave her a quick kiss on the cheek then shut her door, circling his truck to climb behind the wheel. Rather than start it, he twisted to face her. "That bump on the head knock the grumpy into you?"

Kasi's arms were crossed, and she was silently fuming. His question, however, knocked some of the wind out of her sails, and her shoulders drooped.

"No. I'm sorry. I just..." She sighed. "I didn't need to go to the hospital. I told Keith I was fine. The last thing we need is another fucking bill. And now I've lost a couple hours of sales because the stand isn't open."

"Pete opened the stand on time, and Remi's probably there by now, taking over so he and his brother can finish picking the beans for tomorrow's deliveries."

Kasi's eyes widened. "Oh."

Her astonishment told him just how accustomed she'd become to doing everything on her own. It hadn't even occurred to her to ask for help.

Levi frowned, certain Kasi wouldn't have said anything about the money if she wasn't so rattled and pissed off. It certainly answered his concerns about her family having financial difficulties. He tucked that information away to discuss with her later. For now, he had bigger fish to fry. "By the way, those stitches in your head seem to say something different about you needing medical care. Your brother was right to bring you here."

"Fine. Whatever," she said dismissively, leaning back against the seat wearily. "Can you just take me home?"

Levi studied her face, the dark circles under her eyes even more pronounced than they'd been yesterday. "Keith said you passed out again."

She turned her head to look out the window, not bothering to answer him.

"Did you eat today?" he asked.

Kasi continued to look away from him, even as she shook her head.

Levi growled, pissed. "Did you go to bed right after I left last night?"

The slight hesitance before she nodded let him know she was lying.

"Want to try answering that again? Maybe with the truth this time," he said sternly.

Kasi's eyes darted in his direction, some of her anger resurfacing. "I needed to take care of some things, okay?"

When he left last night, he'd expected Kasi to crawl into bed and—hopefully—dream of him. Because that was sure as hell what he'd done. "What things?"

"Levi. I need to get home."

"Then answer my questions."

Kasi was a stubborn woman, but Levi was pretty damn sure he could out-stubborn her right now. He was determined to help her, but she was fighting him every step of the way.

She blew out an exasperated breath. "I needed to pay some bills, and then I did a bit of cleaning because I haven't had time in the last few weeks. It was getting to the point where I could write my name in the dust on every flat surface in the living room."

Levi's temper went from zero to sixty. "You stayed up to clean?! Dammit, Kasi. What the hell is wrong with you? You can't do it all."

"So you keep saying," she fired back. "But the fact is, Levi, I can. Because I *have*. For eight fucking months! Now take me home."

Kasi turned away from him once more, and he knew by the determined tilt of her chin she was finished with this conversation.

That was fine by him.

He'd told her she was his and he'd fucking meant it. It was time to show her exactly what that involved.

He started the truck, pulling out of the hospital parking lot. Kasi was silent, the uninjured side of her head resting against the passenger window. He kept his eyes on the road until they passed the turn to her family's farm. He expected her to kick up a fuss, but when she didn't say a word, he glanced in her direction.

She was asleep.

Good. That would make this trip a lot easier.

Taking the turn to Stormy Weather Farm, he drove slowly, not wanting her to wake until they reached their destination. When he pulled up in front of the vacant cabin where he'd just been working, he turned off the engine and unfastened his seat belt.

Kasi jerked awake, frowning in confusion as she looked around.

"Where are we?" Her voice was huskier after her too-short nap.

"We're at one of the cabins on my family's farm."

"Why?"

Levi climbed out of the truck, crossing around the hood to open her door.

She shook her head. "I'm not getting out, Levi. I need you to drive me to the stand."

"You're not going to work today."

Her eyes flashed with anger. "That's not your call to make."

Levi leaned into the cab of the truck, reaching across her to unfasten her seat belt. Kasi tried to push his hand away, but her strength was no match for his.

Grasping her waist, he tugged her from the truck and lifted her into his arms, intent on carrying her inside. He was careful to be gentle, not wanting to hurt her. Unfortunately, Kasi wasn't making it easy, fighting him every step of the way.

"Let me go!" she demanded, slapping at his hands and arms, then pushing against his chest. He juggled her a bit, trying to get a firmer grip, determined not to drop her.

"I mean it, Levi," she said, pinching his arms.

"Hold still, Kasi," he snapped. "Or as God is my witness, I'll rip down these shorts and spank your ass, concussion or not."

His threat stunned her to silence—for all of three seconds— before she doubled down on trying to escape his hold.

"Dammit," he cursed, shifting so that he could toss her over his shoulder, firefighter-style.

"Levi!" she screamed, pounding her fists on his back.

He lifted his hand and smacked her ass, hard, while walking toward the cabin.

When she gasped—but didn't complain—he spanked her three more times, then he opened the door and carried her inside, not stopping until they were in the bedroom.

Bending forward, he dropped her onto the mattress, prepared for her next attempt at escape. He placed a firm hand in the middle of her breastbone and held her down, dodging the legs she was kicking his direction.

"What the hell do you think you're doing?" Her fingernails dug into his wrist, but he didn't release her. Instead, he straddled her knees, tightening his thighs so her legs were immobile.

"Calm down, Kasi. Right now."

"I'll calm down when you let go of me and take me to the stand!"

Levi shook his head. "That's not happening."

"*Please*," she demanded. "I have to—"

Levi cut her off with a kiss. He kept it soft and gentle, even as his body clamored for more. Every time his lips touched hers, it fired off some primitive part of him that sought to claim and capture.

Kasi struggled a moment or two more, but whatever fight she had left was clearly spent. And despite her complaints, she didn't hesitate to join the kiss, pressing her lips against his, her tongue stroking his.

When they parted, he stroked her cheek, smiling.

"You can't kiss me whenever you don't like something I'm saying," she said. She didn't return his smile, but her scowl was gone.

"We're gonna have to agree to disagree on that one, little bear. But that's not why I kissed you."

"Why did you, then?" she asked.

"Because I can't resist you," he confessed. "Every second I'm with you, I just want you more."

Kasi drew in a soft breath, and he could practically see her brain trying to process his words. "Oh."

"You have to sleep, Kasi."

"I don't have ti—"

"You do," Levi insisted. "You do have time because I'm forcing you to make it. You've passed out twice in the last few days. If you're trying to work yourself to death, you're doing a hell of a good job of it."

Levi released his grip on her, sitting next to her on the bed. Kasi remained on her back, her legs hanging over the edge of the mattress, staring at the ceiling to avoid looking at him.

"Do you know how I felt when Paul called and said you'd hit your head? When he told me you'd been bleeding?"

Her body sagged in exhaustion and her gaze slid to his face. "I don't understand why you care." There was no malice in her tone, just genuine confusion. "Three days ago, we were nothing more than neighbors. Just acquaintances."

"I told you how it was with my dad. How he knew the second he saw Mom."

"Levi, you've seen me a thousand times in the past twenty-plus years."

"You were a kid for most of those years," he pointed out.

"Because I'm thirteen years younger than you."

Levi ran a hand over her hair, trying to find the words to explain it because the truth was, he'd been just as blindsided by this instantaneous need to be with her. He hadn't been looking for love. Hell, at thirty-seven, he was starting to think he'd never find his woman.

"You're a woman now, Kasi. A strong, beautiful, intelligent woman. I'm not sure how I missed that the past few years, but when you fainted, when I caught you, whatever was blinding me just fell away, and I knew I'd never felt anything more right than holding you in my arms."

"I'm not..." Kasi bit her lower lip. "This is too fast. I'm not... ready."

Levi shifted, reclining on his side next to her. He drew his fingertips over her cheek. "I'm trying not to rush you. And yes, I'm failing," he added with a wink. "So for now, let's just leave it at I care about you, Kasi. A lot. You could have been seriously hurt. Head injuries are nothing to fuck around with. I'm glad Keith forced you to go to the hospital."

"Okay," she said. "I get it. I need to sleep more. I need to eat better. I promise I will."

Her words might have carried more weight if she'd

managed to maintain eye contact. As it was, she was studying the ceiling again like it was the most fascinating thing she'd ever seen.

"I'm getting tired of you lying to me, Kasi, but that's not something I can fix right now. You're bruised and concussed, so those consequences I told you about will have to wait until you're healed."

He thought he saw a glimmer of—fuck him—desire, but she locked it down quick. Not that it mattered. He'd seen it, and it had the effect of throwing tinder on a dying fire. Sweet Jesus. He couldn't wait to take her to his bed. A grocery list as long as his arm started playing in his head as he considered all the ways he'd make his sexy girl come.

But now wasn't the time for that. His gaze locked on her bruised forehead and tired eyes. He placed a soft kiss on the side of her head, wishing he really could make it better with just that touch.

She sighed, and it was the saddest sound Levi had ever heard another person make.

"You're not taking me home, are you?" she asked woodenly.

He shook his head. "Not right now. No."

"What do you want?" He hated how resigned she sounded, but he refused to back down. Even if she couldn't see it, he knew what he was doing was for her own good.

"So fucking much, Kasi. But for now, I just want you to go to sleep."

She nodded. "Okay. Only for a couple of hours. I still need to get home and figure out dinner for Daddy."

Levi didn't respond to that because, despite the fact she had no problem lying to him, he refused to lie to her. She wasn't taking a short nap, and she sure as shit wasn't making dinner.

When he didn't answer her, Kasi tugged her cell from her back pocket and set an alarm before placing it on the nightstand. Then she sat up slowly, toed off her sandals, and climbed on top of the duvet.

If he wasn't so frustrated and worried, he might have laughed at her corpse-like pose as she lay on her back, her hands folded together over her chest.

Levi stood up, reaching for her hand. She slipped hers into his without thought—something he liked—but she resisted when he tried to pull her up.

Two minutes ago, she couldn't get off the bed fast enough. Now she wouldn't leave it.

"What are you doing? You said you wanted me to sleep."

"I do," he said, "but I want you to be comfortable." Once she stood next to the bed, he pulled down the duvet.

Kasi's hands flew to his when he started unbuttoning her shorts. "Wait."

Levi shook his head. "Your clothes have blood on them, Kasi. You're not sleeping in them."

"Fine." She continued to try to pull his hands away. "Go away, then, and I'll take them off."

Levi grinned. "Nope."

"Levi."

Once again, he won the battle, mainly because her energy was completely shot. It took less than a minute to tug off her shorts and pull her T-shirt over her head. Kasi stood in front of him in just her bra and panties, attempting to shield herself with her hands, her cheeks flushed bright red.

"You don't have to be shy with me, little bear. You're beautiful, and very soon, I'm going to see it all anyway."

"Cocky asshole." This time, he heard her loud and clear, and he chuckled as he reached behind her, unhooking her bra with one quick flick of his fingers.

She gasped, holding the cups up. "How the hell did you do that? I can't get *myself* out of my bra that fast."

Levi gave her a shit-eating grin, but she shook her head before he could respond.

"Forget it. I don't want to know."

"Thought you might be more comfortable without it on. I know my cousins always swear the bra is the first thing to come off when they get home from work."

Kasi clearly agreed but refused to let him know that. Instead, she narrowed her eyes and quickly returned to bed, pulling the covers tightly around her body, before drawing the bra off and dropping it to the floor.

When she managed to establish eye contact again, her expression had morphed from annoyance to sadness. "This thing between us...it can't happen, Levi."

It was the first time she'd genuinely tried to push back against the future he saw for them.

"Give me one good reason why not."

This time, she held his gaze as she rattled off her list. "Because I'm too busy for a relationship. My life is a dumpster fire. Because up until a few days ago, you viewed me as one of your cousin Remi's little friends. And because..." She paused, then gave him a look that was downright contrary. "I'm not interested."

Levi couldn't help it. He laughed. "I asked for *good* reasons, little bear. Not lame ones and outright lies."

Kasi rolled her eyes, then winced in pain.

"You have a headache."

She lifted one shoulder. "The doctor gave me something for it at the hospital. It's starting to kick in."

Levi walked to the windows, closing the curtains so that the room would be darker, even though, nestled as deeply in the trees as the cabin was, there wasn't a great deal of sunshine getting in anyway. This particular cabin was one of the original three hunting cabins that had been on the property when his great-grandfather purchased the land. It had been renovated at some point, updated with modern appliances, but it still had a rustic feel to it that Levi liked.

Returning to the bed, he fluffed her pillow, tucked the duvet around her more tightly, then gave her a kiss on the forehead before leaving. He turned at the bedroom door to look back at her one last time. Unsurprisingly, she'd already drifted off to sleep.

Tiptoeing back to the nightstand, he grabbed her phone, taking it with him.

Closing the door behind him, Levi walked over to the couch and sank down, his thoughts jumping from one thing to another.

Sadly, none of his contemplations were peaceful.

Kasi was working herself to exhaustion day after day, and he was struggling to figure out a way to stop that. He'd thought helping with the chores would alleviate some of her stress and allow her more time to rest, but all he'd accomplished was freeing her up to do more...like dusting the fucking furniture at midnight.

It was also clear her family was in trouble financially. Levi wasn't sure how bad it was, but it couldn't be good if it was keeping her up at night, stressed out. Considering a huge portion of their farmland hadn't even been planted this year, he feared their money problems were only going to get worse.

Someday very soon, he was going to sit down with Kasi and have a long chat about the chores and the finances. They'd come up with a plan together, one where she was crystal clear about the fact she wasn't doing everything alone anymore, and he would be helping her.

Once he settled his mind to that, the third and final thing rattling around in his brain started to take precedence, and he was disturbed again.

In a hot and bothered way.

Jesus. Christ.

Seeing Kasi just now in her bra and panties had literally taken his breath away. He'd tried to convince himself he should be a gentleman and not look. After all, she was injured and hurting.

That lasted all of a second and a half before his inner caveman kicked the gentleman to the curb, drinking in every gorgeous curve on her body. Her breasts were full, the perfect size to fill his hands, and her waist nipped in, creating an hourglass shape, that showcased her gorgeous ass. His dick stirred and started to thicken despite the fact it was not seeing any action today. Or in the near future.

Kasi still needed time to come to grips with what Levi had figured out in mere seconds.

They were meant for each other.

So he closed his eyes, gave his cock a "be patient" speech, then started making a mental list of next steps.

Kasi was too thin, her ribs protruding more than he liked. He had every intention of making sure she ate three meals a day from this point on. There would be no more leaving Kasi to her own devices. She'd proven today she couldn't be trusted to take care of herself.

So from now on, he'd spend every morning at her house, eating a big breakfast with her. Lunch would be a bit trickier, especially with the busiest part of the harvest approaching, because he would be working at the vineyard all day. Hell, if he had to, he'd have lunch delivered to her.

Dinner would be the same as breakfast. He'd join her at her house, or she could eat with him and his brothers.

As for the chores, they'd divvy them up between him, Kasi, her brother, and...

Levi mentally added her father to that list. He wasn't

entirely sure how to help Mr. Mills, but it was clear his children tiptoeing around him wasn't helping.

He recalled Kasi telling him how her father had always worked from the list his wife provided. Maybe what he needed was that kind of structure again. It was worth a shot, at least.

Feeling better now that he had a plan, Levi returned to the bedroom, peering inside. Kasi was sound asleep, looking more peaceful than he'd seen her in nearly a year. Closing the door behind him, Levi picked up his phone and walked outside.

Sleep was only the first thing she needed.

It was time to start providing the rest.

Chapter Six

<hr>

"You've been a naughty girl, Kasi."

Kasi glanced over her shoulder at Levi and gave him a mischievous grin, one that was certain to get a reaction from him. "So, what are you going to do about it?"

Levi's eyes darkened with a lust so thick, Kasi could barely breathe.

"You know exactly what I'm going to do," he responded in that deep, dark-chocolate voice of his, so rich and thick and yummy.

Kasi took a step back when he approached her, not due to fear but because there truly was a thrill in the chase. He paused, but only for a moment before taking another step. Kasi matched his movements until she reached the kitchen table, putting a chair between them.

"My daddy is upstairs," she murmured, aware that was only adding to the excitement coursing through her.

"You should have thought about that before you tugged on the lion's tail, little bear."

He certainly resembled a lion, his long hair loose and hanging in his face, his thick beard in need of a trim.

"Keith could come home any minute," she added, even though her brother wouldn't be home until the wee hours.

"Then he's about to get one hell of an eyeful," Levi taunted, lifting the chair she was using as a shield and pushing it aside.

Kasi lifted her hands, placing them on Levi's broad, muscular chest, sorely tempted to lean forward and sink her teeth into the firm pec she felt beneath his cotton T-shirt.

"Are you going to take your punishment like a good girl?"

Kasi smirked. "I thought we already determined I was naughty."

Levi chuckled, and it occurred to her the low sound should be more threatening than it was. In fact, it didn't scare her at all. It only turned her on more.

He reached out, gripping her upper arms in his strong hands, tugging her closer and lifting her on tiptoe at the same time. He lowered his head until she could smell the sugar, cinnamon, and apples from the pie they'd eaten for dessert on his breath.

She lifted her face, closing the distance, so ready for his kiss.

It never came.

Kasi gasped as Levi spun her around so fast she was lightheaded. Before she could react to his quick movements, his hand was between her shoulder blades, pressing her chest and face flat against the smooth surface of the kitchen table.

"Levi," was all she managed to say before his hand came down on her ass, spanking her with a strength that should have hurt.

And it did. A little bit. But not enough for her to ask him to stop.

The heat from his blows worked its way through her system, her clenching pussy soaked. She needed him so desperately. It felt as if she'd die without his cock, pounding inside her.

"Please," she gasped, but Levi didn't acknowledge the request, his hand rising and falling on her ass. Kasi lifted onto her toes on each return, adding her own force to his. Her breathing grew ragged and stars formed behind her closed eyes.

God, she wasn't going to come, was she?

From a spanking.

Was that even possible?

Levi paused, bending over her back, his breath hot in her ear. "Are you going to be my good girl?"

That question should not be so fucking hot, but Kasi was helpless to the way every part of her responded to it. She wasn't sure what did it for her more—the way he wanted her to be a good girl, or the fact he wanted her to be his.

My good girl. Not a good girl. She noticed the difference and she liked it...a lot.

"Yes," she hissed. "Please. I'll be good. I promise."

Levi nipped her earlobe. "I know you will."

She started to push up to her elbows when he rose, but Levi's hand landed on the nape of her neck, pressing her harder against the table.

"I didn't give you permission to move."

She pressed her palms flat against the table, her cheek resting on the cool surface. Her body jerked when she felt his fingers reach around her waist, working the button on her shorts free.

Finally.

He removed her shorts and panties with one quick pull, the material pooling around her ankles.

She started to kick them away but froze when Levi drew one finger along her slit, stopping when he reached her clit, stroking it.

. . .

Kasi gasped as she sat bolt upright, blinking rapidly in the dark room, her heart still racing.

Fuck.

It was a dream.

She was tempted to lay down, close her eyes, and find her way back. She even slipped her hand beneath the duvet, ready to help things along.

But then she realized this wasn't her bed or her duvet or her room.

Where the hell was she?

The answer hit her the exact same time Levi's voice cut through the silence.

"That was quite a dream."

She glanced next to her, quickly tugging the sheet around her when she realized she was naked from the waist up and giving him a peep show.

"You're in bed with me," she said, stupidly stating the obvious.

Levi sat up, and she could see from the faint beam of light shining through the cracked-open bathroom door that he was shirtless as well. "You hit your head, Kasi. I wanted to stay close and make sure you were alright."

Today had not been one of her better days, which was saying something, considering how much they'd all sucked lately. She had tossed and turned the previous night despite her exhaustion, too worried about her family's financial situation... and too worked up over Levi's kisses.

In the end, she'd given up trying to sleep, climbing out of the bed she'd only just climbed into a couple hours before. She spent her morning—which began at three a.m.—moving around the kitchen like a zombie, baking for the fruit stand and making breakfast and lunch for her father, before heading to the barn to load the produce baskets into the truck.

That was all she remembered before waking up on the dirt floor of the barn, wiping what she'd initially thought was water from her eyes before realizing it was blood. Then Keith walked in and basically lost it, yelling for Pete and Paul to help him get her to the truck despite her insistence she was fine. It had been a lie because her head was pounding and her ears ringing loudly.

It wasn't until Doc put in the stitches and gave her some pain medication that she'd started doing a mental tally of how much the hospital visit was going to cost them. Her mood turned black after that, and she'd taken it out on poor Monty, Keith, and—she grimaced—Levi.

"I'm sorry I was such a bear earlier," she said, feeling guilty for her behavior. She was usually a nice person and considered herself to be pretty pleasant. When she wasn't running on fumes anyway. Which was next to never these days.

She held the sheet against herself, taking mental stock of her injuries. Her scalp, where Doc had put in the stitches, was tender and she felt a bit stiff, but other than that...

She hadn't felt this good in days. No—weeks.

"You were hurting...and living up to your name," Levi said good-naturedly. "I'm a pain in the ass when I'm hurt too. Now," he said, giving her that charming grin that had her considering adding her panties to that pile of clothes by the side of the bed. "Tell me about that dream. What was I doing to you that had you so breathless and flushed?"

Kasi narrowed her eyes, determined to wipe that arrogant, sexy smile off his face. "What makes you think I was dreaming about you?"

She expected him to laugh. What she *didn't* anticipate was his sudden fierce scowl.

"I'm going to let you in on something, little bear. I'm only just now discovering that I'm a possessive, jealous asshole when it comes to you, so I don't want another man showing up in your dreams any more than your real life."

Kasi's heart started to race again because...wow...swoonworthy.

"Fine," she said softly. "Maybe I *was* dreaming about you. That doesn't mean it was a sex dream."

Her response wiped away every trace of anger, his grin larger than life. Levi ran one finger along her bare arm, leaving a trail of goose bumps in its wake.

"Oh, it was definitely a sex dream. What was I doing to you?"

She was glad the room was so dark. She hoped that meant he couldn't see her blushing. "Nothing." Hell would freeze over before she admitted that she'd dreamed about him spanking her to the precipice of an orgasm over her family's kitchen table.

Her family's table.

Dinner.

Shit!

Kasi jerked around, looking for her phone, then glanced toward the curtains. It was dark outside. "What time is it?" she asked.

Levi shrugged. "Maybe midnight."

"Midnight!" Kasi shrieked, throwing her legs over the side of the bed. "I told you to wake me up. Where's my phone?" She bent down, feeling around the floor for her clothes while struggling to keep herself covered by the sheet.

"I turned off the alarm and took it to the living room. I've got it on a charger out there."

Kasi gave up the search for her clothes, whirling around to face him. "You had no right to do that."

Levi leaned closer to her. "I had every right. You passed out *again*," he stressed the last word, "because you aren't getting enough sleep and you aren't eating. From this point on, I'm taking charge."

She laughed, though there wasn't a bit of happiness in it. "Bullshit."

"Keep fighting me on this, Kasi, and I'll flip you over and introduce you to those consequences I told you about, concussion or not."

He'd mentioned those consequences just before she fell asleep earlier. No wonder he'd been the star of her dreams.

The rebellious part of her was tempted to push him, simply because she wanted what he was threatening.

So. Fucking. Bad.

But the practical side won out because, well...she'd gotten a lot of sleep, thanks to him, so her thoughts were crystal clear and not foggy with exhaustion for the first time in forever.

"I need to go home, Levi," she said, striving for a calmer tone.

"No, you don't."

Kasi turned around again, trying and failing to find her clothes on the floor. Did Levi move them? "I have to get back. There are so many things I didn't do. Things I *need* to do."

"Remi ran the stand for you today."

"That was sweet of her." Kasi was grateful for her best friend's help. Not that Kasi had been much of a friend of late. Prior to Mama's death, she and Remi had been thick as thieves, always going out to the movies or to ladies' night at Whiskey Abbey after they both turned twenty-one. They hadn't done either of those things in the past eight months, Kasi too bogged down with work.

Not that her never-ending list of excuses for not going out had stopped Remi from trying. Hell, lately she didn't even attempt to draw Kasi out, showing up at the farmhouse instead, armed with a bottle of wine that they split as she helped Kasi bake for the stand and regaled her with gossip and funny stories. She'd been too tired to truly appreciate her bestie's attempts at lifting her spirits.

"But Dad—"

"She made dinner for your dad," Levi interjected. "Apparently, she coaxed him out of his bedroom and the two of them ate together on TV trays while watching *Jeopardy*. She said he was way too amused by how many answers she guessed wrong. He mentioned that your mother was some kind of *Jeopardy* savant."

"She was. We always told her she should try out," Kasi replied absentmindedly, too hung up on what else he'd said. "Daddy ate downstairs?"

"He did," Levi replied.

She was instantly overwhelmed with a strong sense of regret. In the weeks following Mama's death, Kasi had tried a million different ways to draw Daddy out of his room, but he always refused. After a while, she'd stopped trying, too busy with her own chores, too lost in her own unending grief. She'd thought the way things were now meant they were the new norm.

But what if they weren't? What would happen nowadays if she pushed and prodded him like Remi had?

Oh God. What if Daddy hadn't been hiding in his room due to grief but simply in need of someone to draw him out?

"I'm going to bake her a pie." Kasi was perfectly aware even that wouldn't be thanks enough for what her best friend had done today.

"She'd like that, but it isn't necessary. She was glad to help because apparently, she's made a lot of offers that haven't been accepted."

Kasi *had* rejected most of Remi's offers to help. The only exceptions were those wine nights, which were too few and far between.

"As for the rest," Levi continued. "Keith took care of the animals, then helped Pete and Paul finish harvesting the beans. They've got them packed up for delivery, and your brother has promised me he'll handle those for you, since neither of us want you driving for a few days. You're prone to passing out."

Kasi frowned. "You didn't tell him about the other day in the fruit stand, did you?"

Levi crossed his arms. "I did."

"I didn't want him to worry."

He scoffed, unmoved. "He's not a kid anymore, Kasi."

She rolled her eyes. "So he keeps telling me."

"He went out with some friends after his chores were finished, but he was back by nine to relieve Remi. He's home with your father. So, there's no need for you to rush out right now."

There were plenty of reasons for her to go home but the longer they sat there, the more self-conscious Kasi became about her near-naked state.

And his shirtless one.

His pecs were every bit as bite-able as she'd dreamed.

"Where are my clothes?" she asked.

"Your shirt is in the trash. I tried to wash it but the blood-stains wouldn't come out. I had better luck with your jean shorts. They're hanging over the porch railing, drying."

"How am I supposed to get home with no shirt?"

Levi rose from the bed, looking hotter than a man had the right to in a pair of faded jeans. There was something oddly intimate about watching him walk around the bedroom shirt-less and barefoot.

He grabbed something from a chair in the corner, returning to her side of the bed.

"Asked my brother Jace to stop by with a few things. He brought you one of my shirts to wear." Levi pulled it over her head as he spoke, grinning when she pulled the large shirt down over the sheet to make sure she didn't give him another peek at her tits.

"Didn't realize you were so shy," he teased.

"Didn't realize you were such a perv," she retorted.

Levi laughed, then offered his hand. She took it, climbing out of bed, allowing him to lead her to the kitchen. His shirt hung to mid-thigh, so she didn't have to worry about flashing her panties. She started to ask where her bra was but decided fuck it. She wasn't so well-endowed that she couldn't walk around without it, especially since she'd lost a bit of weight. It figured she'd lose it the one place she didn't want to.

"Jace also dropped off some food. I wanted to feed you something as soon as you woke up." He opened the refrigerator, pulling out some sliced cheddar cheese and ham, as well as a stick of butter. Grabbing a loaf of bread from the counter, he put together a couple sandwiches, buttering the bread before plopping them onto a griddle on the stove. Her mouth watered as the smell of melting cheese and butter permeated the air.

While the sandwiches were grilling, he opened a can of tomato soup, dumping it into a pan to heat as well.

"Want something to drink?" he asked, opening the fridge once again. "We have water, soda, and Rain or Shine IPA."

"Water, please."

Levi grabbed a bottle for her and one for him, placing them on the table before he finished cooking and plating their midnight feast.

It wasn't until he'd placed the soup and sandwich in front

of her that she realized she hadn't even offered to help. She'd been too distracted by his six-pack abs and the strong muscles in his back.

"This smells delicious. Thank you," she said, picking up her spoon just as her stomach let out a loud rumble. "I'm starving."

"Did you eat at all today?"

She considered lying, but decided against it since Levi seemed to have a sixth sense when it came to her truth telling... or lack thereof.

Kasi shook her head. "I wasn't hungry when I woke up." She didn't bother to add she'd gotten out of bed at three a.m. "Then I got busy with baking."

Her stomach had been tied in knots lately over the farm's finances and the extreme lack of money coming in. In addition to the tax debt, they were still making payments on the new tractor her father had bought just a few months before the fire. The tractor—like the corn—had been a casualty of the blaze. There was nothing more painful than making monthly payments on a useless hunk of charred metal.

The meager amount of savings her family had in the bank had been used to pay for Mama's funeral, a shockingly expensive endeavor. Between the service, the casket, the plot, and the headstone Daddy had insisted they order immediately, that nest egg, which had been pitiful to start with, was completely gone.

While Kasi was relieved they hadn't lost a day's worth of earnings from the fruit stand, she knew it would be nowhere near enough to pay off their personal property tax debt. If she didn't find a solution soon...

No. Fuck that. She was NOT marrying Scottie Grover.

This was all her fault. They should have plowed the burned fields and planted corn in the spring, but at the time,

Daddy had been lost in his grief, hunkered down in his room. Keith had been running wild all over the county, trying to escape from his own misery, like he could outpace it if he just drove that motorcycle fast enough. They were down to the one tractor—the old one that was on its last legs. And she hadn't known enough about the farm side of her family's business at the time to make any decisions. She'd always helped her mother with the baking and the stand. Keith took care of the animals and helped at harvest time. But the actual choices of what to plant when and where had always been something Mama decided, and Kasi had never cared enough to pay attention.

Levi grunted, clearly annoyed by her poor eating habits. "By the way, Jace headed over to your farm after dropping off the clothes and food."

"Why?"

"He offered to help with a couple of things on that honey-do list you made me."

Kasi put her sandwich down without taking a bite. "He didn't have to do that. Shit, Levi, I told you that *you* didn't have to do it. I can take care of those things."

Levi wiped his mouth and hands, then leaned back in his chair, his legs kicked out in front of him. "I asked him to take a look at the tractor because Pete said you'd been having some trouble with it. Jace is a good mechanic. He replaced the transmission belts, filter, and pads, tinkered with the gearbox, and changed the oil. Sounds like whatever he did was just the trick because Pete said it hadn't run that well in years."

Dealing with the old tractor had been one of the major items on Kasi's to-do list, but she'd kept shoving it down because she feared getting it fixed would be costly.

"That was..." Kasi was overcome with relief. "I'm baking him a pie too."

Levi laughed.

"And please tell him to send me the receipts so I can reimburse him for all the replacement parts."

Levi shook his head. "I already took care of that."

Kasi narrowed her eyes. "Then *you* send me the receipts."

He laughed again, acting like she'd made a joke.

"I mean it, Levi."

"I know you do, little bear. But this is just another one of those things you're going to have to stay mad at me for because I'm not giving you the receipts."

"How much was it?"

Levi ignored her, tilting his head toward her plate. "Finish eating."

The gnawing anxiety she felt whenever she thought about money was back. Now she wasn't just in debt to the town but to Levi as well. Freaking awesome. "I'm full."

Levi pushed her plate closer to her. "Finish every bite."

The stern look he gave her told Kasi this was yet another argument she wouldn't win. She picked up the sandwich and took a large bite. Then another and another, until it was gone. Once the plate was clear, he pushed the bowl of soup closer. She scowled at him but didn't complain, picking up her spoon and shoveling in every drop of that as well.

"Good girl," he murmured, once she'd finished eating, his words sending her straight back to her sexy dream.

Levi cleared the table, putting the dishes in the sink before returning to his chair.

"I sure as hell like those blushes of yours."

Kasi raised her hands, covering her cheeks.

"Which reminds me," he said, reaching across the table to pull her hands down, gripping them in his firm grasp. "You never did tell me what I was doing to you in that dream of yours. From the way you were breathing heavy and squirming around, it must have been something good."

"I'm not saying. It's too...mortifying."

Levi shook his head. "Nothing between us is embarrassing, Kasi. This is who we're going to be to each other. There's not a thought, dream, worry, or fear of yours I don't want to hear about. And the same holds true for me. I'm going to tell you everything. We're going to dig so deep into each other, we won't know where I end and you begin."

Kasi couldn't quite make herself believe all the incredible things Levi was saying. For one thing, his abrupt about-face when it came to their relationship status was giving her whiplash. For another, she wasn't sure she should accept what he was offering. Her life was a shitshow, and it didn't seem fair to drag him into that.

No matter how much she wanted to.

"Tell me just one thing about it, and I'll give you one of Mom's homemade salted caramel cookies."

Kasi's eyes flew to the counter, and sure enough, there was a clear plastic tub with half a dozen of her all-time favorite cookies. "You would deprive a woman with a concussion her favorite cookie?"

Levi's eyes crinkled, amused by her attempt at guilting him out of a treat. "I absolutely would."

"You're a monster."

Levi tightened his grip on her hands. "Maybe so, but you can't deny you like my monster. He gets you all hot and bothered, doesn't he? Tell me something, little bear. If I had slipped my fingers into those cute panties of yours right after you woke up, how wet would you have been?"

Soaking, she thought.

Drenched.

Then she realized that state hadn't changed. Watching him cook for her shirtless had kept her arousal going strong.

Despite the flames licking her face, Kasi gave Levi what he

asked for. Or at least a crumb. "I was dreaming about those consequences you've mentioned."

Levi's dark eyes went black. "You dreamt of me spanking you?"

She nodded, looking away.

Levi didn't let her get away with it, cupping her jaw, forcing her to face him. "Were you over my lap?"

Kasi shook her head, suddenly wishing she had been. "I was bent over the kitchen table at my farmhouse."

Levi swallowed deeply, and she watched his Adam's apple bob. "Were your pants down around your ankles?"

"Not while you were spanking me, but after..." She paused, reimagining her dream with his vision of how it would go down.

"So you were bent over, face down, while I spanked you."

"Yes," she whispered.

"And after?"

"I woke up," she confessed.

"That's a shame. You want me to tell you how it would have ended?"

Kasi should end this here before things between them got out of hand. Until she figured out what this was between them, and decided what it should be, she was the worst kind of masochist to allow him to plant even more seeds in her feverish, lust-drunk brain.

Unfortunately, her head moved, nodding rather than shaking, and she was completely helpless to make it change direction.

"Once I'd finished painting that sweet ass of yours red, I would have stripped off your pants and panties, then knelt behind you, pushing your thighs apart so I could see that pretty pussy."

For a second, she wanted to ask him how he knew it was

pretty. He'd never seen it, but the smart-ass question vanished when he continued speaking.

"I'd run my tongue along that soaking wet slit, drinking down every drop of your juices, then I'd tease that cute little clit of yours until you were riding my face, begging me to fuck you."

Kasi clenched her legs together, pursing her lips to stop herself from doing that begging right now.

"Your first orgasm would be on my tongue, the second on my fingers. I'd fuck you with one, then two, then three, stretching your tight cunt until you were screaming for more."

"God," she breathed, hanging on every word. No one had ever talked to her like this. Shit, she'd always been convinced that men didn't say stuff like that in real life, those words confined to the pages of a romance novel.

"Only after you were hoarse from crying out my name would I stand up and fuck you. You're going to feel so good around my cock, Kasi. But be warned, I'm not a gentle lover, and while I might be a strong man typically able to remain in control, I'm afraid that won't apply when it comes to you. I want you too much. So I'm going to fuck you hard—hard enough that you'll feel the effects of it weeks later."

A small squeak escaped before Kasi could call it back.

Levi smiled, lifting their clasped hands to his lips. He drew one of her fingers into his mouth, sucking on it until she was gasping, struggling hard to breathe. How could he make such a simple thing so sinfully sexy?

"Levi." She was intent on begging for everything he just described. She was panting, for God's sake, her pussy dripping.

So she was shocked—and thrilled—when Levi released her hands.

Yes!

No words were necessary.

Levi led her back to the bedroom, pulled the duvet down, helped her in, then circled to the other side, climbing in next to her.

Kasi shifted toward him, disappointed when Levi gave her the quickest, most platonic kiss she'd ever received before saying, "Good night."

"But—" she started.

"Kasi. You have bruises all over your body, stitches in your forehead, and a concussion. And while I'm glad you were able to steal about ten hours of sleep, you still need at least twice that to make up for the way you've been running yourself ragged lately. You need rest."

"I don't want to rest."

Levi grinned, then tapped the tip of her nose playfully. "Every single thing I said to you just now is going to happen, but not tonight. You'll have to give me a rain check on making your dreams come true."

She narrowed her eyes, but the truth was, now that she was back in the ridiculously comfortable bed, her energy was already starting to wane.

"Fine," she said, grumpily. "But I make no promises on that rain check," she lied, turning away from him.

"You're giving me the rain check," he insisted in that arrogant tone of his.

"What about my cookie?" she asked, somewhat petulantly. If she wasn't getting him, the least he could do was give her a treat.

"Another rain check."

She sighed.

Levi shifted next to her, wrapping his arm around her middle and pulling her back against his chest. She'd never been held by a man in bed in her life. That was the first thought she had when Levi's breath evened out, sleep coming for him quickly.

Her last thought before she joined him in dreamland was a simple one.

He was going to win yet another argument.

Because she was totally giving him that rain check.

Chapter Seven

Levi walked inside the fruit stand just as Kasi was closing. As had become their routine, he helped her load the baskets and trays into the truck, then waited while she locked the stand.

Since Keith was using the Lucky Penny Farm's ancient truck as he continued to chisel away at the list Kasi made them, Levi drove Kasi to the stand right after lunch, helping her open then promising to pick her up at closing time.

Waking up this morning with her nestled in his arms was the best thing he'd ever experienced. After their midnight dinner, they'd crawled into bed and fallen fast asleep. Levi had anticipated a restless night, his body clamoring for things Kasi simply wasn't physically well enough for. Instead, he'd wrapped his arm around her and drifted off in record time. He was convinced his good night's sleep was the result of Kasi being exactly where he needed her to be.

Safe and sound in his arms.

Unfortunately, after fourteen hours of deep sleep, Kasi had awoken with the birds, asking to return to the farm. Given the lack of dark circles and the sunny smile of her face, he gave in to her wishes. He'd made some calls yesterday afternoon, arranging for his brothers to cover his daily chores for the next few days because he refused to allow Kasi to relapse.

He was going to owe his brothers a hell of a lot more than pie for their help, but when he'd explained that Kasi had passed out and the family needed help around the farm, they insisted the Millses needed him more than they did, and that they'd keep things running smoothly in the meantime.

His family was the greatest. And the icing on this cake was the fact they all knew and loved Kasi already, given her close friendship with Remi. She'd been a permanent fixture on the farm when she was younger, an honorary Storm for most of her life. He couldn't wait to change that status from honorary to official...but he suspected Kasi would laugh him out of town if he tried proposing to her after only a few days.

After driving Kasi home, they'd spent the morning together in her kitchen, baking. Then they shared breakfast with her father and Keith.

Levi had been pleased when Kasi insisted on her father joining them at the table. He'd noticed last night how shocked she'd been by Mr. Mills' willingness to eat dinner downstairs with Remi. Apparently, Kasi had taken it as a sign the man simply needed a push to emerge from his room. While breakfast was a quiet affair, Levi noticed how happy Kasi had been to have her family sitting around the table together.

With the breakfast dishes washed and put away, Levi and Keith sat together going over Kasi's honey-do list, each taking a couple items apiece to tackle.

While he hadn't offered to chip in, Mr. Mills sat at the table listening to their plans. Levi had hoped he might want to join them, but as they rose to head outside, Kasi's father had climbed the stairs, returning to his room.

Levi tried to tell himself that Rome wasn't built in a day. The fact Mr. Mills had eaten dinner with Remi last night, and breakfast with them this morning, gave him hope that perhaps he was turning a corner on his grief.

"Keith still working on the fences?" Kasi asked as he shut the tailgate of the truck once it was loaded.

Levi nodded. "Yeah. Y'all have a fair amount of fenced property, so I suspect it'll take him a couple days at least if he needs to do a lot of mending." Lucky Penny Farm was surrounded by wooden fencing that hadn't been tended to for a few years at least. As such, there were a lot of broken and fallen boards. It was a big job, and a hard one, so Levi had expected it to fall to him. He'd been pleasantly surprised when Keith offered to take on the hefty chore.

"I'm glad he's doing it. Mr. Grover's made more than a few comments about the state of our fence over the past couple of years. Maybe this will get him off our backs."

Levi scowled. "Never will understand how a family can have so much and still be miserable." The Grover family had moved to Gracemont over two decades ago, bringing with them a big pile of old money. With it, they'd bought up a huge plot of land and started a farm, where they bred high-quality horses. They were also looking to start a training facility, with hopes that one day a Grover Farms horse would compete in and win one of the Triple Crown races.

"They really are unhappy, aren't they?" Kasi agreed.

"Yeah. I typically try to give them a wide berth. Of course, it's not that hard nowadays. Not since I kicked Scottie's ass. Since then, he's greatly curtailed his visits to the brewery and winery, only showing up occasionally when we have a special event that he thinks the mayor should attend. As if anybody ever needs to see that blowhard," he grumbled.

"Remi told me about the ass-whooping right after it happened." Kasi giggled.

"The asshole was coming on too strong with Lucy. So I punched him in the jaw and threatened to call the sheriff if he didn't get off our land."

"I wish I'd been there to see that."

Levi wrapped his arm around her shoulders. "Not a big fan of the mayor?"

Kasi's eyes darted away from his briefly. "Not really."

Levi opened her door, helping her into the truck as she rolled her eyes.

"You know, I've been climbing into cars all by myself for twenty years."

Levi pulled the seat belt over her, snapping it into place. "Yeah. But if you did it on your own, I couldn't do this." He gave her a soft kiss, intending for it to be short and sweet. That attempt failed the second his lips touched hers. He'd missed the hell out of her this afternoon, and they'd only been apart five hours. Not even that because he'd snuck down to the stand twice during work breaks to steal a few more kisses.

Kasi's enthusiastic response to his kisses was what kept him coming back for more. Now that the shock of his newfound devotion was wearing off, she'd stopped fighting this thing between them, accepting his kisses and adding her own heat to them. Her tongue sought out his first, and he felt the edges of her lips tip in a smile when he nipped at it playfully. Her fingers fisted his hair, holding him close to prevent him from stopping. It was a wasted effort. He wasn't going anywhere.

The kiss lingered long enough that Levi hit a crossroads. Faced with either putting the brakes on or stripping Kasi's shorts off and taking her right here on the front seat of his truck.

Levi pulled back, forced to adjust his jeans.

Jesus. Ten minutes in his woman's presence and he was

rock-hard, every drop of blood in his body hanging out due south.

Kasi gave him a knowing grin when he straightened and attempted to walk normally—he failed—around the front of the truck.

Once he was in the truck, Levi fired it up and pulled away from the stand. "Hey. I wanted to talk to you about something. I spent the afternoon with Pete and Paul, plowing one of the burned fields, incorporating the cover crop back into the soil. Have you given any thought to what you might want to plant there? There are some good fall crops you could put in if you want to start something now. Carrots, radishes, lettuce, stuff that can survive the first frost."

Kasi glanced out the passenger window as they drove down the dirt driveway to the farmhouse. "I hadn't thought about that. Maybe I should ask..." She stopped, biting her lower lip.

"You should ask your dad." Levi had been around enough the last few days to realize it was time Kasi and her family started to fix what was broken. Keith, while still a sullen son of a bitch, had been staying home more and contributing. Levi was calling that a win because every chore Keith took on was one less for Kasi.

She remained quiet rather than respond to his suggestion. He could tell she'd dismissed it out of hand. Then...he recalled her telling him it was *Mrs.* Mills who'd had made the major farm decisions. Maybe if she pulled her father in on the decision, he'd start taking an interest in the farm again.

"You should talk to him," Levi pressed.

Kasi nodded slowly. "I will." Given the way her gaze was locked on the driveway in front of them, he knew she'd just lied. He was tempted to call her on it and introduce her to those consequences she seemed to like the sound of, but he decided to let it slide.

Not the idea but the lie.

Levi had no intention of helping Kasi maintain the current status quo with her father. Something needed to give. So, he forged on with the other idea he'd come up with while plowing.

"Hey, it's Theo's night to cook, which means he's grilling," Levi said with a grin. "That's all he ever does. It can be twenty below zero and the asshole will still fire up the grill."

"You guys take turns cooking?"

"Yep. With seven of us, that means we each only have to cook one night a week, so it works out well."

"I can't imagine cooking for seven grown-ass men," she said, shooting him a mock horrified expression.

"It's not that hard once you get the hang of it. Tonight, he's making hamburgers and hot dogs."

"That sounds good. I hope you know I don't expect you to eat with us every night, Levi."

He frowned, aware she'd missed the point of his conversation. "Kasi—" he started.

"I held back two pies for you this morning," she continued. "The extra is for Jace, to thank him for fixing the tractor. They're in the house. If you'll wait a second, I'll run in and get them for you before you go home."

Levi shook his head. "I wasn't planning to eat without you, Kasi. I'm inviting you, your dad, and Keith to join me and my brothers."

"Oh." She frowned. "I'm not sure—"

"Kasi, it's time to create a new normal. Because this current one sucks." Levi pulled up in front of her house and put the truck in park before turning it off. He twisted to look at her.

"I don't know what you mean," she lied. She knew exactly what he meant. He could tell by the way she avoided looking him in the eye.

"Things changed after your mother passed away. That's to

be expected, but..." Levi raked a hand through his hair. "It shouldn't have changed *this* way."

He half expected his comment to piss her off, but he noticed her temperament had calmed considerably since her good night's sleep.

"You're right," she agreed. "It shouldn't have. The problem is, I don't know how to fix it."

"With baby steps."

"I've already taken a few of those and they haven't ended well," Kasi admitted.

"Meaning?"

"Daddy started sleeping upstairs the day Mama died. He said he couldn't sleep in their bedroom when the sheets still smelled like her."

"That room at the end of the hall downstairs. Was that theirs?" Levi had wondered about the closed door, and the fact he'd never seen anyone go in or out of it.

Kasi nodded. "Yeah. I thought eventually Daddy would go back, but it's the one thing he's been decidedly strong about. He said he built it for her—her dream bedroom. He put the addition on the house when I was still in elementary school. Whatever Mama asked for, he included. He put in a big bay window that overlooked her flower garden, so in the spring they could sit on the window seat together and watch them bloom, and there was a dressing table with a mirror, just like she'd seen once in a magazine. It's got an en suite bathroom, too, with double sinks. Mama always raved about the fact there were two sinks. I swear, with the exception of the kitchen, that bedroom was Mama's happy place."

"It sounds nice."

"Yeah. But no one was there to watch the flowers bloom this spring. The door stayed closed, and the room sat empty all the way until May. That's when I took the first baby step. The bedroom was starting to feel like a shrine, a place we all tiptoed around, careful to avoid, and I... I couldn't do that anymore. So, I grabbed a bunch of boxes and started packing Mama's clothes. Then I washed the sheets, opened the windows and aired the room out, trying to breathe new life into it. I hoped maybe with Mama's things gone, Daddy might..." Her voice quivered.

"You thought if you took out the reminders, he'd move back. He'd get better."

Whatever sadness Kasi had been fighting was gone, replaced with resignation. Which Levi found worse.

"It didn't help. I left the door open when I was done, but the next time I walked by, it was closed again. For a few days, I played a game, leaving it open, only to return home to find it shut once more. I thought it was Daddy closing it, but the more I thought about it, the more I started to suspect it was probably Keith."

"Keith?" Levi asked.

"He caught me loading her clothes into my car to take to Goodwill about a week after I cleaned the room, and he unleashed on me. He was angry that I'd touched her things, that I was getting rid of them. I told him he could go through the boxes and take out anything he wanted. I tried to reassure him that I was only giving away her clothes, but he... Well, he hopped on his motorcycle and sped off. He didn't come home for three days, and I was scared shitless, worried something horrible had happened to him. I stopped opening the door after that."

Kasi leaned her head against the headrest, the weariness that had been absent today returning with a vengeance.

Levi was going to have a long, hard talk with her brother. Very, very soon.

"I'm sorry he did that to you. And I'm sorry to ask you to try again, but..."

"You're asking me to try again," she said tiredly.

He nodded. "This time, I'll take the baby step with you. It's just dinner, Kass."

"I guess we can invite them, but I doubt they'll come."

They got out of the truck and walked into the house together. Keith was in the kitchen, sitting at the table eating an apple and drinking a soda.

"Hey," Levi said. "Would you be up for having dinner at my place tonight? My brother's grilling hamburgers."

Keith's gaze slid to Kasi. "What about Dad?"

"He's invited too," Levi said, answering for her.

Keith smirked. "Tell you what. If Dad goes, I will."

Levi wanted to call the little punk to task, but it was hard to do that when Kasi was looking just as doubtful. "I'll be right back."

Levi left Kasi and Keith in the kitchen and headed upstairs.

Mr. Mills was sitting by the window, looking out at the front yard. Levi wondered if he'd been watching him and Kasi talking in the truck.

"Hey, Mr. Mills," he said, knocking on the doorframe.

The man turned to face him. "Hello, Levi. You still here?"

Levi supposed that, prior to her death, Mrs. Mills would have added Levi to her honey-do list for her husband, insisting that Mr. Mills pull him aside to ask his intentions regarding their daughter. And she would have been right to do so because he'd been around a hell of a lot the past few days...and he hadn't brought Kasi home last night.

"Yeah."

"You been here all day?"

Levi nodded. "Keith and I have been trying to take a chunk out of that list Kasi made us."

Mr. Mills smiled sadly. "Trina always made lists like that for me."

"There are still quite a few things on there. We sure could use another pair of hands."

Mr. Mills didn't respond, but he also didn't say no. Levi figured he'd planted the seed, so now he just had to hope it took root.

"Kasi, Keith, and I are doing dinner at my place tonight, and we'd love for you to come along. My brother Theo is cooking."

Mr. Mills was silent for a few moments. "I'm not sure..." He glanced over his shoulder, back at the yard.

"Just going to be me and my brothers. Theo's grilling a pile of hamburgers and hot dogs, and I'm sure he sweet-talked my mom into making us a big batch of her potato salad."

That captured Mr. Mills' attention. "The kind with the little red potatoes and bacon?"

"Yup," Levi replied. Looked like food might be just the motivation Mr. Mills needed.

"I do like your mom's potato salad," the man admitted. "She always makes it for the annual yard party at the fire station."

Levi grinned. "Every year she tries to sign up for something different, swearing she can make other things, but the ladies in the auxiliary have a fit, insisting people would stop coming if her potato salad wasn't there."

Mr. Mills chuckled. "That was probably Katrina's doing. She knew it was my favorite. Trina always tried to replicate it, but she never quite got the recipe right."

Levi noticed the sadness that always seemed present in the older man's eyes lifted briefly as he recalled the happier memory. It convinced him that he was doing the right thing by pushing the Mills family out of this rut. "She should have asked Mom for the recipe. She would have shared it."

Mr. Mills shook his head. "Trina liked making a game of it."

"Kasi's been working hard around here, so I thought it

might be nice to give her the night off from cooking," Levi added, not above using a bit of manipulation. Because if Mr. Mills refused the invitation, he knew Kasi would too.

"She has," Mr. Mills murmured. "I guess...I could..."

Levi got the sense Mr. Mills was giving himself some sort of internal pep talk, and it made him wonder when the man had last left the farm.

"It'll only be an hour or so. We'll have you back here in time for *Jeopardy*," Levi pressed, pulling out every card in his arsenal of tricks. They'd most likely be longer than an hour, but now that he'd gotten this far, he was determined he wasn't leaving this room without the man.

Mr. Mills nodded slowly, his words scattered, as if he was struggling to gather his thoughts. "Okay. I...I'll, um... For Kasi."

Thank God.

Levi couldn't wait to see Kasi's face when he walked downstairs with her father. He waited as Mr. Mills put on his shoes and ran a comb through what little was left of his hair. He probably should have left the man alone to do those things, but he didn't want to run the risk he would change his mind.

Together, they descended the stairs. Levi got a kick out of Keith and Kasi's matching looks of sheer astonishment. Unfortunately, Kasi's faded quickly, turning to something that looked a lot like guilt, which was not Levi's intention.

"Ready to go?" Levi walked over to wrap his arm around Kasi's shoulders.

She nodded. "Let me grab the pies."

"I'll get them," he offered, picking one up to hand to Keith, who was still staring at his father like he expected the man to yell, "Psyche!" or something.

Grabbing the second pie, Levi headed for the front door. "We can all ride in my truck, and I'll bring you back after."

"It makes more sense for us to take our own car," Kasi said. "That way you're not running back and forth."

Levi grasped her hand. "I was coming back anyway, so I'm driving."

Kasi gave in, but not with a whole lot of grace. She narrowed her eyes, muttering, "You're going to have to let me win some of the arguments."

Levi chuckled. "I'll keep that in mind."

The drive to his place was fairly quiet but not awkward as a country station played on the radio, Kasi humming along to the old Dolly Parton song, "Here You Come Again."

When they arrived, Levi could see the smoke rising from the grill beside the house, Theo wielding his spatula like it was some sort of magic wand.

"Hey!" Theo called out as they walked toward him. "Glad you could join us." Levi had texted his brother earlier to warn him he was issuing the invitation and to throw on some extra meat.

Mr. Mills and Theo shook hands.

"Great to see you again, Mr. Mills," Theo said. "We've missed seeing you at the brewery. Sam's about to launch his new pumpkin ale in a couple of weeks, and we were hoping you would come and sample it."

Mr. and Mrs. Mills used to come to Rain or Shine Brewery once a month for a "date," both fans of trying the new flavors.

"That sounds good. We'll... I'll, um..." It was clear that Mr. Mills recalled who his usual tasting partner was because he paused, blinking a few times, his eyes glistening.

Shit. They hadn't been here three minutes and it was already falling apart.

Kasi quickly intervened. "We can do a tasting together, Daddy. Maybe for your birthday at the beginning of October."

"That sounds like a great plan," Levi added. "We can make

a party of it. Throw in a couple of those fire-roasted pizzas my cousin Mila's famous for."

Mr. Mills nodded noncommittally, but Levi made a mental note to make sure that happened.

Theo glanced at all of them, obviously regretting his part in making Mr. Mills sad. Then his brother shared a confused look with Levi. He hadn't gone into a lot of details about Mr. Mills' mental state when he'd asked his brothers to help cover his chores this week. Instead, he'd simply implied the family had gotten behind after Mrs. Mills' death.

Fortunately, Theo didn't let the awkwardness linger. "How do y'all like your hot dogs? The right way, or burned to a crisp like this lunatic?" Theo jerked his head toward Levi.

Keith and Mr. Mills both chose what Theo considered the right way, but Kasi said she was Team Levi when it came to hot dogs, preferring hers burned to a crisp. If he didn't already know she was perfect for him, that would have sealed the deal.

They stood around as Theo manned the grill, chatting about the weather and the ongoing grape harvest. Several of Levi's brothers joined them, enjoying the cooler air. Today's weather was an August unicorn, giving them a break in the ninety-plus-degree days by gracing them with this one, a mild seventy-five. Maverick arrived armed with beers for Kasi and Mr. Mills and a soda for Keith.

Once the food was ready, they piled into the dining room, all of them claiming a seat around the long walnut table. Levi saved Kasi a spot next to him, while Mr. Mills and Keith sat farther down the table, conversing with Sam and Theo, though it was his brothers who were doing the lion's share of the talking as Mr. Mills listened, nodding a great deal and occasionally adding a comment here and there. Keith had mentally checked out, glancing down at his cellphone, which he'd placed on his lap under the table.

Despite being the only woman at the table, Kasi was at ease with his brothers, which wasn't surprising considering she'd spent a great deal of time on the farm when she was younger. She and Jace—who was close to her age—started gossiping about kids they'd gone to high school with, reminiscing about pranks they'd pulled on teachers, and the day they'd both played hooky with Remi to go see the premiere of a *Star Wars* movie.

When Mr. Mills chuckled at something Theo said, Kasi glanced at Levi, flashing him the most beautiful smile he'd ever seen. Unable to resist, he leaned in close, kissing her. It wasn't a long kiss, but it certainly couldn't be mistaken as a platonic one when he ran the back of his finger over her cheek as she blushed.

In addition to Mr. Mills' mental state, Levi hadn't spoken to his brothers about his feelings for Kasi. Mainly because it had only been a few days, and he'd spent the majority of that time with her. It occurred to him now, as he looked around the table, that his brothers had interpreted his desire to work on Lucky Penny Farm as him being neighborly and helping a family friend in need. That impression was shattered with his kiss, and now he felt the weight of too many eyes on him.

Given the age difference between him and Kasi, and the fact that Levi had never paid much attention to her before this week, he understood his brothers' expressions. Jace was curious, Maverick confused, and Grayson downright shocked.

Theo, of course, was amused, even going so far as to give Levi a wink.

Once dinner was over and the pie served, Levi and Kasi drifted to the front porch. They'd dawdled over dinner too long, so when Levi suggested they watch *Jeopardy* here with dessert, rather than miss it, Mr. Mills was quick to agree. Levi got the sense it wasn't his love for the quiz show that kept him watching it religiously. In some ways, it felt like the man's tribute to his late wife, or as a way to keep her alive in his heart.

Mr. Mills joined his brothers in the living room to watch as Everett, their resident brainiac, rubbed his hands with glee, bragging he was going to clean the floor with all of them. Trash talking ensued, even though Levi was certain no one would even come close to competing. Everett was a walking encyclopedia, but his brothers were nothing if not competitive. Jace volunteered to be the scorekeeper as they started figuring out how to make a proper game of their viewing, complete with their own set of rules.

Keith, uninterested in watching, opted to take a walk around the farm on his own.

Rather than watch, Levi and Kasi decided to enjoy the night air as they sat together on the front porch swing. He tucked his arm around her as they gently swayed.

"Thank you for tonight, Levi," Kasi said. "I didn't think… Daddy looked happy, didn't he? I'm kind of hoping…" She was struggling to put her thoughts to words, but she didn't need to. Levi knew what she was thinking. She hadn't anticipated that her father would be able to hang in there the way he had without relapsing into his sorrow, and while it pleased her, there was a part of her that still didn't expect it to last.

Kasi leaned toward him, placing her head on his shoulder. Even though she'd gotten plenty of sleep yesterday and last night, he could see she was starting to get tired. This morning, when they were baking, he'd suggested they double all their recipes so that she could take tonight off completely. He'd done so in hopes that she could get a full night's sleep for once, but it didn't hurt that it had also freed her up for his invitation to dinner.

"What do your brothers think about us?" she asked softly.

Obviously, he hadn't been the only one tuned into their audience.

"I haven't had a chance to talk to them, but I'm not worried. They love you, little bear. Always have."

"Yeah, but that affection is based on the fact I'm Remi's best friend. They might have different feelings about...this."

"They won't, but even if they did, it doesn't matter. The only person whose feelings I care about are yours."

She gave him a sideways glance. "You know you're going to have to give me some time to figure out those feelings, right? You only sprung this caveman side of yours on me four days ago and I'm still not entirely sure what's going on."

Levi chuckled. "I'm aware of that. That's why I'm willing to give you a few more days to catch up."

"Wow. All of a few days. You are so generous." Before he could reply, she raised her hand, covering a yawn.

He kissed the top of her head. "As soon as the show is over, I'll drive you home. You need another early night. No more burning the midnight oil."

"That sounds nice...in theory. I don't think I realized how tired I've been lately until today, when I felt well-rested."

The sounds of cheers reached their ears, and Everett's crowing told them who'd made the most correct guesses.

Everyone drifted to the front porch, laughing. Mr. Mills stepped next to Everett, commenting that it had been like watching the show with his wife. Then the edges of his eyes crinkled, thanks to his wide smile, as he added, "Trina would have given you a run for your money."

Levi heard Kasi's soft intake of breath, aware she was waiting for sadness to accompany those words, but her father's smile held as he thanked them for a wonderful night. Keith rounded the corner just as they were saying their goodbyes, walking straight to the truck and leaning against it with an impatient, bored demeanor. Several of his brothers gave Kasi a hug, the others shaking Mr. Mills' hand, telling him he was welcome back anytime, then bragging about whose dinner menu for this week would be worth the drive up the mountain.

The trip home was just as quiet as the one to Stormy Weather Farm, everyone pleasantly full and drowsy.

When they arrived back at the farm, Mr. Mills excused himself, proclaiming it was past his bedtime. Keith, who'd apparently hit his limit on spending time with adults, hopped on his motorcycle to go "chill with some buds."

Levi and Kasi walked to the living room, sinking down on the couch together.

"You planning to come back tomorrow?" she asked.

He nodded, resting his arm along the back of the couch behind her. "Yup," he said, leaning closer so that his lips were near her ear. He gave her a soft kiss on the cheek.

"You don't have to, you know," she said, not for the first time. Kasi was still struggling with accepting his help. "I'm sure you have a million things you need to do on your own farm."

"In case you didn't notice tonight, I have a big family. All of whom are happy to cover some of my chores while I help you."

"Yes, but that's not fair to them," she insisted.

"Kasi," he murmured in her ear.

"Yeah?"

"I'm coming back. My plan is to put a big-ass dent in that list of yours before harvest time really kicks in at the vineyard."

"It's too much."

"It's not much at all, little bear. So just say thank you and kiss me."

She turned her head toward his. "Thank you," she whispered, placing a too-quick kiss on his lips.

Levi had spent most of the night looking forward to spending time alone with her. Now, he had her right where he wanted her. Leaning in, he let go of the reins, taking what he wanted, gripping the back of her neck, showing her how long a good kiss should last.

The best part was, Kasi was right there with him, just as hungry, just as needy as he was.

Their kiss was no gentle thing. There was no slow build-up. Their lips clashed together right at the crescendo, the kiss so overpowering, Levi couldn't believe the windows weren't rattling in their sills.

Her hands made their way to his hair as he grasped her waist, needing her closer.

One second, he was sitting beside her; the next, he'd pushed her to her back, caging her beneath him on the couch, kissing her relentlessly, endlessly. It would never be enough for him.

Kasi was the first to break their connection, turning her head to suck in several large gasps of air. Levi didn't need to breathe, so he put his lips to better use, drawing them down the side of her neck, his tongue teasing the racing pulse point he found there.

Kasi parted her thighs, her legs wrapping around his waist so that his crotch was nestled in her heat, muted only by the denim of her shorts and his jeans. He rocked against her, letting her feel the bulge, letting her know what kind of effect she had on him. Levi loved the soft moans and whimpers coming from her, especially when she started tilting her hips, trying to add more fuel to the fire.

He hadn't intended to let things go this far. Shit, he hadn't planned to do more than steal a good night kiss from her.

Now, like always, what Levi expected to happen never materialized the way he envisioned. Because in just four short days, she'd become his obsession, and his desire for her had reached fever pitch.

In. Just. Four. Days.

Kasi turned her face toward him, peppering his cheek and neck with desperate kisses as Levi tried to regain control.

If they didn't stop now, he wouldn't be able to pull back, and there was no way he was taking her here on her family's couch, with her father right upstairs. No, when he took her for the first time, it was going to be somewhere private, where they would be free to yell each other's names, pound the headboard of the bed against the wall, and squeak the mattress as loudly as they wanted.

And God help him, that time better come really fucking soon.

Kasi tightened her grip in his hair when he tried to push off her.

"Not here," he murmured. "Not yet. You still have to catch up to me, remember?"

"I'm there," she panted.

Levi chuckled, reaching up to untangle her fingers from his hair. "Physically, maybe, but I'm talking about emotionally. And uh, locationally."

Kasi blinked several times, and Levi watched as his words penetrated. Then he saw her gaze dart to the entryway to the living room. They were in plain view of the staircase.

"Oh," she breathed, blushing. "Oops."

Levi kissed her cheek. "Yeah. Oops. At thirty-seven, I don't relish the idea of getting my ass kicked by your dad for defiling his daughter in the family living room."

Kasi giggled. "Like that would happen. He likes you." Then she quickly covered her mouth, trying to hide another yawn.

"You need to go to bed. You're tired, little bear."

She released a long, slow, very regretful sigh. "I might be tired, but I can assure you, I'm way hornier."

Levi groaned, his cock unhappy at being denied yet again.

Still...

He sat, pulling Kasi up as well. Then they rose together, Kasi slipping into his arms, while he held her tight.

"Not going to feel right sleeping without you," he murmured.

She released him, smiling. "You better go before I throw myself at you."

Levi narrowed his eyes. "You don't fight fair. Because damn, Kass, I do like the idea of you throwing yourself at me."

Kasi grasped his hand, tugging him toward the front door. They shared another kiss, and then he forced one foot in front of the other, all the way to his truck.

Kasi remained at the door, waving to him as he pulled away.

Four days in and he was a goner.

She'd captured his heart.

Hook, line, and sinker.

Chapter Eight

Levi pushed back from the table, grabbing his and Kasi's plates before she could.

"I can get that, Levi," she said, rising as well.

"You cook. I clean." He'd made the same offer every night for the last four nights, and now, as every time before, Kasi ignored it, working beside him as they cleared away the dinner dishes.

"Let me go get Daddy's tray, and then we can start the dishwasher." Kasi headed upstairs, while Levi grabbed a washcloth to wipe the dinner table.

Ever since dining with his brothers, Kasi's father had joined them at the table for dinner. However, tonight he'd turned down their invitation, remaining in his bedroom. He claimed he had a headache, but neither Kasi nor Levi believed that. It appeared there was no rhyme or reason to his down days.

Kasi returned downstairs, looking troubled.

"Everything okay?" he asked.

She shrugged, gesturing to the tray of food, which was basically untouched, but she didn't say anything.

While Levi remained hopeful that they were turning a corner, not a lot of progress had been made in the last four days. Mr. Mills hadn't joined him and Keith as they tackled their chores on the farm, and he still spent far too much time in his room. Even though he'd eaten dinner with them at the table, he didn't contribute much to the conversation, only replying when asked a direct question.

Levi walked over to her, giving her a playful hip bump. "It's my turn to cook tomorrow for my brothers. I'm making a pile of pork barbeque, and Mom's making us her homemade coleslaw to go with it. I'd like you, your dad, and Keith to join us again."

Kasi hesitated. "I'm not sure..."

"Baby steps, Kasi. Remember? We're not packing it in at the first sign of defeat. We're going to keep trying."

She considered that for a second, then smiled. "You're right. We're not." Then she narrowed her eyes. "Now you've got me changing pronouns. Still not sure how me," Kasi pointed to herself, "became we." Her finger waggled between the two of them.

He caught her finger with his, linking them together, giving her a kiss that let her know exactly how they became a *we*.

When they parted, her eyelids were heavy with desire, and he understood just how overrated words were. From now on, every time she questioned this thing between them, he was going to show her just how right it was.

Grasping her hand, Levi led her out of the kitchen. "Come on. Let's go to the living room. We'll be more comfortable there."

For the past four days, Levi had split his time, working mornings on Lucky Penny Farm before returning to Stormy Weather after lunch, tackling things there while Kasi ran the stand. Then, each day, he made his way back down the mountain in time to help her close. He continued to help her prep the baked goods after dinner, but with two of them working, they were able to double their output, making enough pie crust, bread dough, and cakes to last for two days.

Tonight was their off night, meaning, they had time to snuggle on the couch before he headed home.

He'd made some serious headway on her list, managing to make a lot of the repairs needed to the outbuildings, house, and some of the farm equipment. Keith had finished fixing the fence, a major job that had taken him the better part of the last four days. He was still caring for the animals as well. His attitude hadn't improved, but as long as he was working and not being outwardly rude to Kasi, Levi decided to leave it alone.

Unfortunately, tonight, Levi had hit the end of the line as far as helping her because harvest time was upon them, since the majority of the grapes had ripened. That meant, he needed to be on Stormy Weather Farm full-time starting tomorrow until they all were picked. This was the time of the year when nearly everyone in the family, as well as a dozen seasonal workers, converged on the vineyard to begin the backbreaking work of picking the grapes by hand.

Levi hated the idea of not being able to see Kasi as much during the day, and he worried about her returning to bad habits, working too hard, staying up too late, taking too much onto her slim shoulders.

He sank down on the couch, pulling Kasi onto his lap as she laughed.

"There's plenty of room for me to sit on my own cushion," she said, though he noticed her sinking down more comfortably as she spoke.

"You're right where you're supposed to be." Levi backed that proclamation up with a kiss.

Every night for five nights, they'd sat together on this couch, kissing each other senseless until he was forced to slowly disentangle them before he took her right here, no matter *who* was in the house. Nowadays, he'd added an extra item to his list of pre-bedtime routines. Because in addition to showering and brushing his teeth, he had to jerk off in an attempt to avoid blue balls. His nightly showers involved his hand, body wash, and the memory of Kasi's sweet kisses and tempting touches. It was the only way he could manage to go to sleep.

At this rate, the callouses on his hands weren't just going to be the result of a hard day's work, but thanks to a relentless hard-on constantly in need of relief.

Until Kasi accepted that this thing between them was forever, Levi held back from taking them to the next level. He'd approached her with all the subtlety of a tornado, so she was still struggling to see this as a genuine relationship, viewing it instead as what he could only assume she thought was him scratching an itch.

It didn't help that Levi hadn't had any long-term relationships in the past, and Kasi knew it. No doubt she was using his track record against him, probably convinced he'd move on before long because he could sense her holding back from him emotionally.

Which made sense, he supposed. She'd just lost someone she loved deeply, her heart still bruised from the pain of her mother's passing. And on top of that grief, she was stressed out about the farm. He had hoped she would talk to him about the things causing her anxiety, but so far, she'd been stubbornly tight-lipped, determined—despite his assurances he was there for her—to deal with a lot of things on her own.

Levi was trying to give her time, trying to be patient. The problem was, he was all in, and he couldn't understand why she couldn't see and accept that, couldn't follow his lead.

Kasi shifted on his lap, twisting until she straddled his thighs. Levi hadn't done this much dry humping since he was a teenager. He longed to strip her out of her tight shorts and panties and drive his cock deep inside her.

Her fingers glided through his hair as they kissed. Levi slipped his fingers under her shirt, stroking the soft skin of her midriff before going higher. Kasi moaned when his fingers found her nipples, pinching them through the lace of her bra. She arched her back, a silent invitation to pinch harder, and he accepted it. Then he lifted her shirt, his gaze locked on her hard nipples pushing against her bra. Unable to resist, Levi sucked one into his mouth, soaking the material.

"Levi," she breathed.

"You're so beautiful, Kasi." He turned his attention to her other nipple, giving it the same attention.

She gyrated on his lap, driving her crotch again and again over the bulge in his pants, searching for her own relief.

Levi felt his grasp on control slipping because stopping didn't feel like a viable option tonight. He needed her too much. Needed so much more of her.

So...he decided to up the ante.

Mentally, he made a deal with himself, promising he'd pull back before the point of no return. He hoped that was a vow he could keep.

Slipping his hand between them, he released the button on her shorts, then tugged down the zipper.

Kasi jerked when she felt his fingers slip under the elastic of her panties, stroking her clit.

"Oh!" She was breathing heavily, her cheeks flushed with need. "Oh God."

Levi dipped his finger lower, slipping through her arousal. "Nice and wet," he murmured.

Using some of her juices, he returned to her clit, twirling his finger over it, harder and harder.

This was the first time he'd unfastened her pants, aware

that doing so would make it nearly impossible for him to put a stop to things when he should. He figured as long as his pants stayed on, he could manage.

Maybe.

Kasi's body writhed above him as he continued to work her clit, determined to see her come. He'd dreamed of it so many times, it was hard to believe he hadn't already seen it.

"Levi," she whispered, cognizant of the need to be quiet, too aware of her father just upstairs.

He growled because he didn't want her silent, didn't want her worrying about her father overhearing them.

This was why he hadn't let things go this far before.

It was too late now, though, because his girl was right there. He could see it in her almost-desperate expression, hear it in her panting breaths, feel it as more juices flowed over his fingers. He slid through her slippery slit once more, pushing one of his fingers inside her tight—Jesus Christ, *too*-tight pussy. He was glad he hadn't started with two because he would have hurt her.

That thought didn't have time to linger because mere seconds after he penetrated her, she fell apart, her body tensing as her head fell back, a low, soft keening noise slipping from her lips.

Levi watched her through it all, as his cock throbbed with a painful need that was almost blinding.

It took Kasi a minute or two to land, to regain focus, and when she did, she gave him the sexiest, most satisfied smile he'd ever seen. Especially when he lifted his finger to his mouth, sucking it inside. "Delicious."

"Levi," she said, her voice husky. "That was incredible." She leaned forward, resting her forehead on his shoulder, her body trembling slightly in the aftermath of her climax.

He held her, the two of them silent, Levi trying to quiet the nagging voice in the back of his head insisting that something he couldn't believe was true.

"Kasi."

"Hmmm," she hummed.

"Have you had sex before?"

She lifted her head slowly but didn't answer.

There was no fucking way a woman as beautiful as Kasi was a virgin. It simply wasn't possible. And if so, what the hell was wrong with the men in Gracemont?

"My mama was pretty strict," she said. "And very overprotective. To be honest, the only friend she ever let me sleep over with was Remi because she knew your parents and grandparents and trusted them to keep an eye on me. Of course, that's not to say Remi and I didn't sneak out, but that was just to steal a bottle of wine from the vineyard."

"Is that supposed to be an answer to my question?" Levi knew it was, but he needed her to keep talking before he gave himself away. His inner caveman had emerged with a vengeance and was currently beating his chest in true Tarzan style.

Kasi had never slept with anyone else. A woman's sexual experience had never mattered to him before, and to be honest, it wouldn't have mattered this time.

But goddamn...

He was going to be her first, last, and only.

Kasi shrugged. "You want me to say it? Fine. I'm a virgin. But not an intentional one. It's just like I said. Mama was overprotective, and I've always had a lot of chores on the farm. Even before she passed away."

"You've never had a boyfriend?" Levi thought back, but that fact wasn't something he would have noticed because he hadn't ever looked at her and thought *mine*. She'd been under-aged for most of their acquaintance. The thirteen years between them was a hell of a lot less significant now that they were both adults, but prior to that, it had been as wide as the damn Grand Canyon.

"I've gone out with a few guys, done some dating, but none of them were..." She bit her lower lip, and Levi could see she had something more to say.

"None of them were..." he prompted.

He thought she'd been flushed when she came, but that color didn't hold a candle to the red in her cheeks now.

"None of them were you." She spoke the words so quickly, he wasn't entirely sure he'd heard her correctly.

"Me?"

Kasi blew out a slow breath. "I had a crush on you when I was younger."

"I know."

"You knew?"

Levi chuckled. "You started hovering when you were in high school, always trying to catch my attention, even when Remi was trying to get you to do something else." He ran his knuckle over her pink cheek. "And this blushing started whenever you talked to me."

"Ugh. That's embarrassing!"

Levi shook his head. "No, it's not. It was sweet. It's just... I thought the crush ended at some point. I mean, I'd never gotten the sense that you were interested in me since you became an adult."

"I saved you a pie every damn day," she pointed out. "For years."

"Doesn't exactly sound like someone who's," he finger-quoted the last bit, "not interested in me."

She laughed. "You already called me out for that lie."

Levi chuckled as he gripped her ass, tugging her closer, then wrapped his arms around her. "You're right. I did. And I guess I should have realized you still had feelings, but up until a few days ago, I didn't know you were saving the pies. I only suspected. What did your mother think about your feelings?"

"She teased me about it a little. I think, like me, she knew nothing would ever come of it."

"Like you?" Levi didn't care for that response at all.

"You're older than me, Levi. And you'd never given any indication that you were looking for a relationship. I think a lot of the matchmaking mothers in Gracemont have put you in the confirmed bachelor column. Plus, Mama knew and trusted you, so she knew you would never take advantage of my schoolgirl crush."

"You're not a schoolgirl anymore."

"You're right," she agreed. "I'm not."

"You think she wouldn't have approved of us as a couple?" That idea bothered Levi a lot. One, because he'd always respected Mrs. Mills, and two, it was clear her mother's opinion was important to Kasi.

Kasi grinned. "Mama was ten years younger than Daddy. Honestly, I think this—the two of us—would have made her really happy. She liked you. Always said you were a good man and a hard worker, just like Daddy. I know her biggest hope for me was that I'd find a love like what she and my father shared."

A weight lifted from Levi's shoulders. "I wouldn't say I was a confirmed bachelor. I was looking."

"Not very hard. I mean," Kasi waved jazz hands in the air, "*hello*, I was right here the whole time."

Levi wrapped his arm around her neck, messing up her hair playfully. "The difference in our ages doesn't matter to me now. But you had a bit of catching up to do before I opened my eyes and realized who you were to me. Do those thirteen years bother you?"

"Not at all," she confessed. "Honestly, I think a lot of my

lack of dates and interest in guys closer to my own age was their immaturity. It turned me off."

Levi gave her another kiss, trying to let the dust settle on what he'd learned. That was when he realized that waiting to move them to the next level was more important than ever.

She might not have been intentionally saving herself, but the fact was...she had. Which meant he needed to prove to her that he was here for the long haul. He didn't want her to have any questions about him or—God forbid—regrets if he took things too fast for her.

Placing his forehead against hers, he sighed. "I should be going."

There was a brief flash of panic in her eyes. "Because of what I told you?"

"Jesus, no." Levi gripped her face in his hands. "Little bear, I want you so fucking much it hurts, but this isn't the place or the time. When I take you for the first time, it's going to be special."

Kasi scoffed. "I don't need special, Levi."

He narrowed his eyes. "Yes, you do. And so do I. I haven't lived like a monk, Kasi. There have been other women in my past." Levi liked the flash of jealousy in her gaze. It meant she was starting to feel what *he* felt. Because just the thought of any other man looking at her had him seeing red.

"I don't need a list of your conquests," she said, huffily.

He chuckled. "Yeah, well, before you go getting your panties in a wad, I can assure you as far as lists go, mine's relatively short. I'm no Maverick."

That admission prompted a grin. "Don't take this the wrong way, but your brother's sort of a manwhore."

Levi laughed. "No 'sort of' about it." Maverick's reputation as a ladies' man was well-known in Gracemont, as well as most of the surrounding towns. "But what I'm trying to say is that, while there have been others, emotions weren't a part of the package. Those nights were about shared attraction and nothing else. You're different, Kasi. And I want you to know that. Want the opportunity to show you just how different and special you are."

Kasi smiled. "I like the sound of that."

"So when we're finally together, it's going to be in a bed, and we're going to have all night. No, fuck that, we're going to have days."

She shivered. "Days?"

"Days. But, Kasi, a crush is one thing. Reality another. You need to be sure of your feelings for me. I won't let you do anything you might regret later. So take your time, sort this out in your head...and in your heart. Okay?"

"Okay," she whispered.

Levi stole another kiss, careful to keep it quick. Then he helped her stand before refastening her shorts. Kasi walked him to the door, bidding him good night, and tonight, as he did every night, Levi fought against the desire to return to her. It was starting to feel as if they were hooked together by a giant rubber band, and the farther away he got from her, the tighter the pull, the harder it was to resist snapping right back to her side.

Levi drove home in silence, not bothering to turn the radio on because his thoughts were loud enough.

When he pulled up in front of the farmhouse, he was surprised to see all the lights on. Glancing at the clock on the dashboard, he realized it was still early. He hadn't been home before eleven o'clock once this past week, his brothers all in their bedrooms by the time he tromped in.

Walking in, he made his way to the living room, where five of his brothers were hanging out on the oversized sectional and recliners, drinking Rain or Shine beer and watching an old *Alien* movie.

"Hey," he said, claiming an empty spot on the sectional, thanking Sam, who followed him into the living room and handed him a beer.

"Thought I heard your truck pull up," Sam said, reclaiming an empty recliner.

"Wait a second. You still live here?" Theo laughed, making it clear Levi was quickly becoming a stranger in his own house.

"Very funny," he retorted.

"So..." Sam muted the movie, and Levi prepared himself for the long-overdue inquisition. "You and little Kasi Mills," his brother mused aloud with a shit-eating grin.

Levi narrowed his eyes at his brother. "Do you need to put *little* in front of her name?"

Sam shrugged. "Don't need to, but it's funnier if I do."

Given the chuckles of his other brothers, obviously Sam was right.

"Assholes," Levi muttered good-naturedly. He didn't take offense because razzing each other was the norm in this household.

"Seriously, though," Everett piped in. "You dating Kasi?"

Levi shook his head. "No."

Given the six dubious expressions fired in his direction, Levi hurried to explain.

"Dating is too mild a word for what Kasi and I have. Dating makes it sound like we're taking a test drive to see where things go. I already know where we're going. She's it for me. The one. The end game. Forever."

Grayson whistled, long and low. "Damn. Never thought I'd hear you say those words."

"I swear it happened just like it did for Mom and Dad. One

minute, I'm standing there minding my own business, the next, the blinders fell off and I just knew."

"They just fell off, huh?" Jace, like Theo, was laid-back and capable of taking most things in life in stride. Levi wasn't sure he'd ever seen his youngest brother riled up, so he wasn't surprised when Jace gave him a grin and added, "Wicked."

For seven boys all raised by the same parents, Levi was constantly amazed by how different he and his brothers were. As the oldest, he'd always been a bit more serious, trying to set what he hoped was a good example for his brothers.

After him came Sam, who was just one year younger. Granddaddy always referred to them as Irish twins. Sam was a lot like Levi, though softer spoken and a hell of a lot more introspective, which was saying something because it wasn't like Levi was a big talker. Sam was also creative, something that had served him well as brewmaster at Rain or Shine Brewery.

The mild-mannered mold Levi and Sam shared was broken when Theo arrived two years after Sam. Theo never met a party he wasn't the life of, and his loud laughter was the permanent white noise in their house, which was why he was the perfect brother to serve as "the face" of the brewery, training the servers, hiring entertainment, and schmoozing their patrons as they indulged in tastings. Sometimes, Levi thought people came to the brewery to hang out with Theo as much as they did to drink the beer.

Maverick, their resident playboy, came next. The man had been blessed with a face made for Hollywood, and he loved women—all of them—a lot. Levi was starting to suspect their expert-winemaker brother was perilously close to working his way through every eligible lady in Gracemont, as well as the neighboring towns. God only knew what Maverick would do once he'd run out of women to charm and seduce.

After Maverick was Everett, their book-smart, computer-geek brother. As a kid, Everett had made a career of getting out of doing work on the farm, coming up with some ingenious excuses for why he couldn't go outside. His outright aversion to manual labor was something none of the rest of them could begin to understand, but they'd stopped bitching about it when Everett declared himself the farm's marketing and IT guru. He'd put both Rain or Shine Brewery and Lightning in a Bottle winery on the map in the last decade, drawing in countless visitors as well as widening their distribution circles.

Levi's youngest brothers, Grayson and Jace, were polar opposites despite their kid brother statuses. Where Jace was all smiles and laid-back, Grayson was a grumpy, no-nonsense perfectionist, who preferred order and control above all else.

Jace had recently started training to become a brewmaster under Sam, filling the void left when their cousin Lucy found true love with not one man but two. It had taken a little getting used to, but it was clear Miles and Joey were both head over heels for Lucy, and they were great guys to boot.

So when Lucy followed them to Philadelphia, it was Jace who'd stepped in to fill her shoes. Prior to that, he was a jack-of-all-trades, taking on the countless, endless jobs that always popped up on a farm of this size. He was a master mechanic, so he was instrumental in keeping the equipment at both the brewery and winery running smoothly.

Grayson, on the other hand, worked with Maverick in the winery, and despite their vastly different personalities—Maverick with his suave nature and appealing smile, and Grayson's permanent resting bitch face—Levi suspected of all the brothers, those two were the closest, the best of friends.

"You saying this was love at first sight?" Grayson asked.

"Dad always said that was how it was for him and Mom," Sam pointed out.

"Can't be love at first sight," Everett countered. "He's known her forever and *seen* her a million times."

His brother was right. Levi leaned his head back against the couch cushion. "You're right. I have. So maybe it's more accurate to say it was love at first touch. When she passed out in that fruit stand, I reached out to catch her and..." Levi raked a hand through his hair. "Something came alive inside me. About an hour after that, I was hugging her in her kitchen, and a future I never imagined started playing in my mind. One that included a wife to care for and babies."

"She's a lot younger than you," Jace pointed out, though his grin told Levi that his kid brother was just saying it to give him shit.

"I'm aware of that," Levi grumbled, unwilling to let anyone toss that in his lap as an excuse as to why he and Kasi shouldn't be together. "And it doesn't fucking matter."

Jace laughed. "You're right. It doesn't. But that doesn't mean some people around town aren't going to say it."

"Don't give a shit."

"I like the idea of love at first touch," Maverick said. "Even though, I think part of you must have known she was yours even before that. Because, dude...how many years have you been driving by that stand to buy one of her pies?"

"At least three," Levi confessed. Had he known she was his? He hadn't thought so at first, but there was no denying she'd always been the bright spot in his day. While they'd never talked much, he looked forward to their silly song and dance about the change and seeing her had never failed to make him feel...happy. Of course, he'd chalked that up to her sunny disposition and delicious pies. Now his brother's comment left him wondering if his daily trips to the stand had been less about pie and more about...keeping an eye on her.

Grayson, clearly uncomfortable with all this talk about love, changed the subject. "What's going on with her dad?"

Levi realized he owed them an explanation because he was hoping to convince Kasi, Keith, and her father to join them for dinner tomorrow. "He's had a hard time bouncing back since the death of his wife. A *real* hard time."

Grayson nodded, his brows furrowed with concern. "Can't have been easy on Keith or Kasi, either. I mean...I can't imagine losing Mom or Dad." He ran a hand through his hair. "Fuck. It would kill me."

Every head in the room nodded in agreement. Levi knew it was probably odd for all seven of his brothers to still live on the farm where they were born, but family was the most important thing in his life. It was extremely rare that a day passed where he didn't see and speak to both of his parents. He sought them out when he needed advice or whenever he was feeling stressed or depressed. They'd been his rocks, the foundation on which he'd built himself into the man he was today, and he was grateful for their love and guidance. The same held true for his brothers as well.

"Kasi has spent the last eight months since her mother's death taking on almost all of the chores around the farm. Working herself to the point of exhaustion," Levi explained.

Sam scowled. "What about her brother?"

Levi sighed. "Keith seems to have gotten stuck on the 'anger' level when it comes to the five stages of grief. He's spent most of the time since his mother's death running away from the farm, getting into some trouble around town."

"So Kasi's been running the whole farm?" Everett asked. Levi glanced around the room, his heart swelling at the expressions on his brothers' faces, all of them as concerned about Kasi as he was.

"Yeah. She's passed out twice in the last week. She's been

getting four hours of sleep a night, on average, and never takes a day off. I'm not certain, but I'm pretty sure there are money concerns, so that's adding to her anxiety." Levi rubbed his chin, toying with his beard. He was long overdue for a trim—hair and beard. "I've been trying to help as much as I can because too many things have fallen to the wayside. It's why I've been spending so much time there." He paused. "Thanks again for picking up the slack for me here."

Theo, who was sitting next to him, leaned over, bumping his shoulder against Levi's. "We're always going to have your back...and Kasi's."

Levi knew that but it was nice to hear. "Problem is, the heart of harvest time is upon us, so I'm going to have to curtail my trips to Lucky Penny Farm to help her. I'm worried she'll revert to bad habits, not sleeping enough, forgetting to eat."

"Then we'll take it in turns," Everett said. "We can all find time during the next few weeks to check on her, to stop by and lend a hand."

Levi smiled widely. "You'd do that?"

Theo grinned. "Of course, we would. We're family, and we look out for our own. Sounds like little Kasi Mills is about to become our first sister."

Levi punched Theo on the arm good-naturedly as payback for the "little" joke, but inside, he felt a huge weight lifted from his chest. He'd been worried about leaving Kasi on her own for too long, but with his brothers' help, he had a feeling things were going to be okay.

Sam lifted his bottle of beer. "To little sisters."

Everyone followed suit, toasting before taking a sip.

Levi took a drink as well, grinning.

Best family ever.

Chapter Nine

Kasi sat at the kitchen table, staring at the figures in her hands, trying to ignore the way her fingers trembled slightly. She'd spent the past few days reading everything she could about fall crops, trying to determine which produce would be the best to plant now in hopes of recouping some of the money lost after missing the spring planting. In addition to choosing a crop, she needed to find a buyer for it, needed to decide how many acres to plant, and then she needed to find the money to buy the seed.

She groaned and put her head down on her arms, her mind swimming with too many numbers and too many "what-ifs." What if she picked the wrong crop? What if she couldn't sell it? What if this was the wrong thing to invest her family's money in? What if she hit the point where she couldn't afford to pay the Riley brothers?

She wished—for the millionth time—she'd taken more of an interest in the farm back when her mother was still alive. She wished she'd engaged Mama in conversations about the running of the farm because now she was left with precious little information to guide her decisions. Her mother was truly one of the most intelligent people Kasi had ever known. So smart in fact that she rarely wrote things down. Mama hadn't left behind a bunch of notes about the farm's processes or plans because they were all in her head, and that was enough.

It was why Kasi had spent a large part of the spring trying to piece together which distributors supplied them with seeds and fertilizer, as well as which vendors they sold their produce to. Kasi had a working knowledge of the local vendors because part of her chores included deliveries, but she hadn't been fully clued in on their larger purchasers.

She was tempted to call Levi to ask his opinion, but she knew he was busy. He was knee-deep in the grape harvest, and she hated to keep dumping her problems in his lap. In two short weeks with him, she'd let herself get far too used to letting him handle things around the farm, and she refused to keep doing that.

She'd started the conversation with her father about crops this morning over breakfast, but the topic had sent him to a dark place, as he said those decisions had been Mama's. Then he'd risen from the table, his food untouched and tears in his eyes.

Losing Mama hadn't just broken her father's heart; it had stolen every ounce of his desire to live. He was floundering without her, unable to put himself back together. Kasi wished she could find a way to help him, but she was struggling with their new existence as well.

She glanced at the clock, aware her depression wasn't simply driven by Daddy's relapse or her stress over the farm. It was because she hadn't seen Levi today. He'd called earlier to tell her they'd had a problem with the destemmer, and it would set them back if it wasn't repaired quickly. He and Jace planned to work on it once it was too dark to pick grapes.

She smiled when she thought of Jace. The sweet guy had

stopped by yesterday afternoon when she was working at the fruit stand to bring her a sandwich. Said he'd needed to run some errands in town and thought she might be hungry.

Two days before that, Theo had dropped off some of Rain or Shine's new pumpkin ale for her dad to try, along with her favorite salted caramel cookies, claiming he'd swiped them from his mom's kitchen while they were still warm.

This morning, Everett had shown up to look at her computer, simply because she'd mentioned to Levi that it had been glitching and she was afraid she'd downloaded a virus. Everett had done a scan, removed the malware, then uploaded virus protection software for her. She'd been incredibly touched by their kind gestures and help.

Despite harvest time kicking into overdrive, she and Levi had still had dinner together every night this past week. They'd eat together—either here or at Levi's—sometimes with Daddy and Keith, sometimes alone.

Then, every other day, Levi would stick around to help her prepare baked goods for the stand. She loved working in the kitchen with him. He would turn on the radio, the two of them singing along as they baked. They'd steal kisses and talk about their day.

Last night, Levi had run his finger along the edge of the mixing bowl, collecting some of the leftover icing from the cakes he'd made. He'd placed a little of the sugary frosting on her lips, bending lower to kiss it off. She wasn't sure how he'd managed to make a "sweet" kiss so absolutely sinful. After that, he'd pushed his finger—the one with the rest of the icing—between her lips, growling in that sexy way of his as she sucked it clean.

While their baking nights were fun, it was the other nights, their "off nights," as Levi had taken to calling them, that were her absolute favorites. Following dinner, Levi would lead her to the living room, where they'd push each other to the edge of their control, kissing and touching. Every night, he'd bring her to climax with his talented fingers, stroking her clit, filling her pussy with them. She'd never considered herself a sexual person. Sure, she was no stranger to masturbation, but it wasn't like she did it nightly or even weekly. Hell, before Levi, she didn't feel the need to come more than once every month or two.

Now, it was as if he'd released a rabid beast inside her. Her body was in a constant simmering state, and all it took was one touch from him to bring her to full boil. And she now needed those orgasms nightly. Like, NEEDED.

She tried to tell herself it was because the orgasms helped her fall asleep quickly and sleep more deeply, but that was total bullshit. The truth was, she craved that moment when it felt like her spirit was leaving her body, floating on a cloud of sheer bliss. The lifetime of orgasms she'd given herself were lukewarm in comparison to the way Levi made her feel.

With just one finger.

Levi had insisted he wouldn't take things between them to the next level until they had the time to do it right...in private. But given the craziness that was their lives, she was afraid that opportunity would never present itself.

And while she was oh-so ready for a physical relationship with him, she was still struggling to believe this was all real. Kasi wasn't sure if her lack of belief was because she'd spent too many years living under the shadow of an unfulfilled crush. She'd worked hard to convince herself nothing would ever happen between her and Levi as a way of managing expectations, and apparently she'd done such a good job. She couldn't dismiss all those very good reasons she'd had for why they wouldn't work as a couple.

She also couldn't let go of the fact that neither she nor Levi had ever been in a long-term relationship. How on earth could he be so damn sure about them after two weeks when he'd never had a relationship last that long? Part of her, the self-preservation part, worried that perhaps Levi was trying to convince himself this was love at first sight because he was so determined to have a relationship like his parents'.

What if he was trying to shape this into something he wanted because the woman he dreamed of meeting hadn't presented herself yet? He was thirty-seven, and if what he said about not intentionally choosing to remain a bachelor was true, maybe his actions and words were based simply on the desire to be married.

Maybe his clock was ticking. Did guys have clocks?

Even if none of that was the case, the thirteen years that separated them still loomed as a potential issue in her mind. She told Levi the age difference between them didn't matter, and from her perspective, it didn't. But that didn't mean she wasn't worried he'd come to his senses sooner rather than later when he realized just how young and inexperienced she was. How could she hope to keep a virile man like Levi satisfied?

And, as a fun cherry on top of all her reasons to slow this train down, there was the financial burdens that sat on her shoulders like a two-ton weight. If she didn't figure out a solution to their problems soon...

Kasi rubbed her eyes. She'd thought the fact she was sleeping better—and longer—would help her face her anxieties, but it seemed the more well-rested she became, the better able she was to see just how fucked-up everything seemed.

Something needed to give, but damn if she knew what. She couldn't keep living with this unending pressure on her chest. She glanced at the Crock-Pot but didn't rise because she wasn't hungry. Her stomach was tied too tightly in knots.

Levi would give her holy hell if he knew she'd skipped

dinner. She'd made her father a tray earlier, delivering it to him without even bothering to invite him to eat with her, too worried she'd transfer some of her depressed feelings to him.

Before she could get up and force herself to fix a bowl of the chili she'd made, there was a knock at the door. Her heart skipped a few beats as she hastily rose, rushing to the front door.

Maybe Levi managed to fix the destemmer more quickly than he'd anticipated.

She stumbled a step or two when she entered the foyer and saw Scottie standing on the front porch. If he weren't looking right at her, she probably would have immediately retreated to the kitchen, hiding there in hopes he would think no one was home.

Kasi opened the door and gave him what she hoped passed for a friendly smile.

"Hello, Scottie."

"Kasi," he said, nodding his head once before glancing over her shoulder, clearly waiting for an invitation to enter.

"Would you like to come in?" she begrudgingly asked, even though she knew he was here about the back taxes again, and she was no closer to paying them this week than she'd been two weeks earlier. She had, however, just tonight come up with the proposal for a payment plan that she hoped would work.

Scottie stepped inside, looking around the house with a crinkled nose like he thought the place smelled bad. It occurred to her that, despite being neighbors for twenty years, Scottie had never been inside her house, all their meetings since the fall occurring at the fruit stand.

She glanced toward the stairway, hoping Daddy didn't come down. Keith was still working outside, but she knew he was likely to come in at any moment. She didn't want either of them to see her talking to the mayor. It was bad enough she was freaking out over their lack of money. She wasn't about to saddle her father or brother with the same stress.

"If you're here about the personal property taxes—" she began. If this was any other person than Scottie, she would have taken them to the living room and offered them a drink. But as it was, she wanted him out of here as quickly as possible.

"I am," he interjected. "I was thinking perhaps we could discuss them over dinner tonight."

"I've already eaten," she lied.

Scottie leaned closer. "Then how about dessert?"

God, he said *dessert* suggestively, like he considered himself a sweet treat.

"Tonight's not a good night. I still need to do a lot of baking for the stand."

Scottie's jaw clenched. He really didn't like being rejected.

"I've been crunching the numbers," she hastily said, trying to change the subject. "And I'm going to call Herb tomorrow to see about setting up a payment plan."

Scottie didn't reply at first, but given his frown and the way his lips were pursed tightly, she could tell he was about to discard the suggestion.

"We would only need about six months," she continued. "A year at most. We're going to start planting carrots, and once we sell the yield from that—"

"I hate to burst your bubble, Kasi, but the town council voted a few years ago to do away with payment plans because too many people were taking advantage of them. Herb couldn't agree to that even if he wanted to."

"Oh."

"As I said, the town is only able to function as well as it does due to the tax money we collect. This isn't the kind of thing you can nickel or dime your way out of, Kasi. Plus, you didn't just miss one year. You missed two."

"I know, but—"

"I've spent some time considering your dilemma, trying to figure out a way I could help you. We *have* been neighbors for nearly two decades, after all."

Kasi wasn't sure how to reply to that. They may have lived next door to each other for nearly two decades, but Scottie had always struck her as the kind of guy who wouldn't spit on a person if they were dying of thirst, and she'd never seen any trace of neighborly concern from the man prior to last fall. Which was when he'd started stopping by the stand, giving her that smarmy smile he thought was flirty and charming but actually made her skin crawl. Counting tonight, he had asked her out a dozen times and alluded to marriage a few times, which she'd flat-out discounted.

She'd always turned down his invitations to a date, claiming she was too busy with chores, which was true.

"Okay," she said, wondering—and almost hoping—he was proposing a loan because that would be preferable to marrying the idiot. Of course, knowing him, it would most likely be one of those high-interest loans that only benefited him because she could totally see Gracemont's mayor in the role of loan shark, shaking people down for more cash. Which would only land them in deeper financial trouble farther down the road.

"The perfect solution is still staring us both in the face because it's something that will solve not only your problem but one of mine as well."

The look he was suddenly giving her had her stomach twisting itself in knots because she knew where this was going. She shook her head. "No."

"Yes. You and I will get married."

Kasi had a bad habit of laughing when she was nervous. The bark of laughter that followed his proposal was completely the wrong response and she knew it the second it happened.

Scottie's smile faded and his eyes turned black with anger. "You think that's funny?"

"No, I don't," she hastened to say. Then she searched for some excuse for the laugh and came up with nothing.

"I wouldn't joke about something as serious as marriage."

Kasi was out of her league in this conversation because...

What. The. Fuck.

"I know you wouldn't. It's just marriage seems like a rather extreme step to take. We're not in a relationship."

"And whose fault is that? I've asked you out countless times."

It was on the tip of her tongue to point out that a man with half a brain, who was a hell of a lot less narcissistic would have figured out by now that she wasn't interested in him. Scottie unfortunately possessed all the ego and none of the smarts.

"It's the perfect answer," he pressed on. "Our farms adjoin. After you and I wed, we simply tear down the fence and make one big farm. By joining your family's land together with mine, Grover's Farm would become the largest farm in the county."

Kasi didn't like the way he used the words "after you and I wed," like it was a foregone conclusion that the nuptials would happen. She also didn't know why the combined land suddenly became Grover's Farm instead of Lucky Penny Farm.

"But your family doesn't farm your land," she pointed out. "You breed horses."

"That's right. And we hope to extend our business to include training as well. In order to do that, we need more land."

"But we need our land for crops," Kasi countered.

"And yet you failed to plant anything this spring in the fields that burned. All that land is just sitting there doing nothing."

"My mom died!" Kasi spat out, hating the way Scottie put

her on the defensive, the way he spoke to her like she was an idiot.

Condescending prick.

"I know that, sweetheart."

"I'm not your sweetheart."

Scottie sighed, like she was being the irrational one here. "I'm not blaming you or insinuating you've done anything wrong. A cute little thing like you shouldn't have to worry about such things."

She was two seconds away from kicking this misogynistic asshole in the nuts.

"But the fact is, your family is in financial trouble," he continued. "You understand how serious failure to pay is, right? Your home and the land are facing foreclosure."

Nausea clogged Kasi's throat at the thought of losing the farm. Her father had spent his entire life here. Hell, he'd been born in the bedroom where he was currently sleeping.

Losing Mama had nearly destroyed him.

Losing his home?

God. There would be no coming back from that.

"Foreclosure," she whispered, the word tasting like poison on her lips.

"Yes. But that danger goes away if you marry me because I'll pay the tax bill. And then, you don't have to worry about planting anything ever again. I promise there's far more money in horses than in the crops you sell. And the best part is, your brother and father could still live here."

"And the fruit stand?" It was a stupid question because the second she asked it, she could tell Scottie viewed it as her agreement.

"Kasi, once we start having children, you'll be too busy to run that stand. Besides, you won't need to. I have more than enough money to support us."

"No." There were so many vomit-inducing words in this conversation, she wasn't sure she could hold the bile back.

"This is the only solution. You must see that."

She didn't see that at all, but she was struggling to find ways to reject him without saying some really rude words. While she had no intention of marrying the asshole, she wasn't sure just how vindictive the man might become.

Scottie must have confused her silence for consideration of his proposal because he continued to make what he must've thought was an excellent case. "You'll move into my wing in the family home."

Oh, of course. Because there was nothing more inviting than marrying a thirty-year-old man who still lived with his mommy and daddy.

"And your father and brother will be right next door, so you can visit them whenever you want. Your dad can keep a garden, and I know your brother is fond of animals. Perhaps he'd want to start working for me and my dad with the horses. There are always stalls to clean out."

Suuuuuure. Keith would definitely sign up to shovel shit on the Grover's Farm.

Kasi wanted to reject the idea outright, but her head was still swimming in numbers. Too many numbers. All starting with negative signs.

Foreclosure was no longer something looming out there in the distance. Scottie had pulled it out, plopped it in front of her, and made it a reality.

Hopelessness washed through her. "I think I'd prefer to talk to Herb first...about the payment plan."

"He'll say no," Scottie insisted with such conviction, she couldn't help but believe him. "Marriage is an extreme answer."

"This is a very generous offer, Kasi. Do you know how

many women would jump at the chance to be Gracemont's First Lady?" Scottie scowled, annoyed that she wasn't rushing to accept and kissing his feet for making the offer.

He'd been an insufferable asshole before becoming mayor. Now, his haughty arrogance and pompous self-worth were off the charts.

"I'm sure there are, but I still need to explore other options first."

Scottie sniffed. "Don't take too long."

She nodded, certain no other ten-minute conversation in her life had ever left her so completely drained, especially when he bent forward and gave her a kiss on the cheek.

Scottie turned and showed himself out. She heard muffled male voices outside, and then the door opened again. For a split second, she was afraid Scottie had changed his mind on giving her time, so she was relieved when Keith walked in. Even if he was scowling at her.

"Why was the mayor here?" The amount of disdain lacing the word *mayor* proved her brother felt exactly the same way she did about Scottie.

Kasi blanked for a second, then came up with a lie. A lame one, but it was the best she could do. "His mom wanted a recipe. I copied it down for him."

Keith stared at her, and she forced herself to hold his gaze because if he didn't buy that lie, she didn't have the brain capacity to come up with another.

Mercifully, Keith shrugged, then came at her from a different angle. "Where's your boyfriend?"

Kasi sighed. "What's your problem with Levi?"

He scoffed. "I don't like how he thinks he's in charge around here, acting like my father. FYI, Kass. I have one of those."

"At least he's helping out, contributing something."

"Are you saying I'm not?" Keith fired back. "I just spent a week fixing the fucking fence."

"And would you have done that if Levi hadn't told you to?" She was tired of tiptoeing around Keith's bad attitude.

"You know what?" he said, storming by her. "Fuck this. And fuck *you*."

He punctuated those words by stomping upstairs then slamming his bedroom door.

Yeah. Fuck her.

Kasi started to drag herself to the kitchen, intent on cleaning up dinner and putting the food away. She'd just lost her appetite in a very big way.

She wasn't two steps inside the kitchen when there was another knock at the door.

"Grand Central Station tonight," she grumbled, ready to send whoever was there, packing. She wasn't in the mood for any more people-ing tonight.

Or so she thought.

Until she saw Remi smiling at her.

"Remi," she said, opening the door.

"Hey, bestie. I haven't seen you in ages. Was that Scottie I just passed coming down the driveway?"

"Yeah."

"That dick really won't take a hint, will he?" Remi knew about Scottie's continual requests for dates—as well as her refusals—but she hadn't mentioned the marriage talk because before tonight, it had been completely absurd.

"No. He won't," she replied.

"How's your head?"

"Much better," Kasi replied, touching her brow. The stitches were the dissolvable kind, and considering they were right at her hairline, it was easy to forget they were even there.

"So what's with the weary face?" Remi knew Kasi better than anyone, the two of them closer than sisters.

"Nothing new. Just the same shit, different day."

Remi lifted the bottle of wine in her hand. "Damn. Maybe I should have stolen two bottles from the winery."

Kasi grinned. "Is it really stealing if you own the winery?"

Remi smirked. "The way Nora evil-eyes me every time I help myself sure makes it feel that way." She started to hand her the bottle, but Kasi shook her head.

"No. You know what? Wine isn't going to cut it tonight. Nothing short of shots is going to save the day."

Remi's eyes widened in excitement. "Are you saying what I think you're saying?"

Kasi nodded. "It is Wednesday, isn't it?"

Remi cheered, pumping one fist in the air. "Hell yeah. Ladies' night!" Then she looked down at her outfit. "I dressed for wine in your kitchen," Remi said, as she grabbed Kasi, dragging her toward the stairs. "You're going to have to loan me a shirt that's a lot sluttier than this one."

Kasi laughed, letting herself be pulled along in Remi's wake.

Remi was just what the doctor ordered.

An hour later, Kasi found herself perched on a tall stool at Whiskey Abbey—Gracemont's only bar—waiting for Remi to return with their drinks.

She smiled widely when Remi placed four shot glasses on the table between them. "Lemon drops."

Kasi knew without a doubt she would pay dearly for tonight, but she couldn't find it in herself to give a shit. She'd hit her limit on crappy days, so for this one night, she was shutting it all out, drinking shots, dancing her ass off, and just fucking letting go. It had been way too long.

She picked up one of the glasses, tapped it against Remi's, then on the table before tossing back the alcohol. The vodka burned until she popped the sugar-covered lemon slice into her mouth. "Mmm. Mother's milk," she joked, feeling the tension in her shoulders loosen for the first time in ages.

"It's been forever since we've been out like this," Remi said.

Since before Kasi's mother died.

But that didn't need to be said. She and her best friend exchanged a sad look, then Remi did what she did best. She found a way to make Kasi forget.

Picking up the second round of shots, she handed one to Kasi. "One more, and then you're going to tell me what the hell is going on between you and my cousin Levi."

Kasi giggled. She'd been dying to talk to Remi about the entire Levi situation, but she hadn't found the time between working her ass off on the farm and in the stand, and making out every night with said cousin.

They did their glass-and table-tapping routine in unison before slamming down the second shots, sucking on the lemons to kill the taste.

"Damn, I needed those," Kasi said, leaning back in the stool.

Remi waved her hand, calling the waitress over to order two more shots each.

"I'm not sure that's such a good idea," Kasi said, after the waitress headed for the bar.

"Sure, Kass. Because if there's one thing I'm known for, it's my good ideas," Remi joked, her comment accurate. What Remi was famous for—and why Kasi adored her so—was her ability to always take things to the most extreme level of fun.

"So," Remi said, snapping her fingers in Kasi's face. "Levi deets. Now."

"A couple of weeks ago, Levi came to pick up his pie. Just like he always does," Kasi began. "And I passed out."

Remi frowned. "I thought you passed out in the barn."

It really had been too long since she'd talked to her best friend. "I passed out twice. The barn was the second time."

The concern in Remi's eyes touched her. "Are you okay?"

Kasi nodded. "I've been burning the candle at both ends the past few months." More like eight, but she didn't say that. "It caught up to me. And then Levi caught me. Literally. I was going down and when I came to, I was on the ground, my head in his lap."

"I'm glad he was there. You could have been seriously hurt." Remi's eyes slid to Kasi's stitched forehead.

"I know that, and I'm taking better care of myself now. Levi's orders."

Remi lit up at that. "His orders, huh?"

"He's become decidedly bossy when it comes to me."

"Shit. I swear if this was anyone but one of my cousins, I'd be all over you for every single dirty tidbit, but I'm not sure I want to hear about Levi pulling your hair, smacking your ass, and making you call him daddy."

Kasi crinkled her nose, laughing, as she reached out to playfully smack Remi's arm. "Ew. He doesn't make me call him daddy."

Remi lifted one eyebrow. "But he pulls your hair and smacks your ass?"

Kasi bit her lip as Remi raised her hand quickly. "No. Fuck. I changed my mind. I don't want the Levi details. I eat Sunday dinner with that guy."

Kasi snorted. "Fine. Although there aren't that many details to share anyway. He's just helping me out around the farm. And..."

"Aaaaaand?" Remi prompted.

"He calls me little bear, and every night, we make out on the couch like a couple of teenagers who just discovered hormones."

"Little bear?"

"He says I'm a fighter, that I'm strong. I swear to God, every time he says it, my nipples get hard."

"Shut. Up!" Remi howled with laughter. "That is so fucking amazing. But...just making out?"

Kasi grimaced. "So far."

"Which means you've still got that V card to play."

Remi was perfectly aware of Kasi's lack of bedroom experience, and equally aware of how much Kasi wanted that to change. It was something they'd discussed countless times, always ending with Remi making a list of available "doable" guys in Gracemont and the surrounding towns, while Kasi turned her nose up at pretty much all of them.

Levi had never made the list because, like Kasi, Remi obviously hadn't seen him as a viable option. Though whether that was based on the age difference or the fact he'd truly never shown any interest, or both, Kasi didn't know.

"I'm hoping I don't have my virginity for much longer," Kasi confided.

Remi squealed with delight. "Oh my fucking God. How awesome would that be?! Losing it to Levi. You've had a crush on him forever."

"And yet he never made your list of potential candidates."

Remi shrugged. "I figured he'd never go there."

"Because of the age difference?"

Remi tilted her head. "Maybe. But mostly because he's a

workaholic who's never really shown much interest in dating anyone seriously."

"That makes sense because I'm not sure how serious this is. I mean, it's all very new. I love the things he's saying." Kasi grinned.

"Like?"

"Like, I'm his."

Remi's eyes widened, and she fanned herself.

"But I'm not letting myself get carried away."

Remi frowned. "Why not get carried away?"

Kasi shook her head. "There's such a thing as being out of someone's league, and then there's me and Levi. We're a million miles apart, and I don't have enough dating experience...or any experience. What if we take things to the next level and he's..." She paused. "I don't know. Bored or disappointed or something."

"That could never happen. You're smoking hot. Besides, if Levi says you're his—which, by the way, is so fucking hot—then he means it because my cousin doesn't lie."

As far as reassurances went, Remi had hit it out of the ballpark. Because Kasi wanted every single word her best friend had just said to be true.

"That helps," Kasi said, even though there was a tiny part of herself that told her she needed to hold back on the emotions. And not because of Levi but because of herself. Her life was still a disaster, and it didn't look like that chaos was going to end anytime soon.

Did she have the right to drag Levi into the middle of all that? Especially if she couldn't figure out how to pay the bills. Right now, her family was in actual danger of losing their farm and home.

And while Kasi wasn't considering Scottie's offer because... gross. That didn't mean she wasn't facing some hard decisions...

like where they'd go if the farm was foreclosed. The only family they had who would take them in was her mother's brother, Dave, who lived just outside of Nashville. The idea of uprooting and leaving the only home she'd ever known tied her stomach in knots, but they might not have any other choice.

"So you and Levi are dating?" Remi asked, mercifully pulling Kasi back to the present. There would be plenty of time —too much time—to think about what came next, tomorrow. Tonight was just for her. Shots and girl time and no thinking about the future...or the past. God, she'd missed being this girl. This carefree, happy one without a worry in the world.

"I...I think so," Kasi said. Neither she nor Levi had really given this thing between them a name, but it sure felt like dating.

"Here you girls go." The waitress delivered their next rounds of shots.

"Thanks." Remi picked up one of the glasses, waiting until Kasi followed suit. "Here's hoping there's lots of hot, sweaty sex in your very near future."

Kasi laughed as she tapped her glass against Remi's. The third shot slid down without burning, the alcohol doing exactly what Kasi needed, melting away all her anxieties.

"Just be a good bestie, and *don't* tell me about it," Remi added with a grin.

Chapter Ten

Levi slapped Jace on the back as they walked into the farmhouse together.

"Thank God for your mechanical mind," he said to his youngest brother. "I was afraid it was going to be a long night if we couldn't figure out what was wrong with that destemmer."

Jace grinned at the compliment. "Yeah, well, Theo and Maverick provided me with some pretty strong motivation."

Levi chuckled. "Still planning to hit the bar?"

Maverick had declared earlier in the day that after working their asses off for weeks, they all deserved a little downtime. And because it was Maverick, he decided that time should be spent at Whiskey Abbey for ladies' night.

Then the destemmer had gone down.

Technically, the destemmer was Maverick's domain as winemaker, but the poor guy had been putting in seventy-hour work weeks since early summer. So Levi told his brother to keep his plans for the night, and that he'd fix the machine. Mercifully, Jace had volunteered to stay home to help as well.

"Hell yeah, I'm going. I'm only about a half hour behind them," Jace said, checking his watch. "I can catch up quick."

Levi glanced into the living room where Everett and Grayson sat on the couch, each with a controller in hand, playing *Call of Duty.*

"Already finished?" Grayson asked, spying him and Jace in the doorway.

Levi nodded, jerking his thumb toward Jace. "Wonder kid here had it sorted out in record time."

"I'm heading to the bar," Jace added. "Y'all sure you don't want to join me?"

Both of his brothers shook their heads.

"Having the game of my life. Kicking this miserable bastard's ass," Everett replied with a shit-eating grin. Everett was the epitome of a homebody.

"You're not kicking my ass," Grayson grumbled before turning back to them. "I'm perfectly happy on this couch. Too tired to deal with people."

Levi didn't bother to point out that was pretty much always the complaint when it came to Grayson. His younger brother was one of those people who could live quite happily on a deserted island for the rest of his days, never once longing for companionship or conversation.

"Your loss," Jace said. "Always lots of pretty girls there on Wednesdays."

Everett and Grayson waved them off, then returned to playing their game.

"Guess it's a waste of time to ask if *you* want to come," Jace said to Levi as they reached the stairs.

Levi wiggled his eyebrows. "Total waste of time. I'm going to call Kasi to see if she's still up. If she is, I'm heading to Lucky Penny Farm to steal a good night kiss or twenty."

"You're pussy-whipped," Jace said good-naturedly. "But

that's all right. Just means there are more girls at the bar for me, Theo, and Mav."

Levi pulled his phone out of his back pocket just as it started to ring. "Speak of the devil," he said, showing his brother Theo's name on the screen.

"What's up, Theo?" Levi said as he and Jace started climbing the stairs.

"I was wondering how the destemmer repairs are going," Theo said.

"Just finished."

"That was quick. Jace?"

"Yup."

"In that case, thought you might be interested in joining me and Maverick at the bar," Theo said.

"Nope. Just told Jace I'm heading over to Kasi's."

"It would be a wasted trip," Theo replied.

Levi frowned. "Why?"

"Because your girl is here with Remi, and the two of them look like they're trying to set some kind of record for most lemon drop shots pounded in a single evening."

"Kasi's at Whiskey Abbey?"

Jace had been about to enter his bedroom, but he stopped when he heard Levi's question.

"She sure is. Dancing up a storm and looking as pretty as ever. Thought you might want to know that, considering there are more than a few young bucks circling her and Remi on the floor. Assholes look like sharks going in for the kill—and fucking Scottie Grover is leading the charge."

Levi hadn't felt an ounce of jealousy in his life before falling for Kasi. But after hearing his brother mention other men jostling to get Kasi's attention, his green-eyed monster roared to life.

"Keep the assholes away from her," Levi said through

gritted teeth. "I'll be there as soon as I can." He hung up the phone.

"Meet you downstairs in fifteen?" Jace asked, obviously hearing enough to know Levi would be going to the bar. "I need to grab a shower really quick."

"Same," Levi grunted. "But make it ten."

Jace laughed and gave him a thumbs-up.

~

THIRTY MINUTES LATER, Levi and his kid brother walked into Whiskey Abbey. Given the number of cars in the parking lot, he'd say ladies' night was an inspired idea on the part of the bar's owner, Abbey Wagner.

Abbey was a Gracemont transplant, moving into town a decade earlier. After retiring from government work, she'd decided she wanted a slower pace of life, somewhere away from the hubbub of Washington, D.C. She claimed she'd always wanted to run her own bar, so she made her way to Gracemont, where she'd spotted a For Sale ad in the newspaper for a bar.

Prior to renovating the older building and breathing new life into it, Whiskey Abbey had been a sagging, run-down dive simply called The Bar, and the only patrons of the previous place had been a dozen or so grizzled old guys who preferred shots of whiskey to spending time with their wives.

Abbey had changed all that with her establishment, finding ways to entice most of the residents of Gracemont to stop by for a drink at least once during the week.

On Tuesday nights, she ran a music bingo game, Thursday was trivia night, and on Fridays and Saturdays, she always had some local musical talent performing. And while all those nights drew in decent crowds, the one night that seemed to overshadow them all was Wednesday—Ladies' Night—where there were drink specials for the women and the floor was crowded as everyone kicked up their heels to country music.

Levi nodded when he spotted Theo waving to capture his attention. He and Jace made their way through the crowd. Levi kept glancing toward the dance floor, trying to find Kasi, but he couldn't see her. There were too many damn people out there bumping and grinding.

Maverick pulled out the stool next to him, gesturing for Levi to sit, while Jace claimed the other empty chair next to Theo. "We ordered beer as soon as you said you were coming because this place is slammed, and the poor waitresses are behind. They just delivered these a couple of minutes ago, so they should be nice and cold," Maverick said, pointing to the round on the table between them.

Levi nodded his thanks, taking a sip as his gaze traveled around the room.

Theo pointed to a table on the opposite side of the bar. "Kasi and Remi just took a break from dancing. They're over there."

Levi spotted her in an instant, his dick sitting up and taking notice of the deep red blouse she was wearing. It had a plunging neckline, treating him—and every other guy in the place—to a generous peek of her cleavage. He now understood why the sharks had been circling.

Most days, Kasi pinned her hair up in a ponytail, so he'd only seen it hanging loose around her shoulders a few times in the past couple of weeks. Tonight, she'd gone the extra mile, curling her straight hair so that it was full and fluffy and shiny. His fingers itched to see if it felt as soft as it looked, then he imagined himself kneeling behind her in bed, pulling on those long strands as he took her from behind.

Jesus. Something was going to have to give. Lately, he couldn't go more than ten minutes without thinking about his girl, and every time he did, he had to start reciting the times table in his head to ward off the erections that always accompanied thoughts of Kasi.

He shifted in his seat, his jeans cutting into his now half-hard cock. He needed to look away from her until he managed to get himself under control, or else it was about to become obvious to everyone in the bar he was sporting one hell of a boner.

Unfortunately, looking away was impossible because he'd never seen Kasi looking so happy, so carefree, so...young. She was wearing makeup, her long lashes lined and thickened with mascara so that her bright blue eyes popped. She was laughing at something Remi had said, the two of them sitting together, their heads close so that they could hear each other over the loud music.

He was about to turn his attention back to his brothers when he spotted Scottie Grover making his way over to Kasi and Remi's table.

Levi growled.

"Down, boy." Maverick placed his hand on Levi's shoulder.

But he growled again when Scottie stopped next to Kasi. It wasn't so much the fact the douchebag mayor was talking to his girl that pissed him off, though he could admit that was definitely irritating the fuck out of him. It was the way the smile faded from Kasi's face when Scottie started talking to her.

Scottie pointed toward the dance floor, clearly inviting her to dance.

Levi started to stand, but again Maverick's hand was there, holding him in his seat.

He glared at his brother, ready to shove him off, when Maverick said, "You forget who she's with."

Levi frowned, then turned back just in time to see Kasi

shaking her head as Remi shooed the man away, not bothering to feign the slightest bit of politeness.

Remi, as well as the rest of the family, knew all about the fight Levi and Scottie had last fall when the asshole had grabbed Lucy, forcing himself on her. Remi might be the youngest of the Storms, but damn if she wasn't the fiercest. When she'd learned Scottie had hurt her big sister, it had taken him and two of his brothers to stop her from driving down the mountain and straight to the mayor's office to kick his ass. Since then, she'd made a career out of finding ways to cut the man down to size, with barbs that would bring a stronger man to tears.

Obviously she was doing that now, as Scottie's face turned red, a blend of embarrassment and anger. Within seconds, Remi had sent the man packing, and Levi's jealousy waned when he read Kasi's lips, watching as she said, "thank you" to Remi.

Levi took a minute to watch the two women together, the same warmth he felt whenever he was near Kasi filling him.

When he'd first heard she was at Whiskey Abbey, he'd felt a twinge of worry. This thing between them was still new, and while his feelings were fully engaged, and he didn't feel a speck of doubt about her being the one for him, Kasi wasn't there yet.

"You know, they haven't noticed us sitting over here," Maverick said. "Should we invite them to join us before you wind up starting a barroom brawl?" His brother tilted his head toward the girls' table, where Levi saw two more men approach, offering to buy them drinks.

Remi wasn't as quick to send these guys away.

"Think they'll be pissed if we interrupt their girls' night out?" Jace asked.

"Doesn't matter if they are," Levi said, rising. "It's time to set the men in Gracemont straight on Kasi's lack of single status."

"The men or Kasi?" Theo joked.

Levi scowled, then said, "Yes," prompting all three of his brothers to laugh.

"Oh man. This should be fun." Theo rubbed his hands together like he was getting ready to watch a boxing match.

Jace and Maverick rolled their eyes at Theo's excitement, but this time, his brothers let Levi make his way across the bar unhindered.

Levi recognized the two men chatting with Kasi and Remi. Hell, he knew everyone in Gracemont, so he was perfectly aware that Henry Martins and Ezra Kenner were nice guys and harmless, but that didn't mean he wanted them flirting with his girl.

Levi couldn't stop his chest from expanding with pride and love and happiness and a fuck-ton of other emotions when Kasi spotted him walking in her direction. Her smile reappeared, and damn if it wasn't brighter than before. He didn't stop until he was sliding behind the tall stool she was sitting on. Wrapping his arm around her waist, he leaned forward to give her a kiss on the cheek.

"Having fun, little bear?" he murmured in her ear, seeing the confused looks on Henry and Ezra's faces, as well as the extremely amused one on Remi's.

Remi schooled her expression quickly, narrowing her eyes at him. "What are you doing here? Because if you're planning to steal my girlfriend away on the one night I've gotten her in months—"

"I'm not stealing *my* girlfriend from you," Levi stressed the pronoun, then gestured across the bar to where his brothers were sitting, still watching them. Theo waved, grinning widely.

"The boys wanted to blow off some steam after a hell of a long week."

Remi had spent a few days with them in the fields, so she knew exactly how hard they'd been working.

"I'd intended to head to your place to steal a good night kiss," he said to Kasi, "until I was informed you were here. So I made a little detour."

Kasi clearly didn't mind his detour. "I thought you'd be working on the destemmer until late."

That was exactly what he'd told her on the phone. "Yeah. Well, I was blessed with the greatest mechanic on the planet for a brother. Jace fixed the thing in no time."

"He really does know his way around an engine," Kasi concurred. "Our piece-of-shit tractor is running like a dream ever since he worked on it. Paul swears it's like having a new tractor."

"Fellas," Levi said, acknowledging the two men who were now awkwardly shifting on their feet, wondering where to go from here. "Having a good night?"

"I will be if I can get this one out on the dance floor with me," Henry said, smiling down at Remi.

She rolled her eyes playfully, even though it was obvious Henry was getting that dance.

"We never miss ladies' night. So...you and Kasi, huh?" Ezra asked.

Levi nodded.

"Not going to say I'm not disappointed. I was happy to see you back out," Ezra said to Kasi. "It's been a while."

"It has," she agreed.

"Well, you caught yourself a good one." Ezra gave Levi a friendly punch on the shoulder. "Happy for you two."

The two men quickly moved on after Remi promised to find Henry later for a dance.

"Marking your territory?" Remi asked.

Levi snorted. "Damn right." Then he leaned close to Kasi again. "You didn't mention going out when I called earlier."

Kasi gave him an adorable grin, looking at him over her shoulder. "It wasn't even a plan until about an hour ago. Remi showed up with wine, intent on chilling with me in the kitchen, but I knew that wasn't going to cut it."

He frowned, suddenly worried. "Why not? Bad day?" She hadn't given him that impression when they'd spoken on the phone.

The shadows in Kasi's eyes answered the question for him, but he noticed they passed quickly.

"Not really," she said. "Just...more of the same."

He'd spent enough time with her to know exactly what that entailed, so he assumed her father had hidden in his room most of the day. And it was probably a good bet that Keith had been a little shithead. Those two things were the primary reasons Levi had been pushing harder this year with the harvest, pulling longer hours in hopes of finishing sooner.

He wanted to get back to the routine he'd established the week prior to this one, splitting his days between the two farms. Levi knew that wasn't going to work in the long-term, mainly because he couldn't keep asking his brothers to cover chores for him, but damn if he wasn't determined to make it work for as long as he could. Because even with makeup on, he could still see the faintest hint of the dark circles under Kasi's eyes that said she wasn't getting as much sleep as she needed.

"I'm glad you took the night off to enjoy yourself. You deserve it." He took a couple steps away from the table, ready to excuse himself because he really *didn't* want to crash girls' night. She needed it badly, and he knew from personal experience that Remi was good for the soul, the perfect person to cheer up Kasi and ensure she had a great time.

Then he tallied the empty shot glasses on the table, taking in the flush on Kasi's—and Remi's—cheeks, thanks to the vodka. He tipped her head back with a finger under his chin. "Did you eat dinner?"

He expected her to say yes because she'd promised to take care of herself...so when her eyes lowered, darting to the side, he narrowed his own.

"Kasi."

She lifted one shoulder. "I wasn't hungry earlier. Then Remi came by, and we started getting ready to go out, and I forgot."

Levi pressed a quick kiss to her forehead. "I'll order a couple of apps for you and Remi when I get back to my table. You need something in your stomach to soak up the alcohol."

"You're not hanging with us?" Kasi asked, clearly disappointed.

"Do you want me to?" He was pleased as hell to think she did.

"Of course," Kasi said.

Levi's gaze slid over to Remi, who laughed. "I said you couldn't steal her. I didn't say I wouldn't share her."

He chuckled. "I'd love to join you. Should we move over with Mav, Theo, and Jace? They have a bigger table."

"That sounds like fun," Kasi said.

"Now that you've said appetizers, I'm starving. Let's order a few of them. I want cheesy bacon fries, wings, and the big pretzel. Then you guys can get something for yourselves," Remi joked as she stood, picking up her last full shot glass.

Kasi grabbed her shot as well, taking the hand Levi offered as he guided them through the crowd. Levi plucked a couple available stools from nearby tables, adding them to the one he was sharing with his brothers.

Jace smiled when the girls joined them. "Hot damn. Now it's a party!"

Theo waved down a waitress, ordering a couple pitchers of Rain or Shine IPA, which Abbey always kept on tap, as well as too many appetizers.

The six of them ate and drank, laughing and talking, while Levi sat next to Kasi, his arm slung around the back of her stool. She kept leaning into him, her shoulder pressed to his chest, their closeness allowing him to catch the occasional whiff of her strawberry-scented shampoo, as well as the sweet smell of lemons on her breath from the shots.

Because of Kasi's longtime friendship with Remi, it truly felt like she was one of the family, his brothers teasing her the same way they teased their female cousins.

As the evening wore on, Maverick was the first to peel off, spotting a cute blonde across the bar. It didn't take the charming bastard more than three minutes to get her on the dance floor, the two of them pushing the limits when it came to dirty dancing.

Remi followed Maverick's example, finding Henry to drag him out for the dance she'd promised earlier.

Theo and Jace remained at the table, both uninterested in more than chilling out with a beer and people watching.

"You want to dance?" Levi asked, when a slow song came on, Carrie Underwood's "Like I'll Never Love You Again."

Kasi nodded enthusiastically. "I love this song."

The two of them made their way to the floor, and Levi smirked when he spotted Scottie watching them. The mayor shot him a dirty look, obviously still pissed about Levi punching him. It had happened nearly a year earlier, but apparently the fucker held a grudge.

Levi wrapped his arms around Kasi's tiny waist, tucking her close to him. She placed her hands on his shoulders for a minute or so before shifting them to his hair. He'd noticed during their nightly make-out sessions that she was a fan of his long hair. He dipped his fingers beneath the hem of her blouse, desperate to touch skin.

The past week had been an experiment in torture and control as they continued to push the envelope on the couch. Kissing had given way to exploring each other's bodies—her fingers drawing patterns on his chest, his toying with her nipples, tickling and stroking her breasts and stomach. From there, they'd upped the ante to her straddling his thighs, pressing her pussy against his crotch, both of them cursing the material in their way.

Last night, he'd pushed her to her back, caging her beneath him on the couch, as he shoved her T-shirt up, dragged her bra down, and feasted on her breasts for a good half hour while Kasi squirmed beneath him, breathlessly begging for more. He'd never spent this much time with a woman without having actual sex, and while Levi loved pushing her hot buttons and taking the time to discover her erogenous zones, he needed her.

Needed her like he needed air and water.

He lowered his head, resting his cheek against hers, grinning when she giggled.

"Your beard tickles," she admitted.

When he'd first arrived at Whiskey Abbey, Levi could tell Kasi was tipsy, thanks to the lemon drop shots. However, that buzz appeared to have waned. She'd had a fair amount of the appetizers, and she'd drunk the two large glasses of water he'd poured for her. Her focus was crystal clear when he cupped her cheek, pressing his forehead against hers.

"Come home with me tonight," he whispered.

If she'd still been under the influence of the alcohol, he wouldn't have made that request. Kasi was a virgin, and he was determined to make her first time as special as possible.

Kasi's smile grew, and she nodded enthusiastically. "Yeah. Okay."

He tilted his head. "You sure?" he asked, wanting to make it perfectly clear what he had in mind.

"So sure," she quickly replied. "So, *so* sure."

He smiled and kissed her, the two of them giving Maverick and the blonde a run for their money on public indecency. Once they parted, he grasped her hand, dragging her to the table despite the fact the song hadn't ended.

"In a hurry?" she asked, laughing.

"Sweet Jesus, Kass. I'm only human, and these last couple of weeks..." He didn't bother saying more. Mainly because she was nodding in agreement.

"I think I'll die if you and I don't... I need you inside me," she whispered.

Levi closed his eyes, sending up a silent prayer that he managed to make it home. Right now, there was a fifty-fifty shot he'd take her in his truck in the damn parking lot.

Only Theo and Jace were at the table when they returned, Remi and Maverick still dancing with their partners. Levi pulled out his wallet and tossed several twenties on the table. "That should cover mine and Kasi's part of the bill. You okay to catch a ride back with Theo?" he asked Jace.

His brother nodded. "Yeah. We were just discussing that. We'll drive Remi home too. Theo will bring her back here in the morning to pick up her car."

"Good," Levi said, glad they were getting Remi home safely. Like Kasi, she'd switched from shots to water, but she'd still consumed enough that she wouldn't get behind the wheel of a car. "We're heading out. See you later."

"You kids be good," Theo called out. "And use protection!"

Kasi laughed, but Levi didn't have time to do more than playfully flip his brother the middle finger over his shoulder.

Her hand was gripped tight in his as he dragged her toward the exit with too much haste, Kasi half jogging to keep up with his long strides.

"Levi," she said, trying to slow him down.

The second they stepped out of the bar and into the parking lot, he pushed her against the side of the building, lowering his head to kiss her. He didn't have a fucking clue how he was going to make it to the farm without taking her. He'd never wanted a woman with this much desperation. Somehow he'd managed to bank his desires so far because time and location had never been on his side.

Tonight, it was all systems go—and his dick fucking knew it.

Kasi moaned into his mouth, her fingers clenched tightly in his T-shirt, her arousal matching his. They continued to kiss—God, the word *kiss* was way too mild for what they were doing—until some jackass wolf-whistled and another person told them to "get a room."

Levi pulled away slightly, loving the way Kasi's eyelids were heavy, the way she gasped for air. It took her several seconds to focus on him.

"I want you so bad," she confessed.

"Fuck, Kasi. You're killing me." He forced himself to put a few more inches between them. "Come on," he said, reclaiming her hand. "The sooner I get you home, the sooner I can strip you out of these clothes."

Kasi grinned. "I like the sound of that."

They crossed the parking lot and Levi opened the passenger door of his truck, latching her seat belt after she climbed in. She didn't bother to point out—again—that she was capable of buckling herself.

He liked taking care of her. Not because Kasi needed it but because he did. He hadn't downplayed her importance to him.

She was his, and he intended to make sure she never wanted for a single thing. He planned to spend every moment of his life easing her burdens, spoiling her rotten, filling her up with as many babies as she'd give him, and growing old with her. When he looked at her, he didn't see days or years. He saw decades, a lifetime.

Crossing in front of the hood, he climbed behind the steering wheel and turned the truck toward Stormy Weather Farm. They were quiet on the ride. Levi didn't know what was going through her mind, but he was currently running through a grocery list of all the things he wanted to do to his sexy, beautiful girl.

Kasi looked at him curiously when he turned down a less-used dirt path rather than following the paved driveway all the way to his farmhouse.

"We're going to the cabin we stayed in a couple weeks ago," he said in response to her unspoken question. "My farmhouse isn't any more private than yours, little bear."

She grinned. "It's *less* private with seven of you living there," she pointed out. "I thought the cabins were typically booked this time of year."

Levi nodded as they pulled in front of the cabin. "They are, but this one needs a bit of a facelift," he said, as he turned the truck off. "My brothers and I have been replacing some bad boards in the porch, scraping and painting the outside windowsills whenever we have some time, while Mila plans to give it a fresh coat of paint inside once harvest season is over."

Climbing out, he met Kasi on her side before she could get out of the truck. She giggled when he lifted her so that her legs wrapped around his waist, his hands gripping her ass as he carried her inside. On the way, Kasi peppered his cheeks, chin, and neck with kisses, and the erection he'd barely held at bay on the drive to the cabin returned with a vengeance.

Kasi wriggled, expecting him to put her down once they were over the threshold, but Levi tightened his hold, squeezing her ass cheeks, not stopping until they stood in the same bedroom where he'd tucked her in following her trip to the hospital.

Once there, he put her down, cupping her cheeks in his large hands. "Point of no return, Kass," he said softly. "You sure about this?"

"There is nowhere else on earth I'd rather be than right here, right now, Levi."

Those were the best words Levi had ever heard. He bent lower, kissing her. Unlike the kiss at the bar, this one was gentler, calmer.

Having her here helped him temper his needs.

But only a little.

Because the second her tongue found his, the instant her hands reached around his midsection and gripped his ass firmly, it was fucking on.

Levi deepened the kiss as he slow-walked her to the bed, not stopping until the back of her legs hit the mattress. Kasi pulled away, glancing behind her before facing him once more with a smile that was equal parts breathtaking and seductive.

"You're beautiful," he murmured, his lips sliding along her brow, down to her ear. "And you're mine. Now take off those damn clothes."

Chapter Eleven

Kasi soaked in his declaration that she was his like sunshine after a long, cold rain.

What would she give to truly be his...forever?

She desperately wanted the future Levi saw so clearly, but there were too many negative thoughts clouding her vision. Uncertainty about her family's situation, fear of being hurt if Levi changed his mind or realized she wasn't the one, as well as the never-ending trepidation about giving her heart to someone.

Losing her mother had nearly destroyed her, broken her heart in a way she'd never experienced. And she could admit to herself that she hadn't truly picked herself back up since Mama's death. The pain was still there, only slightly more manageable than in the weeks right after the funeral. She wasn't sure her heart would recover if Levi broke things off with her. Adding new pain to the existing wounds would kill her.

Of course, all those reasons weren't helping her keep her distance because Levi was too easy to be with and too easy to fall in love with.

No matter how many times she told herself to play it cool, play it smart, she failed. Because even with those mental pep talks running on repeat in her mind, her heart was already slipping away from her, falling just as hard and fast for Levi as he said he was falling for her.

This evening had been a roller coaster of emotions and a whirlwind of activity. Kasi's life these past eight months had begun to feel like one endless day of the same monotonous routine. Nothing different ever happened. Or if it did, it was always something shitty that never failed to add misery to the boredom.

Levi changed all that, adding excitement and fun to her world, as well as offering her support and compliments and beautiful words that wiped away the agony she'd begun to believe had left a permanent stain on her heart.

Maybe she didn't know what tomorrow was going to bring, but by God, tonight she was going to be selfish, going to take what he was offering because she simply couldn't say no.

Kasi lifted her hands, pulling off her blouse as Levi took a step away, giving himself a better view. Once she slipped the last button free, she slid the silky blouse over her shoulders, dropping it to the floor.

Levi's eyes were glued to her breasts. The desire darkening his gaze and the way his jaw tightened made her feel like the most beautiful woman alive. She'd never given a whole lot of thought to her looks, always accepting that she was passably attractive, pretty enough in her mind, but not drop-dead gorgeous, not the type of woman to turn most men's heads.

The way Levi drank her in said he saw her as so much more than that.

She reached behind her back, unfastening her bra, adding it to the growing pile of clothes at her feet. Any shyness she felt around Levi had vanished over the past couple of weeks as their encounters on the couch progressed. He had seen her bare breasts just last night, when he'd lifted her shirt.

Her nipples pebbled in the cool air of the cabin as she recalled the way he'd taken them into his mouth, sucking on them, nipping at them, driving her out of her mind with the sensation.

While she was technically still a virgin, that didn't mean she didn't have experience with other aspects of sex. She'd made out with a few guys during high school and after. Kasi had gotten pretty good at dry humping and over-the-pants hand jobs. She'd even had a couple guys play with her tits, but always through the barrier of her bra. In truth, she'd never considered her nipples an erogenous zone, never played with them herself in the quiet of her own bedroom when she brought herself to orgasm with her fingers or a vibrator.

Levi had shown her the error of her ways last night, his touches, kisses, sucks, and licks so intense, she'd come close to climaxing. From just breast play.

She expected Levi to touch her as she stood before him shirtless, or to begin stripping off his own clothing, but he did neither. Instead, he tilted his chin up just once. "Keep going."

His deep, velvety voice shot through her system like champagne. She never failed to get light-headed and giddy whenever he whispered sweet nothings in her ear or told her all the dirty things he was going to do to her when he got her alone.

Levi was a master of drawing hot, horny, kinky pictures in her mind, a porntastic Picasso.

She reached for the button on her jeans, slipping it loose before sliding down the zipper. Levi's gaze was locked on her hands, following her progress like his life depended on him not missing a single second. She wasn't sure he'd blinked in the last few minutes.

Kasi shimmied her hips, dragging her jeans and panties

down together, her need too strong to draw this out. Once the denim and lace hit the floor, she toed off her sandals, then stepped out of the rest of her clothes.

She expected to be nervous, standing before Levi completely naked when he hadn't shed a single article of clothing, but instead she felt...powerful.

Especially when Levi dropped to his knees in front of her, his eyes taking in her bared pussy. He'd yet to see that part of her, though he'd touched it. He never did more than open her pants, never pulling them down, telling her that his self-control was a finite thing and if he started seriously exploring below her waist, he'd never be able to stop himself from taking her.

He leaned forward, kissing the top of one thigh before moving to the other, skipping over the part she wanted him to touch the most.

Kasi reached down, gripping his strong shoulders, digging her fingers into the soft cotton of his shirt. "Take it off," she said, plucking at it.

Levi shook his head as he looked up at her with a stern expression that was so fucking sexy, she feared she might spontaneously combust.

"Sit on the side of the bed, sweet girl, and spread those legs wide."

"God," she whispered, trembling with need as she followed his command, sitting on the mattress, parting her legs.

"Lay down," he added.

Kasi fell to her back, aware of just how vulnerable this position was, and equally aware that it wasn't a bad vulnerable. She was opening herself up to a man she trusted with her life. She felt safe...and free.

But she was still entering uncharted territory, no man having ever seen her completely naked or touched her most intimate part with—

She gasped when Levi's thumbs parted her labia, his face close enough that she could feel the heat of his breath.

"All shiny and wet," he murmured. "Just for me."

Levi ran his tongue along her slit, from her anus to her clit.

"Holy shit," she breathed, her voice quivering with need, suddenly discovering just how much she'd been missing out on.

Levi stroked her with his tongue, over and over, until Kasi was writhing on the bed, out of her mind with desire.

"Please," she said on a gasp, tugging at his hair, trying to drag him up her body.

Levi lifted his head, chuckling darkly. "Oh no, sweet girl. We're nowhere near that part. And you're going to have to beg a hell of a lot more than that before we get there."

"I need you," she barked, unable to temper her tone. She'd never been this desperate to come. Hell, some nights, if she couldn't get herself there with her fingers or her toys within a few minutes, she'd give up, choosing sleep over an orgasm. Considering her self-induced climaxes had been tepid at best, that stood to reason.

But now, she was certain she would literally perish if he didn't...

"Fuck. Me. Now."

His eyes narrowed, the alpha male he made no attempt to hide shooting her a warning glance. Levi was in charge here, and he let her know that without uttering a single word.

Why would he when his actions were much more effective?

He nipped at her inner thigh, the brief, sharp sting of pain her punishment for trying to wrest control from him.

"Please," she tried again.

Levi bit the other thigh. Not hard but enough to leave a red mark.

Suddenly, she was overcome with the craving to do the

same. To dig her teeth into his flesh, to leave tangible proof that he was hers.

He'd made that "mine" proclamation quite a few times in the last two weeks, but tonight was the first time Kasi understood the true power behind that word. How those four letters could evoke so many emotions—from obsession to desire, from jealousy to passion—was beyond her. All she knew was tonight...Levi was hers too.

When she didn't speak again, Levi returned his attention to her pussy, driving his tongue inside her, thrusting in and out several times, showing her with his mouth exactly how he planned to take her. His thumb found her clit, circling it several times before finally applying the perfect amount of pressure. Her hips jerked upward in response, her pussy clenching.

Levi moved his free hand to her stomach, pressing on it to hold her more firmly to the mattress while he drove her arousal to the peak with his tongue and thumb.

Kasi erupted like a volcano, her orgasm coming out of nowhere, shocking her system as if she'd just touched a live wire.

"Ah!" she cried out loudly, grateful Levi had found them a private place to be together. There was no way she'd be able to get through tonight in silence.

She shuddered as the last vestiges of her climax faded, lying limp on the bed while waiting for Levi to rise from the floor, undress, and join her.

He didn't do any of that.

Instead, he lowered his head and began to kiss her again, his tongue gliding to her clit, toying with the ultra-sensitive nub until she saw stars.

Her hands flew to his hair, pulling it. "I can't," she gasped. "Not again! Not so soon."

Levi lifted his head. "Yes, you can."

"Levi," she started to protest, sure another orgasm right on the heels of that last one would destroy her.

"Kasi. It's your first time. We're not rushing this. When I take you, I'm going to make damn sure you're ready for me and that the pain is as little as possible."

She sighed. "I may be a virgin in the sense I've never been with a man—unintentional, remember?—but there's no hymen. I have a vibrator and a dildo at home."

He gave her a crooked grin. "Next time you take those toys out, we're going to play together. No more getting yourself off without me. And I'm glad you told me about that experience, but we're still doing this my way."

Levi backed that assertion by pinching her clit, the sharp touch a blend of pain and pleasure she really liked.

She groaned.

Levi's eyes narrowed with sudden interest. "You like that. When I'm rough with you."

She considered his bites and pinches, then nodded because there was no way in hell she could hide the truth of that statement. That sense of vulnerability was back as she opened the door for Levi to things she'd never told anyone before. When she masturbated, it was always rough, her fantasies tending to go to darker places. The make-believe lovers in her mind were strong alpha men who took what they wanted without apology.

For a time, she worried there was something wrong with her. Because there was no question the fantasies that turned her on the most, that never failed to bring her to orgasm, were the ones where she was kidnapped or chased or tied up by a man determined to claim her—with or without her consent. The dirty words her fantasy men always whispered were graphic, threatening, things that should scare rather than arouse.

"I like when you're rough," she whispered. "I like when it hurts."

"You like it as in, it turns you on?"

"My fantasies..." she started. "They're not tame."

Shit. Why had she revealed that? She frowned, but before she could try to backtrack lest her confession bothered him, he spoke.

"You can be damn sure we're going to unpack that comment more later," he said. "But for now...all I want you to do is concentrate."

With those words, he took her clit back into his mouth and her head fell back.

Concentrate, indeed. What choice did she have? It was impossible to think about anything except how good this felt. Especially when he pushed two fingers inside her.

"God," she gasped, as he took off the kid gloves, driving his fingers at the same relentless, hard pace she used when playing with her dildo. "Yes!"

Between his fingers fucking her pussy and the wicked, wicked things he was doing to her clit with his mouth, Levi brought her right to the edge within minutes.

"Give me one more," he urged, lifting his head even as he continued to pound his fingers inside her. "One more orgasm, and then we're going to be very intentional about getting rid of that virginity of yours."

She might have laughed if she could have spared the breath, but there was no more air in her lungs. Her body shifted into overdrive as a second climax roared through her. She'd been a fool for thinking the first one powerful.

"Jesus. Christ," she choked out, as every nerve ending in her body lit up like a goddamn Christmas tree.

Levi continued stroking her, his fingers gliding along her

inner muscles as they clenched, drawing out the orgasm until she feared she would faint.

Something she couldn't do—again—because she'd reassured him she wasn't the kind of girl who passed out all the time.

"Please." Kasi's voice was hoarse from her cries.

"Fucking gorgeous," Levi murmured.

She opened her eyes, looking down to where Levi was still kneeling between her outstretched legs.

"You're perfect, Kasi," he said.

Tears welled in her eyes. The last person to call her perfect was her mother, who never held back from telling her she was the perfect daughter.

Mama used it not as a way of making her feel like she had to do everything right, but as a term of endearment, or for comfort whenever someone made Kasi felt stupid or inferior or less. In Mama's eyes, she was perfect just the way she was, and Kasi had never felt more loved than the times when her mother would envelop her in her arms, nearly smothering her in her large, pillowy breasts, and whisper those same words in her ear.

Kasi pushed herself up, reaching out to Levi, wrapping her arms around his shoulders and hugging him tightly. "So are you," she whispered.

Because he was. Perfect for her. So perfect.

Levi returned the embrace for a moment before pulling away and giving her a look that was almost feral. "Crawl onto that bed, little bear, in the middle."

Kasi wished she knew what it was about that demanding tone in his voice that had her hopping to obey, so anxious to please him. She quickly did as he said. Placing a pillow against the headboard, she sat in the middle, watching and waiting for him, so ready for what came next.

She should have been physically spent—those first two

orgasms were no joke—but instead, she was completely energized and still horny as hell.

Levi reached behind his head with one hand, tugging his shirt off with a strong tug. She'd seen him shirtless countless times in her life. Farmwork was hot in the summer, so it wasn't unusual for men to shed layers as they worked.

The summer her crush on Levi sparked, he'd been twenty-seven, and it was the first time she'd truly looked at a man and appreciated what she was seeing. The years had only improved him, honing his muscles to chiseled perfection, his tanned skin golden brown.

Levi winked when she finally managed to peel her eyes away from his chest to look at his face again.

She laughed, then repeated his chin tilt gesture. "Keep going," she said, repeating the same command he'd issued earlier.

Levi sank onto the edge of the bed, reaching down to tug off his shoes and socks. Unable to resist, she leaned forward, placing a kiss on his shoulder, her breasts rubbing against his bare back. This was the most incredible, intimate moment of her life, and she never wanted it to end.

Rising, Levi turned to face her again, and Kasi bit her lip as he unfastened his jeans. The denim dropped to the floor, revealing his commando state.

Not that Kasi gave that more than a passing thought because...

"Holy shit."

Levi smirked. "You're good for the ego." He gripped his extremely large cock, running his hand along the shaft from base to tip a few times as she watched.

"I probably should have invested in a bigger dildo," she murmured.

Levi barked out a laugh. "This is gonna fit just fine."

Placing one knee on the mattress, he gripped her ankle, tugging until she fell to her back before climbing over her.

His cock bobbed, smacking her stomach as he pushed her legs apart, settling on his knees between them.

She was diving right into the deep end with Levi and his monster dick. Again, she thought that idea should frighten her, but all it did was make her empty pussy clench with need.

Resting on his elbows, Levi kissed her, in no apparent hurry to move to the next part, even though she thought he must be hurting. His hard-on was so...well...*hard* that he must be overwhelmed by the need to fuck.

Levi's fingers gripped her hair, fisting it tightly enough that her scalp stung. He was obviously taking her words about liking it rough to heart, and she adored him for it.

She jerked when he bit her lower lip during their kiss before tugging on her hair again. The stinging pain sent jolts of pleasure straight to her pussy, which was dripping by now.

She groaned, digging her nails into his shoulders, giving him a tiny taste of his own medicine. Levi's growl told her that he liked the pain as much as she did.

Breaking the kiss, Levi pushed up enough that he could take his cock in his hand again. She held her breath as he dragged the head over her slit, sliding it through her arousal, coating it. He slid it up and down, causing her to moan every time it stroked her clit. All her girlie bits were super-sensitive and it wouldn't take much for him to give her another—third!—orgasm.

"Are you on the pill?" he asked after the sixth slide.

"I get the shot," she said, silently thankful for her bad periods for the first time ever.

On his next glide, Levi stopped, the head of his cock resting at her entrance. He paused, their gazes connecting.

She smiled. "Need more begging?" she teased. "Because I'm more than ready to—"

Levi cut her off, not with words but with action, when he slammed inside with one rough, hard, amazing thrust.

She'd reassured him he wouldn't hurt her, and while she wasn't in pain, she also wasn't accustomed to feeling this...full. Between his length and his girth, there didn't seem to be a place inside that he wasn't touching.

Levi paused, giving her time to adjust. Or maybe the pause was for him.

His eyes were closed, his expression one of absolute bliss.

She cupped his cheek, stroking his beard. Levi's eyelids lifted as he held her gaze.

"I've never been inside a woman without a condom," he admitted.

Just like when she'd discovered the power of the word *mine*, Kasi now understood how Levi must feel, realizing he was the first. It was heady to think he was giving her something he'd never given anyone else.

"Good."

Levi grinned at the possessiveness in her tone. "You gonna be a jealous girlfriend, little bear?"

"Extremely," she warned, her response clearly pleasing him.

"Good," he said, giving her word back. "Now hold on."

Levi withdrew until only the head remained, and then he thrust back in deep. This time, there was no pause, no restraint, as he took her with all the force she'd requested.

Her fingers gripped his upper arms, digging into his thick muscles. She had no choice but to hold on because this was unlike anything she'd ever imagined, ever dreamed of.

Every stroke was harder than the first, stoking embers inside her that burst into flames. Less than a minute passed before she felt herself flying apart. Her back arched, even as Levi continued his brutal, beautiful assault.

"Fuck," he said through gritted teeth. "You're squeezing the life out of me. So. Fucking. Tight."

Kasi couldn't reply, couldn't remember how to speak. Her body thrummed, the orgasm lasting for decades, eras, eons, and she panicked slightly, wondering if a person could die from too much pleasure. Her heart was thudding at a dangerous pace, and her pussy throbbed so rapidly, so continuously, she feared it might never stop.

"Levi," she cried. "Too much. Too good!"

He shook his head. "Never," he declared, though mercifully he slowed his thrusts, giving her some time to recover.

Finally, after a few minutes, she regained control. Levi was still inside her, still moving, though much slower. She blinked several times, trying to focus her vision.

Levi smiled when she managed to find his eyes. "There you are."

"I thought I was going to die," she confessed.

He wrapped one strong hand around the side of her throat. "Is that what the panicked look was about?"

Was that why he'd slowed down?

"I had no idea it could feel that good, that it could go on for so long," she admitted, her words breathless as she struggled to fill her lungs with air.

"To be honest," he confessed. "Neither did I."

She giggled because it felt crazy that they were having this conversation with him still slowly fucking her.

"Levi," she said. "Come inside me."

He closed his eyes briefly. "Best offer ever."

He increased his pace, though he didn't take her as hard as before. For which she was grateful. She was stretching muscles she didn't know she had, and he was no small man.

She was going to feel the effects of this night for the next few days.

Kasi lifted her legs, wrapping them around his waist, the position tilting her hips so that he began to hit a different place inside. She gasped at how good it felt.

Dear God. There was no way she was going to come again, was there?

Levi gave her the answer to that unspoken question when he reached between them, rubbing her clit.

"Come with me," he grunted.

And she did. Instantly.

Levi was with her this time, his groans and panting breaths mingling with hers as his hips jerked one last time, coming inside her.

They remained connected, motionless as statues for a few moments before Levi lowered himself to his elbows again, kissing her senseless.

When they parted, he placed one last kiss on the tip of her nose, and she laughed. Then he dropped to her side, drawing her body over his so that he could tuck her against his chest.

Kasi rested her hand flat on his bare chest, her fingers absentmindedly caressing his soft skin as she let what had happened sink in.

She wasn't a virgin anymore.

She'd given it to Levi Storm, who'd revealed himself to be a force of nature in the bedroom.

She also went ahead and accepted that she'd fallen victim to that cliché about one man ruining a woman for all others.

Because there wasn't a guy on the planet who could top that. *Ever.*

They lay there in silence for so long, Kasi thought Levi had fallen asleep.

She was physically exhausted enough that she should have

drifted off instantly, but her brain wouldn't shut down. It was too excited, too happy, too determined to relive every second of what had just happened.

Kasi startled briefly when Levi broke the silence.

"About those fantasies..." he mused.

Kasi buried her face in his chest, groaning. "Oh my God. Please forget I said anything."

He chuckled. "Not a chance in hell. You piqued my interest. Besides, if you don't tell me what they are, how can I make them come true?"

She lifted her head. "You would do that?"

"Little bear, how do I make you understand? There's nothing in the world I won't give you."

And there went her heart.

So much for holding on to it.

Kasi placed a soft kiss on his chest, then rested her chin there, looking at him with a mischievous grin. "You really sure you want to know?"

Levi pushed a strand of hair out of her face before drawing the back of his knuckles along her cheek. "Hit me with your best shot."

So she did.

Chapter Twelve

"Oh my God, Levi," Kasi breathed.

Levi tested the rope binding her wrists to his headboard...and tightened it more.

Kasi's chest rose and fell rapidly, her body writhing on the bed so seductively, he thought he'd lose his mind.

"I didn't realize," she said, panting, "when I told you my fantasies, you'd try to make them all come true immediately."

Levi chuckled. It had been a week since he'd taken Kasi's virginity, and a week since she'd rattled off a list of fantasies that proved his girl's dreams were a hell of a lot less innocent than her body.

He hadn't intended to start knocking things off that list right away, given she was new to sex, but she'd planted all those damn seeds. So many that the images of her fantasies had woven their way into his psyche, until he was nearly consumed by the desires she'd drawn in his mind.

Pursuit. Capture. Submission. Bondage. Punishment.

Every single word she'd spoken had practically imprinted

on his dick, the fucking thing functioning at half-mast this week, never getting completely soft. Ever.

So that was why he'd cornered her in the barn on Sunday afternoon. They'd been completely alone—Keith at a buddy's house and Mr. Mills tucked in his room—and before he could think through his actions, he'd bent her at the waist and told her to hold on to a shelf, while he spanked and finger-fucked her to an orgasm.

Those fantasies were also why, when she'd shown up at his farmhouse earlier tonight—on her own and as a surprise—he'd decided to reward her impetuousness by dragging her upstairs and tying her to his bed.

"Oh my God," she repeated, louder, when he wrapped his lips around one of her nipples.

He'd told her to remain perfectly silent, since all six of his brothers were home—some downstairs in the living room, some in their bedrooms.

Levi narrowed his eyes. "Not a sound," he reminded her.

Kasi pursed her lips closed but, given her flushed cheeks and the way she pressed her legs together, Levi didn't expect her to succeed in remaining quiet when he really got started. His girl was a yeller. And he liked it.

"Please," she whispered, attempting to wrap her legs around his waist, to draw him down to her. She had some serious submission issues that he needed to address. Levi wouldn't call himself a Dom or anything. Sex with past lovers had always been an equal give-and-take of pleasure, but with Kasi, Levi didn't just want to be in charge. He *needed* to.

"That's it." Levi rose from the bed, searching the floor until he found what he was seeking. Picking up the panties he'd pulled off her only a few minutes ago, Levi balled them up and approached her. "Open your mouth."

Kasi's gaze drifted to what he was holding. When she realized what was in his hand, her eyes widened briefly and a low moan escaped.

He bent over her, bracing one hand on the mattress. Kasi's lips parted quickly—willingly—and she offered no resistance when he pushed her damp panties into her mouth as a gag.

"See how sweet you are?" he asked, aware she was tasting her own juices on the cotton.

Kasi nodded, her vision slightly unfocused.

Seven days. That was how long they'd been lovers.

Levi had taken her every single one of those days, addicted to her scent, her soft moans, her kisses, and her oh-so-tight pussy.

Tonight, he'd worked later than usual, not returning home until nearly nine. He realized by the time he'd have showered and driven down the mountain, Kasi would be crawling into bed. The dark circles under her eyes had begun to fade, but Levi wouldn't rest until they were completely gone. He'd heard the disappointment in her voice when he called to tell her he wasn't coming to see her. It bothered him so much, he'd been on the verge of telling her he'd changed his mind when she spoke first, saying something like "a night apart won't kill us."

Those felt like the most wrong words Kasi had ever spoken.

And she must have come to the same conclusion because thirty minutes after saying goodbye and hanging up, she'd been knocking on his door, laughing when she realized he was putting on his shoes, planning to come see her.

She looked slightly shocked when he'd immediately dragged her to his bedroom, not even giving her a chance to say hello to his brothers, then shown her the soft rope he'd bought at the hardware store with her in mind.

The sweet girl had initially made a token attempt at being demure, pretending to be scandalized by the suggestion, even though her grin gave her away. Then she'd taken off all her clothes and placed herself on her back in the middle of his bed, her hands resting on the pillow beneath her head, palms up in surrender. His own personal, beautiful lamb to the slaughter.

Kasi mumbled something around her gag that sounded like "pulley, pulley." Given the pleading look on her face, he figured out she was saying, "Please."

Levi shook his head, then lowered his face until he could issue a sharp nip to her earlobe.

Kasi stopping begging, falling silent.

"Good girl," he breathed into her ear. "No one hears your orgasms except me. If my brothers heard..." He let his words fall away, noting the menace in his tone. This newfound jealousy was going to take some getting used to.

Levi slid down her body, running his tongue through the valley of her breasts and dipping it into her belly button—prompting a giggle—before hitting the jackpot. Her hips lifted, her legs spread wide as he knelt between them.

She gasped, but the sound was muffled enough that Levi let it pass without comment.

Going down on Kasi had become his favorite pastime, as he loved the unabashed way she responded to his licks, bites, and pinches. For several minutes, he used his mouth and fingers to drive her to the edge. Whenever she got close, he backed off, denying her the orgasm she craved.

Peering over her body, he grinned as she threw her head back in frustration. Without the gag, Kasi would have given him one hell of a dressing down. Her silence told him just how deep she wanted to travel into this fantasy.

He'd been blown away by how easily she'd thrown open the door to her darkest desires...and by how closely they mirrored his own.

Kasi wanted to be chased and taken without verbal consent. Levi wanted to hunt.

Kasi wanted to be bound and gagged, edged until she was out of control. Levi wanted to tie the knots.

Kasi wanted to be called baby girl and spanked. Levi wanted her over his lap.

She also wanted to be praised and called his good girl, and damn if Levi didn't already consider the woman his.

Their gazes connected when she lifted her head, curious about why he'd stopped.

"The only place you're coming tonight is on my dick," he warned her.

Kasi nodded eagerly before a muffled moan escaped as he lowered his face to her pussy, diving in for more.

After half a dozen near misses, Levi finally showed her some mercy. But only because he was at the breaking point himself.

He rose from the bed, stripping quickly. Her body relaxed when he returned, and he was thrilled by the complete trust she showed him. She was bound, gagged, completely at his mercy, and yet when she looked at him, all he could see was trust. No fear or apprehension painted her expression. Instead, Kasi told him with her eyes that she knew he would take care of her, that he would never hurt her.

Crawling between her outstretched thighs, he guided his cock to her wet, hot opening. Kasi lifted her legs, wrapping them around his waist, giving him easier access.

Missionary had become one of Kasi's favorites because it meant the head of his dick stroked her G-spot on every return.

While a large part of him wanted to continue the teasing, wanted to draw this out longer, he decided tonight should be a quickie. For one thing, it was getting late and they'd both worked long hours today. And for another, his brothers were in the house, and Levi didn't fool himself into thinking they'd achieve complete silence so, yeah...best to get her there fast.

Levi thrust in roughly, just the way Kasi liked. He knew what his movement would prompt, so he'd been ready. Covering her mouth with his hand, he further muted her loud groan of pleasure.

Kasi's eyes flew open when she felt his hand. He might have thought he'd pushed her too far, if not for her pussy clenched tightly around him. She liked his hand over her mouth, the action pushing her even deeper into her fantasy.

Fuck, if this woman wasn't perfect for him.

Levi kept his hand in place, moving his hips faster, his thrusts short but deep, stroking her G-spot over and over, until her eyes fell shut and she tumbled headlong into her orgasm. Typically, Levi slowed his motions at this point, mentally holding on for dear life to keep from following her into the chasm. Tonight, he let her pull him down, his body jerking once, twice, three times as he unloaded his come inside her.

Levi gave her a quick kiss on the cheek before drawing the makeshift panties gag out of her mouth. The smile Kasi blessed him with—while tired—was full and bright and breathtaking.

"That was amazing," she whispered, her hands quickly slipping down his chest and around to his ass the second he untied her.

Levi fell to her side, drawing her into the crook of his arm as he placed soft kisses on the top of her head. He tried to find his own words to describe what they'd just shared, quickly realizing none of them did the evening justice.

In the end, words weren't necessary because Kasi was asleep within seconds, her soft breath tickling the hair on his chest.

He lay there for at least an hour, willing his own slumber to arrive. He'd risen at the ass crack of dawn, working in the vineyard, so he couldn't understand why he was so wired. Because, Jesus, if a hard day of work followed by explosive sex couldn't produce a sound sleep, what the hell could?

When his restlessness threatened to wake Kasi, Levi gently disengaged himself, sliding out from beneath her.

Rising from the bed, he stepped over to the window, glancing out at the valley below. There was only a faint bit of light provided from tonight's half-moon, so it wasn't hard to see the headlights that flashed in the distance.

Because the family wanted to ensure their homes remained private, they had opened the brewery and the winery below them, on the side of the mountain. That meant, the only traffic on the roads beyond both businesses was from family, friends, and the patrons who stayed at the B&B or rented the cabins sprinkled all around the mountainside.

Their vantage point above the businesses also afforded them a bird's-eye view of the properties below. While there was a grove of trees between the house and the brewery, they'd been cleared back enough that Levi still had a fairly decent view of half of the rear, as well as one whole side of the building. He could also see a piece of the parking lot.

Headlights flashed again.

Someone was down there.

Levi quickly and quietly dressed, stealing one last peek of Kasi, who was sound asleep. She was a beautiful woman, but never so much as now, when she looked so peaceful.

Stepping out into the hallway, he closed the door then traveled down the hall. Levi knocked softly on Theo's door.

"Yeah?"

Levi opened it, peering in. Theo was shirtless in just lounge pants, sitting propped on a pillow, looking at his phone.

Theo glanced up when Levi caught his eye, then his brother gave him a guilty grin as he turned the cell screen toward him. "Candy Crush. It's fucking addictive. Don't judge me."

Levi chuckled. "No judgment here. Hey, did you close the brewery gate when you locked up?"

Theo frowned. "Of course, I did. Why?"

Like Levi's, Theo's bedroom faced the front yard. He rose from the bed, joining Levi by one of the windows. "I saw head-lights in the parking lot."

"Don't see anything now, so—" Theo paused when, once again, headlights flashed in the distance, clearly coming from the brewery. "Shit. I'll go check it out."

"I'll come with you," Levi offered.

Theo threw on a T-shirt and slid his feet into a well-worn pair of sneakers. "Too old to go all night?" he teased, referring to the guest currently sleeping in Levi's bed.

He punched his brother on the shoulder. "Actually, I'm so good, I wore her out."

Theo snorted, then struck an Incredible Hulk pose. "Must run in the family."

Theo and Levi took the dirt path through the woods, the most direct route between the farmhouse and the brewery, walking at a brisk pace.

Once they reached the edge of the woods, they paused, taking in their surroundings. All they could see now was the dim yellow light cast from the lamppost out front. Given they stood behind the building, the majority of the parking lot was blocked by the brewery.

They were about to head to the front when they heard hushed voices a few hundred yards away from them.

Once Levi's vision adjusted to the darkness, he was able to make out a lone shape moving at the far end of the building from where they stood.

"Window?" Theo whispered.

Levi nodded, his thoughts traveling the same direction as Theo's. There was a window at that end of the building that opened into a newly created office. Theo was in the process of hiring an events manager for the farm's businesses, and since he would also serve as that employee's supervisor, the family had decided to put a new office next to Theo's in the brewery. Either that new window hadn't been locked, or whoever was currently leaning into it had jimmied it open.

Staring beyond the figure, Levi spotted two motorcycles. That explained the headlights.

Theo made a gesture with his hand, indicating that he'd go the long way around the building, while Levi made his way quietly along the line of trees. Once they were in position, they'd trap whoever these guys were between them.

Levi considered holding Theo back and suggesting they call the sheriff, but it was clear the thieves weren't big guys. Most likely, it was a couple of local teenagers stealing a case of beer.

Teens were the reason they'd installed a gate on the parking lot in the first place. Last year, a few guys from the local high school had decided to use the huge lot for makeshift drag races. Levi wasn't sure how the idiots thought they could get away with something like that for more than one night. The peeling tires and sharp squeal of brakes had woken his entire family—in all three farmhouses.

Levi heard the telltale sound of clinking bottles as a second person passed a case of beer through the window.

Yep. It was kids stealing beer. He watched as Theo stealthily crossed to the side of the building, making his way to the front before disappearing from view. Levi gave his brother until the count of fifteen to make his way around the front of the brewery and sneaking closer.

The thieves didn't seem content with just one case because, as Levi watched, another was handed out.

"We said one case. How are we going to get both of these home?" the guy standing outside asked his accomplice. "No way we can carry all of this on the bikes."

Before his buddy could reply, Theo stepped around the corner—prompting the kid outside to run directly into Levi's arms.

The boy had his hoodie up, his face lowered, but damn if the kid didn't put up a fight, kicking Levi in the shin...*hard.*

Levi grasped the boy's arm, lifting him slightly and shaking him. "Settle the fuck down," he growled. Glancing over the boy's shoulder, he saw Theo had the other kid by the scruff of the neck.

He turned toward Levi and called out, "It's Archie Carter."

He scowled when he heard the name of Keith's best friend. Reaching up, Levi tugged down the hoodie, unsurprised to find Kasi's brother glaring up at him.

"You good?" he yelled back to Theo.

"Yeah. Me and Arch are going inside the brewery to place a call to his dad."

Archie's shoulders slumped in defeat. "Please don't do that, Theo. He'll kill me! Seriously."

Levi knew Gerry Carter quite well, as the two of them had been teammates on Gracemont High School's football team, when Levi was a freshman and Gerry a senior. As such, he knew Gerry, a local carpenter, would put the boy to work on whatever construction project he was currently on, giving the kid the shit jobs to ensure Archie never did anything like this again. Regardless of the boy's freaking out, Levi was quite confident Archie would survive the night after Theo's call.

That was when Levi realized his brother got the better end

of this adventure, especially when Keith tried to shake off his grip again.

"What good is running going to do? I caught you red-handed. It's not like you can lie your way out of this," Levi pointed out calmly, silently debating with himself on exactly how to handle this situation.

Unlike Archie, who was facing definite punishment, Levi wasn't sure the same would hold true for Keith. He recalled Kasi's comment that her mother had been a strict parent, the one to mete out all discipline. When he paired that with the fact that most of Keith's infractions since Mrs. Mills' passing had been related to Kasi—who definitely hadn't shared the details with her father—it was easy to see the boy hadn't faced any consequences for his actions of late.

So Levi was left with two choices: tell Kasi what her brother had done and force her to handle it, or deal with this situation on his own.

He knew instantly which option he was taking.

He held out his hand. "Key."

Keith frowned, confused.

"Give me the key to your bike."

Keith scoffed. "Fuck off!"

Levi moved fast, his grip on Keith's arm impenetrable as he shoved the boy against the rear wall of the building. "Key," he repeated through gritted teeth. "You're not getting off this mountain until the two of us have a talk. Man to man."

Whatever adrenaline or anger Keith had been holding on to faded, and he reached into the front pocket of his jeans, pulling out the key.

Levi slipped it into his own pocket. "If I let go of you, are you going to be a stupid jackass and try to run? Bear in mind, I know where you live."

Keith sighed. "I won't run."

Levi loosened his grip then let go, braced and ready to nab the kid again if he was lying.

Keith slumped against the back of the brewery. "We were only taking a case. Or..."

Archie had clearly been the greedy one, going back for the second case.

Levi glanced over, shaking his head. "And how did you plan to get a case of beer off the mountain on motorcycles?"

Keith lifted his chin toward his bike. "Strapped duffels to the back of them."

Now that he was closer, Levi noticed the canvas bags hanging on the motorcycles.

"You forget you're underage?" Levi asked.

Keith rolled his eyes like the smart-ass he was. "You telling me you never drank when you were my age?"

Levi and his brother Sam had snuck more than their fair share of beers from their dad and granddad's stash when they were in their teens. Enough that both men had probably noticed. But since he and Sam always consumed that beer at home, never operating a vehicle afterward, they'd never been formally busted.

Instead, his dad had pulled them aside and told them he'd cut up their driver's licenses himself if he ever caught wind of them driving under the influence. Told them there was nothing wrong with drinking a beer from time to time as long as they were smart about it and didn't drink to excess.

Given their close proximity, Levi could smell the tang of beer on Keith's breath, which told him that he and Archie had already helped themselves to some of the beer or—more disturbing—they'd drunk beer before deciding to drive up the mountain on their motorcycles to steal from Levi's family.

"I never broke into a business and stole beer," Levi said,

rather than answering Keith's question. "You ride your bikes around the locked gate?"

Keith's silence told him they did.

"How much have you already had to drink?"

Keith opened his mouth, ready to deny having any, so Levi saved him the bother of trying.

"I can smell it on your breath."

Keith closed his lips as if to block the scent.

"How much?"

"Only one," Keith said, though Levi didn't believe the kid. Why would he? Keith had done nothing but go out of his way to be a thorn in Levi's side, and he'd done a great job making Kasi's life difficult.

"One?" he repeated.

"Yes," Keith insisted. "One, okay? Me and Archie cracked open a couple when we got inside, so we could decide which ones we wanted..."

"To steal," Levi finished when Keith didn't.

"Are you going to tell Kasi?"

Levi hadn't expected that question. Or rather, he hadn't expected the tone behind it, the sadness lacing the words.

Rather than reply—because honestly, he hadn't made up his mind about Kasi's involvement—Levi crossed his arms. "What the hell is going on inside your head, Keith? Why are you doing all this shit?"

Keith looked away, and Levi figured silence was the only response he was going to get...so he was surprised when Keith ran a hand through his hair and replied, "I don't know why."

It was a quiet admission, and Levi considered pushing for more. Then he realized Keith seemed to be genuinely searching for an answer, so he simply stood there, giving the kid time to think.

"I miss her."

Any annoyance or anger Levi harbored toward Kasi's kid brother vanished in an instant after those three small words. "I know you do."

Keith refused to look at him, swallowing heavily. "I know this will make me sound like a pussy, but my mama was my best friend."

Levi shook his head. "Doesn't make you a pussy at all. I'm close to my mom too."

"It's just...when she died," Keith blinked rapidly, fighting hard not to cry, "I got so fucking *mad.*"

"Anger is a big part of grieving," Levi started.

Keith shook his head. "No. I wasn't mad because she died. I was mad *at* her for dying, for leaving me. If she was sick, why didn't she go to the doctor? And then I got mad at my dad for just...fucking disappearing. And..."

"And Kasi?"

"I got mad at her because she didn't cry at the funeral. Not once. It was like she didn't care at all!"

Levi reached out and put his hand on Keith's shoulder. "That's not true, Keith. You know that. Kasi is just as devastated as you are."

Keith scoffed. "Yeah, right. She didn't shed a damn tear. Then, a few days after the funeral, she goes right back to work like nothing happened. Like Mama never existed at all."

Levi recalled Kasi recounting the days following her mother's funeral. How Keith had struck out, how her father had taken to his room, how she'd been left to try to hold them all together. Keith had interpreted his sister's strength as apathy. Nothing could be farther from the truth.

"Kasi misses your mother every bit as much as you do. People grieve differently, but that doesn't mean their pain isn't just as real. Kasi has spent the last eight months fighting like hell to hold it together. For you and your dad."

Keith lowered his head. "I know that."

"You do?"

For the first time, Keith lifted his face, his gaze meeting Levi's. "Yeah, but by the time I realized that, it was too late."

Levi frowned, confused. "Too late for what?"

"I said some really awful things to her. Kept getting into trouble around town. I've been this person for so long now, I don't remember how to be..."

Levi squeezed his shoulder again. "Who you used to be?"

Keith nodded.

"I don't think you're ever going to be the guy you were before your mom died, but you were never going to be him forever anyway. That's just a part of growing up. Experiences change you, mold you. It's up to you how you let the bad times shape you, Keith."

The kid's lower lip quivered. "I don't like this shape."

"Then change it."

Keith shook his head. "You don't know what I said to Kasi. I can't ask her to forgive me for it. It was...too mean."

Levi didn't share that he knew exactly what Keith had said, how he'd blamed her for their mother's death. "She's your sister, and she loves you. More than that, she *misses* you. You say you're sorry to her, and I can guarantee you'll get a clean slate. That's how family works."

Keith fell silent for a moment. "What if I don't deserve a clean slate?"

Levi smiled. "Your sister is headstrong. If she wants to give it to you, by God, she will. And she won't rest until you take it."

Finally, Keith smiled, laughing a little. "You're right. She will. She got that from Mama." Then he sighed. "Are you going to tell Kasi about this?" he asked again.

Levi shook his head. "No. I'm not."

"Thanks. And I'll try to stop being such a pain in the ass.

'Cause I think she's got something else going on that's stressing her out."

"Like what?" Levi asked, concerned.

"I don't know. It's got something to do with the mayor. He keeps stopping by the house and the fruit stand. I think he's bothering her."

Levi recalled Scottie shooting him dirty looks at Whiskey Abbey. He'd thought the man's disdain was due to the Lucy dustup, but now he wondered if it had more to do with Kasi.

"Why is he stopping by?" Levi asked.

Keith shrugged. "I don't know. I asked Kasi, but I think she lied about the reason."

"What did she say?"

"Few times, she said he was just drumming up votes for reelection."

"Sounds plausible to me," Levi countered.

"The last time, she said Scottie was stopping by to get a recipe for his mom."

Levi nodded, relieved that it sounded like Keith was making something out of nothing.

Keith narrowed his eyes at Levi's lack of concern. "*You* ever seen Mrs. Grover cook anything?"

That comment gave Levi reason to pause. Because Mrs. Grover paid one of the local women to prepare meals for her family and, while Gracemont was typically slow to change, a couple young people had started doing DoorDash deliveries around town because the Grovers ordered out enough to keep them busy.

Keith continued proving his point. "She brought that fancy-ass sushi from that expensive restaurant in Leesburg to the town picnic. Sushi, for God's sake. And when Mama died, and all the women in Gracemont were dropping off casseroles and other food, Mrs. Grover had a pizza delivered to our house.

We've been neighbors for nearly twenty years, and she couldn't even be bothered to come pay her respects in person. Not that I give a shit," he was quick to add, "but you have to admit that's cold."

"It is."

Uneasiness settled over Levi as he considered what the real reason for Scottie's visits might be. He supposed Kasi could have been telling her brother the truth. After all, Scottie *was* up for reelection. And it was possible his mother had wanted a recipe to pass on to someone *else* to make for her.

But Kasi never mentioned Scottie stopping by to him. Why?

Unfortunately, he didn't have time to think about it because right now, there was another Mills sibling to worry about. He walked over to the window Keith and Archie had pried open with a crowbar. He bent over to pick it up, and Keith's shoulders sagged with shame.

"I'll pay to replace the window," Keith said.

"You're right. You will. But not with money. It's harvest time, and we can always use a couple extra strong backs. Don't make any plans for Saturday, and tell Archie to do the same."

Keith groaned, making it clear he'd rather just come up with the cash, but he didn't refuse.

Levi tossed the crowbar aside, reaching down to pull a couple of beers out of the case Archie had abandoned when he'd tried to run. Popping the caps on them, he walked over to Keith and handed him one, the two of them leaning against the back of the building side by side.

"Theo will probably give Archie a ride home when he realizes you two have been drinking. You can hop in with them or crash on my couch," Levi said, as he tapped his bottle against Keith's. "By the way, we're not telling your sister about this, either."

Keith grinned, the two of them taking a drink.

"You going to marry Kasi?"

Levi nodded without a moment's hesitation. Because that was *exactly* what he was going to do. "I am. You okay with that?"

Keith's response came just as quick. "Yeah. Better you than Scottie."

Levi hated that answer as much as he liked it.

What the hell was going on between Kasi and the mayor?

Chapter Thirteen

K asi stared at the bills, then turned her attention to the ledger her mother had always kept. Mama was old school when it came to keeping track of their finances, unwilling to embrace the concept of online banking, claiming crunching the numbers kept her brain sharp.

Kasi planned—at some point—to move them into this century by setting up online bill pay and inputting their financial information on a spreadsheet, but as with everything else, she simply hadn't had the time to do it yet.

She scrolled through their bank account online. She'd taken the time to set that up, as it had driven her out of her mind to try to work with her mother's—honest to God—handwritten checkbook register.

Now, just like yesterday, the numbers didn't add up. Because the money they were taking in was nowhere near enough to cover this pile of bills. And given their current operation, it never would.

So, she was left with a chicken or egg situation. Drain their accounts to pay the tax bill and keep the farm—even though they wouldn't be able to plant anything in the empty fields or keep the Rileys on—or plant the fields to earn the money to pay the bills and keep the farm running.

The last one was the smart option. It was also the one that required time. Time she didn't seem to have, according to Scottie. The town wanted their money now.

Of course, there was a third option, but the thought of accepting Scottie's proposal made her sick to her stomach.

Which left her staring down the barrel of the last resort. Do nothing, lose the farm, and move the family to Nashville to live with her uncle.

She rubbed her forehead wearily. Something had to give, but she'd be damned if she could figure out what. When nothing came to her, she put her head down on her arms on the table and sighed.

She hadn't seen Levi since the night before last, when she'd driven to his farmhouse for sex. She didn't even try to sugarcoat her reason for needing to see him. They'd spoken on the phone, said their good nights, and ten minutes later, she and her hormones had been barreling down the road, headed for Stormy Weather Farm.

Levi had lit a fire in her, and the thing was blazing out of control. Not that she gave a shit. It was nice to actually feel something amazing and energizing. For too many months, she'd been running on fumes, exhaustion her permanent state.

All that had changed the past few weeks as Levi helped her organize her life in such a way that she could steal a couple hours of extra sleep each night. He'd done it by helping her around the farm, by streamlining her baking schedule, and by ensuring Keith did his fair share of the chores.

He'd brought fun back into her life and helped her find her laugh again. She'd hated how rusty it had sounded at first.

Of course, in the end, Levi's help had really been for

naught. Because Kasi was happily sacrificing those extra newfound hours of sleep for sex.

Sleep was for suckers, she thought, as she lifted her head, smiling to herself.

Last night, Levi had worked until nearly ten, and when she'd offered to come to him again, he refused, insisting she needed rest. She wanted to argue until he pointed out that he needed sleep too. That was when guilt kicked in. Harvest season was the busiest time of year for Levi, as his family and their crew of fifteen workers, plus some seasonal laborers, went through the back-breaking task of handpicking the grapes. Because their winery was perched on the side of a mountain, the use of a harvester wasn't possible. Levi mentioned even if it had been, they couldn't have afforded the extremely expensive piece of equipment.

The idea that he'd been working long hours and still making time for her warmed her all the way to the bones. Before Levi, she didn't know how cold she'd been inside. Cold and lonely and depressed.

None of that had been present since he'd crash-landed into her life. Or maybe she'd crash-landed into his that day she'd passed out in his arms.

So when Levi had admitted he needed rest, she'd shoved aside her disappointment and tried to temper her horniness. She owed him a decent night's rest after the ones he'd given her.

Kasi had tried to shield her frustration over not being with him, but Levi had this uncanny ability to read her. Sometimes she felt like she was his favorite book, one he'd read so many times, he knew all the words by heart. Because he'd chuckled when her response to his "we'll see each other tomorrow" was met with a grumpy "fine." The only thing missing from her reply had been a petulant foot stomp, which she hadn't been able to do because she'd been lying on top of her bed. She didn't bother to point out to him that she was fully dressed because she'd intended to drive to his house.

Levi had managed to wipe her grumpy tone out in a hot minute when he introduced her to the power of phone sex.

God, she'd never managed to give herself such a mind-blowing orgasm on her own, but the way Levi growled his demands, telling her exactly what he wanted her to do, had driven her to climax in record time.

The best part was, he'd been right there with her, stroking himself, letting her hear how much her moans and soft cries turned him on.

When she was younger and imagined having sex, she hadn't considered much more than the physical aspects of the act. Levi had taken her preconceived notions and turned them on their head because good sex was a hell of a lot more than inserting slot A into slot B. He seduced her with his words as much as his touches, ensnaring her thoughts as well as her body by encouraging her to open up about her desires without fear.

Kasi still couldn't believe how forthright she'd been that first night, telling him things she'd never imagined speaking aloud to a lover. After all, there were fantasies, and then there were *fantasies*.

For a while, she'd even worried her more extreme desires were wrong. Until she and Remi had fallen into a bottle of wine one night and started talking. When she told her best friend about her capture fantasy, Remi confided she often had the same one, and the next thing Kasi knew, they were knee-deep into a porn movie with that very theme on Remi's laptop.

She wasn't sure what had prompted her to share those secrets with Levi, whether it was the afterglow of some amazing orgasms or the fact that she trusted him so completely. Probably both. Kasi knew Levi well enough to understand that he would always listen to her without judgment, without laughing or belittling her. And his response to her revelations had proven her trust hadn't been misplaced. Because she'd unwittingly released a beast. Her *perfect* beast.

When Levi admitted that her fantasies matched his, she worried he was just saying that.

She knew now he was NOT just saying that. Because holy shit.

After this last week of stolen sexual encounters, she thought she should be walking funny.

But it wasn't just the physical intimacy that had her floating on cloud nine. She'd always suspected sex would bring a certain measure of closeness between two people, but with Levi, the edges of where she ended and he began were becoming blurred. He hadn't just taken her body; he'd reached into her head and stolen her fantasies, her dreams, and even her fears. Then he'd broken into her heart and nabbed her love too. He was claiming every single part of her. And she liked it. A lot.

Kasi ran a finger over her lower lip and closed her eyes, replaying the goodbye kiss Levi had given her yesterday morning. Even now, her lips were slightly puffy from the power behind it. Levi kissed her like she fucking mattered. God, after months of feeling invisible—a cog in the wheel that no one noticed unless something didn't get done—being the center of Levi's universe was heady and addictive and...

She was getting carried away again.

Letting herself play out a future that...

She lowered her head in her hands once more. A future that wasn't in the cards.

"What are you doing?"

Kasi startled when Keith walked into the room.

"Just paying some bills," she said, gesturing to the pile.

"Need some help?"

She blinked a couple times, trying to figure out if she'd heard him right. She'd gotten the feeling he wanted to talk to her a few times yesterday, but every time he seemed on the verge, he clammed up again.

Kasi had been tempted to come right out and ask him what was going on, but the past eight months had left her trigger-shy when it came to her brother, unwilling to subject herself to more of his ire.

"Nope," she said. "I'm all good. Just finished actually." Because unless the bank and the utility companies and the city government were okay with being paid in fruits and vegetables, she didn't have much else to offer.

"Okay. I...I, um..." Keith paused again, doing the same thing he'd done all day yesterday. "I'm going to Josh's tonight. Unless you need help around here."

Wow. Two for two on nice offers.

Though, she got the sense that what he said wasn't what he'd intended to say. Once again, she considered pushing the issue. "I finished most of my chores. Did you—"

"Animals are fed," Keith said, cutting her off.

"Thanks. Keith...is everything okay with you?"

"Yeah. I wanted to tell you—"

This time, it wasn't Keith who stopped himself from speaking, but a knock at door.

"I'll get it," he said.

She followed Keith out of the kitchen and swallowed down a groan when she spotted Scottie standing on the porch.

Keith opened the door, the scowl that had been absent the last couple of days firmly back in place. "What are you doing here?" he asked belligerently.

Kasi quickly stepped forward. "Hi, Scottie. Um, Keith, weren't you heading out?"

Her brother hesitated, and Kasi worried he might change his plans. She didn't want him to find out about the back taxes until she had a handle on the situation.

She gave herself an internal "ha ha" because there was no handle. Nothing to grab onto. This ship was going down unless a miracle presented itself.

"Maybe I should…" Keith started.

Kasi felt him wavering. "Josh is probably waiting for you. Weren't you guys going bowling with some of your buddies?"

Keith nodded before shooting Scottie another dirty look.

Kasi needed to get her brother out of here. The next few minutes were going to be awkward enough without Keith adding more fuel to the fire.

She feared the mayor was here for his answer, one she didn't want to give him because she knew it would set him off and she really needed more time. While the collecting of taxes wasn't his job, he still had a great deal of pull around the government offices, and he could encourage Herb to move things along faster than the commissioner's typical snail's pace if his ego was bruised.

She sighed.

She wasn't going to marry him.

It was as simple as that.

What wasn't simple was facing what came *after*.

The idea of packing up their beloved home and moving to another state made her physically ill, but that was what it might come down to.

She'd briefly considered asking Levi for a loan, but she rejected that idea the second she had it. This thing between them was too new and, well, she had too much damn pride to ever make that request. Her family's problems weren't Levi's. She'd done nothing but lean on him since the day he'd stopped her from faceplanting in the fruit stand. It wasn't fair to ask for more, and there was a big difference between moral support and money.

It had been her intention to keep things between her and Levi casual because her life was currently a complete clusterfuck. The problem was, Levi hadn't let the casual thing stand, taking them from friendly neighbors to lovers at breakneck speed. She should probably be walking around with a parachute, considering the freefall she and Levi had taken the past three weeks.

Jesus.

The fact it hadn't even been a month should prove things were moving too fast.

How did she let herself get so swept away by him?

"I can postpone until tomorrow night," Keith offered. "If you need me to stick around."

Kasi waved him off. "Good heavens, no. There's nothing going on here. You've been working hard the past couple of weeks. Go have a good time." She placed her hand on his back, gently shoving him toward the door. Or at least she meant for it to be gentle. She had to add some force when he offered genuine resistance.

"I'll see you in the morning," she said, when Keith finally cleared the doorway.

He shot Scottie one last cold look. "Okay. Call if you need me," he said, stressing the words more than she thought necessary.

If Kasi wasn't so anxious about the upcoming conversation with Scottie, she might have found time to be touched by her brother's overprotective words. She'd missed that part of him most of all since Mama's death. Despite being her kid brother, younger than her by six years, Keith had always gone to bat for her, stepping forward to protect her if he ever felt like she was in trouble or being threatened.

"I will," she reassured him, closing the door. Keith hesitated on the porch, and she feared he was going to turn around. But he finally moved forward, heading for his motorcycle.

Kasi twisted to face Scottie and leaned on the closed door, taking a couple steadying breaths.

"Can I get you something to drink?" The idea of entertaining Scottie was low on her list of what she considered a good time, but she wasn't above stalling.

Scottie shook his head. "No. Thank you."

"Why don't we go into the living room and sit down?" She gestured to the left, pushing away from the door, as Scottie followed.

She took a quick study of the furniture, then opted for the lone armchair in the room, unwilling to encourage Scottie to sit next to her.

He claimed the center of the couch, directly across from her.

"Well," she hedged, praying for some flash of lightning, some inspiration that might save her.

Nothing came.

"What's going on with you and Levi Storm?" Scottie asked, when the silence drifted too long. His brows were furrowed with obvious annoyance.

"What?"

"Levi? I saw the two of you dancing at Whiskey Abbey. You looked pretty familiar with each other, kissing him on the dance floor. You realize the man is barbaric, right? A brute who doesn't have two brain cells in his head to rub together."

Kasi flushed with anger. "That's not—"

"Besides, he's too old for you," Scottie interjected. "The man is pushing forty."

She swallowed down what she wanted to say to that jibe, fighting hard to keep her cool because her back was up against the wall here. She wanted to rip him a new one for insulting Levi.

"I've been best friends with his cousin Remi forever," she said, in an attempt not to answer the question. "And—"

"So you're dating the man?" Scottie pressed.

Kasi hesitated. There was no love lost between Scottie and Levi, so telling him they were dating was a bad idea.

But the idea of denying it wasn't a possibility.

While she and Levi hadn't put any labels on their relationship, she couldn't downplay it. They may not have said the labels aloud, but they were still there, bright as the midday sun. Levi obviously considered her his girlfriend, and dammit...she wanted to be his.

She'd given herself to him, and not just her body. Her heart had been his for most of her life, and these past few weeks had been some of the best she'd ever had. If this thing between them had started earlier, if they were further along, maybe she would have felt more comfortable talking to Levi about this.

But how much could she continue to take from him before it became too much, and he walked away?

The silence lingered too long, so Scottie filled it. "Everything you're doing just proves you need help, Kasi. Apparently, it's not just your brother who's running wild, vandalizing, breaking and entering, stealing stuff."

"He's never stolen anything," Kasi replied hotly.

The slimy smile on Scottie's face instantly set her on alert. "Levi didn't tell you about him and Theo catching Keith and Archie breaking a window at the brewery night before last? Sounds like they did a bit of damage before stealing some beer."

Kasi frowned. She was at Levi's that night. He'd been in bed with her. "That's a lie."

"No. It's not. Archie's dad, Gerry, is good friends with Sheriff Anderson. You know what a hard-ass Gerry is. He asked if the sheriff would put the fear of God in his boy because he didn't like the path he was on. Sheriff scared the kid a bit, told him what sort of jail time he was facing if the Storms decided to press charges."

"They're pressing charges?"

"Possibly."

Levi said he couldn't come the past two nights because of the harvest. Had he lied? He obviously wasn't a fan of Keith's bad attitude, but he wouldn't press charges against her brother, would he?

Unfortunately, the fact he hadn't told her about the break-in left her in doubt. Why would he keep that a secret?

"If they do press charges, Keith could be in some legal trouble. That's not cheap. He's eighteen now, so he would be tried as an adult," Scottie added.

God, was that why Keith had been so contrite just now? Because he knew big trouble was coming and he was trying to soften her up? Then she recalled how he'd started to say something but stopped. What if he'd tried to tell her about the theft and the pending arrest but chickened out?

Before she could reply, she heard heavy, slow footsteps on the stairs. She rose just as her father peered into the living room.

"Heard voices," Daddy said softly, his attention directed to some point over her left shoulder.

There was a new puffiness around her father's red-rimmed eyes that told her he'd been crying. That was when it occurred to her that she hadn't seen Daddy yet today. Keith had taken breakfast and lunch up to his room, and unfortunately, dinner was going to be late as she'd forgotten to turn the Crock-Pot on prior to heading down to work the fruit stand.

"You remember Scottie, Daddy," she said, rising and

crossing the room to him. "Are you okay?" she asked in a quieter voice.

The faraway look in Daddy's eyes was something she hadn't seen recently, the vacantness fading a bit with each passing day. He'd been more like himself recently, joining them at the table for meals and, this past week, even spending a few hours each day in the fields with the Riley twins.

It had given her hope. Hope that was now dashed as she looked into his eyes.

"Daddy?"

He didn't respond. Instead, his gaze was transfixed on the doorframe between the living room and the front foyer, studying the tick marks, initials, and dates covering it. She hated seeing him so desolate.

"Every year," Daddy said, running his finger over the tick marks. "Your mother marked your height every year on your birthday."

Kasi nodded, quickly swiping at her runny nose, her throat closing. "I remember."

The marks started near the bottom, Mama's tradition beginning the year Kasi was two and able to stand on her own, and it had continued right up until she'd graduated from high school. Since it had become apparent she'd hit her maximum height sophomore year, the last three tick marks drawn in the same spot, Mama had stopped measuring her.

A strong cramp twisted inside Kasi's stomach when she realized no one had gotten Keith's birthday measurement in March. She thought back on that day, recalling Keith had been in an exceptionally bad mood, which was saying something for him. He'd refused to eat dinner with her, hadn't touched the birthday cake she'd baked him, and spent most of the day moping in his room, yelling at her to leave him alone whenever she tried to pull him out.

Had he been waiting for her to add a tick mark to the doorframe, to continue the tradition?

Kasi hated herself for forgetting.

"She always made birthdays special," Daddy said, still talking, though Kasi got the sense he wasn't necessarily saying these things to her. She wasn't even sure if he'd noticed Scottie sitting there. No, it was as if he was lost in his own thoughts and speaking to himself.

"She did," Kasi agreed, her voice thin as she swallowed back tears. She would shed those later, in the privacy of her bedroom.

There was a ghost of a smile on Daddy's face. "I loved her birthday cakes. The whole house smelled so sweet."

Kasi drew in a breath, her mind tricking her into believing she could actually smell one of those cakes baking right now. Powdered sugar, butter, vanilla. The greatest combined scent on the planet.

Daddy glanced around. "Everywhere I look...I see pieces of her. There's so much of her in every corner of this house."

It was true. Mama had loved their home, and she'd taken great pride in it. As Kasi followed her father's gaze around the living room, she took in the throw blankets her mom had crocheted, hanging over the back of the couch. She let her eyes travel to the fireplace mantel, jam-packed with framed photos of them—picnics, special occasions, school photos. Her mother changed them frequently, saying she'd been so blessed with happy days and a wonderful family that it was impossible to limit each frame to just one photo. Kasi knew every frame on that mantel probably had at least three more pictures stuffed behind the one being displayed.

Then she studied the special cross-stitch her mother had made. The words, "Two lasting gifts we give our children are roots and wings," colorfully emblazoned on the cloth.

"She would have been fifty-seven today," Daddy whispered.

Kasi gasped, his words cutting through her like a thousand blades.

It was her mother's birthday.

And she'd forgotten.

Kasi clenched her hands together, desperate to keep them from shaking. Bile clogged her throat and for a second, she feared she was going to be sick.

How could she have forgotten?

"Daddy," she said, forcing the single word out. She needed to say something, but all she could think of was, "I'm sorry," and she was too ashamed to admit she hadn't remembered.

For the first time since entering the room, Daddy looked at her. "You're so much like her, Kasi."

She blinked back the tears, but it was hard. So hard. She hadn't cried in front of anyone since Mama's death, holding the emotions at bay because her father and brother needed her to be strong. It had felt like a way of honoring her mother's memory because Kasi had never, not once, seen her mom cry.

Daddy placed his hand on her shoulder. "You make this house a home too."

Kasi felt those words like a punch to the stomach, especially as the smell of tonight's pot roast—her father's favorite—drifted from the kitchen.

She was losing their home.

She looked away from Daddy, turning her face toward the foyer, hating that Scottie had been a silent witness to all of this. It wasn't like him to remain quiet for so long, the blowhard always interjecting his unwanted thoughts and opinions into most conversations. God only knew what he was thinking.

"You're a good daughter. I think I'll take dinner in my room tonight." Daddy turned away from her, heading back up the stairs, unaware of the nuclear explosion he'd set off inside her.

She'd been so wrapped up in Levi, and so stressed about money, that she'd forgotten her mother's birthday.

How could she forget?

She'd *never* forgotten.

Kasi watched her father climb the stairs, noticing how much he'd aged in the last eight months. He wasn't an elderly man, but his stooped shoulders and slow gait made him seem like he was thirty years older than he was.

"You *are* a good daughter," Scottie said from the couch.

Kasi took a moment to try to pull herself together, but it was pointless. She was devastated, destroyed, done in.

Just...done.

She forced herself to turn and face him, wishing she could tell him to get the hell out. All she could think about was locking herself into her room and crying her heart out for the next three lifetimes.

"Scottie," she said, gesturing to where her father just stood. "This isn't a good time. Can you come back—"

"It would be a shame for your father to leave his home. He was born here, wasn't he?" Scottie asked as he rose, joining her in the doorway.

Kasi nodded. The mayor had done his homework.

"Scottie—" she started again. She couldn't do this. Not now.

"Marry me, Kasi, and he can live out his days here. He'll never lose the memories of your mother. It's clear he's still impacted by her death. How hard will it be on him when he has to leave this place? I think it would be a lot like losing her all over again."

Kasi's chest tightened. Suddenly, the idea of packing and leaving here felt impossible. For months, she'd lived with a shell of the man who'd been her father. And with the exception of today, there had been a glimmer of hope that he was returning to them, finding his way out of his grief.

If they lost the house...

There was no way Daddy would come back from that. She'd lose him forever. The same way she'd lost Mama.

"Plus, I can help Keith, hire him the best lawyer to make sure he doesn't go to jail."

"I..." Kasi's throat was constricted, the walls closing in on her. "I can't do this right now," she whispered, turning her head away because she refused to cry in front of Scottie.

Scottie patted her shoulder in a way he probably thought was comforting but made her want to throw up. "My offer is the best one you're going to get. I'm the only man who can help you through this. Get some rest, sweetheart. I'll be in touch very soon."

Scottie's face transformed, not with a smile but with a smirk. Probably because he believed he was on the cusp of getting exactly what he wanted, something that happened more often than not in the spoiled asshole's life. The only time she'd ever heard of him not getting his way was when Lucy turned down his proposal, and Levi had punched his lights out.

Her surroundings started to go gray as Kasi gave in to the numbness that had become her coping technique since Mama's death. When things became too painful, she pushed all the feelings deep inside, shutting them away, closing her thoughts down. It was that or fall apart, and part of her had always feared that if she gave in to the emotions, she wouldn't be able to pull herself back together.

She barely noticed when Scottie pulled an engagement ring out of his pocket.

"Scottie," she said, shaking her head.

"I know you're not ready to officially accept. Just take this as a reminder. I can make all the bad things go away, Kasi." He forced the ring into the palm of her hand.

Kasi glanced at it with a detached eye, acknowledging the fact it was large and gaudy and completely not her style.

She was vaguely aware of Scottie giving her a kiss, just a brush of his lips against hers, but enough to make her skin crawl. Then she heard him say his goodbyes, though the words sounded like they were coming to her through noise-canceling headphones. Mumbled, low, hard to hear.

Kasi didn't show him out, didn't say anything, didn't move, not even when she heard the front door close behind him and the sound of his car fading as he drove away.

She remained frozen in that doorway, her eyes following the tick marks, from that first one on the bottom to the one on top. A lifetime lived in inches.

Then she considered how there wouldn't be any more marks. She would be stuck there, just like that, forever.

She slipped Scottie's ring into the pocket of her jeans, hating the weight of it, the feel of it, the emptiness of it.

Out of sight. Out of mind.

If only.

The numbness started to lift, despite her best efforts to wrap it around herself, the pain forcing its way through.

Kasi slid down the doorframe, her body trembling in agony, her heart shattered into a million pieces. She rested her head on her knees, racked by the tears she couldn't hold in anymore.

Her coping technique failed her as every single thing she'd done wrong crashed in on her at once.

She shouldn't have slept with Levi, shouldn't have let herself believe that they could have a future together.

She shouldn't have let things get so bad on the farm.

She shouldn't have let her father down, letting him shut himself in rather than pulling him out the way Levi and Remi had done. She'd left him alone to suffer in his self-imposed sanctuary instead of being there for him. She'd done the same to Keith, failed him in too many ways to count, and now he was facing jail.

And she shouldn't have left Mama alone in the kitchen that day. Maybe if she'd been there...

Kasi crawled to the couch, tears pouring from her like heavy rain, dropping from her face to the carpet. Climbing on the couch, she curled into a ball, the pain too much to bear.

Months of sobs erupted, and she did nothing to hold them back, six words beating into her brain and on her heart like a sledgehammer.

I shouldn't have left Mama alone.

Chapter Fourteen

Levi glanced at his phone when he pulled up outside Kasi's house, grinning like a damn fool. Usually rain during harvest season pissed him off because it put him behind schedule. But last night's summer shower was just enough to score him a few hours off this morning as they waited for the grapes to dry.

He decided to put that time to good use, hoping he could entice his girl into joining him in a little predawn hanky-panky in the barn. Looking around, he realized how much he'd come to love this farm.

Levi had recently started growing hops on a small patch of land. Rain or Shine Brewery didn't need a lot of hops, so it worked out fine. However, if he had more available land, he could increase his yield to sell to other breweries in the area. His dream was to eventually move Stormy Weather Farm away from outsourcing the things needed for them to produce their wine and beer. Unfortunately, that seemed destined to *remain* a dream because there simply wasn't enough land for them to plant all the things he wanted—like apple trees, barley, berries, and even jalapeños.

Farming had always been his passion, and while he loved working with the vines, he was starting to feel the pull to branch out and explore different kinds of farming. He'd enjoyed his time here, working with the Riley twins, cultivating many different types of produce. There was a science to farming that had always fascinated him. He'd perfected the chemistry of growing grapes, and now he was chomping at the bit to try something else, to learn something new.

He sighed and let that thought go. As Dad was fond of saying, "If wishes were horses, beggars would ride."

Levi was aware that five thirty in the morning was way too early for a visit. But, like him, Kasi's days started before the sun even thought about making an appearance.

Or, at least, they usually did.

There were no lights on inside the house. Not even the front porch light, which was always on.

Maybe she'd overslept.

Considering the long hours she kept, it wasn't like anyone could blame her if she snoozed through the alarm once or twice.

If Levi could be certain she was oversleeping, he'd turn his truck around and head home because there was no way he was waking her up, relentless erection be damned. Those dark circles were lingering beneath her eyes again. If he wasn't so sexually satisfied, he might feel some guilt about that. Because he knew exactly whose fault those reappearing circles were.

He grinned.

Yep. Impossible to feel guilty for keeping her up late this past week.

Clearly, he was a selfish man, and he didn't see that changing anytime soon. Because now that he'd had Kasi, Levi wasn't going to be satisfied until they were living under the same roof and sharing the same bed every night for the rest of their lives.

If he had his way, they'd already be there because there wasn't a doubt in his mind that she was his. This relationship was firmly stamped with the word FOREVER in all caps.

Unfortunately, he got the sense Kasi needed more time to wrap her mind around that truth. Which stood to reason. From the comments she'd made about her past, Levi was pretty sure he wasn't just her first lover, but her first boyfriend as well. It was going to take Kasi some time to understand exactly what it meant to be in a relationship.

Levi sighed as he considered that, wondering if another week would be enough time. He was too impatient to wait much longer.

He rolled his eyes. While a month felt like plenty of time to him, Kasi would likely pitch a fit if he gave her the engagement ring he'd had his eye on at Becker's Jewelry Store.

He glanced at the house again and contemplated leaving. He couldn't make himself do it...because ultimately, he was uneasy about the darkness. His Spidey senses told him something wasn't right.

Fuck it. There was no way he could leave until he knew his girl was okay.

As he stepped out of the truck, he was momentarily blinded by the headlight on Keith's motorcycle.

The young man parked next to him, giving him a sleepy smile. This was the first time they'd seen each other since the night Keith had broken into the brewery. Levi was glad to see the easiness they'd established as they'd shared those beers was still there.

"Done with the harvest already?" Keith asked.

Levi shook his head. "Nope, but I got a little bit of a

reprieve, thanks to that midnight rain shower. We're going to give the grapes a few hours to dry in the sunshine before we start picking again. Came to see Kasi."

Keith glanced toward the house, and his frown told Levi he wasn't the only one worried about the lack of lights.

"She should be up by now," her brother mused.

Keith and Levi walked to the house together, climbing the front porch steps. Keith's frown grew even more pronounced when he discovered the door unlocked. "Kasi always locks up."

Levi tried to hold his sudden anxiety at bay as they stepped inside the silent house. "You check the kitchen, and I'll go take a peek in her bedroom."

Keith nodded.

Levi climbed the stairs to the second floor two at a time. Kasi's bedroom door was open, the bed made. It looked like she hadn't slept in it. His heart started to race as he quickly walked down the hallway, gently opening the door to Mr. Mills' room. The man was snoring, dead to the world, as the muted TV lit up the room.

Returning downstairs, Levi pulled up short when he saw Keith standing in the doorway to the living room. He pointed, and Levi followed his gaze to the couch, where Kasi was curled up in a ball, sound asleep.

Finding her might have set Levi's mind at ease...if she wasn't surrounded by a pile of used tissues.

"She sick?" Levi whispered.

Keith shrugged. "She wasn't when I left yesterday evening. Something's not right, Levi. Scottie..."

"What about Scottie?"

"He was here when I left."

Levi's chest tightened as he recalled Scottie trying to force himself on Lucy. "Tell you what. Why don't you go tend to the animals? I'll find out what's going on here."

Keith was reluctant to leave, so Levi placed his hand on the boy's shoulder.

"I'll take care of her, Keith."

His shoulders relaxed as he nodded. "Yeah. Okay. Cool." Keith slipped into the kitchen, using the back door that led to the barn.

Levi quietly walked over the couch, hating how frail Kasi looked. She was fully dressed, her knees pulled to her chest, so that she was tucked in a ball. Her head rested on the couch cushion at an awkward angle, no pillow beneath it. It looked like she'd pulled one of the throws over herself, but somewhere in the middle of the night it had fallen to the floor.

Levi picked up the blanket and covered her as he knelt, gathering some of the tissues surrounding her and putting them on the coffee table behind him.

Running his finger gently over her forehead, he whispered her name. "Kasi."

It took a minute or two for her to fully rouse, and he wondered how late she'd stayed up. Her eyes were puffy and red, and it was clear she'd been crying.

What the hell happened?

"Kasi," he said again.

"Levi?" Her voice was hoarse, rough. She rubbed her eyes, struggling to open them, given how swollen they were.

Had Scottie hurt her? A sudden murderous rage heated his blood at the thought.

He moved to join her on the couch as she sat up, wincing as she rubbed her stiff neck.

"What are you doing here?" Her words were groggy, wooden.

"Rained last night. We've delayed picking for a few hours."

She glanced around the room as if trying to get her bearings. The fact she wasn't leaping up to start working told Levi that whatever was going on, it was bad.

"What time is it?" she asked.

"Five thirty. Keith got here the same time as me. He's taking care of the animals."

She nodded.

"Kasi. What's wrong?"

She shook her head, refusing to look at him.

"Kasi," he said again. "Keith said Scottie was here last night. Did he—"

"He didn't do anything." She turned her face farther away from him, staring at the doorway, so that he was looking at the back of her head rather than her profile. "It's just... I can't do this anymore."

"Do what? Dammit, Kasi. Look at me."

Levi watched as she braced herself, her spine straightening, her shoulders dropping.

When she turned to face him, he knew he wasn't going to like what she said next. Which was bad news for him because he'd never seen so much determination in her expression.

"I don't want to see you anymore."

He scowled. "Why?"

She closed her eyes, only for a split second, but it was enough to give her away. He didn't know why the hell she was trying to break up with him, but that tiny wavering reaction convinced him she didn't want to do this.

"This is going too fast, Levi. I let myself get carried away." Every word she spoke came slowly, like she was measuring them before speaking them aloud.

"Bullshit. Try again. Why are you doing this?"

"I just told you. We need to be practical. We have nothing in common."

"What prompted this? Scottie?"

"No."

"Then what?"

Kasi's jaw was clenched tight, and the way she tilted her head told him she was done talking.

Levi felt his anxiety give way to anger.

"You owe me a fucking explanation, Kasi. Two nights ago, I had you tied to my bed, coming hard on my fingers, my mouth, my cock."

Her cheeks flushed, but Levi couldn't be sure if the color was there because of arousal, embarrassment, or fury.

"I don't owe you anything," she said, her anger suddenly matching his.

"Wrong answer."

"Apparently, all my answers are wrong!" she shouted, rising from the couch and waving her arms in frustration.

"Because you're not telling me the truth!" he countered loudly.

"Neither are you!"

He frowned. What the fuck did that mean? He'd never lied to her. Before he could question her, Kasi threw her head back and scoffed. "Maybe I'm just not that into you."

Levi laughed, though there was no humor behind it. "That's the biggest bunch of bullshit yet."

"Arrogant much?" Her voice wobbled a bit on the end, ruining the effect of her insult. When his gaze drifted down, noticing her trembling hands, she narrowed her eyes and quickly crossed her arms. She was trying to pick a fight, trying to provoke him enough that he'd leave.

And that was when Levi realized she wasn't mad at all. The look in her eyes was one of...God...sheer devastation.

What the hell happened?

"You're not going to tell me why you're doing this?"

Her shoulders slumped as she shook her head. "It doesn't matter why. None of this matters anymore."

He growled. "Like hell it doesn't."

Levi reached for her, grasping Kasi's hand firmly in his. She tried to tug it back, but he tightened his grip, dragging her out of the living room and across the hall to the kitchen.

Kasi dug her heels in, but she was no match for his strength.

He didn't stop until he'd pulled her into the walk-in pantry, slamming the door behind him, shutting them in.

"What the hell are you doing?" Kasi reached for the door-knob, but he captured her right wrist, then the left, twisting her until her back was pressed against the door, her hands trapped against the surface, over her head.

"I'm fucking you until you come to your senses."

Kasi's eyes widened briefly, and this time, there was no question about her blushing cheeks. Her tight nipples, pushing through the thin cotton of her T-shirt, was all the proof he needed that she still wanted him.

Something had upset her.

Upset her enough to make her run.

But Kasi was in for a rude awakening because there was nowhere she could run that he wouldn't find her.

"You get one chance," he said, his voice low, threatening. He'd swallowed enough of her lies this morning. "Tell me you don't want this."

He had never taken a woman in anger, and he wasn't about to start with Kasi, the first woman he'd ever truly loved.

Kasi looked away.

"Eyes on me," he snapped.

Her gaze flew to his, her chest rising and falling more rapidly now.

"Tell me," he demanded.

She closed her eyes, trying once again to escape. Levi

shifted slightly, pressing his thigh between her legs, applying pressure to her pussy.

When Kasi gasped and whispered, "God," he had his answer. However, he was still too pissed to let her off easy.

She met his gaze again, and he stared her down.

Kasi licked her lower lip, her gaze sliding to his mouth. She was begging to be kissed.

"I'm waiting."

She drew in a slow breath, and for the first time this morning, she told him the truth. "I want you. I shouldn't but I can't stop want—"

He slammed his lips to hers, kissing her with enough force he suspected they'd both have bruised lips.

Kasi's mouth opened, accepting him as he pushed his tongue against hers.

He released her hands, shoving his body more fully against hers. Kasi's hands fisted in his shirt, trying to pull him even closer as she ground her pussy against his hard thigh.

The kiss lingered, lasting one minute, then two, then three. Levi couldn't get enough of her, of her muffled whimpers when his fingers closed around her hair, twisting her head this way and that to deepen the kiss.

When they finally came up for air, Levi grasped the hem of her shirt, pulling it over her head, then he tackled her bra, unfastening it and letting it drop.

Kasi was busy as well, untucking his shirt from his jeans, shoving her hands under it, her nails scraping his chest hard enough to sting.

His kitten's claws were out today.

Once she was naked from the waist up, he decided to mark a bit of his own territory, drawing his lips along the side of her face, down her neck, before biting her shoulder.

Kasi's response was half gasp, half groan, so he did it again, then stroked his tongue over the red mark.

Levi pulled his shirt off with one hand, loving the way Kasi moved forward immediately, her teeth finding his pec, biting hard. He held her face to his chest.

Despite her innocence, Levi found it difficult to hold back his rougher tendencies with Kasi. Mainly because she'd made it crystal clear that she didn't want soft and tender from him.

Kasi's hands slid to his waist.

"Unfasten my jeans," he commanded.

She did as he asked, her hand slipping beneath the denim to pull out his cock. It was rock-hard and throbbing with a hunger that was almost painful.

"You're not leaving me," he stressed. "This isn't over."

She blinked several times. "It should be."

He shook his head. "No, it shouldn't. Now, touch me. Take hold, little bear."

She closed her hand around his thick cock, stroking it tight enough that he saw stars.

He worked the button and zipper free on her shorts, dragging them and her panties down before shoving his thigh between hers again, the wet heat of her pussy slick as she started grinding on him.

Kasi continued to rub his dick as he shoved his jeans off. The second they were gone, he grabbed her ass, lifting her against the door. She shifted, her legs wrapping around his waist, his cock bumping her stomach.

Levi kept a tight grip on her with one hand as he guided his dick to her pussy.

Kasi's head fell back, banging against the door when he thrust in to the hilt, hard and deep. Her hands gripped his shoulders, hanging on for dear life as Levi fucked her with more force than he'd ever used with a woman.

He couldn't shake free of the desperation crashing in on him as he thought it again.

She'd tried to leave him.

She might still be trying.

Those words wouldn't let him go as Levi unleashed every weapon in his sexual arsenal to prove to her just how fucking perfect they were together.

Over and over, he pounded into her body, tilting her ass until he was able to stroke that secret spot inside that always sent her over.

Kasi's nails raked his shoulders, his upper arms, her hips jerking in time with his thrusts, as she begged him to take her even harder.

Too much harder and they'd break down the door at her back.

God help them if her father or brother ventured anywhere near the kitchen because neither of them were holding back their grunts, their moans, their curse-laden demands for "more" and "harder."

"Fuck," Levi said through gritted teeth. "Your pussy is so fucking tight, Kasi. It's like you've got me in a vise grip."

"Harder," she gasped. "Please. God. I need...I need..."

"What?" he prompted.

"I need it to hurt."

Levi paused for only a second, trying to put his finger on her tone. Did she want it to hurt because it turned her on? Or was she seeking punishment for something?

He couldn't tell...but in the end, it didn't matter. Because Kasi took what she wanted anyway. She bit his chest again, this time hard enough to break the skin, a tiny bead of blood welling there.

"Do it," she all but growled.

Levi pulled out, ignoring her brief cry of dismay. It only lasted until she realized he wasn't finished with her.

He yanked her around until her face and chest were pressed against the door.

"You want it hard?"

"Please," her voice quivered with need.

Levi reached around her body, pinching her nipples roughly, pulling on them tightly as she cried out.

Then he gave her clit the same treatment until she rose on her toes.

Kasi's hands pressed flat to the door, sliding down the wood as he grasped her hips, tugging them toward him until she was bent at the waist.

"Yes," she hissed when he slammed inside her once more.

He was no small man, but damn if her body wasn't made for him.

Levi set his beast free, giving her exactly what she asked for, burying himself deeper and deeper. He wanted her to feel this fucking all day. No, all goddamn week. He wanted her to remember exactly who owned her with every step she took.

Because, despite what she said, what she thought, this wasn't over.

It would never be over.

Kasi yelled his name as she came, but Levi didn't give way, relentlessly pounding her through that orgasm and the one that followed right on its heels.

His balls drew tight, and he knew he was reaching the end as well.

When Kasi reached the peak for a third time, Levi chased her over, tumbling head over ass into one of the strongest, most painfully blissful climaxes of his life.

Kasi's pussy clenched around him, drawing out every drop of come. She was on birth control, but that didn't stop him from sending out a silent prayer that his swimmers were stronger than the contraceptive.

His desperation had him seeking other ways to tie her to him.

Kasi remained bent over as their orgasms faded, her forehead pressed against the surface of the door as she panted, breathing heavily.

Levi released her hips, and perfect red marks where his fingers had gripped her caught his attention. Those were going to be bruises.

He searched for some semblance of guilt or regret, but he had none. He wanted her to see them, to remember how they'd gotten there.

When Kasi started to rise, he offered her assistance, wrapping his hand around her upper arm to steady her. He hated the way she tensed at that touch.

After all the ways he'd just had his hands on her, why was she bristling over help?

"Kasi," he started.

When she twisted around, her gaze found his, steady and sure, and he feared he'd lost this battle.

He chose the word "battle" intentionally, allowing it to console him—because he wasn't about to surrender. He'd wage this war for the rest of his life if necessary.

"Why didn't you tell me about Keith?" she asked, her tone challenging, angry.

He was confused. "What about Keith?"

"The break-in. The beer he stole."

Levi's brows rose. He was surprised her brother had come clean, but he was glad he had. Perhaps the walls the Mills siblings had built around themselves were starting to crumble.

"He asked me not to tell you." Was this what Kasi had meant when she'd accused him of not telling the truth?

"After everything he's gone through," she said, her jaw clenched. "Losing our mom... I just don't understand why you would press charges."

Levi scowled. "What the fuck? I'm not pressing charges. Who told you I was pressing charges?"

Now it was her turn to frown. She didn't reply, but she didn't have to when he recalled Keith saying Scottie had stopped by.

Obviously, the mayor was trying to drive a wedge between them. The sheriff had come by the farm yesterday to talk to Theo when he'd heard about what the boys had done, but both men decided the punishment of making Archie and Keith work off the debt, picking grapes, fit the crime just fine.

Perhaps it was time for Levi to pay a little visit to Grover's Farm. Sounded like he and Scottie needed to have a little man-to-man talk, either with words or fists.

"Kasi—" he started, ready to set her straight on Scottie Grover, but he was interrupted by his phone ringing. He ignored it, as Kasi bent over, quickly pulling on her shorts, then her shirt, not bothering with her bra.

Levi followed suit.

His phone stopped ringing as he pulled on his jeans, but then it started again almost immediately.

"You should answer that," she said.

Grabbing it out of his pocket, he held his T-shirt in his other hand.

Kasi opened the door, walking out into the kitchen. Mercifully, it was empty, the house quiet. He hoped that meant her brother was still outside and her father asleep.

Levi followed, giving her a warning glare that he'd chase her if he had to. They weren't finished with their discussion.

Kasi leaned against the counter, her arms crossed tightly against her middle, as if she was seeking comfort from herself.

Fortunately, her anger seemed to have abated. That might have made him happy if she wasn't now wearing an expression of pure exhaustion. Those damn dark circles were back.

He didn't know why Scottie had lied about the charges or why she'd believed him, but his gut told him there was something deeper going on with her and the mayor. Something she wasn't comfortable sharing with him.

Damn stubborn woman had too much pride. Unfortunately for her, he was a force of nature when he set his mind to it and he was more than prepared to wear her down.

He answered the phone when he saw Maverick's name.

"Not a good time," he barked.

Maverick hesitated, probably surprised by the sharpness of his voice. "Afraid you might need to make some. Boone is here."

Fuck. Levi forgot he'd scheduled to meet with Boone Hansen this morning. If things worked out, Boone would be instrumental in Levi's plans for his future with Kasi. He was tempted to ask Maverick to reschedule, but he knew Boone had probably gotten up in the middle of the night to make the three-hour drive to be here this morning. It wouldn't be right to send him away.

"Okay. I'll be there in twenty."

"Cool." Maverick hung up, and Levi tucked his phone back into his jeans' pocket, studying Kasi's face.

Somehow, she'd managed to wipe away every emotion.

"Kasi," he started, raking his hand through the hair she'd mussed up. "We're not pressing charges against Keith. We would never do that. Never hurt him or you that way."

She nodded sadly, biting her lower lip. "I know that. Or...I should have known that. It's just... I'm sorry," she added with a whisper.

"I don't need an apology," he said, trying to hide just how

much it hurt that she thought for even a second that he would do something like that.

"Yes. You do. But the thing is...that doesn't change things. Scottie proposed last night. I'm...I think I'm going to accept."

"Like hell you are," he retorted, loudly.

"Please, Levi. Please don't make this any harder than it already is."

"I haven't even started to make this hard, little bear."

"My mind is made up. You're not going to change it."

Levi stared at her for a long time, hating the resolve that had crept in and taken residence in every fiber of her being.

"You haven't said yes yet?" he asked.

She looked away from him as she shook her head.

"Then don't. Not until we have a chance to talk. You owe me that much, Kasi."

Her face started to crumble, but she recovered quickly, drawing on that mask of indifference he never wanted to see on her again.

"I have to go—for now—but this isn't over. Not by a long shot."

Kasi offered no reply, her eyes turning toward the kitchen window.

"I'm coming back, Kasi. And when I do, I want real answers."

Leaving right now felt wrong on every damn level, but staying felt just as wrong.

He prayed that giving her some time to settle down might help, might allow her to calm enough to confide in him and tell him what was wrong and what in the hell was compelling her to even consider Scottie Grover's proposal.

Heaven help them both if he couldn't convince her to say no. Because right now, all he wanted to do was toss Kasi over his shoulder, drive her straight to their cabin, and keep her there until she promised to never even think about marrying Scottie again.

Levi walked to her. The way her body stiffened went through him like nails, but he persevered.

Cupping her cheek, he pulled her face upward. It took everything he had not to tell her that he loved her. He did, but didn't want the first time he said those three little words to come now, in the middle of an argument. And he didn't want her to think he was using them to get her back.

When he said them, he didn't want there to be a question in Kasi's mind that they were sincere.

So, he compromised with himself. Bending down, he gave her a soft kiss on the cheek. "I'm coming back," he vowed.

Her resolve cracked, but only for a second. If he hadn't been standing so close and looking at her so attentively, he might have missed the sorrow in her eyes before she locked it away.

"Goodbye, Levi," she whispered.

He left the house, forcing himself to take each step that led him farther and farther away from her.

All he could think as he drove home was how final that goodbye sounded.

Chapter Fifteen

Kasi stared out the fruit stand, her vision not focused on anything as she played last night's conversation with Scottie and this morning's confrontation with Levi over in her mind. She couldn't reconcile how she'd been floating on cloud nine, happier than she'd been in a long time, after waking up in Levi's arms.

Then, today, it was as if the bottom had fallen out of her world.

Fortunately, it was Saturday, which meant a decent stream of people coming through. Staying busy helped but for the last twenty minutes or so, she'd been alone, and it was giving her too much time to think.

She glanced down at her cellphone, resting on the counter in front of her. She'd reached for it at least twenty times since opening the stand. Half of those times, she'd planned to call Levi to beg him to forgive her for doubting him, to tell him she loved him—because she did—and that she wanted to be with him. The other half, she'd been determined to call Scottie to tell him to pick up this godawful engagement ring.

Her hand never touched the cell.

Because despite the whirlwind of emotions ravaging her, there was a category five tornado that overtook all the rest.

The image of her father, standing in that doorway, missing her mother so much, the pain enveloping him was almost tangible. She couldn't take anything else away from him. It simply wasn't in her to do so.

Her father and Keith—and the farm—were all she had left.

That's when she realized it wasn't just her father's feelings that were making this decision so hard. It was her feelings as well. Because their home meant so much to Kasi, as well. It held her entire lifetime of memories.

The farmhouse was the only home she'd ever known, where she'd grown up, where she'd gotten her first kiss—a peck on the back porch from Shane, her first "boyfriend" when she was just thirteen. He'd ridden his four-wheeler from his family's farm nearly two miles away just to say hi. It had been a quick, awkward, no-tongue peck, but Kasi swore to Remi later that she'd seen actual fireworks. And when that eighth-grade romance had ended two weeks later, her mother had comforted her in the living room, holding her when she cried, promising her there would be other boys.

The farmhouse was where she and Remi had gotten ready for homecomings and proms together, blasting Taylor Swift and Lady Gaga while they did each other's makeup and fussed with their hair for hours. Their senior prom dinner hadn't been in a fancy restaurant but in her kitchen. Mama had pulled out a pretty tablecloth, tall candles, and served her, Remi, and their dates sparkling cider in champagne flutes and chicken alfredo on her wedding china.

The kitchen was where she'd spent hours with her mother, learning how to bake, the two of them singing along to Tricia Yearwood and Martina McBride, using wooden spoons as microphones. It was where she'd snuck down as a child to watch her parents slow dance, long after she should have been asleep.

And it was the place where her mother had died.

She'd always known she would leave home someday, but there was a big difference between moving a few miles away with a husband and seeing her childhood home foreclosed on. Whenever she'd been younger and looking ahead, Kasi had envisioned a future where she would continue to bake with her mother, still work in the stand, and visit her parents every Sunday for dinner.

Kasi was no more able to give up her home than her father was.

So the cell had remained on the counter, and she'd spent the last few hours fighting desperately trying to make the most difficult decision of her life.

Kasi wondered how differently she might have felt if Scottie's proposal had come pre-Levi Storm. Would she have viewed it with a more open mind? Would she have even considered it a good thing?

Scottie wasn't an unattractive man—physically—and while he was creepy and stuffy and arrogant and full of himself and...

Yeah.

No.

She would have hated the proposal even if Levi hadn't been in the picture.

"Fuck," she muttered, pushing her hair out of her face aggressively enough that it hurt. She winced, then recalled Levi pulling her hair whenever they had sex. God, that was ridiculously hot.

Everything he did was hot.

Even this morning when he'd dragged her into the pantry against her will.

She snorted to herself.

Suuuuuuure. It was against her will.

She'd never felt so brutally possessed and sweetly cherished. She wasn't even sure how it was possible to feel those two things at the same time, but damn if Levi didn't manage.

It was during the wee hours of last night, when sleep continued to elude her, that she was finally able to see just how deeply in love she'd fallen with Levi. True to his name, he'd stormed into her life and turned everything upside down and inside out.

She rubbed her neck wearily. She might have said the words, might have told him they couldn't be together, but they weren't broken up. Yet. At least not in Levi's eyes.

Even after this morning.

She'd hurt Levi's feelings when she had accused him of pressing charges against Keith. He'd been nothing but wonderful and supportive and...

Shit. Why the hell had she let Scottie, the weasel, plant that seed in her head? Why had she let it take root?

And why was she still considering the asshole's proposal?

Rising from her stool, Kasi grabbed a broom to sweep the stand, her mother's words whispering in her ear.

"Nothing like hard work to clear a troubled mind, Cat."

Kasi smiled sadly as she recalled the silly nickname Mama used for her. Kasi was Cat, Keith was Kit. She'd never thought to ask her mother why, and suddenly she wished she had.

"Just sweep," she muttered under her breath, fighting like the devil to shut her stupid head up. If her mind couldn't find something—anything—fucking happy to think about, then she'd prefer to think of nothing at all.

Once she'd swept the small pile of dust, dirt, and leaves into a pile, she bent down to scoop it into a dustpan, then returned to her stool, sinking down heavily.

Kasi felt the first tear slide down her cheek. She didn't bother to stem the tide, letting them fall. Mercifully, no one stopped by the stand because it took her close to a half an hour to pull herself back together.

Unfortunately, exhaustion had set in hard, so she closed the farm market.

Rather than load the truck and return to the farmhouse, she remained where she was. She couldn't face her father or Keith or Levi or anyone yet.

Because, in the end, she'd let them all down.

So, instead, she put her head down on her arms on the counter and closed her eyes, shutting every miserable thought away, hiding out in the stand, refusing to acknowledge all the shit swirling around outside this shed.

Kasi gasped when a loud rumble of thunder cracked overhead.

She glanced around the dark shed wondering how long she'd slept. Given the sharp pain in her neck, she guessed she'd been out at least a few hours.

Rising, she opened the door, cursing her luck, as the sky opened, rain falling in large drops. Darkness had fallen as well, so it had to be late. Daddy and Keith must have assumed she'd gone to Levi's, considering the two of them had been spending pretty much every single night together since they'd started seeing each other.

Returning to the counter, she looked at her phone. She was shocked to discover it was nine thirty at night. She found a couple texts from Keith, asking where she was, then a final one letting her know he and Daddy had fended for themselves for dinner, eating BLTs. He ended that text with "Say hey to Levi," so she'd been right about why they hadn't thrown up the alarm and looked for her.

In addition to Keith's texts, there was one from Remi, who'd heard from Edith Millholland, who'd heard from Mrs. Grover, that she and Scottie were getting married. Remi's text was followed by at least twenty crying-laughing emojis, indicating her best friend obviously didn't believe the rumor. Scottie's mother apparently shared his arrogance, certain there was no woman on earth who could refuse his proposal.

And then, there were nineteen texts from Levi as well as three missed calls. All of them said basically the same thing. That she was still his and this thing between them wasn't over.

Every single one of the texts felt like a punch to the gut.

Tucking the phone in her back pocket, she grabbed a couple of the empty produce baskets and carried them outside.

One short trek to the truck and she was completely drenched, the rain coming down in a deluge.

"Fuck," she muttered, returning to the stand to lock it. She'd get the rest of the stuff in the morning. Right now, all she wanted was to take a hot shower and crawl beneath her covers. The long nap she'd just taken hadn't put a dent in her exhaustion.

Climbing in the cab of the truck, she pulled her phone from her back pocket, tossed it into the center console, then turned the key. Nothing. She tried again and again and again, but the engine was completely dead.

Of course it fucking was.

Tiredness gave way to temper as she flung the door open and stepped back out into the relentless rain. She slammed the door closed, then kicked the front tire for good measure, cussing a blue streak.

"Mother fucking piece of shit!" She beat her fists down on

the hood, these new tears driven by anger rather than sadness. "Goddammit!"

Headlights cut through her tirade, and she let her fury take control as Levi parked his truck behind hers.

He climbed out and walked over to her.

"What are you doing here?" she snapped.

Levi frowned, clearly taken aback by her anger.

"Truck break down?" he asked.

"No, Levi. I always use it for a punching bag in the middle of fucking storms." Her tone was dripping with sarcasm. Kasi wiped the rain out of her face, pulling the wet strands of hair stuck to her cheeks away with a quick swipe of her hands.

"You crying?"

Kasi blinked a few times before she realized she was. Her tears mixed with the rain, slipping down her face. She wiped her eyes again as she shook her head. "No. It's the rain," she lied. "Why are you here?"

"You know why? We have a conversation to finish."

Kasi shook her head wearily because the idea of trying to have any sort of rational conversation was beyond her right now. She was fucking done in. Period. "I don't want to talk. I don't have anything to say."

"You've got a lot to say. Get in the truck," Levi said, gesturing to his vehicle. "I'll take you home."

"Why? So you can try to fuck some sense into me again?" Kasi taunted, unaware of the effect that challenge would have on her until her face flushed and her nipples beaded. She'd loved every single second of her time with Levi in the pantry. The only time her thoughts calmed was when she was with him. He brought a peace to her world that had been absent since the day her mother died.

Levi raked his wet hair out of his face as he stepped closer, studying her face with an intensity that told her he could see right through her. The rain hadn't abated a bit. Actually, she thought it might be coming down harder.

"Is that what you need?"

She tilted her face as Levi moved into her personal space, less than a foot separating them. "What if it is?" Kasi's heart refused to give up, refused to believe that things were over between them. She needed him.

Levi grasped her shoulders, pulling her breasts to his chest as he lowered his head and kissed her hard enough to bruise.

Kasi gripped Levi by the hair, closing her hands in it tightly. Then, she bit Levi's lower lip, the taste of a metallic tang telling her she'd drawn blood.

Levi pulled away. "So it's like that, is it?"

She nodded, her eyes narrowed.

"Fine. Run."

"What?"

"You plan on running from this thing between us. I can see it in your eyes. But I think you need a lesson."

Kasi's heart raced, not with fear but desire. "Lesson?"

"You can run, little bear. But I'll always chase you. And I will *always* catch you."

Holy shit. Every horrible feeling evaporated as Kasi gave in. She wanted to be his prey, and sweet Jesus, she wanted him to catch her.

She twisted, darting away from the truck, running quickly. She expected Levi to pounce immediately, so she was surprised when she made it to the corner of the fruit stand, hiding on the far side behind a pile of old rotted baskets without being captured. He was toying with her, giving her a head start.

So. Fucking. Hot.

Kasi quickly weighed her options, not wanting the chase to end too quickly. Unfortunately, the area surrounding the stand was open farmland, no trees, nothing to offer a hiding spot except the stand and their vehicles.

Kasi considered that when she heard Levi's heavy footsteps sloshing through the mud. He wasn't even trying to be quiet.

She circled the shed, keeping far enough ahead of him that he couldn't see her as she rounded another corner. Once she returned to where she'd started, she jogged around his big truck, bending down, studying her options from here. She could continue to play cat and mouse around the trucks and stand or turn this into a footrace. One she was certain to lose. She was a fast runner, but Levi—with his long legs—would be much faster.

Unfortunately, it was the only option that seemed to offer her even the slightest chance of escape.

She was just about to take off across the field when Levi stepped around the rear of his truck. Jesus, he'd gone into stealth mode and managed to surprise her.

Kasi squealed as she took off, ready to run, but as she suspected, Levi was on her in an instant. He caught the back of her shirt, his fist closing around the wet material as he yanked her toward him, her back slamming against his hard chest.

"Got you," he taunted in a low, sexy voice, his lips brushing her ear. Her pussy clenched hungrily.

She struggled, attempting to break free, but his hold was relentless.

"Stop fighting," he said sternly. "I caught you. Now you're mine."

Levi grabbed her upper arm, dragging her to the back of her truck before lowering the tailgate.

Within seconds, he'd peeled her wet T-shirt off her body, tossing it in the bed of the truck. He didn't bother removing her bra, opting instead to pull the straps off her shoulders, tugging the cups beneath her breasts.

Levi cupped them in his large, calloused hands, squeezing them, pinching her nipples, and pulling until she rose on her tiptoes, the pain sending electrical jolts along her spine, straight to her pussy.

As he tormented her breasts, Kasi pulled his shirt loose from his jeans, unfastening the button, lowering the zipper, and shoving her hand inside the denim, their actions reminiscent of this morning in the pantry.

Levi hissed with pleasure when she wrapped her hand around his thick cock, stroking it firmly.

Releasing his grip on her breasts, Levi stripped her out of her shorts, dropping them and her panties to the ground. In addition to being soaking wet, now they were muddy, but she didn't give a shit.

Levi pulled her hand away from his dick, twisting her until she faced the truck. With a strong hand between her shoulder blades, he pushed her forward until she was bent over the tailgate.

He wasted no time shoving his own pants to his knees before gripping her ass cheeks and pulling them apart.

"Levi," she cried, loud enough to be heard over the driving rain.

He bent over her back. "Beg me, little bear. Beg me to fuck you. Beg me to claim you. Beg me to prove exactly who you belong to."

"Please," she whispered. She wanted everything he offered, even though she couldn't have it.

"That's not good enough, Kasi." His voice was raw as he let her hear what she was doing to him, laying his pain bare. "I need more. I need it all."

His words broke her. She had to stop this madness because even now...she was still hurting him and she hated herself for it.

"I'm sorry," she said, trying to push up.

Levi's hands lay flat on the truck bed, and his body draped over hers, holding her captive beneath him. "Didn't ask for an apology. I told you to beg."

"Levi."

"*Beg.*"

Kasi gave in...or perhaps she simply gave up. Either way, she couldn't fight this, couldn't fight him. She didn't want to.

"Please," she cried out. "Please fuck me, Levi. Fill me up, take me hard. Make me yours."

In her mind, she finished that final plea with the words she couldn't say aloud.

One last time.

He gave her a quick kiss on the cheek. "Good girl."

Words fell away, replaced by gasps and grunts as Levi thrust to the hilt, then took her exactly how she'd asked. He pounded inside her body, his pace relentless, powerful.

Kasi came within minutes, but Levi never paused, never let up.

The second orgasm flashed quicker but harder, Kasi's bare breasts pressed against the now-warm metal of the truck.

"God," she yelled, her pussy clenching tightly as Levi kept fucking her. Despite coming twice, Kasi's need for him only grew.

It was as if her body knew this was it. The last time. And it refused to stop.

Until her third orgasm.

"Holy. Fucking. Shit," she screamed. It felt as if a nuclear bomb had exploded inside her, and she quivered in the aftermath. One more of those and she would definitely die.

Levi slowed his pace, but he didn't stop. She marveled over the fact he seemed even harder and bigger now.

"Can't...take..." she gasped.

Levi sank his teeth into her shoulder, and she cried out.

"We're not done until I say we are. You're mine, little bear," he grunted in her ear. "I'll mark every fucking inch of you if I have to until you understand." To prove that point, his thumb stroked her anus.

She stiffened, that territory completely uncharted. Levi didn't do more than touch her there, taunting her with the idea.

Kasi shook her head, though it was less denial and more fear and panic. Because sweet Jesus, she really couldn't take any more.

Or so she thought. Her body was still trembling from the previous orgasms, and her clit felt as if it had its own pulse.

Then Levi rose, standing behind her, buried deep. His fingers gripped her hips in a firm hold as he tugged her toward him a few inches. The distance was enough that he could reach around her and touch her clit.

Kasi jerked as if struck by lightning. "God. No."

However, her body refused to say die as it came alive again, betrayed by her pussy and clit, which were overly sensitive to every touch, every stroke.

When the next orgasm hit, she gave herself up to it. Because she couldn't think of a better way to die.

Levi came with her, spilling inside her as he growled every single one of her names.

"Kasi. Little bear. Mine."

He fell forward once more, holding himself on bent arms above her, his tongue finding the spot he'd bitten, softly licking.

The rain had slowed to mere sprinkles at some point. Kasi pressed her forehead to the truck bed, her eyes closed as she let herself revel in these final moments of bliss.

They ended too soon when Levi kissed the back of her head. "Can't you see? We're perfect together."

They were.

Absolutely perfect.

Reality crashed around her, and this time, when Kasi pushed up, Levi let her rise.

She bent down, tugging on her muddy shorts, not bothering with the panties. She pulled her bra up and then put on her wet shirt.

Levi dressed as well, though he had shed a lot less, only needing to pull his jeans back up.

Neither of them spoke as he walked her to his truck, opening the door and helping her inside. He looked at her for a second, and she braced herself for whatever he might say.

The shadows in his eyes told her that he was still leery, still confused.

Rather than speak, he closed her door, then crossed in front of the truck and climbed in. He started it, driving her to her house, the silence in the cab suffocating.

Once he pulled in front of her house, she turned to look at him. "I need you to let me go."

"Never."

"Scottie proposed and—"

Levi barked out a laugh that was pure fury. "And you're not accepting."

"Please," she begged. "Please...trust me when I say ending things here is for the best."

"No."

It was a simple response, two lousy letters, but it was laced with a power that told her Levi had no intention of ever letting her go.

How the hell could she combat that level of determination? Especially when she wanted the same thing he did. She hated sitting here, fighting for something she didn't want at all.

Kasi bowed her head and closed her eyes, digging for something that would convince him. She had nothing, nothing but lies that would hurt him and she refused to do that. It simply wasn't in her.

"Twenty-four hours."

Kasi lifted her head, confused by his words. "What?"

"You're running on fumes, little bear. I can see that. And something bad is going on inside that head of yours. I won't press you or force you to tell me what it is because I want you to trust me enough to tell me on your own. So you have twenty-four hours to sleep and wrap your head around what comes next. I'll be back tomorrow night at this same time, and I hope you'll give me the real reason you're pushing me away. Please, Kasi," he started, the gentleness in his tone her undoing. "Trust me."

She already did. But he was right. Her head was in a million different places right now and none of them were good.

"I'll see you tomorrow." Kasi got out of the car and turned away, walking toward her house, praying he didn't change his mind and follow her, then hoping that he would.

When she reached the front door, she resisted the urge to turn and look at him. Instead, she opened the door, stepped inside, and closed it behind her, trudging wearily to the kitchen.

She should go to her bedroom and crawl into bed, exhaustion kicking her ass. However, her overwrought mind wouldn't let her sleep.

An hour passed as Kasi sat at the kitchen table, staring at the wall in front of her, tears streaming down her face. She'd hit P!nk on her Spotify playlist, hoping the music would cheer her up or at least energize her enough that she could tackle the baking that still needed to be done.

What she hadn't braced herself for was listening to P!nk's "When I Get There," the song the artist had recorded after her father passed away. Thanks to the beautiful melody and hauntingly painful yet familiar words, she had dissolved into a puddle of tears, and nothing short of a boat was going to save her from drowning in them.

Kasi swiped at her eyes, hating that she couldn't stop crying. She'd managed to keep the tears at bay for months, but now that the dam had broken...

"Stop," she murmured to herself, taking several deep breaths. "Stop."

"That's a pretty song."

Kasi startled at the sound of her father's voice behind her and quickly reached for her phone, intent on turning off the music.

Daddy stopped her. "Leave it. I want to listen to the rest."

"I don't think—"

"It's fine, Kasi," Daddy said, sitting opposite her at the table.

They sat in silence as the song played out. Kasi grabbed a tissue, lowering her face, not wanting her father to see her like this. After too many hours of crying, she could just imagine how bad she looked with her blotchy face and swollen eyes.

When the song ended, Kasi tapped the pause button. She took a few moments, trying to compose herself until she felt comfortable enough lifting her eyes to face him.

Daddy remained quiet, but she felt the weight of his gaze on her.

"Daddy," she started, uncertain what she planned to say after that.

"I'm..." Daddy cleared his throat. "I'm sorry, Kasi."

She frowned. "For what?"

"For everything." This time, it was her father who sat with his head bowed. "I fell apart when you needed me."

"That's not true," she countered.

He raised his head. "It *is* true. I never imagined... It never occurred to me that Trina would go first. I was ten years older than her, and she was larger than life, full of energy. I wasn't prepared..."

"None of us were."

"She completed me, Kasi. Before her, I was living, but I wasn't alive. I worked all day, every day on this farm, but there didn't seem to be a purpose to it until she walked into my world. She stepped in and took charge of the things I struggled with. She always said we were the perfect couple because I had the strong back and she had the strong mind."

Kasi smiled sadly, recalling that. Her father was one of the hardest workers Kasi had ever known. He was always the first one out in the field in the morning and the last one home each night. He didn't mind the backbreaking tasks associated with working on a farm. In fact, he seemed to thrive on them.

"You *were* the best couple," Kasi said, her voice thick with tears.

"When we lost her, I felt like I'd lost the best part of me, and all I was left with was..." Daddy raised his hands. "This. A shell of a man. Without her, it felt like it had before we met. Like there wasn't a point to anything. She was everything to me, my reason for getting up every day, for working so hard. She knew my shortcomings, my inability to make a plan, my messiness, my complete lack of organization, but she didn't care. She simply took them off my plate, keeping the budget, paying the bills, plugging all the numbers into that little calculator of hers a million miles an hour. I don't know how to function without her, and for too many months, I didn't bother to try. I shut down."

"You were grieving."

He sighed. "Grieving is no excuse. Because today, I realized I was wrong about something."

"What?" she asked.

"Trina was a huge part of my world, but she wasn't all of it. I have you and Keith. And I've let you down. Both of you."

Kasi rose from her chair, walking around the table to kneel in front of her father. She took his hands in hers. "No. You haven't."

Daddy looked at their linked hands. "I left you to do everything on your own. Then I let Levi step in, doing the things I should have been doing. Your mother…" Daddy lowered his head again. "She'd be so ashamed of me."

"Stop, Daddy. Please." Every word her father spoke slashed through her, cutting her into a million little pieces. "Don't say that."

Daddy looked at her, tilting his head. "You look like me."

Kasi nodded. She did. She'd gotten her father's coloring, hair, eyes, skin tone. Keith, with his dirty-blond hair and hazel eyes, took after Mama.

"But you are just like your mother. Strong. Smart. Caring. Brave. When you look at me, even after all the ways I failed you this year, I can see how much you love me."

"I do love you," Kasi said, not bothering to hide her tears from him now. "You're kind and gentle and so good."

Daddy gave her a sad smile. "Just like your mother," he repeated. "Seein' things that—"

"*Are* there," she insisted.

"I love you, Kasi."

The two of them rose, and she curled into her father's arms, her cheek pressed tight to his chest as he slowly rocked her. They remained like that for several minutes, and Kasi felt the hope that tended to flicker, flare, then fade in regard to her father coming back to them, burst into flame. For the first time since she'd lost her mother, it felt like she'd gotten her father— her real father—back.

Daddy released her, looking down with sad eyes. "Keith heard a rumor today. About you and Scottie Grover."

Mrs. Grover had definitely made the rounds.

"His mother is saying the two of you got engaged."

Kasi sucked in a hard breath, her chest growing tight. "He proposed, but I haven't given him an answer yet."

"Say no," he demanded. "Marry Levi. He loves you, Kasi. He looks at you the way your mother used to look at me. You deserve that. And nothing less."

"You don't understand." There was no way Kasi could tell her father about the tax debt. He was already beating himself up, and while she was thrilled to have him talking to her like this, she was terrified of pushing him back into that dark place.

Daddy cupped her cheek affectionately. "You don't love Scottie Grover, and a marriage that doesn't have that will be a miserable one. I know you think you have a reason for doing it, and maybe you even believe it's a good one, but I promise you, it's not good enough. Not if it means you're going to live a life without love. Nothing matters more than that."

"But we've already lost so much. I can't let us...lose more." She whispered the last two words. It was as much as she could say, but she could see it was enough when her father glanced around the kitchen.

"We have each other, Kasi. That's all we need. The rest is just...stuff," he said, shrugging.

Kasi let those words sink in, willing herself to believe them. The problem was, she loved this damn house and farm. In her mind, this place was family as well, and walking away from it felt like dumping a beloved cat off at the shelter after ten years of cuddling with it on the couch.

Daddy reached for her hand, holding it in his firm grip. "I'm done hiding, Kasi. Done letting you and your brother down."

"You didn't let—"

He squeezed her hand. "I want you to make me one of those lists you made for Levi. Tell me what needs doing around here and I'm going do it."

She nodded, even as she realized that offer was coming too late. "Okay. I will."

Daddy released her hand. "I'm going to take a little walk to the barn, check on the animals. It's time I got out of that bedroom and stretched my legs a bit."

She smiled, wiping her eyes. "I think that sounds like a great idea."

Daddy gently touched her shoulder as he walked by, leaving her alone in the kitchen once more.

She considered the baking she needed to do, then walked out of the kitchen, her father's words playing over in her mind.

As she crawled into bed, she knew what she wanted, what she needed.

Love.

Levi's love.

Chapter Sixteen

Levi sat on the front porch with a cup of coffee, watching the sun come up. In an hour or so, he'd have to move to the field to begin picking grapes for the day. Because of the smaller size of their winery, it wasn't practical to purchase a very expensive harvester machine to expedite this part of the process. Of course, given the fact their winery was located on the side of the mountain, they couldn't use the machine even if they owned one.

Which meant, he spent the end of each summer and the beginning of every fall picking grapes. When he was younger, he loved harvest time, loved being out amongst the vines with his brothers. With each passing year, the bloom on that rose was fading more and more. However, he hadn't realized just how much until he'd spent time working on Kasi's farm.

Levi leaned his head back and closed his eyes, praying he'd made the right decision in leaving Kasi alone last night.

Hell would freeze over before he let Kasi marry Scottie Grover. The guy was a self-absorbed, pompous prick, and there was no way he'd treat Kasi the way she deserved.

After dropping her off at her place last night, Levi had driven straight to the girls' farmhouse. Remi shared the third house on Stormy Weather Farm with her sisters, Mila and Nora. Lucy had lived there as well until this past fall, when she'd moved out to be with her boyfriends, Miles and Joey.

Remi had heard about Scottie and Kasi's supposed engagement through the grapevine, but she considered it such a ridiculous rumor, she'd discounted it. Then Remi confirmed what Levi had suspected. Kasi didn't love Scottie. In fact, Remi was certain Kasi despised the man as much as they did.

She went on to mention that after Lucy, Scottie had turned his attention toward Kasi, something Levi didn't know. Apparently, the mayor had asked her out quite a few times, and Kasi had turned him down consistently.

That idea didn't sit well with Levi because he recalled how badly Scottie had taken Lucy's rejection, becoming physical with her, trying to force his attentions on her. Levi didn't know how far the man would have gone if he hadn't happened on the scene and literally pulled Scottie away from his cousin.

Levi wondered if Scottie was using some sort of intimidation on Kasi, given the fact she'd been absolutely wrecked yesterday morning when Levi had found her on the couch.

Knowing Kasi seemed to believe she had a valid reason to accept the proposal didn't help much because without knowing what it was, he couldn't plan how to proceed.

Right now, the best idea he could come up with was his original one. Go talk to her tonight, and if she persisted in keeping him in the dark and accepting Scottie's proposal, he'd kidnap her and tie her to his bed until she came to her senses. And while that was a damn tempting plan, he didn't think Kasi would take too kindly to it.

Levi was sure Kasi's reason for this ridiculous marriage idea had something to do with her family. She was fiercely devoted to her father and brother. It was one of the things he loved best about her because it proved to him how fucking awesome a mother she would be. So while he tossed and turned most of last night, considering what might motivate Kasi, he knew it wouldn't be a self-serving reason, but more likely her sacrificing her own happiness for her family.

It had taken all the strength Levi had to drive away from her last night, but he'd seen the exhaustion on her face and the desolation in her eyes, and he had refused to push her so hard when she was already suffering. He decided to give her space. Now, he just needed to figure out what the hell he could do to convince her to reject Scottie's proposal.

Levi sighed and took another sip of coffee. His brothers had all retired for the evening when he'd returned from Remi's, but he planned to talk to them today as they worked in the vineyard. He needed advice. Badly.

He turned his gaze toward the driveway when he heard a motorcycle approaching. Levi rose as Keith pulled in front of the house. Shutting off the bike, the young man took off his helmet, then unfastened the satchel attached to the back.

"Come to steal more beer?" Levi half-heartedly joked when Keith climbed the steps to join him on the porch.

Keith gave him a sheepish grin and shook his head. "No. I overheard something that's bothering me."

"Does it have something to do with Scottie proposing to Kasi?"

"Yeah."

"She dropped that bomb on me yesterday." Levi gestured to the rocking chair next to his, the two of them sitting down together.

"You can't let her marry that asshole," Keith said vehemently.

"Didn't intend to."

"So you're not giving up on her?"

Levi scowled. "Never."

Keith's shoulders relaxed. "Good. Because Scottie's not a nice guy. He wouldn't be good to her."

"I agree, but until I get to the bottom of why she thinks she needs to marry him—"

"I think it might have something to do with all of this," Keith interjected, pulling a stack of papers from his satchel. He handed them to Levi.

"Bills?" Levi asked, as he flipped through the pages. He mentally began doing some calculations, and his suspicions regarding the Mills' financial state were quickly confirmed. It appeared they owed a sizeable amount on the new—destroyed—tractor he'd seen in the midst of the burned-out fields, and they were in debt to the town, their personal property taxes unpaid for the past two years.

Regardless...

"I'm not sure I see a connection," Levi said to Keith.

"Me either, but I know Kasi has spent a lot of time poring over those bills, and while she tries to hide it, I can tell she's stressed out. The Grovers have a lot of money."

"You think your sister is marrying Scottie to save the farm?"

Keith rubbed the back of his neck wearily. "Everything Kasi does these days is for the farm, for me, and for Dad. I hate that we've let her take on all that responsibility without helping her. I've spent the last few days trying to find a way to apologize for being such a dick to her, but..."

Levi had never seen such outright despair on a boy's face. Keith was still young, only eighteen. Boys his age should be thinking about girls, going to the movies, and hanging out with his friends. Instead, the kid was sitting here, beating himself up over how he'd acted after losing his mother.

"Just say the words," Levi suggested. "Because I promise,

once they're out there, not only will Kasi feel better, but you will too. You didn't do or say a damn thing that can't be fixed with a heartfelt apology."

He'd said the same thing to Keith that night behind the brewery. Now, like then, Keith didn't look convinced.

"You gotta let go of the guilt," Levi added. "It'll cripple you until you do."

Keith considered that, then nodded. "You're right." He still looked troubled as he turned his gaze toward the horizon.

Stormy Weather Farm had the greatest views on the planet. Ordinarily, the surroundings brought him peace, but this morning, Levi might as well be looking at an apocalyptic wasteland.

"What happens if we can't pay the taxes?" Keith asked, obviously worried about the bills.

Levi rubbed his jaw, his fingers toying with his beard. "Herb at the Commissioner of the Revenue's office usually works with people. Sets up a payment plan if needed." Levi glanced back down at the stack of notices. On every single one, the amount due was the total. "Doesn't look like he's done that here."

"Kasi would have asked," Keith said. "You think he refused?"

Levi lifted one shoulder. "I'm not sure. I don't know much about the way Gracemont does business, but I could ask my dad. He's on the town council."

"Do you think we could lose the farm?" There was a tremor of fear in Keith's voice, and Levi imagined Kasi would likely be feeling that same fear. However, Levi didn't want to lie to the boy.

"The town could foreclose on the house and land, yes."

"What happens then?"

Levi leaned back, slowly rocking. "The farm, the land, all the buildings would go up for auction."

"So anybody could buy it?"

Levi nodded. "Including the Grovers." Which seemed to rule out the tax bill as an impetus for marriage, at least from Scottie's perspective.

"What do we do?" Keith asked. "We can't pay that bill."

Levi stood up, placing a comforting hand on Keith's shoulder. "You leave this with me," he said, lifting the papers. "I'm going to talk to my dad and then pay a little visit to Herb."

The anxiety in Keith's expression cleared, and he smiled. "Thanks, Levi."

"Thank you for bringing this to me. For trusting me with it."

"You're good for Kasi. She's been happier since you, more like her old self. I..." Keith looked down at the floor of the porch. "I missed her."

Levi hoped he got the opportunity to keep being good to her. "I'll be in touch soon, okay?"

Keith stepped off the porch and climbed on his motorcycle, giving Levi a wave before driving away.

Levi took another look at the stack of bills, then headed in the direction of his parents' house, the plans he hadn't been able to formulate suddenly lining up in a straight row in his mind, along with some suspicions. Unfounded, maybe, but the more he thought about it, the more he was convinced he was right about how Scottie had convinced Kasi to say yes.

The path between his house and his parents' wasn't a long one, and soon, he was walking in the back door, straight into the kitchen. He drew in a deep breath, enjoying the smell of bacon frying. Mom was standing by the stove, prepping breakfast for the guests staying in the B&B she and Dad ran.

Levi stepped behind his mom and gave her a quick kiss on the cheek. When she turned toward him, he reached around her back to snatch a piece of bacon from the plate. Mom laughed, even as she shooed him away before he could steal more.

"Off with you," she said. "Shouldn't you be in the field?"

"Not for a little while. And maybe not at all today. Something's come up. Dad around?"

Mom nodded, crossing the kitchen to peer into the dining room. "Rex," she called out.

Dad came in a moment later. "You need me, Claire?" he asked, before spotting Levi. "Son," he said amiably. "You're out and about early."

"Yeah. I was hoping you could answer a few questions for me about the way personal property taxes are collected in town."

Dad was obviously surprised by the topic. "Sure. Why don't we grab a cup of coffee and sit?"

Mom poured three mugs, adding a fourth when Sam walked in. "I was walking by and smelled bacon," he said.

Mom laughed again, tossing a pile of bacon on a plate and putting it in the middle of the kitchen table. "I swear you have bionic smelling," she said to Sam, as they joined him and Dad.

"Is this some meeting I didn't know about?" Sam asked, clearly curious about the serious expression on Levi's face.

"Impromptu," Dad replied. "What is it you want to know about property taxes, Levi?"

Levi showed his father the bills, explaining that Keith had brought them by earlier, worried about his family losing the farm.

"Gracemont isn't very big, so we don't function like other towns that are larger. Farming is a fickle business, and considering how many of Gracemont's citizens own and operate farms, we've always been understanding when shortfalls occur. Bad weather years and failing crops are just a part of nature, and as far as I've always understood it, Herb Cline can offer extensions and he often sets up payment plans for farms strug-gling to pay their taxes."

"That's what I thought," Levi said. "So why isn't he doing it for Kasi's family?"

"That's something you'd have to ask Herb. He just got back to town Friday afternoon."

"Where's he been?"

"He and his son take that annual hunting trip out west, you know that. He's been gone a few weeks."

"Oh yeah. Forgot about that." Levi leaned back in his chair, voicing a concern that had come to him on the walk to his parents' house. "I think Scottie Grover might have taken advan-tage of Herb's absence. Might be interfering."

Dad frowned. "Interfering how?"

Levi didn't answer that question; rather, he asked another of his own. "Does the mayor have anything to do with the collection of property taxes?"

Dad shook his head. "No."

"Would he know which families were behind on their taxes?"

Dad took a sip of his coffee, then shrugged. "It's a small town, son, and Scottie's office is in the same building as Herb's. Not unusual for the folks who work there to talk. Hell, the fact Sheriff Anderson was up here just a day after Archie and Keith's antics the other night at the brewery should tell you that."

"Scottie proposed to Kasi," Levi said.

Sam leaned forward, scowling. "He did what?"

"Keith said the mayor's been stopping by a lot of late. Apparently, he mentioned to her that we were considering pressing charges against Keith."

Sam exploded. "In what world would we do that? Why would he tell her that?!"

Levi agreed with his brother. "What if he knew the Mills family couldn't pay their taxes, and he decided to apply a little pressure?"

While Dad looked skeptical, Sam's mind jumped to the exact same place Levi's had. "Everybody in Gracemont knows the Grovers want to build a training facility on their farm," Sam pointed out.

Levi nodded because that was common knowledge.

"You think Scottie's proposal was based on getting Lucky Penny Farm? That's a pretty big leap, son," Dad said. "Especially considering if the town did foreclose on the farm, it would go up for auction. Why would he marry Kasi when he could just buy the property outright?"

Sam tapped the rim of his coffee cup. "If it went up for auction, there's no guarantee the Grovers would win it."

"That's true. And if there was a bidding war..." Levi looked down at the bill.

Dad clearly wasn't convinced. "The Grovers are wealthy. Chances are very good they would be the winning bid."

"Maybe so, but if Scottie marries Kasi, all he has to do is pay off that bill, which is considerably less than he'd pay at auction," Sam suggested. "Plus, there's no risk of losing and he gets the farm for..."

"For a fraction of what he'd pay if he bought the land outright," Levi finished. "He's asked Kasi out more than a few times the past year. She rejected him every time. I think he found a way to have his cake and eat it too."

"That fucking asshole," Sam muttered.

"Kasi would do anything to make sure her family didn't lose the farm," Levi added. It was the missing piece of the puzzle—and likely proof that Levi had been right. She'd been willing to marry a man she couldn't stand to ensure her dad and brother didn't lose their home.

Dad shook his head. "Fellas, come on. That's a lot of conjecture. You can't accuse Scottie of foul play," he paused, then gave them a smirk, "until we speak to Herb."

Sam chuckled.

Dad didn't. "I know you're not a fan of the mayor, Levi, but—"

"He forced himself on Lucy when she rejected him," he interjected.

Dad raised his hands in immediate surrender. "I know, and you have to believe that pisses me off as much as you. But I also know that a lot of what's driving you right this minute has less to do with Lucy and everything to do with Kasi."

Levi couldn't deny that. "It does."

"She's the one, isn't she?" Mom reached out and took Levi's hand.

He gave it a squeeze. "She is."

Mom's smile lit up the kitchen. "I'm so happy for you. Kasi is a darling girl. So sweet and smart and funny."

"She's all that and more," Levi agreed. "It was just like you said, Dad. One look and I knew."

"You've known her forever," Dad pointed out.

Sam laughed. "That's what Everett said."

Levi rolled his eyes. "I'm not sure how to explain it. It was like I had blinders on and the second they fell away, she was there, and I saw my entire future laid out in front of me."

Mom placed her hand over her heart. "Marriage? Children?" Mom had been dropping not-so-subtle hints for years about her desire for grandchildren.

Levi nodded. "I want all of that with her. If it was up to me, I'd already have my ring on her finger, but Kasi's younger and a lot less experienced when it comes to relationships."

Dad snorted. "Wouldn't exactly say you were an expert,

son. Can't recall you bringing too many girlfriends around in the past."

"Or any," Sam added.

Levi chuckled. "She and I are going to have to teach other how to be part of a couple."

"Gonna have to get Scottie out of the way first," Sam grumbled. Levi loved that his brother was as pissed about Scottie's treatment of Kasi as he was. He also knew without a fact that if his other five brothers had been here for this conversation, they'd be just as outraged.

"I have no doubt you and Kasi are meant to be. It's all just so wonderful," Mom gushed. "And perfect. Because I know you'll take care of each other and spend as many happy years together as your father and I have."

Dad reached over and ran an affectionate finger down Mom's face. "Kasi will make a fine wife, and it will be nice to have her become an official part of the family. God knows she's been an honorary one forever," Dad agreed.

"She has a big heart," Mom added.

"She does. Which is why if I find out Scottie is pressuring her to marry him so that he can steal her family's land—" Levi started.

Dad stood up. "Sam, tell your brothers we're going to need them to cover for Levi this morning in the field." He glanced at his watch. "Herb's office opens at eight. Levi, you and I are going to be there when he arrives."

An hour later, Levi and his father were standing at the counter of the commissioner's office, Kasi's stack of bills resting in front of them. Levi fought to calm his temper when Herb said he didn't realize Scottie had been in contact with Kasi.

"It's my job to collect the taxes from the Mills family, not the mayor's. I gave them an extension the first year because that fire wiped out most of their crop and then this year..." Herb sighed. "Well, I wasn't in a hurry to call and demand money after Mrs. Mills passed. That family has seen more than their fair share of tragedies."

Dad nodded in agreement. "They really have."

Herb held up a yellow legal pad with names and phone numbers on it. "I was just working my way through all the voicemails that came in from when I was out west. I'll admit I've never learned how to make one of those out-of-the-office messages. I have it on my list here to call Kasi back. I had no idea Scottie was pressuring them to pay the amount in full immediately. We set up payment plans," Herb said to Dad. "You know that. The council made that an official guideline a few years ago. Voted on it and everything."

"Have the Millses ever been on a payment plan?" Dad asked.

Herb shook his head. "These past two years are the first time they've ever failed to pay their taxes."

Levi and Dad hadn't mentioned Scottie's marriage proposal or their suspicions that Scottie was preying on the Mills family for his own personal gain.

"Are you aware of Scottie contacting anyone else who was behind on payments?" Levi asked.

"No," Herb replied. "Never. Gotta admit I'm kind of shocked to hear he was overstepping. Just between me and you, no one's ever accused Scottie of working too hard on his mayoral duties. More interested in strutting around town like a bigwig than pushing papers."

Dad crossed his arms. "And there are other people in town on payment plans?"

Herb tapped his pen on the counter. "Several families. You

know how it is. Some years are good, some are bad, but we don't punish those who are behind. We give them time to recoup losses and pay us back. Scottie knows that. Most of the people who live in Gracemont have deep roots here. It's what makes this town so great."

Levi walked over to a large map of Gracemont, hanging on a bulletin board. He ran his finger over it until he found Lucky Penny Farm, clearly marked. Then he drew his finger upward until he found the line that separated that farm from the Grovers'.

Herb frowned, taking note of what Levi was studying. "Wait. Do you think the mayor is interested in getting Lucky Penny Farm? Is he trying to force foreclosure?"

Levi studied the man's face. Herb and Dad were fishing buddies, the two frequently casting lines into the pond on the edge of Herb's property. If he weren't so close to Herb, he wouldn't admit his suspicions, but he trusted the man. "Yeah. I do. The Grovers have made no secret about their desire to expand their horse farm."

"They want to compete with the big dogs, train horses for Triple Crown," Dad added.

"That's a pretty serious allegation, Rex," Herb said to Levi's dad, though he didn't sound exactly surprised. Looked like it wasn't just the Storm family who wasn't fond of the mayor.

"Which is why we're not making it," Levi stressed. "You willing to set up a payment plan for the Mills family, Herb?"

Herb nodded. "Of course I am. Have Tim—or Kasi—call me."

The fact Herb knew to include Kasi in that invitation told Levi that word was spreading about who was really running the farm.

"I'll do that."

Herb shook his hand, and then Dad's. "Fishing Saturday?" Herb asked Dad.

Dad nodded. "I'll bring the beer."

"Good."

Once they stepped back out into the early morning sunshine, Dad turned to Levi. "What's next?" he asked.

"I've got a plan, but I'm going to need the support of the entire family."

"Sounds like we need a meeting," Dad said with a grin.

Chapter Seventeen

Kasi had to hand it to Levi. He'd known exactly the right thing to do last night when he dropped her off and told her to sleep. Yesterday, she'd been an emotional wreck, too shattered inside to piece together a single thought.

This morning, she'd woken up surprisingly refreshed, despite the fact she had zero answers to...well...anything. For some reason, that didn't feel as overwhelming today as it had yesterday.

Probably because she knew Levi was coming over tonight and she'd decided to talk to him about all of it. If there was one thing she had figured out after her shockingly restful sleep, it was that she couldn't do this alone, and while she worried about leaning on him too much, she wasn't going to let that hold her back anymore because she was drowning and she needed help.

Kasi leaned down, drawing a towel over the pie she'd held back special for him. Her baked good selection was painfully small this morning, limited to the few things she'd managed to make this morning. Regardless, she was determined that Levi was going to get his pie.

When she stood and turned back toward the counter, she was startled to discover someone standing on the other side of it.

"Oh. Mrs. Grover," Kasi said. "I didn't hear you come in."

Mrs. Grover didn't reply. Or smile. Or even say hello.

She'd had too much time to consider all the shitty things that would accompany marrying Scottie Grover. So many, Kasi's list could fill a notebook, but number one would be his mother.

Because she was a bitch with a capital B.

Remi had dubbed her Mrs. Cuntcake, a name that was securely stuck in Kasi's mind. So stuck, she was terrified she might let it slip one day, saying it to the nasty woman.

Mrs. Grover's gaze slid down Kasi, taking in her cutoff shorts and faded T-shirt, then back up again. When her eyes landed on the hand Kasi was resting on her iPad—and narrowed—Kasi knew exactly what she saw. Or didn't see.

"Where's the ring my son gave you?"

It was sitting on her nightstand. She'd considered calling Scottie to swing by and get it today, but she'd put it off, not in a hurry to see the asshole so soon again. She wasn't a hundred percent sure she wouldn't punch him in the throat for lying about Levi's family pressing charges against Keith. "I didn't accept his proposal."

"Yet." Mrs. Grover's chin tilted, and she sniffed with clear disapproval. "That was my mother's ring. Don't lose it." The woman glanced around the stand, and it occurred to Kasi this was the first time Scottie's mother had ever stopped in. She'd never visited the original stand, either.

"Is there something you're looking for?" Kasi asked.

"Today's pie special is pecan. I only have a couple left, and we also have—"

"I'm not here to buy anything," Mrs. Grover interjected, as if the idea of buying something from Kasi was completely preposterous. "I came to invite you to tea next Saturday. I have a few ideas about the wedding to discuss with you."

"Again," Kasi muttered. "I didn't accept the proposal." Nor did she plan to. But that was a conversation she needed to have with Scottie, not his bitch of a mother.

Mrs. Grover talked over Kasi, ignoring everything she said. Kasi was starting to see where Scottie got his arrogance and his inability to hear the word, "no."

"As you know, Scottie is running for mayor again in a few months and we felt it would increase his chances of being reelected if he had a wife."

"Isn't he running unopposed again?" Kasi asked, resisting the urge to roll her eyes.

Mrs. Grover glared at her. "Since the wedding will take place at our home, we can hold the ceremony as soon as we want. I've been in touch with a caterer and—"

"A caterer?" Kasi said, shocked by Mrs. Grover's tenaciousness.

"Don't interrupt me."

Kasi wanted to point out that Mrs. Cuntcake had interrupted her first. "When did you talk to a caterer?"

Mrs. Grover sighed heavily. "Last week."

"He only proposed the night before last."

"I know that Scottie has raised the idea of marriage prior to this week, and given your family's unfortunate situation, it's clear to me that the wedding was imminent."

Kasi's temper flared, pissed that Scottie had shared her family's private information with his mother. Sadly, it didn't shock her, but that still didn't calm her fury.

"You're a very lucky girl, Kassandra."

Kasi gritted her teeth, hating the way this nasty woman used her full name, saying it like it was an insult.

"I tried to talk my son out of this proposal, considering the wide disparity in our..." Mrs. Grover paused, either for effect or to add some punch to the next affront. "Social standings."

"You know, it seems to me that your family has just as much if not more to gain from a marriage between us." Kasi refused to let Mrs. Grover intimidate her.

Fuck this bitch.

Mrs. Grover tittered. "Don't be ridiculous. We were going to get your family's land regardless. Once the farm was foreclosed on, we would have bought it. However, if my son has one flaw, it's that his heart is too generous."

It took everything Kasi had not to mimic one of Remi's fake "bullshit" sneezes.

"He couldn't stand the thought of your family losing their home, especially now."

"Now?" Kasi asked.

"Scottie told me about your father's breakdown, his failing mental health, and the issues with your brother's imminent arrest." Mrs. Grover attempted—and failed—to give her a sympathetic look. Primarily because the woman looked very much like a shark who'd smelled blood in the water. No doubt, Mrs. Grover was busy spreading those vicious rumors all over town as well as the false ones about her and Scottie getting married.

Kasi had tried to shield her father from the general public because it was none of the town's business if he was dealing with crippling grief. Obviously, Daddy's close friends knew, but they hadn't spread it around, respecting her father's privacy.

"My father is fine," Kasi said, recalling last night's conversation and the way her father had been up and waiting for her in the kitchen this morning, grinning and asking for his honey-do list. "There's absolutely nothing wrong with his mental health. And Keith isn't getting arrested. The Storms aren't pressing charges."

Mrs. Grover smirked, and Kasi got the sense the woman knew Scottie had lied about that. "So about tea. I'll need you to come to my house at three next Saturday."

Kasi shook her head. "I didn't accept his proposal." Kasi was starting to feel like a broken record.

"But you will. You have no other options. So...Saturday."

This entire conversation was exhausting. Since Mrs. Grover refused to hear what she didn't want to hear, Kasi decided to just brush her off. "Can't make it. I'll be working here, in the stand."

"Get your brother to run the stand. Or just don't open. You're going to close it down once you and Scottie are married anyway because there will be no need for you to work. Your duties as the mayor's wife, as well as the raising of your children, will keep you too busy."

"It's Gracemont, Mrs. Cu—Grover," Kasi said, unable to temper her tone or guard her words. "The mayor's wife *has* no duties."

"Your job will be to raise your children. But don't worry. I'll be there to help you, since your mother is deceased."

Hell would freeze over before she spent her days trapped with this horrible woman.

"Besides," Mrs. Grover continued, "once we expand Grover's Farm and open the training facility on your family's land, you won't have much left to sell." She looked around with obvious disdain. "It will be nice to finally tear down this eyesore. I hate being forced to drive by it every day on my way home."

"The stand will *not* be torn down, and I *will* continue to work here," Kasi said through gritted teeth. "Because I am NOT marrying your son."

Mrs. Grover scowled. "Hmpf. We'll see about that." Kasi harbored no illusions about who wore the pants in the Grover household. Mr. Grover and Scottie lived to serve the high queen.

Mrs. Grover shot Kasi one last dirty look before walking toward the door to leave. "I'll expect you next Saturday at three so that we can make plans for your wedding to my son. It would be in your best interest to be there."

Kasi started to follow, intent on setting the record straight once and for all, but pulled up short when someone else walked in, just as Mrs. Grover exited.

"What the fuck was that?" Remi asked, storming into the stand.

"Um..."

"There's no way in hell Mrs. Cuntcake just invited you over to plan your wedding to Scottie Douchebag Grover."

"Actually, she was, but—"

"No," Remi said, shaking her head. "No fucking way."

"He proposed the night before last. His ring is sitting on my nightstand."

Remi's eyes widened. "You took the ring? Is this a joke? This is a joke."

"No. It's not a joke, but I'm also not marrying Scottie."

Remi stared at her, confused. "Then why did you take the ring?"

Kasi sighed. "Because when he first asked...I was considering it."

Remi frowned. "Were you drunk? No, scratch that question because there's not enough alcohol in the world to make any sane woman marry Scottie."

"You're not wrong about that. It's just..." Kasi pursed her lips, fighting back tears. For eight months, she'd hadn't shed a single one, keeping it together after her mother passed because Daddy and Keith were falling apart and they needed her to be strong. That strength had abandoned her now.

Since the night of her mother's birthday, she was helpless to hold back the waterworks.

Remi reached for her, tugging her into her arms. "Oh God, Kasi. What is it? Whatever it is, we'll fix it. I'll help you and so will Levi."

Those words opened the gate, and Kasi cried on her best friend's shoulder, hating herself for not reaching out sooner. She'd stupidly thought she could handle all of this on her own, pushing away her support system because of an abundance of pride and embarrassment over failing her family so spectacularly.

Somewhere in the midst of her breakdown, she heard Remi call out to someone that the stand was closed. Whoever it was had clearly left.

"I'm sorry," Kasi said, when she finally pulled herself together. She'd left a huge wet spot on the shoulder of Remi's T-shirt.

Remi grinned. "No worries. It's laundry day. You just helped me get a jump on it with this one."

Kasi laughed through the last remnants of her tears. Remi always knew how to lighten a dark moment.

"Why would you even consider marrying Scottie?" Remi asked.

"Because I'm out of options." At that, Kasi let it all out, explaining about the mounting debt, her father's unstable mental state, her missteps when it came to running the farm. She explained that Scottie hadn't just been asking her out since her mother's death, but that he'd been hinting about marriage as a way to get their land. She even told Remi about the break-in and Scottie's lie about Levi pressing charges.

"Levi would never hurt your family like that."

Kasi thought she'd shed every tear she had, but hearing Remi say what Kasi should have known found a few more. "I know that. I think I hurt him, Remi."

"How?"

"By believing he would press those charges even for a second."

"Levi's a big boy. He'll bounce. Why did you believe it?"

"The night Scottie proposed, I realized... I forgot my mother's birthday."

"Oh, Kass." Remi pulled her back into her arms. "Is it any wonder you forgot? You're carrying around the weight of the world right now. I wish you'd told me all of this sooner."

"So do I," Kasi admitted, her voice wobbling. "I'm sorry I didn't."

Remi pulled back, drying Kasi's cheeks, wiping away the tears with her thumbs. "Well, I know now. I'm guessing from the fact you just fell apart in my arms, you haven't told Levi any of this."

The guilt Kasi felt over believing Levi would press charges against Keith was now compounded by the fact she hadn't confided in him, had her lowering her head in shame. "I haven't."

"Don't you think you should?"

Leave it to Remi to hit her with the hard truths. "I should and I am."

"Good."

Kasi gave her best friend a grateful smile, grabbing her for another hug. "I love you."

"I love you too. So give Scottie that stupid ring back, make things right with Levi, then have some of that smoking-hot sex that you are NOT going to tell me about."

Kasi laughed. "Okay. I will."

Kasi stood at the counter, glancing out the kitchen window, grinning when she saw Dad and Keith feeding the goats together, the two of them talking and laughing. When Mama was alive, they would return to the house after closing to start making supper together. Dinners were always a special time when their little family of four sat down at the kitchen table and ate together. She didn't realize just how much she'd missed that until right this moment.

Glancing around the room, she let the memories of her mother that she usually kept locked away, flow through her mind. Rather than reliving the sad stuff, she smiled, recalling all the fun times they'd shared in this room.

Before she knew it, she was standing at the counter, her hands coated in flour as she kneaded bread dough, allowing herself to simply enjoy the soothing motion, the smell of the yeast, the peacefulness of the moment, as she heard her mother's voice talking her through the process.

Really dig in there with the heel of your hand, Cat. Now lift and stretch. That's it, my clever girl.

She got so lost in the memories she didn't realize she wasn't alone until she heard Levi's voice in the doorway.

"Sure do like that smell."

Kasi turned to face him.

Levi tilted his head toward the front door. "Keith was outside. Told me to head on in, that you were in the kitchen."

She hated that Levi thought he needed an invitation to enter the house. During those glorious, too-few days when he was working on the farm, marking things off her honey-do list, he'd started coming and going without knocking.

When she glanced at the clock, she was surprised to discover she'd been working for nearly two hours. In addition to the bread, she'd made a Texas sheet cake, the chocolate confection baking in the oven.

"Levi," she started, searching for a way to explain her behavior and to apologize for the things she'd done and said.

Levi held his hand up. "Let me talk first."

Kasi bit her lower lip, then went to the sink to wash the flour from her hands. Grabbing a towel, she dried them off as she walked to the table to sit. She nodded at the chair across from her. "Okay."

After the way she'd hurt him, he deserved a chance to speak his peace.

Levi sank down, then reached into his back pocket to pull out several folded pieces of paper. He opened them up, laying them flat on the table in front of her.

Kasi scanned the top page, trying to understand what she was looking at. It looked like some sort of rental agreement, but before she could read more than a few words, Levi placed something else on top of it.

A blank check.

Kasi's gaze lifted to his. "I don't underst—" She stopped mid-word. "You know."

Levi nodded. "Keith showed me the bills and I figured it out. But before you accept Scottie's marriage proposal, I think you should know all of your options."

"I'm not accept—" She paused. "What options?"

Levi tapped his finger on the contract again. "Stormy Weather Farm would like to lease the farmland you're currently not using. We've wanted to become more self-sustaining for years, but nearly all of our farmable land is used for the vineyard. Now that we're operating the brewery as well, we've been looking into growing our own ingredients rather than outsourcing. I have a small plot where I've been growing hops. The yield has been good—really good—and while it's enough for Rain or Shine Brewery, I've been approached by other breweries in the area about selling hops to them. I don't have enough land. Just like I don't have enough for the barley, the apple orchard, or berries I'd like to plant. Sam has all sorts of ideas for new brews, and we're both excited about the idea of growing our own ingredients. You can fill in the blank on what you think is a fair amount in terms of rent and I can write you a check right now."

Kasi skimmed the document in front of her. It was a good idea. "Who would farm the land? You're busy with the vineyard."

"We're going to hire someone to manage the vineyards," Levi said. "That's why I had to leave yesterday morning. I was interviewing someone to take over my job as vineyard manager. I'm ready for a new challenge, so I would be working the land here. I know you had to let Jeb and Cal go. I was thinking of hiring them to help me."

One of the hardest things Kasi had done since her mother's death was fire Jeb and Cal. Like the Riley twins, the other farmhands had become an extension of their family, and she knew both men had struggled to find work since. "They're great workers."

Levi nodded. "I know. We hired them to help us with the harvest this year. They've been invaluable."

Kasi was relieved to hear the men had found work, even if it was temporary. Because she'd been eaten alive by guilt over messing up their livelihood. "That's good."

She looked down at the lease, then recalled something else he'd said. "You said I had other options?"

"Yeah. If you want to go ahead with your plans to plant a fall crop and sell it, you can do that too."

She shook her head. "It's too late for that. The tax bill is due in full."

Levi scowled. "No, it's not. If you call Herb Cline at his office, he'll work with you to set up a payment plan. Same as he does for everyone else in town."

Kasi frowned, confused. "But Scottie said..." She sighed. "He lied about that too. I really am the dumbest person on the planet."

Levi's expression turned dark. "No, you're not. He saw a way to get you *and* your land."

"And I almost fell for it." Kasi hated that she'd been so easily duped, but even she could see she'd been low-hanging fruit, ripe for picking, given her fears of failing her family and her lingering grief over Mama.

"You never told me Scottie had been asking you out."

Kasi sighed again. "I didn't think it mattered. I always turned him down." Then her temper spiked. "What a fucking lying asshole. God, I can't wait to shove that stupid ring of his right up his ass."

"You took the ring?"

"He pushed it into my hand. It's never been on my finger, and it never will be."

"Good girl. But you're going to have to get behind me when it comes to Scottie's comeuppance. And considering Remi's anger right now, you might be after her too."

Kasi narrowed her eyes. "You're not doing anything to Scottie. That prick is all mine."

"Agree to disagree, little bear. He hurt my girl, and that won't go unpunished."

"Your girl," she murmured, loving the sound of that way too much. She pressed her forehead against his, breathing in his fresh, masculine scent, so grateful he was giving her not only a second chance but choices. Good choices of ways to save her family's farm.

Levi leaned back, giving her a wicked grin. "While you consider those options I just laid out for you, I think it only fair to point out that if you accept my family's offer, I'll be here all day, every day."

She laughed, the weight that had been pressing on her chest for months lifting completely. "Is that supposed to be a selling point?"

Levi reached out, grasping her wrist and tugging until she had no chance but to stand and step toward him. The second she did, he pulled her down onto his lap, wrapping his arm around her middle. "Damn right, it's a selling point. Sign the lease, Kasi, and we can work on this farm together."

"It's not my decision to make," she said. "It's my dad's."

"You're wrong, Kasi," Daddy said from the back door.

Kasi looked up as he and Keith walked in together.

"It's your decision," Daddy continued. "Yours and Keith's. You're the ones who've been keeping this farm afloat, same as your mother did in the years before."

Keith shook his head. "No. It's been all Kasi. She's done it all, so she should decide. So long as she doesn't pick Scottie."

Levi growled as Kasi giggled. "That option is way off the table."

"Thank God," Keith muttered before giving her a sad grin. "I'm sorry, Kasi. For the way I treated you. The stuff I said. All of it. I'm just so sorry."

Kasi blinked rapidly. How she still had tears left was beyond her. "No apology necessary."

He grimaced. "That's not true at all. Maybe we could talk later?"

Kasi nodded, as she smiled. "I'd like that." Then she realized she was still sitting on Levi's lap. She squirmed and tried to stand, but Levi tightened his grip, keeping her in place.

"Stay still," he admonished.

"Levi," she muttered. "My dad—"

"Stay where you are, Kasi," Daddy said, grinning. "Nothing wrong with a man holding on to his woman." Daddy walked to the table to pick up the lease. He scanned it the same way Kasi had. "This is a good idea," he said to her. Then he glanced at Levi. "You know, it doesn't make much sense for you to commute to work every day, Levi."

Kasi laughed. "His farmhouse is a fifteen-minute drive, tops. And it's not like there's traffic."

"I think your father is right," Levi chimed in, resting his chin on her shoulder as she rolled her eyes. "Commuting sucks."

"Are you two ganging up on me?" she asked.

"Nope. The three of us are," Keith said.

"I want to thank you for all the work you've been doing around here lately, Levi. And for putting that pretty smile on my daughter's face," Daddy said.

Levi gave her a quick kiss on the cheek. "It's been my pleasure."

Daddy glanced toward the hallway. "You know, there's an empty room just down that hall."

Kasi gasped. "Daddy, that's your—"

"I'm never moving back into that room," he interjected. "It was built for two people. A couple," he added, putting his hand on Levi's shoulder. "A *married* couple."

Kasi's eyes widened at her father's way-less-than-subtle hint, but Levi just laughed.

"I plan on putting a ring on that finger immediately." Levi lifted her hand, rubbing his thumb over her ring finger.

"I like the sound of that," Daddy said, brushing beneath her chin with his knuckle. "Keith, what do you say we head to the store and pick up some fried chicken for dinner. I've got a craving."

Keith, grinning from ear to ear, nodded enthusiastically. Her brother was as delighted as Kasi to have their father back.

Daddy and Keith said their goodbyes, leaving her alone with Levi.

"Would you like something to eat?"

Levi shook his head. "Nope. We need to head out."

"We do?"

He placed Kasi on her feet then stood up. Before Kasi knew his intentions, Levi tossed her over his shoulder.

"What are you doing?" she asked, giggling as he headed for the front door.

"Taking you to our cabin. You and I have some making up to do."

Chapter Eighteen

The ride to the cabin was a quiet one, only the radio filling the silence.

Kasi suspected Levi, like her, was relishing the closeness.

Once they arrived at the cabin, Levi opened the door of the truck for her, like he always did, and they walked inside hand in hand.

Kasi stood awkwardly, waiting for him to make the first move.

Levi closed the door, then pushed her toward the couch. "Come on. I can see you've got some things on your mind that you need to get out."

Kasi nodded, all too aware that while Levi had swooped in and fixed her family's problems, she hadn't done anything to repair what she'd broken.

She dropped down on the couch, turning to face him when he sat next to her, their thighs touching.

"I hurt you yesterday."

Levi started to shake his head, but she wouldn't let him lie to her just to spare her feelings. "I know you would never hurt me or my family. I have no good excuse for accusing you of that, for thinking the worst, other than Scottie snuck in when I was down and almost out. I shouldn't have let him in. I'm so sorry."

Levi leaned forward and gave her a soft, sweet kiss. "Forgiven."

He leaned back, his arm resting on the cushion behind her. "Why didn't you tell me about the tax bill?"

She lifted one shoulder. "Because I knew you'd try to fix things, and I'd already let you do too much for me and my family. I didn't want to keep imposing on you."

Levi scowled. "Imposing on me?" He twisted until one leg rested bent on the cushion between them. "Asking your man for help isn't an imposition, Kasi."

"I..." She'd known from the start that it was taking her longer to adjust to their new relationship status than it was Levi. It was the main place her inexperience stuck out like a sore thumb. But he also had to give her some sort of leeway. After all, it had only been about three weeks since their first kiss, for God's sake.

"It's not that easy for me," she tried to explain. "Ever since my mother died, I've been taking care of things on my own. It's what I'm used to. So handing control over to you, for things I felt like I should be doing, was hard."

"Do you trust me, Kasi?"

She nodded her head without hesitation. "Completely."

"If I came to you in need of help, would you give it?"

"Of course," she replied, understanding where he was going. "But—"

Levi pressed his fingers on her lips. "There's no but to it. You wouldn't hesitate to help me if I was in trouble, right?"

She grimaced, then admitted defeat. "Right."

"So why is it wrong for me to want to help you when you need it?"

She folded her arms over her chest. "It's not, but—" she tried again.

"But nothing."

"But I'm doing it too much!" she exclaimed. "My life is a hot fucking mess, and I'm sorry, but it's too much to ask you to keep working long hours, bail us financially, and catch me every time I pass out."

Levi grasped her hips, pulling her until she faced him, straddling his lap. "It's not too much at all. There's nothing in the world you could ask for that I wouldn't move heaven and earth to get for you. I love you, little bear. I want to take care of you, and I want you to take care of me. For as long as we both shall live."

"You love me," she whispered, though it wasn't a question. She'd felt his love from the moment she opened her eyes after fainting in his arms.

Levi untucked her T-shirt, his fingers drifting beneath the soft cotton so that he could stroke her skin. "I'm head over fucking heels in love with you. And since you're still struggling, let me lay things out for you so there's no more confusion. You belong to me, Kasi, which means I want it all. Your heart, your body, your problems, and your trust. I want my ring on your finger, you in my bed, and my baby inside you. What I feel for you isn't some lukewarm affection. It's not a mistake or a misunderstanding. It's an unstoppable obsession. Do you understand?"

She nodded, words failing her. Because *dayum*.

"That's how I see our future," he continued, "and I'm a stubborn son of a bitch, so you can count on it happening just like that."

"What else do you see?" she asked.

"I'm going to take your father up on his offer. Going to move in with you."

"You're aware my father will live there for the rest of his life, and I have no idea what Keith's plans are for the future."

"I come from a big family, Kass. There were nine of us in one house when we were all kids. And since we became adults, my brothers and I have shared a home. Living with only three other people is going to feel much quieter by comparison."

"You don't mind sharing a home with them?"

"They're your family, little bear, and soon they're going to be mine too. Multigenerational homes are the norm around here. You know that. Besides, you live in a big farmhouse, and there's plenty of room for all of us. Think how nice it would be for our kids to grow up in a house with their granddaddy."

Kasi blinked back tears because that was the most wonderful thing she'd ever heard. "Daddy would love that."

"So no more trying to walk away from me, Kasi," Levi stressed.

"Because you'll chase me?"

He nodded. "Always. Now tell me you love me so we can go to the bedroom."

She laughed. "So cocky. How do you know—" Kasi didn't have the chance to finish before Levi stood, twisting until she was on her back on the couch and he tickled her. She batted at his hands, desperate to escape, even as squeals of laughter erupted from her.

"Tell me," he demanded.

"I love you," she said, gasping for air.

Levi stopped tickling her instantly. "Good girl."

He grabbed her hand, helping her rise and tugging her toward the bedroom while she laughed at his haste.

Within seconds, they were both undressed.

Levi followed her onto the bed, Kasi lifting her arms to pull him over her.

"Want you so much," she whispered.

"Same," he said, his kiss proving it.

Kasi gasped when he wasted no time guiding his cock to her pussy, pushing inside in one slow glide that didn't stop until he was completely buried.

He gave her only a second or two to adjust before he began thrusting. Unlike the last two times they were together, they moved more slowly, enjoying the motions rather than fucking like it was the end of the world.

Which, to be fair, was what Kasi had thought the past few days.

He kissed her as he glided in and out, their tongues dancing together.

"You're mine," he insisted, his hands gripping her hair tightly. "And I'm never going to let you go. You ever try to leave again...I will chase you, little bear. I'll capture you, claim you, fuck every part of you over and over until you understand there's no me and you anymore. Just us."

Kasi closed her eyes, feeling slightly light-headed at the thought. She loved this dominant, alpha side of Levi, loved the way he took control of her sexually. She'd never imagined having the opportunity to make her fantasies a reality, but now, Levi had her adding more kinks to the list.

"Just us," she breathed, loving the intimacy, the closeness. Kasi didn't understand just how lonely she'd been before Levi, but now she could see how truly empty her life had been.

"I love you," Levi said again, his lips near her ear, his teeth nibbling at the lobe.

She could hear those words a hundred times a day for the rest of her life and never get sick of them.

Kasi ran her fingers through his hair, closing her fists around the long strands. "Love you too."

When Levi reached between them to stroke her clit, she was a goner. Her back arched as her orgasm swept through her like a tidal wave.

"Look at me when you come," Levi demanded.

She forced her eyes open and found his. He was there too. She could see it in his hungry, almost-pained expression.

"Kasi," he groaned, his climax blending with hers. "Little bear."

She lifted her head, kissing him, over and over and over.

"Love you," she breathed. "Love you so much."

Levi dropped down beside her, wrapping her in his arms.

"You're giving Scottie that ring back," he said in his deep, demanding voice.

"Damn right, I am," she said, laughing softly.

"And you're marrying me."

"Damn right, I am."

"Good. Now get some sleep because I'm going to wake you up in an hour or so to do all of that to you again."

"Damn right, you are," she joked, even as her eyes drifted shut.

So damn right.

LEVI SAT at a tall table in the corner of the large patio that jutted out from the entire front of the brewery. It was a gorgeous September Saturday, and it looked as if most of Gracemont had descended on the mountain to celebrate.

Rain or Shine Brewery held an Oktoberfest celebration for six weeks every fall, starting in mid-September and lasting through October. Since today was the kickoff of the event, Sam and Jace were behind the bar, serving tastings of their latest German-inspired beers, talking about the flavor profiles and ingredients included.

Mila was outside by the pizza oven, baking approximately four thousand pizzas for the hungry masses, while Remi waited tables. Hell, even Theo and Levi's dad were pitching in, delivering food and bussing tables because the place really was packed.

Lark McCoy, a local Gracemont girl, had recently started playing her acoustic guitar and singing on the weekends. She was incredibly talented and definitely part of what had drawn people in today. She was currently singing a cover of "Me and Bobby McGee" that would have brought Janis Joplin to her knees. Theo had been damn smart to hire her.

Like his brother, Levi had made his own smart hire recently, handing his job as vineyard manager over to Boone Hansen. Boone had been working as an assistant in a large vineyard just outside Williamsburg, but because there'd been no room for advancement, the man was happy to come here, where he would be able to make all the decisions. He was in the process of selling his house while looking for a place in Gracemont so he could take over Levi's duties at the beginning of the year.

Technically, that was when Levi intended to officially move in with the Mills family, but in truth, he was already spending every night there, and a fair amount of his clothes were hanging in the closet in his and Kasi's new shared room.

Life was good, he thought, as he leaned back, gazing out across the valley. There wasn't a cloud in the sky, so the view stretched out for miles and miles.

Life would be even better if Kasi had managed to give Scottie back his damn engagement ring. However, the man—overly confident about acquiring Lucky Penny Farm—had been out of town all week with his father, apparently in meetings with a man they hoped to hire as a horse trainer. Levi couldn't wait to see the look on Scottie's face when Kasi kicked him to the curb.

Kasi sighed happily next to him. Keith and her dad were running the stand today, as they both declared she needed a day off.

Kasi and her brother had finally sat down to talk about losing their mother, their shared grief, and Keith apologized again for his hurtful words.

Between that and her father emerging from his room to work on the farm again, Kasi's smile was so huge and bright these days, Levi suspected astronauts could see it from space.

"I think this one is my favorite," she said, pointing to one of the small tasting glasses. They'd ordered today's special Oktoberfest flight so they could sample them all.

He grinned. "I still say this one is the best," he argued, pointing to the first one they'd tried. Levi wrapped his arm around the back of Kasi's stool, leaning toward her, intent on giving her a kiss on the cheek.

Kasi, however, had other ideas, turning her head at the last minute, their lips touching. They'd spent hours this past week kissing and cuddling and, well, fucking. Levi couldn't spend five minutes with her without giving in to the need to touch her, and every night, they fell into bed together like two lovers who'd been apart for years. He was grateful her father's bedroom was on the second story and the other side of the house. Though that hadn't stopped Levi from needing to cover her mouth with his hand or use a gag. Of course, those actions were only half based on the sounds she was making, the other half because it turned her on. Big-time.

His girl had a voracious sexual appetite, and damn if she wasn't adventurous as hell. There were times he worried he couldn't keep up with her, and he considered himself a virile man.

"Ugh. Do you have to rub your happiness in everyone's faces twenty-four seven?" Remi asked, though her grin told them she wasn't really complaining.

"We do," Kasi said solemnly. "It's part of our relationship agreement. Showing off without restraint."

Remi snorted. "Horny bitch."

"Jealous cow," Kasi countered, as both women broke into peals of laughter.

"Hey," Theo said, walking up to their table. "Been too busy to stop over here to say hello to you two. Still sucking face nonstop, I see."

Levi chuckled. "Apparently, we've got a bit of a reputation. Great crowd," he added, changing the subject. "Looks like Sam and Jace hit it out of the park this fall with their beer lineup."

"And then some. Abbey called first thing this morning to ask for three more kegs of the pumpkin lager. Said she drained the first one in three days," Theo said.

"You've done a great job with Oktoberfest," Kasi added. "Again."

"And mercifully for the last time. I finally hired an events coordinator for the farm businesses. She starts in a couple weeks. I'll be glad to hand those duties over. Party planning isn't my thing." Theo winked. "I'm better suited to being the life of the party instead."

Remi hip-bumped Theo, since both their hands were filled with trays of dirty glasses. "I thought I was the life of the party."

Remi and Theo looked at him and Kasi for the ruling on who ruled parties, but they shook their heads in unison.

"Not stepping on that hornet's nest," Kasi said.

"Chicken shit," Remi said. "I'm going to take these to the

kitchen, then go ask Lark to sing 'Better Together.' I love me some Jack Johnson."

Remi and Theo walked to the kitchen together, still debating which of them was more fun, trying to draw several tables of patrons into the fray.

"You realize this is our one-month anniversary," Levi pointed out.

"How has it only been one month?"

"Best month of my life," Levi murmured, kissing the side of her head, before his attention was distracted by someone walking into the brewery. He frowned. "You still have Scottie's ring in your pocket?"

Kasi nodded. "Yes. I told you, I want to give it back the second I see him. Don't want to have to schedule another meeting just to return it. One and done."

Levi had been annoyed earlier in the week when he realized Kasi was carrying the ring around everywhere with her, but once she'd explained why, he understood. "I'm not mad," he quickly said, before nodding toward the entrance. "Just letting you know we've got incoming."

Kasi turned quickly, spotting Scottie at the same time the mayor saw them.

Scottie scowled as he took in how closely Levi and Kasi were sitting. And because Levi was a jealous asshole, and he really hated the guy, he pulled her stool even closer as he draped his arm around her shoulders.

Kasi giggled, delighted by his power play. Then she gave him a stern look. "Scottie is all mine," she warned him.

Levi shook his head, but before they could argue over who got to give the mayor the smackdown he deserved, Scottie stepped up to their table.

"You're supposed to be having tea with my mother," he said, scowling at Levi's arm around her.

That was what he led with?

"I told your mother I wasn't going," Kasi replied.

"You said you needed to work the fruit stand, but your brother and father are."

Obviously, Scottie had stopped by there first, intent on dragging her to tea with his bitch of a mother. Keith and Mr. Mills—who'd begun insisting that Levi call him Tim—must have told Scottie where to find Kasi. They knew how anxious she was to give back the ring.

"I never agreed to marry you, Scottie," she replied coolly.

As much as Levi wanted to rearrange the smug mayor's face, he was taking a lot of pleasure in watching his little bear sharpen her claws. Glancing around, he realized his brothers and Remi had noted Scottie's arrival, and they were watching them with great interest. Actually, Remi looked like she wanted to do more than watch, but Theo had a grip on her arm, holding her back.

Scottie gestured to the exit. "Why don't we discuss this in private?"

Kasi shook her head. "There's nothing to discuss. You lied about Levi pressing charges."

Scottie narrowed his eyes. "I said they might press charges. I never said they were."

Levi clenched his fist and started to rise because fuck this guy.

Kasi stopped Levi by placing her hand on his thigh before digging into her pocket. She pulled out the engagement ring and thrust it toward Scottie.

"What are you doing?" he asked.

"Returning your ring. My answer is no."

Levi didn't think Kasi intended to speak as loudly as she had, but with each passing day, her fury over Scottie preying on her grief to try to bully her family out of their farm had grown.

It probably hadn't helped that Keith, Tim, and Levi had shared that emotion, the four of them outraged by Scottie's manipulations. As such, she'd had plenty of time to build up a big head of steam.

Scottie glanced around, aware they were drawing an audience because his reply was spoken much softer. "We need to talk," he said to her, before looking at Levi. "Alone."

Kasi didn't bother to temper her volume. "There's nothing you need to say to me that my boyfriend, Levi, can't hear."

Scottie pursed his lips tightly, and Levi could almost see the wheels turning in the man's head. "Returning that ring isn't going to help you or your family," Scottie said through gritted teeth.

"Oh," Kasi feigned surprise. "You mean because of the property taxes? That's all taken care of. Paid in full."

Scottie frowned. "But—"

"I have to admit," Levi said, definitely speaking louder than he needed to, "I was surprised when I realized you said town council had done away with the payment plan option for back taxes. Dad was confused too, considering the council didn't vote to reverse the rules regarding that issue. Is that something you're planning to change if you win the election?"

Several heads turned in their direction, and Levi recognized more than a few of those who were sitting nearby were local landowners and farmers.

"No more payment plans?" someone muttered with alarm.

Scottie shook his head quickly, his hands raised in immediate surrender as he surveyed the people around them. "That's not true. The payment plans are still in effect," he said loudly, before turning back to their table, leaning forward. "Dammit, Kasi," he started. "Stop this."

Levi didn't like how close Scottie was getting...or the look in his eye. It reminded him of last fall, when Scottie had grabbed Lucy. The mayor *really* didn't take rejection well.

"Back up," Levi said, in a deep, low voice.

Scottie held Kasi's gaze for a few seconds longer, clearly trying to intimidate her.

"Right now," Levi added.

The tone of his voice must have penetrated, reminding Scottie of exactly what Levi would do to protect a woman he cared about.

Scottie took a step back, his face flushed with anger.

"Take the ring and get the fuck out of here," Levi said quietly, aware Scottie had refused to reclaim the ring.

Scottie put his hand out, and Kasi slapped it into his palm.

"You tried to take advantage of my family's misfortune, tried to use it to your benefit. You're an asshole." Kasi was quieter, but now that they'd captured everyone's attention, the conversations at the surrounding tables had faded enough that she was still heard.

Scottie sniffed. "I was trying to help you."

Kasi shook her head. "No. You weren't. You were using me to get what you wanted."

Before they could say more, a new voice came over the microphone, as Lark's last song had just ended.

Levi glanced toward the makeshift stage, surprised to find Sam standing there.

"I hope everyone will forgive me for stealing the mic away from our very talented Lark here, but I have an announcement I'd like to make," Sam began.

Kasi glanced at Levi, and he shrugged. He didn't have a clue what his brother was about to say.

"I'm very happy to announce that I've decided to throw my hat in the ring. I'll be running for mayor of Gracemont in the next election!"

Scottie's mouth fell open in astonishment as the patrons of the brewery broke into a loud round of applause, several people shouting and whistling in support.

"He can't," Scottie said under his breath.

"I hope I can count on your support," Sam continued. "And I look forward to talking to you in the coming weeks about ways we can continue our Gracemont traditions, while creating some new ones."

Sam handed the microphone back to Lark, stepping down to shake hands. A few of the older guys slapped him on the back as he made his way around to Levi and Kasi's table.

Sam put his hand out, forcing Scottie to shake it or lose face.

"It's too late to run," Scottie said, still struggling to accept Sam's news.

"I filled out the paperwork yesterday, actually," Sam said. "Just under the wire on the deadline."

Remi rushed over. "I'm going to be your campaign manager," she declared, giving Sam a huge hug.

Everyone laughed.

Except Scottie.

It had become a running joke around town that Scottie only won the mayoral election because he'd run unopposed. It would be interesting to see how he faired in a true race.

Given his suddenly pasty complexion, it looked as if he wasn't feeling too good about his chances.

With too many eyes now on their table, Scottie must have decided it was in his best interest to cut and run. "You'll all regret this," he murmured under his breath.

Levi rose. "Is that a threat?"

Whatever brief burst of bravado he'd found vanished when Levi stepped closer. Scottie shoved the engagement ring in his pocket, then walked away without saying another word, like the coward he was.

"You okay?" Kasi asked, placing her hand on Levi's forearm as Sam and Remi walked away, visiting the surrounding tables to begin the campaigning.

Levi grunted. "I really wanted to punch that guy." Kasi had told him about Scottie's creepy touches and sexist comments.

Kasi giggled. "Can I tell you a secret?"

He nodded.

"When you used that deep, scary voice on him, I got totally turned on."

Levi grasped her hand. "Grab your purse. We're leaving."

"Where are we going?" she asked, even as she stood and allowed him to tow her toward the exit.

"Home. Bed. Now," he said, using *that* tone.

"Oooo," she said, grinning wickedly. "Sounds like there's a storm coming."

"In an hour, there will be a Storm and a Mills coming," he joked, wrapping his arm around her waist. "Walk faster."

Fortunately, he and Kasi had the farmhouse to themselves once they returned, Keith and her dad still working the fruit stand.

A quick glance at the clock as they entered their bedroom told him they had two hours before the two men returned home, and Levi intended to put every single second to good use.

However, two seconds after he shut the bedroom door, Kasi took his plans and twisted them on their ear when she turned to face him and—God help him—dropped to her knees.

"Little bear," he murmured as she reached for the button on his jeans.

Kasi lifted her gaze to his, her eyes sparkling. "I want you. Want this."

Levi cupped her cheek. "Then take it."

Delighted, she gave him a wink, then lowered his zipper. He helped her pull his jeans down, the denim dropping to the floor around his ankles.

Levi didn't bother to kick them off. Instead, he closed his fists around her long hair and guided her mouth to his cock.

He was stealing another piece of her innocence, claiming it for his own. He knew—because she'd told him—that she had never given a man a blowjob before. Now, as always, Levi felt as if he'd found his own lucky penny on this farm, every single day he spent with Kasi better than the one before.

Levi hissed when his girl lost no time, parting her lips and sucking the head of his cock inside. She'd wrapped both her hands around him, covering him from base to just below the head, so that he felt wholly encapsulated by her.

She drew her tongue around the tip, stealing a taste of precome, teasing the tiny opening until he tightened his grip in her hair, tugging on the strands enough to sting. She loved it when he pulled on her hair.

The way her eyes drifted closed, a low moan vibrating around him, told him she hadn't lied.

Then one hand released him, sliding between his legs, cupping his balls as Kasi took him deeper into her mouth.

"Fuck," Levi breathed. He felt rather than saw the edges of her mouth curve in a grin. "Look at me, Kasi," he demanded. "Keep your eyes on me while you do that."

Kasi's gaze locked with his, her eyes watering slightly when the head of his cock brushed the back of her throat. She wasn't holding back, wasn't being timid about it, and he loved it.

He let her set the pace for a couple of minutes, her rhythm slow and steady, before he needed to take control. Using his grip on her hair, he began guiding her on and off his dick, sliding in a bit deeper, pushing her boundaries.

Kasi's eyes drifted shut, clearly enjoying his dominance.

"Eyes," he reminded her, pleased when she instantly obeyed and looked at him again.

Levi pushed in harder and faster, quickly reaching the point of no return.

He didn't want to cross that line. One day soon, sure. But for today...he wanted her with him.

After one more push, he released his hold on her hair and took a step back.

Kasi tried to follow him, frowning. "Levi," she started.

He reached down, lifting her to her feet. She was such a tiny thing in comparison to him. With a firm grip on her elbow, he waited until she was steady on her feet before he began stripping her clothes off.

"I wanted—"

"I know what you wanted," he interjected. "I want that too. But not today. Today is going to be about us."

Once she was naked, he pulled down the duvet, directing her to climb into the bed. He followed, caging her beneath him as he kissed her.

Kasi's hands—as always—drifted to his hair. She admitted a few nights earlier when he mentioned needing a haircut that she loved his long hair and beard, claiming she liked having something to run her fingers through and grab onto.

Levi lined his cock up, thrusting in with a force that left the two of them groaning in unison. He was convinced there was no better feeling than being buried deep in Kasi's body.

Kasi lifted her legs, wrapping them around his waist, her ankles locked at the small of her back.

Reaching between them, Levi stroked her clit, determined to feel her come on his dick at least twice before giving in to his own climax. Of course, it would be a miracle if he was able to hold off because her blowjob left him primed and ready.

Kasi cried out, her fingernails digging into his shoulders. "God. Levi. Yes!"

Her back arched as she came, her pussy clenching his dick so tightly he saw stars.

Levi gritted his teeth and closed his eyes, fighting with everything he had not to follow her over. As she came, he continued caressing her clit and thrusting hard, his actions only serving to drive them both crazy. Her orgasm seemed to go on for minutes, hours.

Her body sank into the mattress when it finally waned, but Levi wasn't in the right frame of mind to give her time to rest. After the meeting with Scottie, he felt his inner caveman clawing back to the surface, determined to make damn sure Kasi understood she was his.

While her attempt to leave him hadn't lasted more than a day, it had shaken him enough to prove just how strong his feelings for her truly were.

He lowered his head to kiss her, even as she fought to catch her breath.

"Love you," he murmured against her lips.

"Love you," she repeated, breathlessly.

Levi gave her one more quick kiss, then pulled out.

Kasi reached up, intent on pulling him back to her, but he shook his head, shifting enough that he could grasp one hip and flip her over.

"Hands and knees."

She moved sluggishly, still trying to recover from her first orgasm.

Levi smacked her ass to encourage her to move faster.

"Mmm," Kasi hummed, her obvious pleasure prompting him to spank her again.

She pushed her ass higher, urging him to continue.

Levi wasn't one to look a gift horse in the mouth, so he gave her what she—and he—wanted. Her soft ass turned a delightful pink as he alternated between her right and left cheeks, smacking her until her head dropped to the pillow beneath her and she trembled with need.

She moaned when he rubbed her tender flesh, caressing it with a soft touch, then adding to the heat by squeezing the firm globes.

"This ass," he murmured.

She giggled, wiggling it.

He gave her one more smack for good measure, then ran the head of his dick through her wet slit. She was practically dripping with need, and so hot he half expected to see steam rising.

"Ready for more?"

"Please," she said, not bothering to lift her head from the pillow. He could only see one side of her face, her eyes closed, her cheeks as flushed as her ass.

"Hold on." It was the only warning he gave as he grasped her hips and slammed in to the hilt.

Kasi cried out, her fingers fisting in the pillow. "God! More!"

Levi pounded in relentlessly. He wasn't going to manage to hold off through another of her orgasms.

She was heaven on fucking earth.

"I'm close, Kasi," he said. "With me," he demanded roughly.

She didn't reply, merely nodded her head. At least, he thought she was nodding.

Kasi's fingers drifted between her legs, stroking her clit, giving herself the extra stimulation she loved so much, as Levi used his grip on her hips to pull her backward into his hard thrusts.

He started to worry she wouldn't get there before him, until —mercifully—she opened her mouth, screaming without sound, as her body contracted and her pussy milked every drop of come out of him.

Levi came so hard, it almost hurt. He grinned, thinking—not for the first time—that Kasi was going to be the death of him. She had him wrapped around her little finger, his balls in her palm, and his heart in her teeth.

The best kind of pain.

Perfect.

Levi pulled away from her, catching her slight wince. A gentleman might feel guilt for using her so hard, but all Levi felt was pride.

Regardless...

"Sorry," he whispered, dropping down next to her on the bed, pulling her toward him so she could use his chest as a pillow.

"I'm not. That was so fucking hot."

"I was rough."

Kasi toyed with his beard as she lifted her head. "Just the way I like it."

He kissed the top of her head. "You were made for me."

She placed several soft kisses on his chest, the two of them lying together.

Peace after passion.

Levi closed his eyes, though he didn't sleep, simply soaking up the wonder of holding his girl in his arms.

In their bed.

In their house.

On their farm.

Life didn't get any better than this.

～

"I'm starving. Let's eat," Levi said, sitting up slowly. He and Kasi had dozed nearly an hour, the sun slipping lower as afternoon was giving way to evening. They'd split a soft pretzel at the brewery, intending to order a pizza before their confrontation with Scottie.

Kasi lay on her stomach, groaning like a teenager refusing to get out of bed in the morning for school.

"I'm comfy," she murmured.

Levi slapped her bare ass playfully. "Come on. Your dad and Keith will be closing the stand soon."

"Hmph," she grumbled, rising slowly.

Once they were dressed, they ventured into the kitchen, opening the refrigerator in search of food. Levi pulled out some steaks Kasi had thawing.

"Steak and eggs?" he suggested.

"Sounds yummy. Let me see if Keith and Daddy are joining us. Then I'll chop up some red potatoes for hash browns."

Her brother quickly replied that he and their father had decided to grab fast food and go see a movie together. While Levi enjoyed their company, he was thrilled to have Kasi all to himself for an evening.

The two of them cooked, their movements around the kitchen natural after so many nights spent baking together. As always, Kasi fired up some music on Spotify and synced it with a small speaker that sat on the kitchen counter.

Once their meal was prepared, they sat at the table, eating as they laughed about Scottie's face when Sam announced his intention to run for mayor.

"I can't believe he didn't tell you," Kasi mused.

"In his defense, we haven't seen each other at all this week. I've been here a lot, and he and Jace were in that brewhouse from dawn to dusk getting everything ready for the Oktoberfest kickoff. I'm not surprised though. Sam is a lot like Dad, committed to Gracemont and a firm believer in community service. I think he'd make a hell of a mayor. Not sure there's anyone in town—with the exception of Edith Millholland—who loves Gracemont more."

"I really hope he wins," Kasi said.

"If the reaction of those patrons at the brewery is anything to go on..."

Kasi nodded in agreement. "Sam's very well liked. Scottie, not so much." She wiped her mouth and put her fork down once her plate was clean.

Levi's ears perked up when a pretty song started playing. He'd heard it a couple times before and had always liked it. Now, as he considered the words, the lyrics took on a new meaning, one that fit him and Kasi to a tee.

Levi held his hand out, helping her stand. "Dance with me. Our song is playing," he said, as he pulled her into his arms, the two of them swaying slowly together.

"Didn't have you pegged for a Swiftie," Kasi joked.

Levi laughed. "Is that who's singing?"

Kasi placed her hand over her heart dramatically, as if he'd wounded her. "How can you not recognize Taylor's voice?"

"Obviously, I'm going to have to study up on her albums. I only know this one because I heard it on the radio a few times. I like the words."

"It's called 'invisible string,' and I love it."

"Invisible string. Yeah, it definitely fits because every time I'm away from you, I feel like the string is pulled so taut, I don't have any choice but to come right back to you."

"I like that," she said, resting her cheek against his chest. "Like the idea that we're tied together. You know, my parents used to slow dance in the kitchen. I always dreamed," she lifted her face to him, "that I'd find a man who would want to dance with me like this."

Levi's heart swelled so much, he was shocked it still fit in his chest. Unable to resist, he lowered his head and kissed her, soft and slow.

"Hashtag life goals," Kasi whispered when their lips parted.

"Love at first touch," he murmured. "You were always destined to be mine, little bear."

She smiled sweetly. "And you were destined to be mine."

Epilogue

Theo rubbed his eyes, then leaned back in his office chair and closed them. He'd been staring at the computer for too long. He'd been burning the candle at both ends the past month or so. Not like that was unusual for August and September.

Most of the year, he spent the majority of his working hours in the brewery, either in his office or the tasting room, but whenever harvest time rolled around, he split his time between here and the vineyards, helping to pick the grapes. Sometimes, it just felt good to get back out into nature.

He should be seeing a light at the end of the tunnel by now, as most of the grapes were picked, but he and his family had decided the time was right to expand the businesses by hiring an events coordinator. In the past, Theo and Nora had worked together, planning special events at the brewery and winery, but because their lists of job duties were already quite large, they were never pleased with the end results, certain every event could be better if only they'd had the time to do more.

Theo had been the one to propose they create a new position, and his family had voted unanimously to bring on the new employee. He'd volunteered to do the hiring, as well as serve as the coordinator's supervisor.

He opened his eyes and glanced at his computer screen again, reviewing the resume of the woman he'd hired, hoping he'd made the right choice. Most of the interviews he'd conducted had been through video conference calls. It wasn't his preferred way of interviewing, as he liked to get to know people face-to-face. However, in order to widen his applicant pool—the list of qualified people in Gracemont was pitifully small—he'd been forced to interview online.

He would know soon enough if he'd picked right, since the new coordinator was scheduled to begin work next week.

Theo stifled a yawn, then decided to call it a day. It was a little before quitting time, but it was his night to cook, and after all the extra hours he'd been pulling, he'd earned an early out. Plus, there had to be some perks to being his own boss.

He reached to turn off his computer when he heard someone say his name.

"Theo Storm?"

He glanced up, trying to place the woman standing in his doorway. She looked vaguely familiar.

"Yes," he replied.

"I'm Gretchen Banks."

Of course. The new events coordinator.

Theo hadn't gotten a great look at her face during the interview because she'd been sitting in front of a window, leaving her face backlit so much she'd been little more than a shadow. Not that he'd needed to see her face because she'd hit it out of the park in her interview, her answers to his questions lining right up with his vision for the brewery and winery.

He stood, walking around his desk. "Gretchen," he said

with a friendly smile. "I wasn't expecting to meet you until next week."

Theo reached out to shake her hand—and when Gretchen placed her hand in his, it felt as if he'd been struck by lightning.

Jesus, he thought, smiling at the petite woman he knew without a doubt was going to be his wife.

It was just as Levi said.

Love at first touch.

LEVI'S STORY is just the beginning! Theo's story is coming in June 2025.

Shelter from the Storm

AND DID you read Lucy's story? Kiss and Tell is available now! Turn the page to read the first chapter of Kiss and Tell.

CALLING all fans of Mari Carr AND Facebook! There's a group for you. Come join Mari Carr's Facebook group for sneak peaks, cover reveals, contests and more! Join now.

AND BE sure to join Mari's mailing list to receive a **FREE** sexy novella, Midnight Wild.

Kiss and Tell

"What a place!" Joey Moretti did a complete three-sixty, spinning around to take in the gorgeous views surrounding him. The large wooden sign with the colorful words Stormy Weather Farm—the t's in *stormy* and *weather* shaped like lightning strikes—told them they had arrived at their destination.

He and his cohost Miles Williams had just made the three-and-a-half-hour drive from Philadelphia to Gracemont in Northern Virginia, as they prepared to start filming a new episode of their show. He could hardly believe that he and Miles were already hard at work on their third season of *ManPower*.

When he'd first landed the gig hosting a cable show, Joey had no idea *ManPower* would become so popular. These days, it was rare that he could go out in public without being recognized by people. Just yesterday, his sister Layla had texted him a picture of herself standing in the grocery store checkout line, posing with a copy of a home improvement magazine featuring him and Miles on the cover.

Along with the selfie, she'd included a one-word text.

Squeeeeeeee!!!!

Joey felt like he'd stepped back into the past as he took in the giant white farmhouse with large navy-blue shutters, surrounded by countless well-kept outbuildings, including an honest-to-God red barn. The place was storybook perfect, with rolling hills, a vibrant view of leaves currently in the height of changing colors, and at least fifteen different-size pumpkins adorning the house's wraparound porch, intermingled with bright yellow mums.

In addition to this farmhouse, there were two other homes situated on Stormy Weather Farm's two-hundred-plus acres, as well as several businesses—Rain or Shine Brewery, Lightning in a Bottle Winery, and some rental cabins.

"Shit, man. That was some climb. I wasn't sure the car was going to make it," Miles muttered. "We're not in Philly anymore, Toto."

Joey chuckled, though he agreed the climb had been white-knuckle steep. The rest of the *ManPower* crew would be arriving tomorrow, but he and Miles had made plans to arrive a day early to meet Levi Storm and his brewmaster, Lou, this afternoon for a tour of Stormy Weather Farm.

Joey had done quite a bit of research on the farm in preparation for the show. The Storm family had settled here four generations ago, and they'd created an amazing legacy in the decades since.

After the tour, Levi, the oldest of the latest generation of Storms, had promised them a home-cooked dinner and a chance to meet the rest of his siblings and cousins. Joey and Levi had spoken on the phone a few times in preparation for the filming, and the man had mentioned the fact he had six brothers. Joey, who was one of five siblings, felt a kinship with Levi instantly. It was apparent the man was as close to his family as Joey was to his own, and the branches on the Storm family tree were as weighted down by countless relatives as the Moretti's.

Levi reminded Joey a lot of his older brother, Tony—confident and take-charge. The kind of guy who never met a stranger. For most of Tony's adult life, the family had called him the mayor because the dude seriously seemed to know every single person in Philadelphia. He suspected the same was likely true of Levi, though to be fair, the population of Gracemont probably didn't reach four digits, while Philadelphia boasted of close to two million inhabitants.

"Never gave much thought to the farming lifestyle but, damn, Miles, imagine waking up here every morning of your life." Joey stared into the distance, amazed by just how many colors Mother Nature had in her palette. The mountain was awash in golden and neon yellows, vibrant reds and bright purples, deep oranges, and at least three different shades of green.

"No thanks," Miles growled.

Joey rolled his eyes, amused by the response though not surprised. Miles was taking in the same view he was, but his best friend was clearly much less impressed, especially when he pulled out his phone to check his text messages.

"Reception sucks up here," he muttered. A city boy from the word go, Miles viewed the mountains and woods and, well, nature in general as space simply waiting to be "civilized" with houses, stores, restaurants, and a fucking Starbucks on every corner.

Miles had grown up in the Ridgewood section of Queens, his playgrounds made of concrete. Joey had spent his childhood in two large cities as well—Philadelphia and, for a time, Baltimore. However, his family had always resided in the suburbs, so he had a working knowledge of how to mow grass, unlike Miles.

When he was little, Joey helped Nonna and Aunt Berta plant seeds in the raised-bed gardens in their backyards every summer. He'd loved watching the tomatoes grow big and turn red, enjoyed searching the sprawling vines for the green beans that Nonna would cook for dinner, and picking the strawberries that never seemed to make it from the yard to the house because he ate them all before he got inside.

Levi had mentioned during one of their calls that on a clear day, they could see all the way to Washington, D.C., the view from here completely unencumbered by other houses or trees. Joey found himself searching the horizon to see if that was true. They were so high, he could almost believe that if he was only an inch or two taller, he'd bump his head on the sky.

Miles scowled at the cell screen, clearly upset, before stuffing his phone back in his pocket.

"Bad text?" Joey asked.

Miles had been uncharacteristically quiet on the drive. He shook his head, then took another cursory glance at the landscape Joey couldn't take his eyes off of. They hadn't made it more than a few feet from the truck because the view had literally stopped him in his tracks. "Should we go knock on the door?"

Before Joey could respond, they heard a female voice calling to them from the porch of the house.

"You're here!"

Joey spun around, blinking several times and even shaking his head. His shocked gasp was audible, drawing Miles's attention.

"You okay, man?"

"It's her," Joey whispered.

"Her who?"

Joey watched as the petite strawberry-blonde woman descended the stairs, walking in their direction, intent on greeting them. She wore faded overalls over a hot-pink long-sleeved tee and her long hair was pulled back in a high ponytail, though a chunk of it had fallen out on one side. She tucked it behind her ear each time the breeze blew it loose again. She wore the girliest Doc Martens he'd ever seen, the boots covered in pink and purple flowers.

She was smiling as she approached—and Joey knew without a doubt, he'd never seen a more beautiful woman in his life.

"Joey?" Miles prodded. "Who is she?"

Joey grinned, unable to look away from her. "The woman I'm going to marry," he replied, only half joking.

Miles turned to look at him, snorting...until he saw Joey's face. Then he looked confused. "You know her?"

"Never met her."

"Jesus," Miles muttered, but before he could give him shit for saying crazy stuff, the woman reached them.

"I can't believe you're both really here," she gushed. "When Levi told us *ManPower* wanted to film a show about Rain or Shine Brewery, we thought he was pulling our leg. Although to be honest, Levi isn't usually the joking type. That honor falls to my youngest cousin, Jace, who's always pulling pranks and cracking us up with his farfetched stories. We're all—the whole family, I mean—big fans of the show. I especially liked the episode where you went lobster fishing in Maine and that big storm rolled up. Oh my God! I suffered some serious second-hand anxiety watching that."

Joey wasn't sure what part of this one-sided conversation he enjoyed more, listening to the woman talk or watching Miles's expressions, which ranged anywhere from awe to horror.

"That was a good show," Joey interjected, amused by how fast the woman was talking. "And terrifying." He crooked his thumb at Miles. "This guy was in danger of puking his guts out the whole time."

Miles grunted because the truth was, they were both green around the gills by the end of filming, and the first thing Joey had done when he got off the boat was beg for ginger ale and saltines to settle his stomach.

"I can imagine. I've seen all the *ManPower* episodes a few times and I still can't watch that one without freaking out. And I know how it ends!" she added, eyes wide with humor. "Oh crap, I'm rambling, aren't I? My grandma always said I was blessed with the gift of gab, but there were times when I'm pretty sure she substituted the word 'cursed' with 'blessed' to soften the blow. She was kind of wonderful like that." The beautiful woman laughed, and Joey couldn't help but join in.

Miles, who hadn't said anything—probably because he couldn't find a break in the conversation—was studying her with furrowed brows. His best friend was a happy-go-lucky guy overall, but during times when he was stressed out or upset, his resting bitch face was fierce. It was in full force right now.

"Well," Joey said. "Obviously, I'm Joey Moretti, and this is Miles Williams."

The woman threw up her arms. "Dear God, I'm an idiot. Just pounced right on you, didn't I? Completely forgot to introduce myself. I'm Lucy Storm, one of the brewmasters."

"Lucy," Joey repeated, surprised. "Wait. You're Lou?"

When Levi informed him that Rain or Shine Brewery had two brewmasters, Sam and Lou, Joey had assumed they were both men.

"You thought I was a guy, didn't you?" she asked. "Lu is short for Lucy, which is the nickname my family insists on using. Fortunately it's not contagious, because everyone else in Gracemont calls me Lucy."

Joey laughed. "I tried for years to get people to call me Joe, but my family refused to conform, and their insistence on adding that damn y *was* contagious. Eventually, I just gave up and embraced it, though every now and then, Miles treats me to the shortened version because he's kind of wonderful like that," he said, repeating her joke.

"How about you?" Lucy looked at Miles. "Any dreaded nicknames?"

Miles shrugged. "My name is straightforward, without much room for creativity."

"That's true, I suppose," she said, her smile wavering at Miles's uncharacteristically gruff tone.

"You have a beautiful home," Joey said.

Lucy looked over her shoulder. "This farmhouse belongs to my cousins, seven guys in one place. My sister, Remi, calls it the frat house."

Joey hadn't lived with his brothers since they were all old enough to move out of their dad's house. He'd roomed with his oldest brother Tony for a time, but that hadn't worked for long as Tony was a neat freak and Joey was cleaning challenged. Or, as his family put it, "a fucking slob."

"I know Levi said he would give you a tour, but he had some trouble with a tractor this morning, so he's elbow-deep in machine parts, trying to figure out what's wrong with it. I volunteered to take charge." She pointed to a beat-up truck that looked older than Joey with the words *Farm Use* spray-painted on the door. "The property is quite large and spread out. How are you guys for steps?" she asked.

"Steps?" Miles repeated, confused.

She grinned as she pointed to her Apple Watch. "You know, the step counter?"

Miles frowned, his tone downright sarcastic. "We've been in the car all morning."

Joey shot his friend a look, wondering where this asshole attitude was coming from. "Miles and I are gym rats most of the time, so steps aren't something we usually look at."

"Oh. I got this Apple Watch last year for Christmas, and I've become obsessed with hitting a certain number of steps every day. I'm too competitive for my own good, even if I'm only competing with myself. I set these ridiculous goals. Drives Sam crazy when we're at work because we'll be sitting down discussing something, my watch will beep, and then, well, I have to get up and start moving," she said, as if that should be obvious. "So...a gym, huh? You mean like weights, or are you treadmill guys?"

"Mainly weights," Joey said, but before he could elaborate, Lucy continued speaking.

"I have to admit, I've never stepped foot in a gym—except the one in my high school. Wouldn't have a clue how to use all those weight machines. Life on a farm is its own workout."

Joey loved Lucy's voice. It was a weird thing to be thinking, but there was something about it that made him want to smile... like nonstop. There was a cheerful lilt to it, and she had the tiniest bit of a southern accent that he found adorable. "I bet it is."

"Anyway..." Lucy started walking toward the ancient pickup. "I think we'd better take the truck. Otherwise, we'll end up walking a hundred miles, trying to take everything in. Why don't you follow me in your vehicle to the first stop, which is the cabin where you'll be staying. We can drop off your suitcases and leave your car there."

"Sounds like a plan." Joey looked at Miles, tossing the keys to his car to him. "You can drive, Miles, while I ride with our beautiful tour guide."

Miles rolled his eyes but didn't argue.

Joey crossed around the back of the truck, claiming the passenger seat, grinning when he realized the thing had a long bucket in the front and no backseat at all. He mentally dibsed the middle spot for himself once Miles rejoined them. He liked the idea of spending a few hours sitting pressed close to Lucy.

God, she smelled good, he thought as soon as the two of them were closed in the cab of the truck. Like lilacs and apples, a perfect blend of the best of spring and fall.

"The cabins aren't far." Lucy glanced in the rearview mirror, checking that Miles was behind them before shifting into drive and starting down the dirt lane. "If you guys are tired, we can delay the tour. Maybe Miles wants some time to unwind?"

Obviously, Lucy had picked up on Miles's bad mood. Joey wasn't sure what the hell had gotten into his friend. While he'd been quiet on the drive from Philadelphia to Virginia, he hadn't been the downright grumpy ass he was acting like right now. Miles was no fan of the mountains, but they'd spent a lot of time in places more remote than this during the filming of the show and he'd been just fine.

No. Miles's mood had darkened when he'd looked at his cellphone. And it had only gotten worse since Lucy appeared. Which didn't make a damn bit of sense, because she was charming and sweet.

"We're good to go on the tour," Joey replied.

"Cool." Lucy gave him a sideways glance. "I guess I should warn you. I tend to talk a lot when I'm excited or nervous, and at the moment, I'm both. I'm going to try to settle down."

Joey chuckled, loving how open, honest, and even self-deprecating Lucy was. There was no pretense with her, no putting on airs.

Lately, Joey had been dating the same type of women—all

around his age, professionals in their chosen careers, sophisticated and worldly. He'd been on a dozen dates in the past few months and not one of them had ended in the bedroom, because Joey hadn't felt any spark or connection to the women. Now it was starting to occur to him that perhaps he'd been seeking out the wrong women to date...which might also account for his failed attempts at finding "the one."

Miles would roll his eyes hard if he heard Joey rambling on about "the one" again, but ever since his only other single sibling, Luca, had found his life partners—Conor and Harper—Joey had become even more determined than ever to find the person he wanted to spend the rest of his life with.

Not that he was *so* determined that he'd settle for just anyone, of course. Joey had witnessed too many examples of true love in his family to ever settle for less.

Aaaaand that was another concept Miles would give him shit for. Because Miles did not believe in true love or soul mates or love at first sight or any of those things Joey knew for a fact existed.

Glancing at Lucy, Joey felt a slight stir in his heart *and* his pants. Both had lain dormant for too long, but now they were suddenly waking up.

"Do me a favor, Lucy. Don't stop talking. I like the sound of your voice."

She blushed as she grinned widely. "Okay, but you might regret that request later."

"I'm pretty sure I won't. Have to admit, I'm looking forward to seeing the farm, seeing where you work. What made you decide to become a brewmaster?"

Lucy lifted one shoulder casually. "I guess a combination of things. I've always loved science, and the chemistry behind brewing beer is fascinating. Plus, there are countless chores and jobs that need to be done in order to run the farm and businesses efficiently. Most of the primary tasks fall to the family, though we certainly have a lot of employees who aren't related to us. I've always been most interested in the brewery side, while my sisters tend to work in the winery most of the time."

"Sisters?"

"I have three, all younger."

"No brothers?"

Lucy shook her head. "Nope, but that's probably a good thing, because with seven male cousins, I'm not sure I could have survived with one more overprotective man in my life."

Joey winced playfully. "Damn. I might resemble that remark. My brothers and I have one little sister, Layla."

Lucy laughed. "I'm going to need her phone number. At least I have my sisters to commiserate with when the guys pull their cavemen routine with our prospective dates, while it sounds like poor Layla is adrift and on her own."

Joey snorted. "Not really. She did alright for herself. Settled into a pretty amazing happily ever after."

"What?" Lucy asked, aghast. "You let a man into the inner sanctum?"

"*Two* men," Joey replied with a wink.

She pulled up in front of a cute cabin, also adorned with pumpkins and mums, celebrating the fact that fall had arrived and Halloween was just four days away. Joey wondered if the decorations had been Lucy's doing.

Before they could continue the conversation, Miles was standing next to the passenger door, duffel bag slung over his shoulder.

Joey got out, retrieving his own bag from the car as Lucy climbed the three steps to the cabin's porch and unlocked the door.

"My aunt Claire runs a B&B on the property with my sister, Mila. They also take care of the cabins. You have Mila to thank for the pumpkins and flowers, as well as the stocked refrigerator. She's got an eye for design, and she loves to make everything pretty. One whole shed behind the farmhouse I share with my sisters is filled with every possible decoration for every conceivable holiday on the calendar." Lucy led them inside as she spoke. "Levi told her she was probably taking it too far when she started decking the B&B in lightsabers, Death Star cutouts, and mini Yodas for Star Wars Day."

Joey folded his hands in front of himself, trying to look like a somber Jedi. "May the Fourth be with you."

"And also with you," Lucy replied, giggling as she crossed herself.

"How many cabins are on the property?" Joey was impressed by the homey feel of the cabin they were going to call home for the next five days.

"There are ten, scattered around various places on the farm. The first three are tucked in the woods and were originally used as hunting cabins...many, many moons ago. When my grandfather took over the running of the farm, he started growing grapes with the intention of opening the winery. Once that happened, he stopped allowing people to hunt on the property. Aunt Claire was the one who suggested we refurbish those older cabins and build new ones to rent to guests, so Uncle Rex scoped out seven spots with amazing views. There aren't many weeks that pass where at least half the cabins aren't rented, and we sell out almost every week in the summer and fall, when the leaves are changing color."

"I was admiring your colorful mountain when we arrived, wasn't I, Miles?" Joey attempted to draw his friend into the conversation because, since entering the cabin, he'd been wandering around, looking completely distracted.

"Yep." Miles jerked his thumb toward one of the bedroom doors. "I'm going to take that one, okay?"

Joey nodded, annoyed when Miles walked away from them.

"Um. Okay." Lucy stumbled for a moment, clearly struggling to make this Miles fit with the man who appeared on her TV screen in every episode. That Miles was all smiles and easygoing, everybody's pal, while today, his first impression screamed impatient asshole.

"Sounds like we were lucky to score a cabin then." Joey tried to distract her from his best friend's rudeness.

"Your producer set up the filming way back in early spring, so we made sure to save the best cabin for you. The other bedroom is over here." Lucy pointed to the door behind her.

"Let me toss my bag in there really quick, then we can start the tour."

Lucy nodded, but her smile wasn't as bright as it had been a few minutes ago.

Joey gave his bedroom a cursory glance, placing his bag on the bed without unpacking before returning to Lucy. Miles had already emerged from his room, but neither he nor Lucy were talking to each other.

"Ready?" Lucy asked brightly, though her tone felt more forced than before.

"Can't wait." Joey reached out, clasping his hand with hers, tugging her along, hoping his enthusiasm would re-spark her own.

She laughed when he gallantly opened the driver's side door for her, bowing as he did so. After she climbed in, he jogged around the hood, bumping Miles out of the way. "I'll take the middle seat," he said, acting as if he was making some sacrifice.

Miles nodded, looking annoyed.

Joey shot his buddy a glare, one that was greeted with a

regretful sigh. At least Miles was aware of the fact he was acting like an ass.

"Sorry," he muttered.

Appeased, Joey slid into the truck, shifting until he was right next to Lucy. Then he rested his arm along the back of the seat, smiling at her as she shook her head at his obvious flirting.

She didn't call him out for it though, which Joey took as a win. Especially when he realized her cheeks were turning pink again. God, he couldn't remember the last time he'd dated a woman who blushed. It was endearing and cute as hell.

"Okay. First stop is the winery. We'll drive by the grapevines as we go. Let me know if y'all have any questions about them," she offered.

"We're just focusing on the brewery for filming," Miles pointed out, his tone less harsh. Not that it mattered, considering his scowl was still firmly in place.

"Oh. I, um, just meant questions in general. Or we can skip that part if—"

"No, no," Joey quickly interjected. "We want to see it all." He narrowed his eyes at Miles. "Don't we?"

"Yeah. We do." Miles nodded and even attempted a smile. A weak one. Then his cell buzzed. He pulled it out and his frown returned. Joey tried to sneak a glance at the screen, but Miles tilted it away from him. He raised one eyebrow, curious about who was texting him.

Miles grimaced, then put his phone away.

Lucy pointed out various things along the way, her knowledge and love of the farm showing as she spoke. Joey was impressed by her intelligence, and by the time they reached the winery, even Miles had started to thaw a little, asking how they harvested the grapes.

"And here's Lightning in a Bottle Winery. My cousins Maverick and Grayson are our winemakers. Maverick is certified in viticulture and winery tech and has over ten years of official experience, although he worked with our granddaddy from the time he was old enough to walk, learning everything he could from him about our vineyards. I thought I'd show you where we process it, the cellars, then take you to the tasting room to sample some."

"Sounds great," Joey said as they pulled up next to a beautiful building with a massive front porch containing an assortment of tables and Adirondacks, with yet another stellar view from the mountain.

They spent an hour walking through the winery with Lucy and Maverick, who took charge of that part of the tour since it was his domain. Then they enjoyed tasting four of the wines, served with a charcuterie board filled with an assortment of meats, cheeses, nuts, and crackers.

From there, they drove by several of the other rental cabins, then took a quick walk-through of the B&B—the second farmhouse—where they met Lucy's sister, Mila, her aunt Claire, and her uncle Rex. According to Lucy, Claire had decided to turn her family's home into an inn after the youngest of her sons, Jace, moved out. Apparently, after raising seven rambunctious boys, Claire found her empty nest too quiet for her liking.

Finally, they arrived at the brewhouse. Joey thought Lucy had been cheerful and happy all day, but once they entered her realm, she lit up brighter than the sun. She introduced them to two more cousins—her fellow brewmaster, Sam, and Theo, who was the brewhouse manager. During the two-hour walk-through of the brewhouse, Joey had been fascinated to learn about the process involved in brewing beer. He'd never considered it a hobby he wanted to try, but after listening to Sam and Lucy, he found himself thinking about buying a kit and giving it a whirl at home.

Just like at the end of the winery tour, Theo, Sam, and

Lucy invited them to the tasting room, and the five of them sampled every beer made at Rain or Shine Brewery.

It was nearly six o'clock by the time Lucy drove him and Miles back to their cabin so they could change for dinner. She waited for them in the living room. Despite the fact it had been a whirlwind day, Joey was full of energy, something he was attributing to Lucy, who seemed truly tireless. He was feeding off her excitement and enthusiasm.

"I hope you're ready for this," Lucy said, as they pulled up in front of the third farmhouse on the property, the one she shared with her three sisters, Nora, Remi, and Mila—all of whom they'd been introduced to during their tour.

"Ready?" Miles asked.

"I tried to tell everyone it would be better for us to meet you in small groups. Unfortunately, a couple of weeks ago, when Mila mentioned hosting the two of you for dinner your first night here, Aunt Claire hopped on the bandwagon, and then let it slip she was making her chili. After that, well..."

"The whole family invited themselves?" Joey asked, amused. Levi had told him about the dinner on the phone last night, but he'd forgotten to warn Miles.

She nodded.

"Sounds like the Morettis," Joey replied, laughing. "The second we hear Nonna is making eggplant parmesan, we crawl out of the woodwork like ants."

Lucy grinned. "Aunt Claire's chili wins the local chili cookoff every single year, and Mila makes homemade cornbread that is literally to die for."

"Sounds amazing." Joey climbed out of the truck on Lucy's side, the two of them waiting for Miles to cross around the front of the truck.

"Do you have a big family too, Miles?" Lucy asked.

While Miles had shed some of his early moodiness, he'd

still been quiet and reserved. Joey planned to corner him tonight before they turned in to find out what the hell was wrong with him.

"No," Miles responded. "My parents are divorced, so for most of my life it's just been me, Mom, and my sister. I have an aunt, but she lives on the West Coast, and we don't see her or my cousins more than once every few years."

"Oh," she murmured almost sadly.

Joey and Lucy definitely shared the same love for big families.

He'd been jerking Miles's chain earlier when he said she was the one he was going to marry. He'd taken one look at the gorgeous woman and fallen head over heels in lust because every single molecule in his body was attracted to every molecule in hers.

However, that statement felt less like a joke the longer he'd spent with her today.

Joey wasn't the type to debunk the idea of love at first sight because he'd witnessed it firsthand with his cousin, Aldo, and his best friend Kayden. Those two guys had fallen for their sweet nurse, Hazel, the second they saw her standing outside a burning motel, all of her possessions consumed in the fire. Luckily for them, she'd fallen right back.

Joey had never experienced it himself, but there was no denying he'd taken one look at Lucy and felt as if he'd been struck by lightning. Which was appropriate, considering they were standing in the middle of Stormy Weather Farm.

"Should we go in?" Joey wrapped his arm around Lucy's shoulders, turning toward the house. He'd been infringing on her personal space most of the day, which was out of character for him. Joey respected boundaries, especially those of women he'd just met. But there was something about her that had him wanting to hold her hand, or tug on her ponytail playfully, or tuck her under his arm as they walked across the gravel drive and up the porch steps.

If she'd given him any indication she was uncomfortable with that, he would have backed off instantly, but so far, all she'd done—God help his libido—was lean closer.

Even better, he got the sense she felt the same attraction because she'd matched him touch for touch, grasping his forearm as she leaned close to be heard over the brewery equipment, lightly smacking his upper arm whenever he said something funny, and shoulder-bumping him in the truck to get his attention when they passed something she wanted him to see.

As they walked toward the house, Joey offered her some reassurance. "Don't worry about Miles being overwhelmed, Lucy. He's spent plenty of time with the Morettis. While the first couple of times were a shock to his system, I think we've worn him down enough that he's prepared to meet your family."

"It's cute that you think I'm not still shocked by your family," Miles said in a deadpan voice. It was his first joke of the day, and Joey and Lucy both laughed.

She reached out to Miles, and Joey was delighted when his friend took the hand she'd proffered. Joey was at ease with her after spending so many hours together, and he wanted Miles to be a part of that. The three of them walking side by side like this felt—

Joey shut the thought down instantly. Because there were places he didn't let himself go, not even in his own head.

They stopped just outside the front door, Lucy grinning at them. "Gird your loins, boys, because the Storm family is a force of nature."

Kiss and Tell is available now.

About the Author

Virginia native Mari Carr is a New York Times and USA TODAY bestseller of contemporary romance novels. With over three million copies of her books sold, Mari was the winner of the Romance Writers of America's Passionate Plume award for her novella, Erotic Research. She has over a hundred published works, including her popular Wild Irish and Italian Stallions series, along with the Trinity Masters series she writes with Lila Dubois.

Follow Mari:
www.maricarr.com
mari@maricarr.com

Join her newsletter so you don't miss new releases and for exclusive subscriber-only content.